D0049262

critical point

ALSO BY S. L. HUANG

Zero Sum Game
Null Set

S. L. HUANG

critical point

TOR

A TOM DOHERTY ASSOCIATES BOOK • NEW YORK

CRITICAL POINT

A Tor Book
Published by Tom Doherty Associates
120 Broadway
New York, NY 10271

www.tor-forge.com

Tor® is a registered trademark of Macmillan Publishing Group, LLC.

The Library of Congress Cataloging-in-Publication Data is available upon request.

ISBN 978-1-250-18036-0 (hardcover)
ISBN 978-1-250-18037-7 (ebook)

Our books may be purchased in bulk for promotional, educational, or business use. Please contact your local bookseller or the Macmillan Corporate and Premium Sales Department at 1-800-221-7945, extension 5442, or by email at MacmillanSpecialMarkets@macmillan.com.

First Edition: April 2020

Printed in the United States of America

0 9 8 7 6 5 4 3 2 1

TO BUZ,

FOR BEING A CATACLYSMIC HELLBEAST

WHO WILL SPARK A VERY NICE APOCALYPSE

critical point

one

I slouched in my chair, putting my feet up against the edge of the desk. *My* desk.

I had an office.

The place felt cavernous and stifling at the same time, and massively permanent, as if someone were pinioning me to this spot with a railroad spike.

I had rented the office because I'd lost a bet with a friend. A friend who was, for some unfathomable reason, far too invested in convincing me to stop doing business in dive bars. He was also campaigning for me to get a social security number, but that was over the line.

Even the office made me feel like I'd been brainwashed.

I hunched into myself, the heaviness pressing at me. Getting dragged into mildly more mainstream habits by my actual friends was one thing. But it had still only been months since I'd agreed to let the man who called himself Simon start crawling through my head every week. And I'd only agreed under duress: namely, the implosion of my own goddamn mind.

Telepathy was the closest word for what people like Simon did, and I'd been on the verge of refusing his help even if it had killed me. No matter how much he swore he would never take control of my thoughts, someone I didn't trust should never have that much access.

Unfortunately for me, it wasn't like trustworthy telepaths were thick on the ground. Better Simon than the ones who wanted me dead. The shadows of conspiracies and killers slithered through the back of my mind, strangling me. Conspiracies that involved my past. Killers who had forced me not to move against them.

And me, stuck in a city I hadn't even managed to save from my own actions, and struggling just to tread water on my sanity. Losing ground while the psychics and ghosts recovered their power.

The room loomed, and I hunched farther into the chair. The walls weren't claustrophobic, I told myself. The office was roughly twelve feet by ten, though I could see the long side was a little more than two inches shy of its stated length. The ceiling was four feet, nine and seven-eighths inches above where I was slouched in my chair. Or 1.47 meters. Imperial was stupid.

Before I could stop myself, I'd calculated the volume of the small room, minus the space taken up by desk, chairs, and me. I multiplied and estimated the number of oxygen molecules. Moles and moles and moles. Not the least danger of suffocation, I told myself. The math wouldn't lie.

If only my bizarre computational ability could fix my brain.

I thought of the bottle of cheap vodka in the bottom drawer of the desk. No, I had a client meeting in a few minutes. The promise of work to distract me was the only reason I was here. However flimsy and trivial a job this was, I needed it. Treading water. I felt sick without even drinking the vodka.

Someone tapped on the door outside, the timid sound barely making it through the wood.

Early. Small favors. "Come in," I called, swinging my feet down and trying my best to look professional. I probably should have worn a clean shirt.

The African American girl who pushed the door open was tall, but clearly young—probably not older than sixteen, and with the beanpole thinness and awkwardly long limbs that come from unexpected growth spurts. She was dressed smartly but not overly fashionably, wearing a jean jacket and various braided bracelets and necklaces that looked homemade, and had her hair plaited tightly back against her head.

And she wasn't my client. The message requesting this meeting had been left by a babbling man with an Aussie accent.

She was probably lost or something. "Can I help you?" I asked with an effort, and was pleased with managing some tact. Kids bring out the best in me.

"Are you Cas Russell?" She said the words hesitantly, and one of her hands gripped the cuff of her jacket like she needed it to anchor her.

"Yeah, that's me. Retrieval expert." Also known as thief, mercenary, and soldier of fortune who could punch a guy in the face as hard as the relationship between impulse and momentum allowed, but I didn't add that. Or the part about being a woman without a memory, someone else's living weapon until my old self had gotten sliced out of my head. I wondered how she had gotten my name. "Do you want to sit down?"

She stepped forward as if she were about to walk the plank and perched herself on the edge of one of the client chairs in front of my desk. "I need your help."

She didn't say any more. I suppressed a sigh. "What's your name, kid?"

"Tabitha."

More silence. "Okay," I said. "Tabitha. Do your parents know you're here?"

"Well, that's what I'm here about," she said, fidgeting. "My dad, he—he's not answering his phone."

"He's not answering his phone?"

"He *always* answers his phone."

I tried to speak delicately. "He may have lost it temporarily, or been busy—"

"No. He always answers when I call." Her face was tight and tense, and her voice quivered slightly. "And he warns us beforehand if he thinks he might be out of touch—and other than that, he's only not answered once, and it was 'cause he was in trouble, and he called me back right after. Now I haven't been able to reach him in two days, and I think he's in trouble again, and his message on his other phone said to come find you—"

My thoughts smashed to a halt with the grace of a car crash. "Wait, what? He said to come find *me*? Kid, who's your dad?"

"Arthur Tresting."

The bottom dropped out of my stomach.

"Are you a friend of his?" Tabitha asked.

I turned away from her, grabbed out my phone, and dialed Arthur's cell. Voicemail. I hung up and tried his office number, the one he listed online as a private investigator. The message informed potential clients he was away from the office for a few days, and sure enough, advised any current clients with an emergency to contact me, complete with the address of the brand-new office Arthur himself had only recently strong-armed me into renting.

Well. Nice of him to tell me. "I'm not even a PI," I growled into the speaker, and jabbed at the button to hang up before tossing my phone on the desk.

Then I turned to face Arthur's daughter.

Arthur had a daughter. I'd known Arthur almost two years now, and I didn't know he had a daughter.

For all the enemies I had been expecting to come feinting out of the dark, this was a sucker punch.

"I'll track him down," I promised her, finding my voice. "Do you have a number where I can contact you?"

She gave me her mobile number, the beginnings of relief sketching her features.

"Did he tell you anything? Or, uh, anyone else in your family?" Was Arthur married? Wife? Ex-wife? I had no idea.

She shook her head. "My sister and brothers don't know anything. Dad never wants to involve us in his work; he won't talk about it. They keep telling me not to worry, but . . . ."

"Better to be safe," I agreed, trying for comforting. "I'll find him." A sick worry had started squirming in under the shock. "What about your mom? Would she know anything?"

"My other dad," Tabitha corrected. "I have two dads. No, they don't—they don't really talk anymore."

So Arthur liked men. In the name of everything holy, how had I never known that he had what sounded like an ex-husband and a family? These seemed like pretty basic things for friends who regularly saved each other's life to know. Forget the shock and worry, I was settling on pissed off.

"I'll find him," I vowed to Tabitha again, even more firmly. *So I can punch him.* "Are you okay getting home?"

She nodded. "I'd better go. My dad will miss me if I'm home too late."

Her dad—Arthur's ex. I seethed with curiosity, but forcibly behaved myself in front of Tabitha. "Go home. I'll call you as soon as I know anything."

"Thank you, Ms. Russell," she said solemnly, and hitching what looked like a school bag on her shoulder, she ducked awkwardly out of my office.

I picked up my phone.

I knew exactly who my next call would be.

"Hey, Cas!" said the voice of the best hacker I knew—who also happened to be Arthur's investigative partner and information broker. "Did you hear David Tennant is doing an event in Los Angeles next month? *David Tennant.* I might have to leave the Hole for that."

"Checker, have you heard from Arthur lately?" I interrupted.

"Uh, yeah, talked to him last week. We don't have any cases right now, though. What's up?"

"Have you talked to him in the last two days?"

"No, why?"

"Me neither. And guess who was just in my office worried she can't reach him? His daughter."

Long pause.

"Checker, did you know Arthur has a family?"

Another long pause. Then Checker said, "Yes."

"And did you find this out through Internet stalking, or am I justified in feeling shafted right now?"

"It's not like that," Checker said a little desperately. "I knew Arthur before everything went down. Before he lost—while he was still with them. Nowadays he never . . . he got private about them afterwards. His business, Cas," he added severely. He cleared his throat. "Which daughter?"

Great. He knew them all by name. "Tabitha."

"I, uh, I think we should be worried. Maybe very worried. Arthur wouldn't ignore one of his kids, ever."

The squirming in my gut got worse, enough that my anger faded a bit. "Do you know what he was working on?"

"Not a clue. I didn't even know we had a case on."

"I'm going to head to his office, then. See if I can find anything."

"Sounds good," said Checker, and I could already hear the quick clack of his computer keys. "I'll see if I can find anything on my end. Does Diego know?"

"Who's Diego?" I was proud of how calmly and precisely I managed to speak.

The clacking of the keyboards stopped for a moment. "Uh, his husband. Never mind, I'll call."

"Still in touch, are you?"

"Stop it." The clacking had resumed, and a thread of annoyance joined the worry in Checker's voice. "You can be petty after we find him."

He was right, but that didn't mean I had to concede it. "I'm capable of multitasking," I snapped. "I'll let you know what I find at his office. And after that I'm going to his apartment. Are you going to give me grief about respecting his privacy on that too?"

"Just find him," said Checker, sounding tired and concerned, and hung up on me.

I grabbed my coat, steadfastly resisting any urge to feel guilt about my snippiness. I checked the Colt in my belt and made sure the hem of the coat covered it completely, shoved a few spare magazines in my pocket and, feeling in a better-to-be-safe-than-sorry mood, a revolver in another pocket. Part of me hoped to find Arthur snoozing at home, but a strong sense of foreboding in my chest warned of how unlikely that was.

Wherever he was, he'd better be alive. He owed me about a thousand damn explanations.

two

SHIT. I'd forgotten about my client meeting. I pulled out my cell as I locked the door of the stupid office behind me, punching in the contact number I had. It was already seven minutes after the hour; maybe he was a no-show anyway.

The phone rang out without a voicemail message. That was weird.

"You're not supposed to be leaving," said a voice with an Aussie accent.

I turned. It took me three scans of the decrepit parking lot to find the person who had spoken. My client—well, I assumed—was scrambling toward me over the gravel: an unkempt Asian Australian man, with shaggy black hair, greasy stubble, and a torn shirt beneath his leather jacket that was even dirtier than mine. "Sorry," I said insincerely, waving my phone at him. "I was just trying to call. Something's come up."

"No. No!" He whipped his head in a frantic headshake. "No, you have to stay!"

"Look, we can reschedule for—"

"No!" he cried, and launched himself at me.

His movement translated into mathematics, clumsy Newtonian mechanics with his mass and velocity throwing themselves forward with no regard for efficiency. He might be bigger than I was, but still, it was insulting. And I was in the mood to hit someone.

I twisted and struck my palm against his hip, building the perfect fulcrum. His body flipped over in a spin an acrobat would have been proud of, and he landed on his back, wheezing.

I stepped into the afternoon sun so my shadow fell across his face. "Hi," I said. "I'm Cas Russell. *Our meeting is rescheduled.* Is that underst—"

My office exploded.

The concussion roared outward through shattering glass and splintering wood and slammed across the lot. The blast flung me into the air, the noise overwhelming everything else. I flailed against it and managed enough of a partial solution to twist and hit the ground hard on my shoulder before rolling out back to my feet.

The explosion had shredded the front wall of my new office, bits of boards hanging by mere splinters against crumbling mounds of plaster. Nothing was on fire, but I didn't want to know what it looked like inside. The small, grimy parking lot had only a few cars in it, but their windows had all shattered, and I could hear car alarms wailing from some distance away. My lungs twinged in the aftermath of the sudden pressure differential.

My would-be client, who had escaped the worst of the blast by being flat on his back, tried to scramble to his feet and dash away. I snatched up a piece of wood rubble from the explosion and threw it.

And *missed*.

What the hell? I never missed. One hundred percent accuracy was one of the perks of having a freakish mathematical superpower. I picked up another piece of debris, concentrated, and tried again. This time the board smacked him against the back of the knees, and his feet flew up, landing him on his back for the second time in thirty seconds.

"You!" I shouted, bearing down on him. My voice sounded strange and tinny. Also, my head hurt. "You just tried to get me killed!"

He mouthed something at me.

I grabbed him by the neck and slammed his head into the gravel. "Who are you?"

His jaw worked frantically, as if he were trying to form words, and he stabbed one finger repeatedly at the side of his head like a jackhammer.

Ears. Right.

The car alarms I was hearing weren't from far away. They were right next to me.

I yanked the guy to his feet and levered one of his arms behind his back to force him along with me. His face contorted in pain as he stumbled to keep up. I brought us to a car that wasn't mine and shoved him to the ground while I jacked it open; glass showered down onto the seats. I shoved my new friend into the back, brushed the glass off the driver's seat, and pried open the dash to touch the right two wires together.

The car thrummed to life beneath us. I couldn't hear it.

Neighbors were starting to poke their heads out. An Armenian guy in an apron who was probably the owner of the car came running, waving his arms, but I was already pulling out, skidding in a 360 to squeal out of the parking lot. At least, I was pretty sure we squealed. My head felt like it was wrapped in wool, muffling all sound to almost nothing. A high ringing phased in over it, as if trying to prove the point.

Christ, I'd have to start tracking my hearing damage. Between firefights and explosives, I was pretty sure some of it was becoming permanent.

We had to switch cars fast; it wasn't like we could stay under the police radar with all our windows blown out. I swerved into an underground garage beneath a run-down apartment building, and within minutes, we were driving back out in a much less conspicuous sedan. In the chaos I'd almost forgotten to haul my prisoner along in the car swap, but he'd tried to run again and I'd clotheslined him into the front passenger seat.

I texted Checker with one hand as I drove:

Office blew up

On the run

Burning this phone

In touch soon

Then I popped the battery out, dropped the phone out the window, and lost us in the summer heat of Los Angeles traffic.

My prisoner moaned next to me, reminding me again that he was there. He tried to reach for the car door handle, but I punched him in the throat.

"No, no," he wheezed between bouts of coughing. "You don't see me!"

"Of course I do," I said. "You blew up my office!"

Come to that, where the hell should I go with him?

Aside from my office, I exchanged monthly cash payments for plenty of shabby little apartments around LA which doubled as both safe houses and interchangeable living spaces. Arthur had also tried to get me to stick to a semipermanent address, but I absolutely had never seen the point to that.

I had to get to Arthur's office and home and check them, but what if those were rigged too? What if the explosion had to do with his disappearance? How likely was that? After all, I had plenty of enemies who'd be more than happy to blow me to kingdom come, and they had nothing to do with Arthur.

The grasping hands of my past reared up again. Flashes of fragmented memory had given shape to doctors and drugs, training and cruelty. Someone had been honing me—honing a lot of us—but I still didn't know who or why. Only that they had been frighteningly similar to the people who called themselves Pithica, the mind witches who'd eventually claimed themselves puppet masters of the world until I'd been dumb enough to throw a spanner into their works.

Or maybe it's closer to home. Maybe someone in the city found out about you screwing them all in the head.

That was a troubling thought. As of four months ago, almost all of Los Angeles had owed me a broken skull, but my mistakes had been psychically erased in the most discomfiting way possible, and most of them appeared to have forgotten. I doubted the telepathic sweep had gotten everyone, though. Some people seemed to have dismissed the rumors of my involvement, given the ultimately bizarre and seemingly inconsistent sequence of events, but I suspected there existed others—people who'd recognized a voice on the radio and now nursed perfectly rational grudges even as their cohorts laughed them off.

Then there were all the people I'd screwed over directly by breaking into their secure lairs and threatening them. I was pretty sure Yamamoto wasn't the only crime lord still taking my rampage as a personal insult, and I hadn't even pointed a gun at him.

But even with all the lurking threats, I still didn't believe in coincidences, or at least only believed in them when they fit the relevant probability distribution. And for my office to blow up *exactly* after Arthur had gone missing . . . especially considering he'd left a message on his voicemail about being connected with me . . .

"You're not supposed to *see* me," moaned my passenger.

I blinked.

Somehow I'd stopped paying attention to him. Weird. Especially considering he was currently my most likely source of answers. The ringing in my ears had died down enough to hear the very loud rap music in the car next to us; it was past time to run an interrogation.

"Yeah, I've heard blowing people up is great for stealth," I said back to him. "In fact, we're going to have a nice little conversation now. Talk and you'll live."

"I don't know anything," said the Aussie man. The emphasis on the words was odd, as if he wasn't used to speaking aloud. "You were supposed to stay. You were supposed to stay and not see."

What?

"Nobody sees," he continued. "I'm *not here*." He started giggling.

Oh. Oh, shit. This guy was . . . not all there. Someone else must be taking advantage of him.

Fuck.

I thought for a minute and then drove to a four-story apartment building where I kept a one-bedroom place on the top floor. The Aussie man whimpered about hidden secrets and invisible friends all the way up.

I didn't want to hurt him again—I wasn't opposed to hurting people in general, but in this case, it didn't seem fair—but when he wouldn't get out of the car, I had to hustle him out with a grip on his jacket. I got him up to the apartment and sat him down in the bedroom. There wasn't a bed, only a couch with one of its cushions missing, but hey, I didn't run a Hilton.

"What's your name?" I tried.

"People don't talk to me," he said. "And I don't talk to people."

"A man after my own heart." I sighed. "Who told you to blow up my office?"

"They told me to do it," he agreed. "And they were right."

"*Who* told you?"

"The one who makes the music," he said. "Playing the songs when you ask."

"Does this person have a name?"

"I'm not supposed to tell anyone. How did you know it was me?"

"You basically told me," I said. "I do tend to notice when people try to kill me."

"No, you don't. It wasn't me. You're wrong."

I gave up.

He had access to the bathroom, and I opened some cans of overly processed food and left them in the room with a spoon and a few bottles of water. Then I locked the door to the bedroom and shoved a wedge under the outside door to the apartment for good measure. The windows in the place were painted shut and four stories up—the only danger of him getting out was if he started making noise and someone investigated. But this building was mostly empty units or people who spent their entire days high, so I didn't think it likely.

Two years ago, I probably would have tied the guy up and gagged him, or at least considered it. "Fuck you, Arthur," I muttered.

Are you sure it's all Arthur?

I stomped down the stairs. No—Arthur had been trying to convince me to have a conscience long before I'd had a telepath in my head regularly. I wasn't going to go there.

Wasn't going to start second-guessing myself.

I'd repeated the same words so often over the past four months that I was sick of them.

Besides, I reminded myself, it was bad enough if it *was* just Arthur pushing at my morals—pretending to be my friend, trying to fix me up to be a model citizen, and not even telling me the basic facts of his own goddamn life. He knew the most personal details about me, after all. He'd been with me all through fighting a worldwide organization of psychics who were only too ready to kill me if given half a chance, and knew all about Dawna Polk, Pithica's telepath who'd clawed into my brain and almost destroyed me. He knew about my amnesia—that I was mired without any memory more than five years back, aside from hellish remnants best forgotten. And he knew about Simon, who I had to keep letting erase me once a week or I'd fragment and blow away on the wind . . . even after I'd found out he was the one who'd obliterated me in the first place. A past I couldn't look at, the capacity for ruthless mathematical violence with no explanation behind such an abnormal skill set . . . whispers of words and images and nothing more to tell me who had made me . . . Arthur knew all of it.

I'd saved Arthur's life so many times now, and he'd saved mine.

He'd never once mentioned he had a family.

three

TELEPATHS. Something sparked in my brain, making me think about Pithica and Dawna Polk and Simon again. Psychic powers—something—I squeezed my eyelids shut, my head aching. I couldn't help feeling like I'd just missed something important.

My mind came up a blank. Damn.

I'd picked up a clean phone in the apartment, and I dialed Checker as I started down again.

"Hello?" he said.

"It's Cas."

"Cas, holy shit—are you all right? What do you mean, your office blew up? What happened?"

"My office blew up."

"Cas!"

"I'm fine. I'm going to head to Arthur's office now." Technically the business was half Checker's, but he telecommuted. "Have you found anything yet?"

"Yeah. There's been no activity on Arthur's cell in the past day and a half, and the GPS copped out not long after that. The last known location is the office. Same for his email accounts—no activity since he was last on his phone. I'm—I'm really worried."

"I take it the, uh, the family didn't know anything."

"No. Tabitha was the last one to talk to him."

I swallowed back my resentment about Arthur's secrets again. I'd reached the ground floor, and I headed back to my stolen car, pinching the phone between my shoulder and cheek as I got in.

"Do you think whoever attacked you—is it related?" Checker asked.

"I don't know."

"Do you think Tabitha's in danger? Or the rest of Arthur's family?"

"I don't *know*."

"Shit, what if they're going to blow up our office too?" His voice rose with alarm. "Maybe you shouldn't—"

"Only one way to find out." I ignored the fact that I'd been thinking the same thing.

"You know," Checker said. "There are, um. Private security firms. Who rent. Um. Bomb-sniffing dogs."

The traffic flowed around me mathematically, speed and density and flux automatically mapping to a space-time diagram, so fortunately, I didn't have to concentrate, because Checker had just thrown me for a loop. "How on earth do you know that?"

"I may have . . . done some research. A while ago."

It wasn't a bad idea. I couldn't do math on what I didn't know existed. "I'm on my way there now. Can you get one fast?"

"Uh, I don't know. Let me call at least, okay?"

"Fine," I said. "In the meantime, I'll pick up Pilar. She can help me sort through your files. Unless you want to come do it." I was a shit investigator, and Pilar Velasquez had been Arthur and Checker's office manager up through a few months ago.

"No, Pilar's better," Checker said. "She knows our files better than we do. But she's at an event tonight—I've been trying to call her, but it keeps going to voicemail—"

"Where is she?"

"The W, in Hollywood. Some sort of hoity-toity political fundraiser."

I snorted. "It's not polite to track people's phones, you know."

"Serves her right," Checker said with no remorse. "We're lost without that woman. Why we ever let her leave is beyond me."

"Didn't you give her the investment to start her event-thingy business in the first place?"

"Not the point," he huffed, then sobered. "Wait for my call, okay?"

"Whatever," I said, and hung up, slewing the sedan onto a side street to turn toward downtown. Again, something itched at me, something I'd forgotten to tell him. Something *important*—

I didn't like not being able to trust my own mind. It was bad enough not trusting the person I needed to have rifle through it regularly.

But whatever I wasn't remembering, it would have to wait—I didn't have time to dwell. I parked in a self-pay lot in Hollywood and left without buying the dash ticket from the machine. Pilar had probably driven; we'd just take her car from here.

Pilar was easily the most organized person I'd ever met, and had worked for Arthur and Checker for a little over a year. She'd continued with them part-time through the early months of starting her own business, but her clientele had taken off so fast, she'd been gone before the two of them could find someone new. Checker had flat-out admitted they liked her so much, they'd been dragging their feet on replacing her.

I supposed it was difficult to find someone good at spreadsheets who was also comfortable getting shot at occasionally and who wouldn't call the police on shady sometimes-colleagues like me.

Colleagues. Even *colleagues* knew about their coworkers' families. What the hell did I count as, then?

When I got to the W Hotel, dolled-up patrons strolled in and out of the twilit evening, all of them constructed to be beautiful and walking to be seen. Women gleamed poreless from their strappy heels to their manicured fingertips. Men sported suits designed to look recklessly casual and hairdos gelled to be artfully messy. A few people of indeterminate gender played up one look or the other with equal flamboyance.

Hollywood at its finest.

I crossed the star-inlaid sidewalk and slipped into the glitzy lobby. Some sort of red-carpet event was going on in a courtyard through the back, but I didn't see Pilar. I started a systematic search of the ground floor for event rooms, keeping an eye out for hotel security. A few of the peacocked patrons graced me with a combat-boots-up stare, but no one tried to stop me.

I caught sight of Pilar's energetic posture and stride flitting between name-tagged hotel staff in a grand, long ballroom filled with round tables draped in tablecloths so snowy, they were blinding. Caterers bustled about setting wineglasses and flatware.

"Excuse me, ma'am, can I help you?" A very large member of the hotel security staff had appeared by my elbow while I was distracted. The subtext of his baritone request was, *If you don't have a good reason to be here, allow me to escort you out. Immediately.*

"I just have to grab my friend," I said, and sidestepped around him.

"Ma'am—"

He reached out a beefy hand to block me.

I didn't hurt him, but I grabbed his wrist and pushed at exactly the angle lacking an equal-and-opposite normal force. The security guard lost his balance, half-pirouetted, and landed on his ass. His face clouded.

"He tripped," I announced to the suddenly staring hotel staff.

"Cas!" Pilar rushed toward me with wide eyes. She had put on some weight since I'd seen her last, and she wore it well, with an air of authority. She also wore a deep purple cocktail dress that was turning heads, and her makeup and hair were a few orders of magnitude sharper than usual. "Cas, honey, I love you, but—what are you doing? And I'm sorry, you really can't be here dressed like that—"

I glanced down at my usual cargo-pants-and-boots ensemble. There was also some broken glass and blood on it I hadn't noticed. "Sorry," I said, not meaning it. "Pilar, Arthur's missing. Checker's been trying to get in touch with you—we need your help with his office. His files—"

Pilar looked stricken. "Arthur's missing? What happened?"

"That's what we're trying to figure out. He just disappeared. Now come on."

"I can't—" Her head swiveled from side to side, and she flailed her hands miserably. "I can't just leave—I'm in charge here! Our client is—"

"Pilar," I said. "It's Arthur."

"Ma'am, do you know this woman?" asked the security guard, who had regained his feet.

"Yes, I do. It's all right. Um." Pilar cast me an agonized expression and then reached out to snag a black-and-white-clad server by the elbow. "Get Catherine for me, now," she said, before turning back. "Give me five minutes to square things here. And can you please wait outside? People are staring."

Ten minutes later, I was zipping Pilar's car onto the freeway while reading a series of texts from Checker, the long and short of which was that he hadn't been able to get us canine help on such short notice, but he was still trying, and would I please be careful and possibly consider waiting even though he knew I wasn't going to.

"Can you please not do that while you're driving?" Pilar said, while tapping out texts and emails a mile a minute herself. I gathered she'd screwed her staff over by leaving.

I ignored her. "Talk to me about Arthur. Was he doing anything off the books? Anything that might have been making him enemies recently?"

"You mean, anything Checker wouldn't know about?" she said.

I hadn't been thinking that, but now I was.

"I mean, I haven't been around in a while," she stammered. "I don't know what would be recent."

"Anything *un*recent?" I said.

She worried her lower lip with her teeth. "I'll look when we get there."

"God*dammit*," I said. "All you fucking people and your fucking secrets. This is not the time."

Her eyes went all huge and wounded.

"Don't give me that look. Because guess who I met today?" I whipped the words at her. "Tabitha."

"What? O—oh."

"'Oh' is right," I said. "How long have *you* known?"

"Known what?" Pilar asked miserably.

"Fuck you."

"I'm sorry—"

"What was it like?" I tried to make the question snide, but for some reason it sounded hurt. "Did he introduce you and say, 'Oh, hey, meet my family, and by the way, tell anyone but Cas'?"

"No, it—it wasn't like that—"

"Forget it," I said. "But you hide anything that could help us find him, and I will burn down your nice new event business."

"*Cas,*" she sighed. I'd apparently ceased to be able to shock her properly. "Okay. Okay. There was this one thing he had me working on, setting up web alerts and stuff, that he wasn't telling Checker about, but I don't know if it's relevant at all, and he started it like a year ago, and I don't think he got anywhere really, but I don't know if recently—"

"Spill."

"Well, it was about—there was that person Checker has a history with, who kept, um, blowing things up."

That definitely seemed to fit. "Which person who kept blowing stuff up?"

"*Seriously?* How many people have tried to blow up you or your friends?"

"More than one," I said. "I can't be expected to keep track of them all."

"Well, but Checker has talked about—do you ever even listen to people? Anyway, I don't know what all their history was, I just know Arthur was trying to find any information he could on D.J., so he had me keep on it and, um—he didn't want me to tell anyone."

"D.J.?" I vaguely remembered who she meant now. "Oh, yeah, we've run across each other a few times. Freelance bomber, utterly batshit, mouth like a filthy sewer." D.J. was like me—a contractor who didn't seem to care mightily how many people died as long as payment came on time. Actually, I was pretty sure D.J. was more amoral than I was, which said a lot. On the other hand, even though we'd run into each other on opposite sides a few times, I'd always had the impression it was because good money was changing hands for the explosions. It made me less leery of meeting D.J. again than I otherwise would've been.

It also meant that even if D.J. was involved here, the mastermind was probably someone else putting out a contract . . .

Wait. Except Pilar had mentioned Checker. Who didn't exactly run in the same violent and not-so-legal circles I did. "Back up," I said. "You said this is related to Checker? How?"

"I don't *know*, I only know what Checker himself has said about it, which isn't much. Something from years ago, I think. And Arthur was working on it like a case, trying to pick up any trail to find where D.J. might be."

"Why didn't he ask me?" That stung. "Criminal contractors are my world, you know. Arthur needs to track down a bomber-for-hire, I should be his first goddamn call."

He probably didn't ask for the same reason he didn't tell you about Diego or Tabitha or anything about this fucking case in the first place.

Arthur didn't trust me.

But the bitterness threatening to flood me was eclipsed by everything suddenly slotting together, every piece of this that hadn't registered at the time pointing to the same conclusion. Pilar was trying to sputter a response to me from the passenger seat, but I didn't hear her. Arthur on D.J.'s trail before his sudden disappearance, Checker looking up bomb-sniffing dogs, and then the explosion at my office . . .

The one who makes the music, an echo of an Australian accent said. *Playing the songs when you ask.*

D.J.

This wasn't just a contract. It was personal.

four

I STARTED to dial Checker. Pilar's hand stopped me. "Please, can we just wait until we know for sure it's the same person?" she said. "Arthur didn't want him to know because—I mean, I don't *know*, but you know Checker's past was pretty rough, so I'm guessing something traumatic . . ."

"I'm sure it's the same person," I said, but I stopped dialing. I didn't know what I'd say to Checker anyway.

You know Checker's past was pretty rough, Pilar had said. But I hadn't known.

Sure, I was aware the guy had a less-than-legal history that had involved gaining a surprising level of money-laundering expertise for someone as young as he was, but in all the nights he'd coerced me into coming over to drink and watch trashy science fiction shows, all the times I'd thought that, maybe, I was starting to have people around me I called friends . . . he'd never gone on about anything deeper than whether they should make another *Terminator* movie. Nothing about his past, or family, or . . . anything.

Just like Arthur.

Or it's like Pilar said, and you weren't listening, a traitorous thought suggested. I slammed it away and kept driving.

I expected to have to wing it when we got to Arthur's office—I didn't have any handy explosives-detection tech available to pick up, and there were limits to what math could tell me about the existence of bombs I couldn't see. But when I pulled into the parking lot, two men were waiting for us: a tall Asian man in a trench coat, and a less-tall, olive-skinned man who was hugging his arms around himself despite the warm night. Rio and Simon.

We got out. Behind me, Pilar rebalanced her weight and put her hand in her purse.

I slipped slightly in front of her. The chill in the air felt like it dipped three degrees even though I could tell it was exactly the same temperature. Pilar was probably the genuinely nicest person I knew, and she'd never even touched a gun before she'd met me, but I still wasn't sure she wouldn't try to take down Rio someday for what he'd done to her.

Or maybe it was exactly because she *was* so genuinely nice that she was this willing to draw on Rio, when I knew for a fact that she'd never in her life fired on another human. After all, there were people who'd consider Rio's murder to be a public service. I wondered if that lurked in Pilar's mind every time she saw him—how many of his victims she'd save if she could only bring herself to pull the trigger. Sure, it wasn't like the people Rio killed were angels, but he did kill an *awful* lot of them.

I'd told Pilar I'd try to keep him away from her. Whoops.

"Stay cool," I said to her out of the corner of my mouth. Would she even have been carrying a weapon when I yanked her from the W?

"I will if he does," she muttered back.

The fact that I still trusted and associated with Rio . . . was this why Arthur had never told me about his family? I was angry all over again.

It wasn't like I was particularly glad to see them either, though. Especially not Simon, who thought he had the right to ransack my brain regularly just to keep me from dying.

"You're stalking me now?" I called out to them as greeting. "Fuck you."

"We did try to call—" started Simon.

Right. I'd burned my phone and hadn't sent either of them an update.

"You failed to appear for your appointment," said Rio, his expression unchanged.

Shit. Until that very moment, the fact that I'd been supposed to see Simon tonight had completely dropped out of my head.

"Yeah," I said. "Something came up."

"Cas," said Rio. "You realize the importance of this."

Simon shuffled his feet on the gravel of the parking lot and ran a hand through his hair. "Cassand—" He cut himself off with a cough. Simon still had trouble getting his head around the fact that I didn't like being called by my full name. For a psychic, he could be pretty dumb. "Cas, if we don't address things regularly . . ."

If I didn't let Simon and his telepathic skills worm into my brain on a weekly-or-so basis, I would go mad from the errant memories of the dead woman who used to own my body. Yes, yes, he'd explained it enough times for me never to want to hear it again.

But I didn't have time right now to spend two hours engaging in his deranged version of psychotherapy. "I'll come see you when I'm done with this job."

"You're always on the job, Cas," said Simon.

"Are you under an imminent deadline?" asked Rio.

This was an excellent example of why Rio was about fifty times smarter than Simon. I focused on him instead. "Arthur's missing. Help me or get out of my way."

Rio might not understand friendship, but he had a theoretical knowledge of it. I imagined the if-A-then-B flowchart he must use whenever he was confronted with such an inscrutable emotion. I was pretty sure his flowchart told him it was a good thing I had friends, and that if one had a friend and the friend was in trouble, this must logically take top priority.

Though if his flowcharts told him something different, I didn't give a shit. I was perfectly willing to bulldoze through Rio and Simon both if they didn't acquiesce in the next ten seconds.

"I am at your service," said Rio. Good. That was good. Rio had a lot more explosives expertise than I did.

"Cas, you know I'll help," put in Simon, spreading his hands earnestly—even though I knew no such thing, and he and his telepathic skills had to be aware of that, the prick. He winced. "I meant, of course I'll help. Where do we start?"

Simon was not someone I ever spent time with voluntarily, but I wasn't stupid enough to turn him down. The problem was, he wasn't ever willing to use his powers unless . . . wait.

Something itched at my brain.

I rubbed my forehead, but it was gone.

"Rio," I said instead, "we're up against someone who likes explosives, and we need to go through Arthur's office. Can you—"

"It would be my pleasure. Remain here," Rio said, and swept toward the outside stairs to Arthur's second-floor office. Yet another reason I liked Rio.

I pointed at Simon. "As for you, stay by your phone. The minute we have someone you could help with, I want you there."

I started to turn away, ushering Pilar with me.

"Wait," Simon said.

"I told you, now is not the time to—"

"No. Cas. There's something you wanted to tell me. I saw it a minute ago, but then it left your mind. I think it's important."

"Ego, much?" I said.

"*Cas.*"

I wasn't sure if it was Simon's abilities or my own brain that filled in his tone, but it did occur to me that when a telepath who claimed he was on my side was trying to tell me I wanted something, I should probably consider it. Next to me, Pilar's expression had creased into worry, mirroring my thoughts.

Goddamn psychics.

"I don't remember wanting to tell you anything," I said to Simon, but a lot less aggressively.

He shook his head, as if he were hearing a fly buzzing but he wasn't sure from where. "There's something wrong. May I?"

I gave him a look that made the skin around his eyes tighten, but I also jerked my head to invite him closer. He stepped up to me and gazed down into my face. "Give me your eyes, Cas. Run back your day for me."

"Right before this, I picked up Pilar," I said, making eye contact and trying not to sneer the words. "I've been on the phone with Checker in between trying to figure out what to do ever since my office blew up. And right before that was when—"

"Stop. You skipped something."

"I skipped a lot of things."

"Start again with when your office . . . God, you're all right physically, right?"

"I'm *fine*." I didn't bother to moderate my tone. "My office blew up, I jacked a car and went to pick up Pilar, and we came here. Talked to Checker in between."

"You skipped it again. After your office—what happened right before and after the, um, the bomb? Was it a bomb?"

"Yeah," I said. "I'd just gone outside, and I was trying to call my client—"

Shit.

My would-be client.

"That's it," Simon said, unnecessarily.

I tried to hold on to the guy's image. It felt slippery, the face blurred, as if I were trying to recall someone from a decade ago.

What the *fuck*.

"I locked him up," I said. Jesus, he was lucky I'd run into Simon, or he would have died of thirst there. "What the hell did he do to me? And *why*? Is he one of you lot?" But his powers seemed much weaker—I'd never have been able to imprison Simon so easily, not if he chose to use his mental mojo on me. Nor Dawna Polk, the leader of Pithica—the memory of how easily and thoroughly she'd been able to rewrite my perceptions still gave me nightmares.

"I don't know," Simon said. "I haven't been connected to Pithica in . . . a long time. This seems different, but I can't place how. And Pithica—they were always refining new technologies. I don't know."

Making new types of psychics. Holy hell.

"We had a deal," I croaked.

Rio had brokered it, to save all our lives: Pithica wouldn't kill us, and we would stop our efforts to destroy them. It wasn't one I would have said yes to, given the choice, but they'd enforced my agreement with a mental block that made it impossible for me to work against them.

I'd insisted Simon remove the actual block months ago. But still— I'd hesitated. I'd told myself that Pithica hadn't only threatened my life and mental sanctity, but Arthur's and Checker's, and without a plan, putting a toe in their direction would immediately equal us all being snuffed from the face of the Earth. They were too powerful.

Maybe that was logic. Or maybe it was fear.

Find Arthur, I commanded myself. *Finding Arthur is the first step, no matter what.* If we had to regroup after that to take on people who could literally rewrite our thoughts . . .

"I'll try to figure out more," Simon said. "The man you can't remember—focus on his face. That will help."

I did, and as soon as Simon told me to, I found it easier. The details of my client's features started to clear. Asian, I thought. And Australian—for some reason, now that I'd remembered him, I didn't have the least bit of trouble with his *voice*. Only his appearance.

"Who the fuck is this guy?" I said.

"I don't know," Simon said again.

"He blew up my office." It was coming back to me now, in hazy half mirages. Had he been working with D.J.? "He tried to kill me, and then I forgot him. After locking him up."

You don't see me, the man had said. He'd meant it literally.

But I also remembered him being . . . out of it, not quite making sense . . . like he'd been manipulated himself. Or was that just my malfunctioning neurons making it seem so?

"Cas," Simon said. "I reiterate my offer to help."

Oh, Christ. I *hated* needing Simon's help.

"Yeah. Okay," I said. I gave him the address. "Go get me some fucking answers. Are you going to be able to *tell* him to stay put, by the way? And not to blow *you* up?"

He knew by *tell* I meant *force*. He hesitated.

"*Seriously?* This guy might be working for Pithica! You can't tell me you have moral qualms about using your goddamned psychic powers against another psychic—"

"I don't think he is one," Simon said. "Not in the same sense that we are. It's something different. And if he isn't—you know I can't do that sort of thing. No matter what."

Can't or won't? Simon and his mewling ethics. "I'll send Rio with you," I said. "There's even the off chance he won't be affected by whatever this is." Rio was immune to Simon's brand of telepathy, but even if this was something different, well, *I* had been able to interact with the guy for some small period of time. Rio would be able to handle keeping him in place. And he'd make sure our prisoner didn't try to kill Simon. Not that people did attack Simon, usually—even if he didn't make a concerted effort to keep himself safe, telepaths' thoughts had a lot of unconscious bleed.

Yet another thing I hated about them.

"Go update Rio," I said. "Tell him he's with you after he clears us here, and that this might be Pithica, but we're not sure yet."

Simon opened his mouth, probably to say something about Rio having told us to stay down here because of *possible bombs*, but then he took in my face and started across the parking lot.

"This could get real bad, couldn't it?" Pilar said softly. "I've heard you guys talk about the Pithica telepaths and how they—they can just make you believe anything, can't they? And you think it's your own thoughts?"

"Yeah," I said.

"Can Simon help us against that, do you think?"

Who knew. I should probably ask him, just to plan contingencies, but getting a straight commitment out of the man without being condescended to was like trying to force a chaotic system to behave, and just the thought of trying to coordinate a defensive plan with him made my mouth sour.

I leaned against Pilar's car to wait. Someone cackled in the back of my head, but I told myself it was psychosomatic.

"Hey, are you going to be okay?" Pilar asked, as if she were the mind reader now. "If you skip the mental therapy thing with Simon, I mean."

"Yes," I snapped. "It's not an exact science." The words were ones Simon himself oft-repeated, and I felt dirty being the one saying them now. But it was true: I wasn't going to start collapsing if I missed a session.

I might start hearing voices again after missing several sessions, but who knew how long that would take.

Rio had finished his sweep of the perimeter and had gone inside Arthur's office now, the heavy metal door wedged ajar. I was certain Pilar hadn't given him the keys—if she even still had them—but a locked door was little more than a nuisance to Rio. Simon hovered on the upstairs landing, talking to him through the crack.

It was coming on dark. A breeze had started up, but the summer air was still hot and dry where it blew against our skin.

"You know, I almost stayed," said Pilar, very suddenly.

"What?" I glanced at her. She was staring abstractly up after Simon, as if she hadn't spoken. "What are you talking about?"

"I almost stayed on," she said. "With Arthur and Checker. I'd been wanting to start my own business forever, and I'd never meant to be an admin all my life, but I almost stayed."

"Okay. So?"

"I had signed up for tactical training."

"Really?"

"Yeah. I was all signed up, and the business was going to pay for it and all—I mean, Arthur wasn't too happy about it, seeing as he got all torn up about ever putting me in danger in the first place, but he did want me to be safer if I could, and he couldn't exactly promise me I'd always be safe working for him. I think he even wanted me to quit, sometimes, but he sort of forced himself to let me make the decision."

"He wanted to *fire* you to keep you safe?" I said.

"It's not completely absurd. Not with what we've been through. He didn't want me hurt."

I thought of the justification Simon had given for what he'd done to me, that he'd *had* to because he couldn't stand the thought of me dying, and something inside me curdled blackly. I couldn't agree.

"Anyway," Pilar continued. "I was about to go to boot camp, and I realized—if I didn't leave now, I would never leave."

"That doesn't make any sense," I said. "Now, does all this have a point, or is it just small talk? Because you know how I hate—"

"I do. I have a point." She chewed her lip for a moment. "Here's the thing. Most of Arthur's cases aren't that bad. It's always when he's working with you that stuff gets dangerous. Like the brain entrainment thing earlier this year. Or even the first case with Pithica, he's told me—"

"Arthur was on that case way before I ever heard of Pithica. This is blatant sampling error!"

"There are a lot more times, Cas, you *know* there have been a lot more times—Arthur helps you out whenever you ask, and things just kind of escalate when you're around, you know? You do tend to think violence is the best answer."

"Sometimes it is," I said hotly.

"Cas, sweetie, I'm not trying to put you down. You've saved all our lives more than once. I'm just saying, I know it doesn't seem fair to you, but I get where Arthur's coming from in wanting to keep his family out of it. Maybe cut him some slack."

"Not a chance."

"It's not even him," she pleaded. "It's his kids. Cut him some slack."

That was exactly why I wasn't going to be cutting any slack at all—once we found him alive and well.

Shit.

The door to Arthur's office opened, and Rio came out, raising a hand to wave us up. "Talk later," I said to Pilar, and we hurried up the metal steps to the landing.

"Cas," Rio said, sliding some sort of sensor wand back into his trench coat, "there are no longer any active devices here that I can detect. However . . ."

We stood in the doorway and stared. The dim evening light played softly over our heads, illuminating the inside of Arthur's office.

The inside of what had *been* Arthur's office.

five

THE ROOM was a wreck.

In kind terms, Arthur was . . . particular. He wasn't so much a neat freak as he wanted everything in its place. Now the large file cabinets had all been wrenched open, the drawers pulled at amok angles. Files littered the floor in a paper carpet. Everything had been tossed off the desks—both Arthur's desk and at Pilar's old station—and the drawers had been yanked fully out and plopped on the floor.

Arthur's tall gun safe had been blown open, too, the metal warped and charred.

"Rio," I said. "How certain are you nothing live is here?"

"Approximately ninety percent," he answered.

I inched forward, motioning Pilar to stay back. Luckily, I knew this room well, and the level of sloppiness here suggested little attempt at subtlety, enough for me to be able to take a set difference. The complement rose to prominence in my senses, allowing me to focus on what had changed.

The locks on the file cabinets, the desks, and the gun safe had all been busted open with varying levels of explosives. "One-trick pony," I muttered, as I edged around to Arthur's desk. The desktop computer still hummed. I reached out and turned on one of the dual monitors.

A login screen flared to life undramatically. No way the ransacker could have gotten past Checker's security, not unless the computer was already unlocked for some reason, which I supposed was possible. Come to think of it . . .

"Isn't there a security system on this place?" I called to Pilar, who was still by the door. Checker's security on his *home* probably rivaled the White House; why wouldn't he have wired the office the same way?

Pilar twisted her hands against each other. "We have one, we do, and it's really good, but it's more for when we're not here. During the day, we mostly have it turned off—we have to, what with clients coming in and out all the time. And even the cameras, Arthur doesn't keep them on when we have people in, because of confidentiality."

I finished my circuit of the office. The set difference had revealed no indication of active explosives anywhere things were out of place. I couldn't be a hundred percent sure, but I thought we were probably in the clear, and on top of Rio's check, that was the best we could hope for.

"Okay, you two can go," I said to Simon and Rio. "Pilar, text Checker and see if he can get anything, anything at all, from either the security system or by hopping on the office intranets. Then tell me where you think Arthur would've been keeping stuff."

"We'll go find the man you took prisoner," Simon promised, turning to leave.

Shit. I'd already forgotten that's where I was sending them.

"Rio," I called.

He turned.

"This guy, he . . ." My memory of the Australian's face was still fuzzy, but I could recall my attempted interrogation now. "I had the impression . . . I don't think he's quite with it. Minimal force, okay? Unless you find out he really is with Pithica."

Rio hesitated. "Cas, if they have broken their covenant with us, this will only be their first step. I submit that I may be more useful to you elsewhere."

He was right, but . . . "Our first priority has to be finding Arthur. Please."

He touched his forehead. "As you wish, Cas."

I took a relieved breath.

A year ago I wouldn't have thought it necessary to caution Rio against employing his . . . usual methods . . . against someone who displayed a questionable mental capacity. But these days, every time I thought about assuming something like that, the image flashed in my head of Rio pointing a gun at Pilar's head, and I warned him off anyway.

He didn't seem to mind. In fact, he seemed to take it as logical, which was frightening in a whole host of other ways.

Rio and Simon headed out into the gathering darkness, and Pilar finished tapping out a message on her phone and picked her way across the paper-strewn floor. "When you say you want to know anywhere Arthur was keeping stuff, what kind of stuff are you looking for?" she said. "Do you mean anything on—on D.J.?"

"Yeah," I said. "That, or any current cases, any files he wanted to keep sort of on hand. Or, on the flip side, anything he wanted to hide. And if he or Checker were still doing any legwork on Pithica without my knowledge, I want that too." Dawna had also given Arthur the mental block, but he might've taken advantage of Simon's presence to get it removed too. Everything was on the table at this point.

A sneaking doubt reminded me that Checker wasn't the only one who had a complicated past. What if instead of D.J., it was my own history Arthur had been looking into?

Was it possible a personalized bomber could be after me? Thanks to Simon, any villains I had known were a faded clutter of disconnected faces. A woman with a scar. Another with steel-gray hair, holding a clipboard. A man with a crew cut holding a stopwatch, nodding approvingly . . .

"Oh. Okay," Pilar interrupted my disturbed ponderings. She gazed around the clutter-strewn office. "Isn't it sort of useless to tell you where things would've been, though?"

"Pilar," I growled.

"Okay! Um." She started pointing. "His inbox used to sit here, uh—I think that's it in the corner. And there was a slot here where I'd put phone messages for him, but I don't know if he uses it anymore. Any really current stuff would've been on his desk or in the top right drawer. Anything sensitive was in the desk file drawer, which was reinforced and only Arthur had the key. This drawer here had a file for miscellaneous papers, which could be anything, and docs that weren't filed yet got put in here." She pointed to another mangled file drawer. "I think that's . . . that's all I can think of? I had places I kept current stuff too, but it doesn't look like he's been using my desk for anything."

She stood staring down at the empty drawers at her own old station, looking a little lost.

"Good," I said. "That's good. Now, stay still and don't touch anything."

I started backtracking the entropy of the room.

The place might look like chaos, but the stacked and scattered papers became coded in probability according to where they'd come from. Someone had searched through the mess before we'd gotten here—several times, if I was reading things correctly—but still, the way the files overlapped, the way the drawers overlapped, the most expected progression around the space . . . it all served to cut out possibilities and narrow the sequence down to a few interchangeable likelihoods.

The room disarrayed itself before me, forward and back, forward and back, in only a few possible combinations. Ones that overlapped significantly.

Finally, a problem I could attack and solve.

I held the backtracking in my head and started moving, picking up documents and folders whenever they came from where Pilar had pointed out, as long as I assumed the most probable events. By the time I reached Pilar's desk, I had an armful of papers.

Her eyes were very round. "Now *that's* a superpower."

"Oh, shut up."

I stared down at the folders for a moment, an intrusive reluctance making me hesitate in handing them over to her. How likely was it any of them would contain sprinklings of my past, my life? Quiet, concerned research Arthur might have been doing, one glimpse of which might destabilize my own amputated mind?

Find Arthur, I repeated to myself. Everything else was secondary.

If my own ghosts or sanity interfered, well, I would have to cowboy up and deal.

I tried not to let myself consider that if the investigation did lead in that direction, I could be the one to blame for the attack on Arthur. For all my righteous indignation about him keeping things from me . . . maybe it would have been better for him if we'd never met.

No. This was D.J. Everything points to D.J.

I handed the papers to Pilar with rigid fingers and had her sit and start going through the pile. Then, to keep myself busy more than anything, I called Checker to see what he'd found on the security system. "Can you get us *any* info on what happened here?" I asked him.

"I'm telling you, I've got no useful data at all from this end." His frustration was palpable through the line. "Arthur's code turned the entire security system off Friday morning, and it's been off since then. Nobody even tried the computers with an incorrect password, or it would have logged. From now on, I'm going to reprogram things to make the damn system notify me if it's off for more than twelve hours. I fought with Arthur about turning it off, you know—I said, it's still confidential if you're the only person who has access to the recordings, and he quoted stuff at me about California being a two-party consent state, and I said, well then, what about just *video,* there's nothing wrong with *video,* and he said he wants his clients to feel like they—"

"I get it, you know nothing," I said, more harshly than I meant to.

Checker stopped talking.

Shit. I also had to broach the topic of D.J. with him, and I didn't know how. I hadn't meant to start off by snapping at him.

It has to be D.J.—bombs, and the connection to Checker, and Arthur researching him. Playing the music when you ask . . .

This was D.J. It wasn't me.

"Thanks for looking, anyway," I said stiffly to Checker. "Maybe we'll find something in his papers."

"You're not good at this, Cas."

"What?"

"Beating around the bush. We've got buildings blowing up, and you want to know if it's my fault."

I hadn't expected him to be so blunt about it, but my mouth pounced on the hypothesis before my brain could moderate it. "Well, you do have a connection to a homicidal bomber, don't you? It's a logical question."

"And I promise you, I'm looking for the answer, okay? I'm pulling all the CSI data from the police investigation at your office, to see if I can find any sort of—of signature match with the building explosions we know D.J. did or—or with other ones. I'm doing everything I can. I swear I am."

"I . . . didn't think you weren't." I swallowed. I'd been insisting to myself that this was D.J. so hard, I'd let what that would mean for Checker fall out of the equation. His anxious self-recrimination made me hate myself.

But it's different. Arthur never held any of that against him . . .

"We need to consider all possibilities," I said. Hypocritically. "And that includes D.J."

"I know."

"Start by telling me if you know anything that would help us track him—or is it her?" I'd never quite figured that out. "Anything that would help us track them down."

"Him. I think," Checker said. "And I don't. I really don't, Cas. I tried—a year ago, when D.J.'s trail showed up again, I followed up on everything, I pulled all the police records—but he disappeared. And then I started tracking—explosions, bombings, anything that might—and I couldn't—God, Cas, between that and trying to track down *your* past, I didn't sleep for months. I was behind on work, everything was going to shit—"

I winced. I hadn't thought I could feel worse, but I knew why I'd missed it all now. I had been holding a grudge against Checker during those months and . . . not speaking to him.

"And I finally said, 'I have to stop, this isn't healthy,'" he continued. "And I stopped. I made myself stop. But the point I'm trying to make is that I wasn't getting anywhere. I wasn't finding *anything,*

I was chasing shadows and then obsessing over them, and *of course* I'm looking again now, but I don't have any reason to believe I'll be any more successful than the last time. And I could spend two days straight telling you about D.J. and still not tell you everything I know, and that wouldn't help you either, but I promise you, if I can think of one single thing that would, I will dial you so fast, I'll sprain something. Okay?"

"Okay," I said. Arthur hadn't stopped looking, I thought. Checker had stopped, but Arthur hadn't. Because that was the kind of thing Arthur did for people.

"Meanwhile, you can skip Arthur's apartment unless you have no other leads. He argued with me about a security system there too, the moron, but I put my foot down, and it's running perfectly fine and shows nothing unusual."

"Okay," I said again.

"Cas, I . . ." He sounded miserable.

Pilar held something up and waved at me.

"I gotta go." I didn't know what else to say, anyway. "We'll update you."

"Yeah," he said, and hung up.

I let the hand holding my phone drop and turned to Pilar. "What've you got?"

She passed me a business card. "Did Arthur ever ask you about this?"

My heart felt like it gave an extra thump as I took the card, but a quick scan of the raised blue text on ribbed cream showed nothing familiar, nothing related to me at all. I tried not to show my relief and read it more closely. The person on the card was some sort of doctor at a place called the Bimini Restorative Wellness Center, with an address out in Ventura County. Arthur had circled the doctor's name in ballpoint, and below it was scrawled, *Mathematical formula—ask Sonya or Cas?*

So not about me—just about math. Math, I could handle. But Arthur had never spoken to me about this.

"No," I said. "He didn't ask me."

"Should we call Professor—"

"I'm on it," I said, my fingers moving on my phone.

"Hello?" said Professor Sonya Halliday. Sonya was a legitimate mathematics professor and a childhood friend of Arthur's, and I was pretty sure she was the reason he'd put up with me to begin with. Maybe I'd just been a stand-in for her all along.

"It's Cas," I said into the phone.

Sonya's voice turned amused. "Oh, my. I do believe this is the first time you've called me instead of the reverse. I'm honored."

"I don't have time for games," I snapped. "I need to know if Arthur ever asked you about someone named . . ." I glanced back at the business card. "Dr. Eva Teplova."

She was too smart. "And you aren't asking him because . . . ?"

"He's missing," I said. "Now, answer the goddamn question. Dr. Teplova. Do you recognize the name?"

"I don't." Her voice had gone strained, as if she were pushing herself to recall the impossible. I was about to hang up on her when Pilar grabbed the phone from me.

"Hi, Professor, it's Pilar. The name Cas was just asking you about is on a business card for a doctor's office at the Bimini Restorative Wellness Center. Arthur wrote a note on it reminding himself to ask you about a mathematical formula. Does that ring any bells?"

I leaned in so I could hear. "A mathematical formula?" Sonya repeated. "Well, he did pose a hypothetical last week that—but I can't see how it would be at all related."

I took the phone back. "*Now*, Professor."

"He asked me whether one could potentially write a formula for human beauty. I told him no, of course. The easy contradiction is to view how aesthetic standards change so significantly between centuries or cultures, or even simply to examine differences in personal taste. Beauty is not even well-defined qualitatively, so could never be quantified effectively."

"You're wrong," I said. "You could come up with something locally defined by aggregate taste in terms of a probability distribution. It would just be . . . very, very, very multivariable."

"You mean use the culture you're based in to set the parameters? But how does—"

"Not now. Did Arthur tell you anything else?"

"No. Not that I can recall. Only that it was for a case." She gave the answers with clipped speed, lacking the dryness I'd come to expect from her. "Miss Russell?"

"Yeah?"

"Please call me when you find him. Godspeed." She hung up.

At least Professor Halliday was decent at knowing when to give me answers and then get off the phone.

I tapped my mobile against my hand, trying to feel through the new information. "Checker said they didn't have any cases right now. But if Arthur told Sonya this was for a case . . . if it was something he wasn't telling Checker about, it must be related to the D.J. thing."

I tried not to feel guilty for being right.

"A plastic surgeon? How?" Pilar said.

"You're assuming this doctor's a plastic surgeon?"

She gave an unhappy shrug. "Mathematical formula for beauty? What else could it be?"

That did seem the obvious connection, but I didn't see how a plastic surgeon would relate to Arthur's search for a bomber.

"There's a TV show where a plastic surgeon changes criminals' faces so they can disappear," Pilar said. "I—I don't know how plausible that is in real life."

Neither did I. "I guess this is where I'm headed next," I said, holding up the card. "You in?"

"Of course! I mean, if you think I'd be helpful."

"There might be flipping-through-files crap. You're better at that than I am." Not to mention handling any human interaction that couldn't be solved by bashing it in the head. I started for the door, but pointed back to the rest of the document stack. "Grab those to finish in the car. And text Checker the doctor's info. Tell him to run background but also to look for any connection to D.J. Or to Pithica," I added. I didn't want to think they could still be involved, but we did have evidence of psychic byplay here, or something like it. In the vindication of concluding Arthur's kidnapper was indeed D.J., I'd momentarily forgotten about the puzzle pieces that didn't yet fit.

The sensation of larger conspiracies loomed. I shook it off. At least I had a definite next step now, one thankfully free of my own ghosts.

Pilar hastened to obey me, but as we left the destroyed office, she said, "Cas, what if—I mean, we've been assuming—"

I stopped so fast, she almost ran into me.

"We've been operating under the assumption that Arthur's still alive," she said softly. "What if we're only going to find him in— in an alley somewhere, or unidentified in a morgue . . ." The words wobbled.

"Is making that assumption productive?" I said.

"No," she admitted in a small voice.

"Then *stop*."

"I keep thinking I should've been here," she said, glancing back at the shambles of her former workplace.

I didn't know what to say to that. Especially given what Pilar had shared earlier; between the lines, her main reason for leaving was that she hadn't wanted to get swept up with *me* anymore.

Instead, I resumed my hurried jog down through the gathering darkness to the car, assuming Pilar would follow. I wasn't going to think about any possibility other than getting Arthur back alive. And if Dr. Eva Teplova was connected in any way to his disappearance, well, she was going to end up needing medical attention herself.

six

THE BIMINI Restorative Wellness Center turned out to be a sprawling ranch with acres of land, and the whole thing had a high iron fence around it that was tastefully aesthetic even as it was topped with spikes. The locked front gate had a card reader to buzz in, with a sign overhead that read, "Welcome to the Best Years of Your Life" in fancy script.

On the inside of the fence, the gate had a guardhouse next to it, but it was empty and dark.

Empty and dark and *open*. That was odd.

"Oh, um," Pilar said. "Are you breaking in? Because I don't want to, like, muck up your entry or anything."

"I don't think we'll need to break in," I said. I slowed the car to a crawl and squinted at the top of the guardhouse. A security camera poked up from the roof like a weather vane, but it had been spun to aim at the sky.

Open, empty guardhouse plus a purposely misaligned security camera—that only meant one thing. And the camera hadn't been shifted back yet, which meant either a very sloppy burglar or that the B and E was still in progress.

I parked Pilar's little Yaris illegally on the side of the road, under a line of sentinel palms. If this went south, we'd have to remember to report her car stolen.

"There's a break-in happening here already," I said to her. "Are you up for this? I don't know what we're going to find inside. Arthur's been kidnapped by a bomber who's already tried to kill me, and we either have telepaths involved here or something close to it."

Pilar had pulled some stale-smelling gym wear from a bag in the back seat and was squirming into it. She tossed her dress behind her, pushed on a hairband, and finished double-knotting her sneakers. "You said we're looking for files or computer stuff. As long as I'm not going to slow you down, I should be there."

I was no longer a hundred percent sure it was a good idea, but Pilar was competent enough not to fuck me up, and she and I *did* have basically orthogonal skill sets. If she still wanted to come, I could use her. "All right," I said. "Follow my lead."

We got out of the car and hurried down the street to the gate. I jumped and grabbed, levering against the iron to clamber up and hop over the spikes at the top. I landed on the drive inside, then held up a finger to Pilar and ducked into the empty, inert guardhouse.

A monitor inside was flicking through security camera footage. All it showed was the smudged starlessness of tonight's sky. I scanned for an obvious button or switch of some sort and found one.

My guess was right. The gate shivered open soundlessly.

Pilar slipped through, and we jogged down a long, curved driveway past a screen of cypress trees. Low buildings came into sight, lit at their outside corners. Scattered patio furniture surrounded glassy pools. On the far side, the lawn sloped up into what appeared to be a golf course.

"There are no lights on," Pilar whispered.

"What?" I said.

She pointed at the buildings. "Inside. It's not that late, and this is some sort of residential facility. But there are no lights in the windows."

I folded my lips together, wondering if we should wait for more intel. On the way over, Checker had described the facility's website as "the totally generic type of thing you put up when you only ever take clients by referral," and Dr. Teplova's virtual presence as "only normal doctor stuff so far." He was digging deeper but hadn't yet turned up any connection to D.J. or Pithica, or any other squirming innards.

Who knew if he would, without us getting into the place in person?

I hesitated. Bombs, I had good odds of being able to handle, but I couldn't help thinking of the last time I'd been up against a psychic. Dawna Polk, aka Daniela Saio, who'd had me completely twisted around and still convinced every thought was my own idea. No way of predicting it or fighting it. No way to know when I'd been influenced, unless someone immune like Rio figured out I wasn't making sense.

Rio and Simon . . . they were the only two people who could plausibly fight a telepath. Maybe it was sheer recklessness to try going into a place without them. But if I had to wait for one of them every time I made a move—

Arthur had already been missing for at least a day and a half.

Fuck.

"Watch your back," I muttered to Pilar. I nodded across at the largest structure. "Looks like the main building. Let's go."

We started across the lawn. Forget golf courses and pools—in drought-stricken California, the spongy sod beneath our feet was the height of decadence. There was no cover, but with no lights or security cameras—or people—the place felt so deserted, it was hard to remember to be cautious.

We were about halfway across the lawn when something barked off to our left, and an animal pounded across the grass toward us.

It wasn't a dog, or any other sort of creature I'd ever seen before. And that was the last coherent thought I had before the pure static of absolute terror eclipsed every sense.

No. Not terror. Panic. Strangling panic, sucking out any logic, any thought, until my brain didn't have a hairsbreadth of space to question *why the fuck I was panicking.*

My Colt bucked against my hand as I fired my entire magazine into the animal as fast as I could pull the trigger. Someone else was firing next to me, and the creature's body twisted as the bullets pummeled it. Screams pierced the air, loud and long and soul-wringing. The world seemed to exist only in the strobe-lit flashes of the gunfire.

The thing that had been charging us slumped and fell with an agonized whine, its hideous snout plowing into the grass. I reloaded and emptied another magazine into its skull. Then I did it again, and again, until I ran out of ammo, and then I pawed for the revolver I remembered in a pocket and emptied that too—

The fur had turned to a bloody mass. It was dead. But I still needed to fight it. The urge was primal, untamed. This thing was *dangerous* and I needed to *fight* it—the panic flooded my synapses, clogging my thoughts, paralyzing me.

I'd hit my knees on the grass at some point. The dark lawn see-sawed before me. And emerging out of it, the figure of a man.

His silhouette yawed and split into an army before snapping back into a single, advancing menace. He was tall. His shoulders were square, his hands at his side, large and empty and grasping.

And he was familiar.

His face sent a wedge shivering into my brain. Both known and not. Both remembered and not. And, like the animal, *more* than the animal, igniting every fear center in my brain, electrifying every nerve, until nothing remained but gross murderous need.

I groped for my guns without knowing what I was looking for. My hands clenched the ground, my nails snapping back against dirt and clay. I tried to rear up, to fight him, the only instinct I had shouting to *kill*, but my consciousness zigzagged.

A shape lurched in front of me, eclipsing him. Another human. Someone dragged at my arm. Shouted at me. I barely managed to stumble up and make my legs move in some sort of semi-coordinated way. Someone was pulling me across the lawn.

Glass shattered, and my feet hit a door lintel. Then my body smacked against a wall, and I half-collapsed to sit against it. Floorboards against my hands. Walls, ceiling. We were inside the ranch.

My breath sawed in and out of my lungs, sandpaper against my throat. Shit. Shit. *Shit.*

"Pilar," I finally got out. I groped with one hand and found her next to me. She grabbed my wrist and squeezed it hard enough to cut off circulation.

We had to get up. The man. He was out there—we had to stop him—*destroy* him—

Oh, God. Oh, fuck . . .

I tried to move. Unreasoned, smothering panic suffocated me at the first impulse. My throat closed, my insides rioting.

He's coming he's coming he's coming

The man's face split into a different one, a younger one, unremarkably different and yet changed in every way that mattered. I saw my own hand reaching out to clasp his . . .

No no no, not now! I struggled away from the errant memory, if that's what it was, its barbs skipping against my consciousness. The only sure knowledge was that he was going to kill us, he was coming, I needed to *fight* . . .

Time slid against itself. Beside me, Pilar was mumbling something through hyperventilating sobs, the same words over and over. "I'm sorry, I'm sorry . . . I'm sorry, I'm sorry, I'm sorry . . ."

We had to get up. We had to move. If not to fight, then to escape—

The fear exploded in me again like a supernova, contracting every muscle, tightening my joints into a wad of useless contortion.

After what felt like an eternity, I managed to struggle for my phone. My fingers felt numb, lacking any tactile sensation. I couldn't see. I leaned into the simplest of mathematics, the geometry of the number array. Eight. One. Eight . . .

Simon picked up almost right away. "Cas?"

"Help," I whispered. The phone was on the floor, but that was okay, because I still was too, contorted on my side. I'd lost track of Pilar again. "Help . . ."

For once in his life, there were no questions, no pussyfooting, no moral objections. "Cas, listen to my voice," Simon said. "You're all right. Relax. Try to think about *why* you're afraid. Not what you're afraid of, but why."

Why . . .

My eyes stopped rolling in their sockets. The knots in my muscles started to unkink.

"Find the edges of your fear, and step outside of it. Like it belongs to someone else. You're just watching. You can analyze it without it controlling you."

As he said it, I found I could do it. Recalling the monsters on the lawn, both animal and human . . . it was still draining, but no longer sent me into a black hole.

"Remember what you're capable of," Simon continued. "And that you have people who will help you. You're all right. Now talk to me. How do you feel?"

"Better," I managed. My hands had curled into talons. I uncurled them. "Better. I have to . . ."

"Are you hurt anywhere? Is there any threat against you right now?"

"Yes—" I shoved myself up to sitting. The hallway we were in was dark and deserted. A French door across from us stood ajar with a broken pane, a breeze whispering through it.

I scrambled up, clutching the phone, but outside the door, the lawn stretched empty and placid into the night. The grass ruffled slightly in the night air.

Nothing else moved.

What—?

From here, I couldn't see where we'd fought the creature . . . animal . . . thing. Part of me gibbered in gratitude at that. But the man was nowhere to be found either. He easily could have overtaken us here, the state we'd been in.

But he hadn't.

"Cas?" Simon asked.

"I'm here . . ."

"Are you all right? Are you in danger?"

"No, we're . . . we're alone." For now. "Keep talking. Fast, please."

"This fear isn't logical." I didn't know how Simon knew that. Maybe because I did, deep down. "Tell me about what caused it. It will help."

"There was—a monster," I started. Its menacing shape rose in my mind's eye. I did as Simon had instructed, and stepped outside the fear, observed it. "No. 'Monster' is inaccurate. A creature of some sort. I don't know what it was."

All I knew was that it had made us afraid.

"You're a person of reason," Simon said. "Science can explain this."

Yes. Science.

"We killed it, and then . . ." And then there had been the person behind it. Equally monstrous, somehow, equally fear-inducing . . . and, I was sure, *someone I knew.*

I was starting to think I had dreamed that part. It wasn't like my past didn't dig its teeth into my waking reality every so often.

I was supposed to talk to Simon when that happened. Let him help me lock it all away again. It was also the last thing I wanted to do right now. If he thought I was slipping, he'd push me to scrub the mission, to delay finding Arthur . . .

"I need you to talk to Pilar," I said through gritted teeth.

"Of course. Put her on." He spoke after just enough of a pause that I knew he'd caught onto my caginess, but he didn't press. Yet.

Pilar was curled on the floor next to me. I poked at her, trying to get her to take the phone, but she almost seemed catatonic. Finally I wedged it under her cheek. I could hear Simon's calm questions. Pilar only made monosyllabic responses, but as long as she could hear him, I knew she'd be okay.

Having a telepath around was good for some things.

And if it took a telepath to counter . . . what the hell was *all that?* An animal wouldn't have the decision-making capability to act the part of a psychic—would it? Could it have been the man who'd been influencing us and not the animal at all? But why hadn't he pursued us? And the more I thought about it, the more it didn't seem like the scalpel of telepathic influence at all, but an indiscriminate, panic-inducing blast from man and beast both. What the hell was going on here?

I kept one unnerved eye on the empty lawn while I took stock. My Colt was on the hardwood floor a few feet away, empty, with its slide locked open. After scooping it up, I cast about for the revolver but couldn't find it. I vaguely recalled dropping it when it had run out of ammo. Or . . . I had thrown it at the corpse of the animal? While shouting? I couldn't remember.

Pilar was sitting up now, the phone to her ear. Her workout gear stuck to her in damp patches, her hair plastered to her face and neck and her makeup in wet streaks of black and tan.

I probably should have thought to offer the revolver to Pilar, but apparently she hadn't needed it. Her CZ was locked open on empty too, but she'd hung on to it—the hand not holding the phone was still around the gun in a death grip. The side of her palm was bleeding, but it didn't look serious.

My extra magazines were all missing, probably dropped at the scene while reloading. I hit the slide release and stuck the empty gun back in my belt. I was feeling reasonably coherent as long as I didn't think too hard about . . . anything we had seen. But it was striking me as more and more eerie that after all *that*, we were still alone in an empty hallway. Everything about this place was all wrong.

I crouched down next to Pilar. "Can you move?"

"I'm all right." She said the words both to me and into the phone, then added to Simon, "Yes. Thanks. Thank you. Okay. Bye."

She handed the phone back to me, and I hung it up before I could second-guess myself.

"I think he wanted to check in with you," Pilar said.

"Too bad." I hesitated. "What did you see out there?"

"I—I don't know. An animal." She shivered. "What do you think it was?"

"Did you see a person?"

"No, just—whatever that *thing* was, but I—why?" The rattled look in her eyes got a little worse, her pupils dilating out more. "Did you see someone?"

"No," I lied.

Pilar had fallen facing the other way from me, hadn't she? She'd reared up between me and the man, when she'd pulled me out and saved both of us. She wouldn't have seen in his direction.

Or I'd invented him.

Another flash in my head, someone who looked like him but different, holding a stopwatch and saying *"go—"*

"Cas? Are you okay?" Pilar asked.

"Yeah. Come on."

Pilar scrambled up with a little help from the wall, and like me, hit the slide release on her weapon before stowing it away. Then she pulled off her soft fabric hairband and wrapped it around her bleeding hand.

For a split second, I juggled the decision of whether to abort and regroup. Running wasn't my style, but with both of us shaken and out of ammo, and a possible enemy lurking who could take us down without a word or a strike . . .

No. We were here. Clues to Arthur might be too. Whatever strange luck had granted us a lack of pursuit, we should take advantage of it.

I led the way down the hallway, my stride firmer than I felt.

The inside of the ranch was all varnished wood and airy architecture. In sunlight, with people, the building was designed to be bright and pleasant with a kiss of rustic warmth. Now, it was like a movie set made out of lifeless props: ghostly and out of place without its intended purpose.

Pilar ran a finger along a windowsill and frowned at the track she made in the dust.

"Don't touch things unless you need to," I said. I was never as cautious about fingerprints as I should be myself, but Pilar probably cared more about not having a criminal record.

"Right," she whispered back, and scrubbed out the finger trail with the edge of her sleeve.

I'd noticed the dust too. A little over five months' worth, by my calculations. The grass outside had been the soft type that didn't need mowing and was probably automatically watered, but here inside, we had evidence of five months without anyone cleaning the place.

We crept through the silent rooms. We'd entered in a meandering back hallway across the building from the main entrance, and I worked toward the front, keeping a floor plan of the place active in my brain and scanning for offices. Most of what we'd passed through so far seemed to have an unspecified use—meeting or event rooms of some sort.

We came across Dr. Teplova's office quite suddenly, double doors with gilded lettering spelling out her name. I pressed down the ornate handle—unlocked—and pushed the door open.

"Oh my God," breathed Pilar, her whisper rising to a slight squeak.

We'd found Dr. Teplova.

Most of her.

Pilar stayed by the door, looking away and breathing shallowly. I stepped carefully into the room, avoiding the blood and . . . other bits . . . splashed across the floor. The dim ambient light from the windows gleamed blackly across the mess.

Still wet. This had happened tonight. Jesus.

"Keep an eye out," I called to Pilar in a low voice. She nodded rapidly and straightened, facing the hall. Probably relieved I hadn't told her to come in.

Fuck, *I* didn't want to go in.

I let the numbers draw out the room for me dispassionately, concentrating on the waveform: the amount of pressure that must have been generated to do this, the milliseconds of time that pressure would have been generated within. Dr. Teplova had been sitting at her desk. A nice heavy chunk of explosive material had been strapped to her chest, and then it had been detonated.

About a quarter of her skeleton was still draped across what remained of the chair, wetness caking it. The rest of her was splayed across the space, outlining the bomb's flow field, expansion fans sprawling their gruesome graphs around the corners of the furniture. I edged over behind the desk and found a picture frame with shattered glass in it fallen flat on the blotter. I picked it up, automatically scanning the corpse to try to reconstruct the topography of its features from the pieces of skull that were still intact.

As little as was left, the reconstruction came together for me within instants, in the time it took me to right the photo. The skeleton's youthful face snapped into conclusion at the same time I locked eyes with the version in the frame.

Memory whiplashed out from nowhere.

"Medicine isn't just healing," said the woman in the photo, only she was a girl with short-cropped hair. "It's making people better."

My hip slammed into the blood-soaked desk, and my elbow came down hard on the blotter, crushing against residue I didn't want to think about. Who was—what the *hell*—

I'd dropped the photo again. This time, it had landed faceup on the floor. My eyes crawled over to it. The woman in the chair had been the same woman as in the photo, as of a bit under ninety minutes ago. Large-framed with sandy hair, one arm slung around a German shepherd. Sharp, intelligent eyes. Smiling. Slyly arrogant.

And oh, Jesus . . . I knew her.

The man outside hadn't been a hallucination. Both of them were phantasms I'd been familiar with in some earlier life, before I'd lost who I was to Simon's misguided attempts at saving me.

Of course, that didn't help me one whit. Who they were, or *what* they had been to me . . . it was all lost in striated layers of deleted identity. All I knew now was everything I had feared—my past was involved here too.

Fuck.

I fought against the sense of titans rising unseen around me. Giants playing a board game where I was only one of the pieces.

Why was my past intersecting with Checker's? What had Arthur stumbled onto?

Investigate now. Think about it later. I pushed myself back to reality. What had Dr. Teplova been doing in this chapter of her life that had gotten her so very dead?

I shivered. I couldn't remember enough to know if I should be frightened by her murder, but if she were like me . . . well, I knew how hard I was to kill. The desk had no lock, but had been painted shut with the carnage. I considered the wisdom of messing with what was sure to be an active crime scene in the very near future, but I'd already disturbed it fairly drastically by accident. I pulled my sleeve over one hand to pry at a corner of one of the drawers until I got it open. Bits of the former doctor glopped down onto the files.

Which were all things like promotional packets and propaganda about the wellness center, nothing I even needed Pilar's help on. This was a place Teplova had sat with potential clients to hook them and put them at ease, not where she'd done the real work of the facility.

Whatever that was.

I left the drawers open and wound my way back to Pilar. "Dead end. Let's go."

The pronouncement sounded brittle to my own ears, but she only nodded tightly. Now wasn't the time to talk, I told myself. I'd get everybody in the loop once we were out of danger. I would.

We took a lucky turn, then, down a hallway behind the doctor's office that looked less shiny and more official. I pushed open the next door to find an open area with desks and file cabinets set up across it as a bull pen-style workspace.

For the first time, the light was on, and a dark-haired woman stood engrossed in the open drawer of a file cabinet.

seven

Empty or not, my Colt was out before I could think about it. Surprisingly, Pilar and her CZ were only a second behind me.

The woman dropped the papers she was holding and whipped her hands into the air. Then her face twisted into anger. "Damn you!" she shouted at us. "God*damn* you! Eva was *helping* people. Go ahead, kill me too, leave more evidence—"

Pilar shifted her gun so it was pointed down and raised her other hand. "Calm down! We're not here to kill anyone, promise. What's your name?"

The woman's eyes flicked to me and then to Pilar and back again. Sharp and unafraid.

I studied her in return. She was *distractingly* beautiful. I found it impossible to guess her ethnicity: she might have been Italian, Asian, Spanish, or Indian, or from an island in the Pacific, or a mix of ancestry aesthetics that had made her the winner of the genetic lottery. The bones of her face cut at breathtaking angles, her eyes large and luminous. Her waist was improbably small and her legs improbably long, and the way her body curved in between struck me as exactly within the error margins of the clearly digitally reshaped models who graced every magazine and advert. Except she was real.

I'd never seen anyone like her, and I lived in LA, cesspool of models and movie stars.

She also wore an expensive-looking scarlet dress, one with a modest cut that was belied by its exactly fitted tailoring. I didn't know anything about fashion, but it was obvious that dress was designed only as a picture frame for the body inside it. It also didn't seem like the type of thing someone would wear to commit murder . . .

I blinked. It wasn't like me to make assumptions that gave people the benefit of the doubt. I refocused on keeping my gun up and aimed—she didn't know it was empty, or that I could kill her just as easily without it.

"You heard the question," I said. "Who are you?" Her face hadn't sparked any dark flashbacks for me, but that didn't necessarily mean anything. Though she didn't seem to recognize me either. I tried not to feel unduly relieved by that.

"My name is Willow Grace," the woman said. Her inflection didn't give a clue as to whether it was a double first name or if Grace was her surname. "You can verify that."

"Wait, are you the same—you are! Aren't you?" Pilar said. "I mean, you're the news anchor. Cas, I've seen her before, on TV."

Wait, what?

"What are you doing here, then?" I demanded. "Some kind of journalistic exposé?"

She brought her hands down a smidge. "I've told you who I am. Do me the same courtesy."

"I'm Pilar, and this is Cas. We work for a private investigator," Pilar said, straining the truth into zigzags.

"Show me your licenses," said Willow Grace.

"I said I work for a PI, not that I am one," Pilar said. "We're—"

"I've got a license," I cut in. "One second." I took my left hand off my gun and pulled a handful of cards out of my pocket.

I managed to riffle through them one-handed by flipping them between my fingers. The first PI license I found didn't have a name similar to Cas on it—goddamn Pilar—but it turned out I had another one. I shoved the rest of the cards back in my pocket and held it up.

"Cassie Wells, PI," I said. I expected Pilar to glare at me, but she gave no outward sign—which was probably good, as I wasn't sure my bravado sounded all that convincing. I wasn't a very good liar even when I wasn't feeling jerked around by unseen foes.

But people respond well to pieces of paper, even ones that are forgeries. "Thank you," Willow Grace said.

Oddly, her acknowledgment made a little nub of pleasure flare in me, that she'd accepted us. That she'd decided to *respect* us. Damn—I hadn't thought I'd respond that way to someone's appearance, but somehow this woman's *face* seemed to make me want her approval.

Steady, Cas.

"I'm here because Eva is . . . was a friend," Willow Grace continued. "And I worked with her. Unofficially."

"What does that mean?" I said, trying to keep the words brusque.

"I brought her clients. Among other things." Apparently no longer concerned with my gun, she dropped her hands all the way. "What are you investigating?"

"Well, now we're investigating Dr. Teplova's death," Pilar said smoothly. "It may have a connection to one of our cases. Will you tell us more?"

"On one condition. I want to be kept out of the police investigation. Don't tell them you saw me here."

"Why not?" I asked.

"Because if they look into me, it would ruin me," she answered bluntly. "In exchange, I'll tell you why, but only under strictest confidentiality."

"You were one of her clients, weren't you?" Pilar said. For some reason, she sounded sad. "That's your secret. You're afraid the media would shred you for it."

"They would." Willow Grace said it very calmly, straightening her spine and meeting Pilar's eyes. "You must know what women run up against in a career like mine. I'm asking you. Do me this favor."

She stepped slowly across the room as she spoke, until she was close enough to put a hand on Pilar's arm.

"No—yes, of course we will," Pilar said, flushing slightly. "Cas, she's right. It won't do any good to out her, and we'd be doing a pretty terrible thing. She's one of the most respected women in news and journalism. Let's not destroy that for no reason."

I didn't care about politics, but it wasn't like I wanted to involve the police either . . .

Willow Grace turned her fine-boned face to me. Her eyes were liquid darkness. Looking at her made it hard to think.

"No." I shook my head, physically and forcefully, trying to concentrate. "You can't be just a journalist. Teplova was—" *Someone like me* . . . "not a normal doctor. What do you know about her? What do you know about her enemies?"

Pilar glanced at me, her forehead creasing.

And Willow Grace's well-shaped eyes narrowed as she studied me.

"You're right," she said finally. "It's not just that. Eva had enemies you can't dream of. If we involved the authorities—"

"You might have saved her if you had," Pilar murmured, showing a shocking level of contrarianism.

"No," Willow Grace said. "I'd be dead too. I can't break this story. I can't broadcast it. All I could do was help Eva stay hidden, and I would have done anything to keep them from finding her. But if you're truly not working for *them* . . ."

Her gaze flicked between us.

"Them who?" Pilar asked.

"You know where Teplova came from," I realized. "You . . ." *I can't break this story*, she'd said. "You had an investigation that led all the way into a black hole, didn't you? Conspiracies. People with *abilities* who were out to manipulate the whole world, who were—who were turning children into weapons. Tell me I'm wrong . . ."

My hand had started shaking against the grip of my gun. Very slightly, too slightly for anyone to see, but I could feel it.

"You know about them too," Willow Grace said slowly.

I am one.

Pilar gasped, the slightest intake of air.

"How did you meet Teplova?" I asked.

"I was her friend," Willow Grace said again.

"You say you protected her. You . . . you got her out." I knew—or had been able to piece together—what Rio had done for me. Flashes of bone-deep knowledge that he had saved me. Hidden me. Looked out for me, before I built a new identity that barely remembered the old one.

This reporter . . . it sounded like she was Teplova's Rio.

Not that Eva Teplova had likely had her whole personality erased like I had, but I felt a thrum of kinship with her. She'd found a way to use her skills quietly to build a good life for herself. And become rich too. I never had any objections to that.

A younger Teplova flashed in my mind's eye again, brandishing a bloody scalpel above a blurred impression of brown and red. Some sort of small animal, a part of me felt sure.

I blinked the disturbing image away. After all, it's not like I had never done anything questionable with my skill set.

"They tracked her down. After all this time," Willow Grace said softly. "When I found her, I knew."

She spoke with a startling lack of emotion. But then, as someone who was friends with Rio, I didn't need people to show their tears on their sleeve.

"Get on the computers," I said to Pilar, finally lowering my gun. "Grab everything you can. Hey. Willow Grace. Do you know the passwords and everything?"

She hesitated. "No."

On the fly, I struggled to make all the pieces jam together. The man on the lawn—an unseen enemy, someone from our joint history? Teplova's murderer, and possibly someone who'd be happy to kill me too?

But the *way* she'd been killed . . . it had lacked all finesse. Messy. Uncoordinated. Same with Arthur's office.

Not to mention, Arthur wouldn't have kept any investigation into *my* past a secret from Checker . . .

"What about other enemies?" I asked Willow Grace. "Did anyone else have disagreements with Teplova?"

"Of course," she answered. "Everyone who knew of her work felt obligated to have an opinion. Which wasn't a lot of people, but when you have a business, you have to spread the word to some degree.

After we became close, and she worked on me, I reciprocated by bringing her other high-end interest. But not everyone reacted well."

Pilar made a small noise. I glanced over, but she was busy with the computer.

"Anyone who would hire a batshit mercenary explosives expert?" I pressed.

Willow Grace's eyebrows lifted slightly.

"I saw how she died," I said.

"She did have wealthy enemies from this phase of her life," Willow Grace admitted. "Their resources would have been extensive. But I don't think—"

"There's more than one piece to this," I cut her off. I just couldn't see *how* yet. The man on the lawn, and the creature and the bombs . . . "Pilar, look in particular for any mention of D.J. or Pithica."

"You still think D.J.'s involved?" Pilar said, but I was more interested in Willow Grace's reaction. Her perfect complexion had paled about three shades.

But it wasn't from the word I'd expected.

"D.J.?" she repeated, her aggressiveness gone almost faint.

Oh, *shit*. Sometimes I hated being right.

"Yeah," I said. "What do you know about—"

A sharp *crack* sounded from outside.

"That wasn't gunfire," I said, and ran for the door.

"This way!" called Willow Grace, and took a turn down another corridor that opened out onto a patio. More *booms* and *cracks*—

We burst outside. The sky was filled with fireworks, spouts of white light pinwheeling into cascades.

I double-checked in my head. It was August. Way too late for Independence Day shenanigans.

The sky cleared momentarily, and then a single firework soared to the center of the starless blackness. It popped into a squiggle, the line of brilliant white dots painting a sideways *S* across the smoggy clouds.

A second lone firework came a moment later, exploding into a sharply angled curve.

Next came a ring in a perfect circle. Then two loops with long tails.

The final one burst into a long, two-pronged fork, the pinpoints of light dripping from the shape and dissolving into the dark.

The message hadn't been all that obvious, but patterns always make themselves clear to me, even ones scrawled on the sky in messy English.

"Sloppy," I said aloud.

"What?" Willow Grace had gone even paler.

I pointed upward. "Letters. They spelled *sloppy*." The display hadn't been a very high one. On a clear night, it would have been visible in Ventura, but today, I estimated the population who were even in a position to see it to be no more than a few thousand—to see it unobstructed, even less. And it had been centered almost right on top of us.

"This was a message for somebody here." I turned to Willow Grace. "Who would they be talking to? Your friend? Her murderer?"

"I don't—I don't know. I swear I don't." I tried to read her expression, but couldn't—shock, fear, confusion? Anger?

A hum rose on the edge of our senses.

"What's that?" said Pilar. She'd come out behind us, poised like she thought she'd need to run or fight.

She wasn't wrong.

"Drones." I turned and shoved Pilar ahead of me back under the eave of the patio and then inside the building, Willow Grace following. My ears teased out the frequencies, calculating differentials in the Doppler effect: small drones, on the order of remote-controlled helicopters you could get at any electronics store. But a *lot* of them—

They came out of the night like a swarm of wasps, quadcopters descending toward the compound with a buzzing whine. Pilar sucked in a quick, tight breath beside me. In one instant, I located everything in the room that might possibly qualify as either a weapon or protection.

But the drones weren't interested in us. I squinted through the windows. I'd been starting to feel a flashback to the last bad guy who had attacked me with missiles out of the sky, but these seemed to be ordinary electronics.

And they were—crop dusting?

The quadcopters crisscrossed the wellness center's campus, powder drifting down from their payloads.

My mind went to all the worst places first—if this were a chemical or biological weapon of some kind, we were dead already. But Willow Grace cracked the French door next to us and touched a finger to the powder drifting down onto the patio.

She stood back up, staring at her fingertip. "It's a binary explosive. Someone's about to destroy this place."

Oh. Crap. The quick search algorithm in my head mapped the shortest route off campus, and I started back the way we had come.

Willow Grace threw out a hand, blocking me. "No! Not that way!"

"Why not?" I riveted on her. "Wait. You *know*. The creature, the man—you know—"

"I don't—I mean, I—" Her studied composure whipped in its moorings. "Not now! Please. I heard the gunshots—did you kill them? Tell me!"

"Not the man," I said. "Is he still—"

"What about the dog? Did you kill the dog!"

"Yes—"

"Where?" Willow Grace had begun to sound panicked. "We can't see it again, even dead. Where did you kill the dog?"

I pointed.

"This way, then," she said, and slipped through the door ahead of us to veer right, down another drive past the golf course, keeping the main building between us and the . . . dog. Thing.

We ran, pounding through the silent hillocks of the golf course. The grass was overgrown here, and the flags and sand traps over-looked us idly like the scattered remnants of a very rich dystopia. The powder from the drones overhead drifted down and coated our clothes and skin within seconds.

I kept all my senses alert for a man who had fear for a face or an-other animal racing at us out of the darkness, but the night was only loud with our breathing and pounding feet and the buzz of the drones above us. My mind whizzed through the other probabilities and urgencies. Setting aside for a moment just how much Willow Grace knew that she hadn't shared yet, the binary explosive meant—what? I didn't know much about them beyond the basics: two chemicals that were harmless when separate, but would detonate with great prejudice once they met. So the initial powder, the one already caking us, would be inert by itself. Another wave of drones would have to come and spray their payload around all at once . . . and then the entire place would go up like another Independence Day display. Without knowing what the chemical compositions were, I couldn't make a reliable estimation of destructive power, but I was guessing *big* and *flamey*.

Assume the same type of drones for the second payload, though, and we'd make it past the fence and out before anything could go off. We were already probably far enough away from the buildings, which was where the drones were concentrating themselves—

"There's a person!" gasped Pilar, pointing.

I swiveled, every nerve ending instantly wiring with adrenaline.

But it wasn't the man from the lawn. Instead, a much smaller, black-clad silhouette was bobbing in and out of the screen of cypress trees a few hundred yards down from us.

A silhouette I recognized. And this time not from my nightmares.

Oh, fuck.

I grabbed the other women to stop them. "Keep an eye on her," I commanded Pilar, pointing at Willow Grace. I wasn't sure whether I meant Pilar should protect her or keep her under guard, but Willow Grace was right about one thing—any more answers on that had to wait.

"Now *run*," I said.

They took off into the night, and I sprinted in the opposite direction, back across the lawn toward where Arthur's daughter was sneaking into the wellness center.

eight

·

I binned all caution and shouted her name, but she was too far away, and the buzzing of the drones had built up into an unbearable white noise. Tabitha kept glancing at them, but was slipping around the buildings on the periphery, pausing to push at windows and doors as though looking for a way in.

Oh, *shit*. If she turned the farthest corner of the building she was at, she'd be in view of the back lawn.

I didn't know what the damned "dog" was, or why none of us could seem to look at it without going into a screaming panic, but I wasn't about to test it on Tabitha—or myself. I thought about yelling again, but I was afraid she'd spook and run in the other direction from me, which was exactly what *could not happen*.

I juked so I was coming up straight behind her and grabbed her in a bear hug. "Tabitha! Tabitha, it's Cas Russell. Your dad's friend. Stop struggling!" I shifted my face in time for her skull not to break my nose.

She froze. "Ms. Russell?"

"Yes. Come with me fast and don't ask questions."

I grabbed her by the wrist and dragged her back toward the main building. And that was when I registered the increased hum, climbing behind the drones already in the air.

The second wave. The ones that would set off the binary.

I ran approximations in my head as comprehensively as I could—possible concussive blast, fire danger, shrapnel, not to mention if we got directly splashed by the second payload ourselves, considering our skin and clothes were dusted with the first chemical . . .

Too much variance. If we ran, we might make it, or we might be toast. Literally. We were way too far within the territory the drones had covered to be sure we could clear any blast radius.

The rising hum of the second wave gave me an inside time limit. We'd be able to get into the buildings, but that wouldn't help; there wouldn't be buildings anymore in a minute. The large, glassy pools would offer protection from a blast through the air, but their surfaces were coated in the powder too, and a concussion through water would be even worse.

Unless I could get the primary agent of the binary *off* the water.

The thought process took less than a second. I cast around—the pools hadn't been well-maintained in the past few months, and some cleaning supplies were heaped by one of the pieces of lawn furniture in a sad little pile. I grabbed at Tabitha again and ran.

I scooped up a pool cleaner from the pile and ran past the first basin to a glassy, perfectly round reflecting pool beyond it, my brain running off estimates of surface tension and molecular density. The water was fifteen feet in diameter. In this hot climate, the basin must have been kept filled exactly to the brim by some sort of automatic mechanism; it met the brick bordering it in a smooth mirror with a fine dusting of the explosive powder over its face.

Fifteen feet across meant a hundred and seventy-seven square feet of surface. I needed enough detergent molecules to displace the water on each square inch of that. I tore open the box of cleaner and socked it forward, transferring the inertia to propel a cloud of powder exactly into the center of the pool.

The cleaner hit the water with a small plop and ripple, and the effect was instant and dramatic. The surface tension chased itself to the sides like it was sucked there by a magnet, and within the space of a heartbeat, the binary explosive powder was only a dense ring around the edge.

The second wave of drones was trundling in above us, fast—a neat, orderly array of death.

"Relax," I ordered Tabitha. "I'm going to throw you."

"You're—I'm—*what*?"

I grabbed her under the knees and shoulders. She flailed a little. I shouted, "Relax!" again and heaved.

Tabitha hit the water in the center of the shallow pool in a belly flop that both prevented her from breaking her neck and caused a nice tidal wave splashing almost all of the powder out onto the brick. I followed immediately, with a running leap that I flipped into landing on my back. The wave equation and vertical oscillations rippled out in my head without seeing them, carrying any of the deadly powder that remained out of the pool and onto dry land.

I twisted and found the slippery bottom with my boots to push upright.

"What's going on?" Tabitha had also found her feet, and her wet face was wide and scared.

"Get ready to hold your breath," I said.

I stood in the slick pool, water lapping at my chest, and watched the drones. Closer and closer, an army above us, until they blanketed the campus, a phalanx that would let loose as soon as it stopped in position. Distance to its nearest likely position divided by airspeed gave us five, four, three—

"Duck," I said to Tabitha, and tackled her under the surface.

Even with almost all the powder off the pool, the concussion hit the water like someone had cannonballed in next to us.

I pressed my hands and feet against the slimy, sloping bottom, keeping myself down with Tabitha flattened under me. A flash of red and gold rippled across the surface along with the blast, and the algae-coated cement vibrated against my palms as the earth shook.

Then everything was blackness and cold.

I kept us under until Tabitha squirmed against me, which I took as a communication she was desperate for air. I let her up, and we broke the surface into a hellscape.

Tabitha immediately took a heaving breath that burst into a cough. The air was clogged with smoke and ash. I looked out over the lawn to find everything from the patio furniture to the buildings had been—disintegrated. Smoking piles of rubble marked where structures had collapsed, small fires here and there. In a few places, the crumbled remains had big enough chunks left to form a mound with the odd timber poking out, but mostly it was just . . . gone. The grass had been seared off, leaving nothing but charred soil.

A haze of ashy dust, combined with the gray-black darkness—now much more complete without the outside floodlights—made the whole scene recede into unreality. I realized too late that even so, I could see clear across the lawn, and I lurched back, the water sloshing with my movement. But the corpse of whatever animal had attacked us had been burned off the face of the planet along with everything else, and there was no sign of its human companion. Even the other pools had been blasted so hard on the surface that they were now only half-full of lapping water.

Holy *shit*.

Tabitha was still hacking. We needed to move. We might be in a remote area, but police had to be on their way—this had not been a small display.

I looked around again as I slopped out of the pool onto soot and rubble and gave Tabitha a hand up. This, I thought, had been somebody showing off.

· . ·˙ . ·˙ . ·˙

TABITHA DIDN'T get her breath back until we were beyond where the line of trees had been. The cypresses had been spared the worst of the blast, so they were still in the shape of trees—but mostly not upright ones. Many of them had been splintered along the base of their trunks by the concussion, and the perimeter looked like a forest graveyard left by haphazard loggers. We finally found the back side of the iron fence, and I boosted Tabitha over before climbing the bars myself.

Fatigue made the effort less agile than when I'd entered.

Stay alert, I ordered myself, but the directive was hard to follow, even with my stamina. How many villains were out here tonight? Which of them might be watching for escapees from this dramatic showcase? Too many shadows, hemming us in . . .

But though every rustle and whisper made my senses jangle, we got out to the street without any more surprises.

My phone definitely wasn't functional after its dunking, and I had no idea where Pilar had gone off to, but I decided the most likely rendezvous point was her car. I turned to lead Arthur's daughter back in that direction.

But Tabitha had used the pause to breathe and cough, and now trotted up next to me. "Wow," she gasped now. "Wow. That was— that was *awesome*."

I stopped so fast she tripped trying to match me and spun to face her. "What?"

"I just mean—what you did! That was so, like—wow!" She goggled at me. "What just *happened*?"

The whole bloody night felt like it crashed down on me in that one instant. After everything—the dog and Teplova and the ghosts from my past and fucking D.J. and explosives, and Tabitha thought it was *awesome*?

"You interfered with my work to find your dad, that's what happened." I nearly snarled the words in her face.

Her expression crumpled. "I didn't mean—wait, he wasn't, Dad wasn't in that—"

"No. I don't think so." I started walking again, fast, and she hastened to keep up.

"You don't *think*—"

"No." The wellness center was definitely tangled up with Arthur's kidnapping, but rather than being one of the abductors, Teplova seemed to be a victim here as much as we were. I thought it most likely we had a common enemy. Or several common enemies.

Besides, except for Dr. Teplova, the center had been deserted for a long time, which was something else I'd have to quiz Willow Grace about. Someone holding Arthur there, in one of the other buildings . . . it was possible, but I didn't rate it as likely.

I ignored the possibility that I just wasn't letting myself consider it. As I'd told Pilar, what would be the point in such thinking anyway? It wouldn't help me find Arthur any faster.

I scanned the night for where we'd left the Yaris.

Pilar was, indeed, at her car. She had her CZ out, and there was no sign of Willow Grace.

"What happened?" I said.

"We got out okay. What happened in *there*? Tabitha, what—what are you—are you guys all right?"

"I meant, where's Willow Grace?" I said.

"Oh! She's in the car. Back seat." She gestured at the car and cast a self-conscious look at Tabitha before tucking her gun away. "You can take over now," she added to me.

I located Willow Grace's profile in the back seat, still and placid, an idealized sculpture of a woman. Good. She had more answers to all this, and I was going to make sure she told me.

A sneaking apprehension wormed its way through my mind. If those answers intersected with my own history . . . Simon had warned me over and over that learning too much about my past would cause my brain to destabilize and derail itself. I'd felt firsthand what it was like for the shell of its old owner to come gabbling back— Valarmathi, she whom Simon had known and loved and saved by destroying her.

She was dead, but that didn't mean she couldn't drag me down with her.

Tough. You'll figure it out. It's Arthur.

If my mental health was the price to pay for rescuing him, well, that's what I had Simon for. He could fucking earn his keep.

"Tabitha, sweetie." Pilar took the girl's hands in hers, drawing my attention back to them. "What are you doing here?"

"I'd like to know that too," I said. I turned to face her, arms crossed.

"I—I wanted to help find Dad," Tabitha answered.

"You almost got us killed." If there was one extra shit complication I hadn't needed tonight . . . "You know how you can help? By staying the fuck out of the way."

"Cas! Shush." Pilar sounded scandalized.

"No," I said. "How the hell do you think 'hey, Arthur, we rescued you but got your daughter killed' will go down?"

Emotion surged, and something in me wanted to say a lot more than that, to yell at this too-reckless teenager until I lost my voice, because even the thought of giving news like that to Arthur wrecked me like I'd been run over by a semitruck. I wanted to be angry at him, not validate every decision he'd made.

Especially if my own old enemies were already responsible for everything that had happened here, screaming forward to hurt Arthur and his family.

Enemies I hadn't had any hand in making. Ones I had no intel on, or control.

"You didn't get me killed!" Tabitha protested. "You saved me. Unless that was—you with the—?" She made a *boom* gesture with her hands.

"No! No, no, no," Pilar said. "That wasn't us."

"But it might've been, and you wouldn't have known," I snapped. "You work at cross-purposes on the same job, you're going to get someone killed. And if you don't know basic shit like that, you have no business breaking into places."

Tabitha's face fell as if I'd just told her she'd failed a test.

"Sweetie, how are you even here?" Pilar said.

"I went to Dad's office." She sounded like she was on the verge of tears. "Have you seen it? It's a mess. And I searched around a little, but it seemed kinda hopeless, so then I went on the computer—I have the passwords because I do homework there sometimes—and I looked at his calendar. And he had written on next Sunday to 'meet with Tabitha's doctor,' and that didn't make any sense because I don't have any doctor's appointments ever except physicals. So I looked at his Internet history, and he did a search for this place." She pushed her hands at the smoky ruin beyond the fence like she was a mime. "I figured it was code, like, he'd put our names so it wouldn't look suspicious, but he knew it wasn't really about us."

Code to stop Checker from knowing, in case he happened to

see Arthur's calendar. Right. A mundane errand related to his kids wouldn't look suspicious.

Fuck, this was a mess.

"No, I meant—" Pilar licked her lips. "How did you *get here*? Does Diego know you snuck out? Did you drive?"

Tabitha toed the ground and shook her head. "I took the bus and then walked."

"Well, you're coming back with us." I grabbed her by the wet fabric of her black turtleneck. Jesus, the bus would have taken her forever; we were in the middle of nowhere. "In the front. Pilar, get in the back with Willow Grace."

I drove us out at exactly the speed limit, away from civilization first and then circling around to head back toward the city by another route to avoid any emergency response vehicles. The streets out here weren't gridded logically, but they tended to follow the mountains in mathematically intuitive ways.

Tabitha started shivering in the front seat. Pilar leaned forward and flicked the heat on. I kept half an eye on Willow Grace, but she hadn't moved, her hands folded over her purse in her lap and her lovely face in an inscrutable mask.

"Tabitha, sweetie—we should call your dad. He's probably worried sick," Pilar said.

"I'm not sure my phone will still work." She pulled it out of a wet pocket. She was wearing a utility belt around her black clothes, with what looked like lockpicks, a flashlight, and a penknife, among other tools. I wasn't sure whether to be impressed or even more pissed off.

"I left mine tethered to the computer," Pilar said. "Oh, Cas—there was no outside network connection, but the wireless card was functional, so I tethered and got Checker in. Hopefully he was able to pull stuff right until the minute it kaboomed."

Hopefully. I supposed the outcome could have been worse—given the number of times we'd been blindsided tonight, Pilar's data pull was the best we could have hoped for.

Though Willow Grace knew more. I glanced at her in the rearview mirror, but she was staring ahead, focused on nothing.

"My phone'll be dead too," I said. "Willow Grace?"

"Beg pardon?" Her eyes riveted to me in the mirror.

"Your phone. Let the kid make a call."

"It's out of battery."

"You're lying." It was a guess, but I wanted to push her.

It worked. The car got as tense as if a live viper had been dropped into it.

Then Willow Grace let out a grim breath. "Yes, I'm lying. I have sensitive information on my phone. Confidential messages from sources, contact information for highly secured people. I'm sure you understand."

All right, that did make sense, I had to admit grudgingly. And at least she'd been up front about it once I asked. Despite having set out to needle her, I couldn't decide if that made me trust her more or less.

After all, I wouldn't have expected Rio to lend a kid his phone just to call her father.

"It's okay," Pilar said to her quickly, interrupting my frowning thoughts. "Tabitha honey, look in the glove box. There should be a new phone in there." When I glanced back at her in surprise, she added quickly, "Arthur does that too, for emergencies. I'm not turning into you."

She said it jokingly, so I wasn't sure why it stung.

nine

I MULLED over what we knew while I drove, and kept a sidelong eye on Willow Grace in the rearview mirror.

She knew more about Teplova's situation than she'd said so far, that much was clear. She might have guesses about how the doctor had been tracked and targeted, and she'd *definitely* recognized D.J.'s name. Plus the "dog" and its master . . .

I remembered her pressing a finger to the ground, declaring a strange powder to be the first half of a binary explosive.

"Hey. Willow Grace."

"You can call me Willow."

"Okay. Willow," I said. "Let's start here. How did you know about the binary?"

"I've reported in a lot of war zones. I'd seen this before."

"Where?"

"The Middle East."

Something flashed on the back of my eyelids: bright lights of a city street, crowds and cars, a woman shouting happily.

"That's the stupid, easy answer," I growled. The Yaris swerved. I wrenched it back on track. "Give me a real one."

Pilar's hand touched my shoulder. "Cas? You okay?"

Shit. My fucking brain and its fucking broken memories.

That question hadn't even been connected to Teplova or Pithica or men whose faces I half-recognized before they shredded me in panic.

Fuck, I needed Simon, or Rio, or at least to get somewhere where

I wasn't at risk of slamming us all into a tree if Willow Grace gave me the wrong answer. The ticking clock on Arthur's disappearance felt like it timed itself with my heartbeat. What use was I to him if I was this broken?

I drove faster, accelerating and decelerating in compressed lurches that weren't technically good for Pilar's car. She winced a few times in the back seat, but didn't say anything. I tossed the phone over my shoulder at her and directed her to text Checker everything we'd learned tonight—then at least the drive time wouldn't be entirely wasted.

Fortunately, we'd hit a late enough hour that the roads were actually functioning as throughways instead of creeping clogged pipelines, but it still took the better part of an hour to get Tabitha home. Her bus journey out must have been absurd. But instead of sympathy, all I could feel was resentment at how she was delaying us in finding her father. If her address hadn't been on the way back into the city, I probably just would have dragged her along with us, but her family wasn't that far from Checker's place and almost directly between the wellness center and where I'd left Simon and Rio.

Small favors.

I pulled up a few doors down from the house, ordered Pilar and Willow to stay in the car, and came around to hustle Tabitha out of the front seat. Her phone conversation with her father had been brief—she'd started out trying to argue with him the same way she had with us, but had quickly hunched subdued in her seat and listened before mumbling about a dozen apologies. I gathered he'd been concerned.

That hadn't stopped her from wrapping her arms around herself once she'd hung up and slouching with her chin thrust out. The part of me that wasn't mad at her wanted to tell her she could go home and be a kid and not worry, but I wasn't a good enough liar.

Tabitha's home was a cozy two-story bungalow with just enough land to contain its footprint and a wild but well-cared-for garden overtaking the tiny front yard. A porchlight beckoned at us, welcoming. And a paved walkway led to a ramp built over the front steps, just like at Checker's place.

It was always possible Diego and his kids knew another person who used a wheelchair, or that this was an artifact left over from when Arthur had still entertained guests here, but the far more likely conclusion was that Checker was a regular visitor. In other words, it hadn't only been Arthur hiding huge chunks of his life from me.

My resentment resurging, I stomped up the ramp to the porch and thumped on the door.

Someone pulled it open almost immediately. I found myself facing a very handsome, very built Hispanic guy who looked to be in his forties, silver just starting at his temples. He was one of those guys who was so fit, it dented my eyes to look at him, and his gray T-shirt was tight enough to show it off. His face, however, was creased with worry, and the minute he saw Tabitha, he sucked in a hard breath of relief.

"Oh, thank God." He grabbed her in a massive hug, which, whatever her feelings about being brought home, she returned just as tightly.

I shifted my weight and wondered if I should just go.

The man—presumably Tabitha's father and Arthur's ex-husband—finally remembered I was there as he released his daughter. "Thank you for bringing her home. Miss . . . ?"

"Russell," I said.

He glanced between me and Tabitha, taking in our wet clothes and his daughter's burglary garb. "What happened? Where were you?"

"She works with Dad," said Tabitha.

I didn't know what reaction I was expecting to a dodge like that, but it wasn't the one I got. Tabitha's father looked at me with raw fear in his eyes.

Christ, did everyone think I was a monster?

"Arthur's missing," I said too loudly. "I think Checker told you? Tabitha asked me to look into it, which I am, but then"—I shot her a severe glare—"she decided haring off on her own would be a *great idea,* and she almost got us—in real trouble."

At least I managed to cut myself off before I said "killed." Sometimes I'm capable of tact.

"I couldn't just do nothing!" said Tabitha.

The fear in her father's eyes hadn't gone away, despite my commendable circumspection. "Thank you, Miss Russell," he said. "I'll see that she doesn't bother you again."

"Good." Tabitha's face went so low and sad at my response that I felt compelled to add, "Because Arthur. Would have my hide. If anything happened to her." Crap on a cracker, if meeting Arthur's family was destined to be this uncomfortable, maybe he had spared me.

Diego took his daughter by the shoulders. "Sweetheart. Go inside, okay?"

Tabitha ducked behind him and into the house. Given his reaction, I half-expected Diego to shut the door in my face at that point, but instead, he came out and closed it behind him.

"How bad?"

"What do you mean?" I said.

"How much danger are we in?" The question almost had a deadness to it, resignation despite his intensity. "How much danger is my daughter in right now?"

"I—" The truth was, I hadn't been thinking about it from that angle at all. "I don't know, exactly."

"But you know not-exactly?"

At least one person was already dead, and his daughter had almost been turned into the scrapings on the bottom of a barbecue tonight. One of the prime suspects in all that was a guy from Checker's past who seemed intent on blowing up anyone with a connection to Arthur. And then there was the man on the lawn and whoever had been targeting Teplova, who sparked just enough familiarity for me to extrapolate that they were all very bad news . . . the lurking threat of Pithica and conspiracies could very well pivot to fall right on Tabitha and her family, without me being able to do a damned thing to prevent it.

Diego was probably right to be worried.

Apparently I'd taken too long to respond, because Diego scoffed and muttered something disgusted-sounding in Spanish that I was quite sure I was not supposed to understand.

"I can get you somewhere safe," I offered. I cringed at the thought of burying their whole family in one of my tiny, dirty apartments, but safe trumped comfortable. "It's a good idea, just in case—"

"Run from our lives? Again?" Diego wasn't looking at me. "I have a job. The children have school, and work."

"So miss a few days. Call it a vacation."

"A vacation," Diego echoed. His voice was shot through with bitterness. "I've come to dread when the next of these calls will come from Arthur, you know. Always the same—he's angered someone by fighting for some higher good, and so we must pay the price, we must run, hide, check into a hotel, miss important appointments, huddle in fear. No. There must be a limit."

I thought of the various bad guys Arthur and I had fought over the last couple of years. How many of them had he worried might be a danger to his family?

Shit. It wasn't like I could drag Diego out of his house by force.

"All right," I said. "In that case, I can send someone to stay with you. Protect you. If you want." Oh, Christ, there was really only one person I could assign to that. Arthur was going to murder me. Not to mention it was terrible resource management—but what choice did I have? "I'll send someone," I repeated. "And I can base here too, to have an extra gun around."

He winced but seemed to accept that. "We have a guest room. Thank you."

"No problem."

He squinted back at me. "What did you say your name was?"

I told him.

"Oh," he said. "You're the gal Charles mentioned, aren't you? The math genius."

"I—wait, who?"

The slightest wry smile touched Diego's mouth, and for the first time, he seemed to relax a bit and take in my presence properly, like I was a human he was talking with on his doorstep instead of a disease come to threaten his family. "Eh. I know he doesn't go by Charles anymore, but forgive me; I'm an old dog."

"You mean *Checker*? You call him *Charles*?" I had vaguely been aware Checker was an Internet-handle-turned-nickname, but I hadn't even known his real name. I wondered what he had told Diego about me. "I, uh. Yeah. Math genius is probably me."

"It's good to meet you. Thank you again for bringing Tabitha back." He sounded more sincere this time. "I'll get you my card so you can call."

Diego stepped back into the house, leaving me on the porch, and he returned a moment later with a business card from a gym. He handed it to me with a civil nod and then moved to go back inside.

"Hey," I said.

He turned.

"You didn't ask how the search is going."

I wasn't sure why I said it. I wasn't trying to attack him, and Christ knew I had a hell of a lot better things to do than stand here on a porch guilt-tripping Arthur's ex-husband. But dammit, this felt wrong.

Diego stood still for a few seconds. Then he said, "How is it going?"

"We're making headway. We were onto something at the place we found Tabitha. And someone from Checker's past might be mixed up in all this, and—" I cleared my throat. He didn't need to know about psychics or creatures or children becoming weapons. "We'll figure it out."

Diego's head came up. "This has to do with Charles? Is he all right?"

"Oh, uh—yeah, no one's given him trouble yet." A thought occurred to me—Diego had clearly known Checker for a lot longer than I'd assumed. "Hey, would *you* know anything about a demolition expert named D.J.?"

Diego inhaled deeply. "That poor boy."

"Who? D.J.?"

He shook his head. "Him too. But I was talking about Charles."

Considering what I knew of D.J., and that he might have just tried to blow us to smithereens, I wasn't inclined to feel the least bit of sympathy for him. Or patience. "Do you know anything Checker wouldn't, then?"

"I don't think so. I don't know much at all, and mostly from Charles." He said something unhappy-sounding in Spanish. "They were friends once. They ran on the same crew."

"Wait, *friends?*"

"Once. Close enough that Charles tried to find him, after moving in with us. I don't think they ever had luck."

People and their fucking secrets. I was going to kill Checker and Arthur *both*. Telling me everything I needed to know, my ass.

"Thanks," I said stiffly. I held up his card. "I'll be in touch soon. Keep your phone on."

He called after me as I stepped down onto the walkway. "Miss Russell. Have the police been contacted? About Arthur?"

I stopped and turned. "Oh. I'm—not sure. I don't think so."

Diego was backlit by the house light in the open door, so I couldn't see his expression. "If you do speak to them, have a care," he said. "Some of Arthur's old colleagues may not be inclined to give you help." One of his hands was gripping the doorframe very tightly.

"I'll keep that in mind," I said.

ten

I tromped down the ramp off the porch until I was out of sight of the front door. I'd taken Pilar's burner phone with me, and I stopped there on the sidewalk to call Rio.

He picked up immediately. "Hello."

"It's Cas—the old phone drowned."

"Cas. Are you well?"

"Yeah. Did Simon tell you what we ran into?"

"Briefly. I would appreciate more detail." That was fair. He probably hadn't gotten much detail from Simon precisely because I hadn't given Simon any.

I took a breath, pressed my eyes shut for a second, and recounted everything that had happened at the wellness center. To my surprise and relief, I was able to do it without my consciousness juddering off the rails. Rio listened quietly until I wound down.

"Have you seen this kind of thing before?" I asked. "Either a binary explosive this destructive, or the . . . whatever those things did to Pilar and me?"

"No, in either instance. This is new technology, and troubling."

I hadn't realized how disconcerting it would be to hear Rio confirm that. He made it a point to have a vast level of global intelligence.

"This Willow Grace says she's seen the binary explosive before," I said. "You think she's lying?"

"Impossible to say. She may truly have seen this somewhere, or she may have been able to recognize the likelihood without having seen the specific chemical capable of this level of annihilation."

New bombs. And we still hadn't figured out how D.J. might factor in. For some reason, I didn't mention that to Rio—I wanted to talk to Checker again first.

"Do you . . ." I wasn't sure what I wanted to ask. "When you were . . . years ago. Did you ever run into Willow Grace? Or Teplova?"

"I have not met this reporter, though I am familiar with her work. She has been a highly regarded force in more than one volatile situation. As for the doctor, I know of no one by that name, though it's more than likely she would have chosen to change identities."

Right. I should have taken her photograph with me or something.

"It sounds like they were trying to fight Pithica too," I said.

"Perhaps. I shall look into it."

Was I imagining the slight emphasis on the pronoun?

My hand tightened on the phone. "Don't tell me to stop, Rio. Don't you fucking tell me to stop."

"I would hardly dare," Rio said dryly. "However, it is only logical to point out that driving yourself into an altered state would hardly be the best use of the people available to you. I can pursue this angle."

"But I remember them, Rio. There could be something—some information, something we can use—"

"Has your sense of familiarity granted you any actionable intel?"

"No, but if I keep trying—"

"Destroying yourself in such an attempt would be of no help to your friend." He said it flatly. Factually.

"You've fought Pithica before we ever did. You could fill in a lot more for me," I tried, knowing already what his answer would be. "We'll be better off if we can pool that. Just tell me what you suspect, and I swear I'll tell you if I start going off-kilter or something. Rio, please, it's for Arthur . . ."

"I am not appropriately equipped to determine what information could be of too much harm to you," Rio answered. "But Simon's knowledge may exceed my own in any case. I suggest you direct these questions at him. He wishes to speak to you anyway."

Of course he did.

Intellectually, I could have guessed that Rio would never have any sort of emotional investment in Arthur's rescue. He was doing it only as a favor to me, and I wasn't ungrateful. But somehow, his complete lack of regret in not answering made my skin prickle like fleas had crawled in under it.

Arthur deserved better. I *wanted* to be better. Jesus Christ, if I wasn't the person he invited to his kids' sports meets, at the very least I should be the one who could haul in every resource to save him from violent kidnappers, the optimum under this metric. If I couldn't even do that . . .

A brief rustling sound on the phone. I felt Simon before he spoke, his concern *pushing* at me even through the telephone connection.

"Cas. Cas," he said. "How are you feeling? Any residual effects?"

Picturing what we'd encountered at the wellness center still made my throat tighten and my stomach fold over, but I brushed it off. "I'm fine."

"Are you sure?" He must have sensed my instant desire to tear his face off, because he continued rapidly, "Okay. Okay. All right. I have, um, information on your prisoner."

"My what?"

"The man you left with us," Simon reminded me. "The one who was probably responsible for destroying your office. Remember?"

A man who'd destroyed my office . . .

A voice on the phone. Australian. An indistinct face, yelling as I dropped him to the ground. The image of me locking an apartment door and leaving him.

The whole reason we'd started to be suspicious of a Pithica connection in the first place.

"Shit," I said.

"We'll keep reminding you," Simon offered.

"Yeah," I croaked. "Do that. Now what about him?"

"His name is Oscar. And Cas, he's seen Arthur. He's alive, at least as of earlier today."

My knees felt like they lost the ability to hold me up, and I almost sat right on the sidewalk. I'd told Pilar, I'd told Tabitha, but hearing it was true . . .

Relief wasn't supposed to feel this awful.

"Where?" I got out.

"I—we haven't worked that out yet. He might be willing to tell me, but I don't think he's fully conscious of everything he's done. You were right—he's had severe psychological trauma."

"Can't you impress upon him that this is *urgent*? Or just—" I bit my lip. I knew what Simon would say to the suggestion that he go forth and rip everything we needed out of Oscar's head.

It wasn't even something I would generally consider ethical, especially with a guy we were concluding was someone else's pawn. But if Arthur died because we didn't get there fast enough . . .

Simon did me the favor of not finger-wagging at me for what he already knew I knew. "I *can* tell you this," he said instead. "I don't know for sure, but I suspect many of his psychological issues are related to the way he won't stick in your memory."

"What?" I said. "How?"

"Well, the mind is a malleable thing, Cas. What would happen to a person's mind if nobody could ever see them?"

Cold crept up the back of my neck. As pissed as my friends could make me, the thought of becoming a ghost . . . unable to make any human connection, anywhere, because no matter what I did, good or bad, tender or cruel, no one would ever, ever acknowledge I existed . . .

Fuck.

"So, it isn't him who's mindwiping people of his face, then?" I said. "Can you tell how . . . ?"

"I'm still not sure. He definitely doesn't have any special, um, powers, if you want to use that word. He's within all the norms for a human."

We're outside the norm, whispered a voice in my head. *But we're still human.*

Not true. "Normal" *has a specific mathematical meaning. So does* "*human.*"

"Cas?"

"I'm here," I barked into the phone, pushing the stray murmurings aside. "Go on."

Simon paused for just long enough that I knew he was trying to handle me delicately. "Cas, speaking of people's psychological variances, you know what you're dealing with equates to a chronic mental health condition. If you need to—"

"*Not now*," I said. I needed to finish this conversation and get back to the car. "Keep going. About Oscar. He doesn't have powers?"

"No," Simon answered. "He just has—I don't know how to describe it. A very forgettable face."

"That doesn't make any sense." Either Oscar was manipulating us or someone else was; this couldn't be something hard-coded.

"*Very* forgettable," Simon said.

Or, wait. What if it was *exactly* something hard-coded . . . "Supernaturally forgettable?"

His tone went neutral and careful. "I'm not sure I know what that word means."

"Cut the crap."

"I think it's more what you would call 'low probability,'" he said. "If I'm using such a phrase correctly."

I got what he meant, and it made me mad that I got it. Simon didn't get to use the terms I would use.

"You mean, it's something that would never happen ever but is still technically possible," I said. "It's *possible* he was born this way."

"Possible, but—I'm not sure if he would have survived this long if he had been. Although there's also the chance his face changed enough in puberty that he was able to interact more normally as a child, but still, it's so . . . specific."

I had the spooky feeling that even if humans multiplied wildly until the universe ended, Simon was saying there was basically a zero chance someone like Oscar would've ever been born.

"So you're saying someone made him into this," I said.

"I think it's likely. If so, he probably had some psychological issues before that, but they're many times worse now."

Which confirmed I'd made the right decision in not being willing to use Rio to help with the questioning. Though when I went back and asked myself if I would willingly sacrifice Arthur to those principles—

"I promise I'll keep at it," said Simon quickly. Even through a phone conversation he'd probably caught wind of my thoughts, the fucker. He cleared his throat. "Do you want to talk about the creature?"

"Only if you can tell me how to fight something like that."

"I . . . without knowing how it triggers such an extreme panic response, I'm not sure. But if you find out more, I may be able to help."

Fat lot of good you are, I wanted to say, but it was so demonstrably untrue even I would have felt stupid. The man from the lawn oozed through my memory again—and then, startlingly, the image of him sitting on a low cement wall, drink in hand and laughing. And I was laughing with him, looking up to him with the warmth of a pupil for her favorite mentor or teacher . . .

"There's some connection," I said hoarsely to Simon. "The doctor at the clinic, Eva Teplova, and—other things. I can feel a—there's some connection, to Pithica, or—" I coughed, biting down on telling him more. Too risky that he would hear me start to slide—he could get it from Rio later. I needed to keep showcasing my sane side around Simon, or he'd never tell me anything. "And now this Oscar guy is tangled up in it all too. So, if this is Pithica, they're, what? Putting a spell on him to make it so—"

"It doesn't work like that," Simon said. "It's not magic. If this is . . . one of us . . . it's someone from Halberd, not Pithica."

Halberd . . .

We are the halberd against the gathering storm, chanted a long-dead memory. I tried to slap it away. What did that even mean? It was gibberish. I needed to focus—

The night around me fuzzed in and out for a moment, like reality was a badly tuned television set.

"Cas." Simon's voice cut through the static in my brain. "Cas, are you with me?"

"Yeah." *Protectors of the species. No—its new definition.* I shook my head hard. "What's the, um. What's the difference?"

"Cas, I don't know if I should—"

"Tell me what you can," I said. "Please."

Simon was silent for a moment. Whether he was startled by hearing sincerity instead of rudeness from me for once, or he could just tell how desperately I needed the information . . . I forced myself to let my words hang in the air and to allow him to think.

"I'll try to limit it to information that won't, um, be a trigger for your memories," he said quietly at last. "Pithica came first, and it concentrated exclusively on enhancement of the brain. In the beginning, it looked like it would be wildly successful."

"It was," I said. "They'd practically taken over the world before we stopped them."

Simon was *intensely* silent.

"Okay, I get it, things you can't tell me lest I start going off the deep end." I mostly managed to keep a cap on my snippiness. "Go on."

"With the technology behind Pithica going so well, the next step was to develop abilities that went beyond the neurological. The Holy Grail was allowing not only enhancements of the mind, but discovering ways for those to interact with enhancements to the human body."

The familiarity dropped through my consciousness like a block of lead.

What did you take?

My medicine.

"Like me," I said numbly. "That's what I am."

The numbers sang under my skin, mathematics come alive, gloving every neuron with theory made flesh . . .

"Cas?"

I forced myself to breathe. To think. Arthur. We had to find Arthur, and I could dwell on anything else later.

"So, you're saying this isn't Pithica," I said to Simon. "They're not violating their deal with us."

More importantly, that meant I wouldn't be bringing down their retribution if I mowed down everyone who got in my way. First bit of good news we'd had about whoever was behind this.

"That's my, well—that's my guess," Simon confirmed. "From what I know, at least. I haven't had contact with anyone from those years in a long while, but this also feels far enough removed not to be involved with Daniela's group. And I don't think Halberd even exists anymore, as such; their people would all be . . . scattered, now. But, Cas—don't take this lightly. If whoever's behind this is related to Halberd, that might mean they're just as dangerous as Pithica ever would be."

Dangerous like me.

At least that felt familiar. Something I could kill.

"Have you heard Teplova's name before?" I asked Simon. "Was she a part of—did you know her?"

"I haven't heard the name, but that doesn't mean anything. She could have been before my time, or separate in some other way. I wouldn't know everybody."

Besides, like Rio had said, Teplova could easily be a pseudonym. And now, like everything else at the wellness center, she was nothing more than a sprinkling of ash.

I tried to reorient, to look forward and formulate a plan. I had to use all this somehow to track down Arthur. And meanwhile, protect his family, which would at least be a slightly better use of one of my best people than babysitting Simon's too-virtuous ethics.

"I need Rio," I said to him. "If I take him, is this Oscar guy going to try to run? Or, you know, try to kill you?"

He sighed. "He's not going to attack me. I mean, people don't in general, but Oscar also likes my company. I think because I can, um, see and interact with him, and him not having had that . . . but I can't guarantee he won't want his freedom. That's not a villainous need."

"Then I'll tell Rio to barricade you two in there together. Put him back on."

A moment later Rio's baritone came back on the line.

"Rio," I said. "I need you to lock Simon and the Australian in together and come babysit Arthur's family."

"I shall do so and head there at once. I can arrive within the hour."

It was like the words didn't have English meanings. They balled up in my head with no sense attached to them. After everything else tonight . . .

"Their location was merely intelligence, Cas," Rio said, misinterpreting my silence. "I have promised not to harm your friends' families, and I will not."

Rio fucking knew about Arthur's family?

Of course. He'd probably background checked all my friends.

"Do that," I sputtered, and hung up.

I texted Diego a heads-up and a description of Rio and then stomped back to the car.

eleven

I DIDN'T think to call Checker to warn him we were descending on his place, but it turned out he'd expected it. All four of us squeezed into the garage he'd converted into his own personal computer cluster. Despite it being well past midnight, Checker was fully dressed and had clearly been hard at work on Pilar's data pull from the wellness center. He immediately put Pilar and Willow on the files as well and sent them in to work in his living room with laptops, though we could still see them clearly on his security monitors.

I'd tried to push Willow for answers again, but she'd recovered her previous calm and claimed only to have heard bits and pieces about Teplova's enemies—D.J.'s name along with nebulous haunted accounts of other foes, including the dogs.

Dogs—*plural*. Apparently. And we'd only killed one of them.

I didn't want to think about what would happen if I ran into a pack of those things.

But Willow insisted the reason she was nosing through the doctor's files when we'd found her was that she didn't have much more information on the night's events than we did. She acknowledged she'd known the clinic had been closed for the past six months, but had no more than a thousand equally likely suspicions as to why, and only said that her friend had called her tonight with a supposed life-and-death emergency . . . and that she'd arrived only to find death.

Either she really didn't know very much, or she was capable of making it sound like she didn't.

"Don't worry, her background checks out completely," Checker said. He scooted his wheelchair back and craned his neck around to watch through the window as the two women went into his house, even though they were clearly visible on the monitors. "I mean, I figured it would, because I've seen her on the newscasts just like everyone else, and besides, if there was anything for anybody to find, people would've been all over her. Like the Brian Williams thing. She's too much of a celebrity not to keep her nose as clean as possible, especially being a woman. But yeah, aside from the plastic surgery secret, which I honestly can't believe she's been able to keep this long, she's as clean as a whistle."

I cared less about clean backgrounds than whether a person was on our side. "I don't think she's working for D.J. or Halberd. But I also don't think she's telling us everything."

Checker pressed his lips together for a moment. "How sure are you?"

"You mean, should I grab some thumbscrews and start tightening them on her fingers and toes? Jesus, I don't know."

He twitched slightly at that. Checker was usually much more antitorture than I was. The fact that he didn't hit me with a sarcastic comeback said everything about how worried he was about Arthur. So did the drawn skin of his face and the tired shadows under his eyes.

I felt the same way myself.

"What's her rep as a journalist?" I asked.

"Solid. One of the best investigative reporters out there. Rising star, on track to become the next Tom Brokaw or something—she only hit the scene this decade, but she's reported from all over the world, battlefronts and natural disasters and disease-ridden hot zones. She's been on sabbatical lately to write a book, and some people have made noises about hoping it meant she was going to run for political office."

"So, if she was investigating Pithica . . ."

"I'd say I wouldn't want to be them."

"She didn't break the story," I pointed out. "They beat her."

"Well, I'm going to hope she's playing a long game on getting sources," Checker said, moving forward to start multitasking on one of his machines as he spoke. "Maybe she'll team up with us after this. I'm actually surprised you haven't heard of her—I know it's *you*, but she's practically a household name."

And she still hadn't been able to save her friend. Teplova had likely called her tonight for help of some kind—the bottomless sort of help a friend of power and prestige and wealth could employ. None of that had stopped the assassins.

I wasn't going to fail my friends the way Willow Grace had. I wouldn't *let* myself.

"All right, let's set her aside for now." I swallowed. "You should know—Simon thinks Teplova might have been. Uh. Like us somehow."

"Like us how?"

"No. Like me and Simon." I hesitated. "Or just . . . like me."

Checker had stopped typing and turned back to me, his face very still.

"I don't think this has to do with me. I mean, I don't think that history is why Arthur ended up looking into them," I said quickly, though I wasn't sure of that at all. "But if whoever killed Teplova killed her because . . . We might be running up against some dangerous people."

"Does this give us something?" Checker asked softly. He was gripping the edge of the desk so hard, his knuckles had gone white. "Do you know anything about—does Simon know—"

"No. I already asked him. All he knows is that it sounds likely this is all mixed up with people who have, you know, our same sorts of . . . talents, but he doesn't know who, or why. Or where. It doesn't give us anything that would lead to Arthur yet."

"What about you? Are you okay?" Checker asked after a moment.

The question startled me. "I'm fine," I said a little too harshly. "Just want to get him back."

He hesitated, then frowned. "That seems like a pretty big coincidence, though, doesn't it? That they'd kidnap *your* friend without there being some sort of, I don't know, connection?"

"Selection bias," I snapped. Refusing to acknowledge the possibility aloud may have been petty, but . . . it wasn't like admitting it would help us find him. The self-recrimination twisted into barbs before I could stop myself. "Do you really think it's so unlikely that *your* old friend D.J. would end up hooking up with some of the most dangerous people in the world all on his own? Arthur would've told you about investigating Teplova in the first place if this were a regular case, so I'm assuming he was tracking D.J. and then got mixed up in the rest of it. Willow says Teplova kept referencing D.J. all panicked."

Checker's head jerked. "Yeah, um. Probably whoever our murderer is just—hired him. I don't know."

"Diego said you knew him pretty well." I felt a vindictive spark as he flinched, and tried to quash it. "Any guesses on his next move?"

"I don't—I wish I knew." Checker's posture had gone so tense, it was as if he were about to make himself shatter. "It was a long time ago. And if he's working for someone else, then—I swear, Cas, I *wish* I could help. If something happens to Arthur because of—or if something's already happened to him—" His words strangled off like they had choked him. "That can't, that can't happen, all right?"

"Oh," I said. "I forgot to tell you. Simon got intel that Arthur was seen alive earlier today somewhere. He's working on the where. But alive."

"Wha—he's ali—you *forgot*? What the *fuck*, Cas!" Checker spun and grabbed for his keyboard, his phone-texting program summoned to the screen before I'd seen him hit a key. "Did you tell his family? Or Pilar?"

"Uh—" I'd been reaching for some sort of emotional high ground in this whole situation, some vengeful absolution—from any responsibility for it, from Arthur's opinion of me and every assumption I'd been screaming to prove wrong. It all socked out of me, leaving me breathless and flat-footed. "No, I—"

"*Forgot.* Right. Fuck you." Checker's fingers clattered on the keyboard, the messages sending faster than I could have spoken them aloud. Heat rushed into my face and the back of my neck, my skin tingling with a thousand tiny needles, a buzzing in my ears.

This wasn't the angriest Checker had ever been at me. But it was the first time I'd felt like this about it. It was worse than having a gun pointed at my face.

Much worse.

I would have liked to blame my forgetfulness on possible telepathic influence, or on whatever Simon was doing—there was something I was supposed to remember, and where had he gotten the intelligence about Arthur again? *Fuck*—but I wasn't having any trouble remembering the actual information. I was just . . . the type of person who would forget to tell Arthur's friends and family about it. Apparently.

The very type of person Arthur thought I was.

"So, you know Arthur's family pretty well, huh?" I said, watching Checker send the texts.

"Yes. Can we do this later?"

"How well is *well?*"

He slapped the keyboard back and met my gaze defiantly. "They were almost my family too, if you must know. Arthur and Diego offered to adopt me."

"*What?*"

"It would have been murder on their health insurance, so I said no. This was right after my accident, and I figured I'd let the state keep paying for the physical therapy. But they took me in, set me straight—saved my life, to be dramatic but truthful about it. Before them, I was pretty much the poster child for 'messed-up teenager,' and it's not an overstatement to say I literally owe them everything. That's it. Happy?" He pulled at his desktop, sliding himself over to start typing at a different screen. "I still have decades of tax records and client data to sort through, not to mention decrypting the rest of what we got. You should start with Dr. Teplova's surgical methods; I'm betting you can—"

"Yeah, give me a workstation." My breath was coming short now, like he'd stabbed me in a lung. Like they all had. "And then take five seconds and tell me what the hell happened, because—"

"What do you mean, what happened?"

"Everything! How many kids does he have?"

"Five."

"And he and Diego, how come they're not sunshine and roses anymore?"

He hunched into himself, still typing. "Not my story to tell."

"Tell me *something,* or I will punch you in the face."

His head came up. "What? No, you won't!"

"Try me. Fucking *try me.*"

He squinted at me in something that wasn't quite a glare, but whatever he saw in my eyes made him falter.

"Fine, I'll give you the public records version," he said. "But *not* because you're threatening me—you should stop saying such shitty things to your friends, by the way—but because you're Arthur's friend too and you don't deserve to be kept in the dark. I wasn't here when it all went down—I'd gone off to be a real adult and try my hand at being a productive member of society, believe it or not; I had some harebrained idea about making sure I could make it on my own without their help. When I get back in touch, I find out hell had frozen over while I was off playing dot-com rich kid—Arthur had gotten boned and thrown off the force, and he and Diego had split up, which as far as I was concerned was one of the top twelve signs of the apocalypse. I found Arthur working nights as a security guard for minimum wage."

"That's when you came back?"

He made a face and turned back to his screen. "Normal life was never a good fit for me anyway. I talked Arthur into starting the business and getting some meaning back into his life, and here we are."

"So Arthur and Diego don't speak anymore."

"They keep it civil, but no, not really. Arthur's in his kids' lives every minute he can be, though. He's a good father."

Yet he had chosen to hide it from me. He had never wanted me to know about the most important piece of himself.

He'd made a conscious decision to cut a carefully Cas-shaped hole around everything that mattered to him most.

"And what about you?" I said to Checker, my voice treacherously even.

He cleared his throat. "I go over for Sunday dinner almost every week. They're still family to me, even if we never made it official."

I almost did punch him, then. "Two years," I said. "That's how long I've known you and Arthur. Two. *Years.*"

"People have a right to have secrets from one another, Cas—"

"This isn't a secret!" The sting in my chest was writhing up until I couldn't stop it anymore and didn't want to. "This is—this is his *family*, practically your family too from what you just said—how far did you have to go out of your way to avoid ever mentioning them in front of me? How far?"

"It was Arthur's call—"

"And what, he doesn't trust me? To know his children *exist*?" I cried. "Jesus, that sort of thing is public knowledge if anyone wanted to look; it's not even like it's something dangerous I could spill to a bad guy. So, what, he just didn't want me to know?"

"He likes to keep his family separate from his work life—"

"And that's all I am to him, right? Someone he can hire to bash in heads when he needs to. Nothing more."

A tool. A fucking gun in his arsenal. One he thought should be illegal if it weren't so regrettably useful.

I'd been reluctant to have friends because they needed things from me and would make me feel shitty if they were inconsiderate enough to die. I'd braced myself for the guilt of inevitably letting them down.

I'd never prepared for . . . this.

"I tried to tell him it was getting ridiculous," Checker said tightly. "So did Pilar. He was just *stubborn;* you know how stubborn he can be. But I'm sorry, Cas. Is that what you want me to say? I'm sorry. Though, come on, it's not like *you* share anything unless you're forced to, so can we call a fucking truce? Now, for the love of human progress, will you please *sit the fuck down* and get to work on finding him?"

I clamped down on my emotions like I was trying to reseal a shaken soda bottle and sat.

My fingers hit the keys with almost enough force to break them.

twelve

CHECKER—OR more likely Pilar—had already been sifting through the files from the data dump and sorting them into directories. Not a whole lot of it was decrypted yet, but the moment I opened the first file about Teplova's surgical methods, I had to admit I saw why Checker had wanted me on them.

It was as I'd told Professor Halliday, way back when all this had started: Eva Teplova had figured out a definition for beauty as a narrow band around the optimum of the Western popular opinion distribution. In other words, she'd figured out how to aggregate which characteristics were most likely to make the largest percentage of the local population awestruck and drooling, at least according to what *currently* made the largest percentage of the local population awestruck and drooling.

I'd told Sonya Halliday how a mathematical formula for beauty might theoretically be achieved. But Teplova had gone beyond theory.

She had done it.

People like me, I thought darkly. But Teplova wasn't a computational machine in the same way. She was more . . . applied. A different sort of genius.

Her face blinked by me again, masked, reaching for a tray of silver instruments at her elbow.

I concentrated on the screen and kept reading. The trickier part seemed to have been finding the functions for mapping a particular face into that narrow band of the distribution using current surgical technology. It looked like Teplova had half-brute forced that part of it by having the computer scan through the finite space of her possible surgical techniques, but her notes indicated she'd also invented a few new ones when she needed to fill in gaps.

That definitely wasn't something I could have replicated. What kind of talent went into medical skill? I didn't even know how to quantify it.

On the plus side, I could understand her methods . . . but that gave me less than no help with anything useful. If Dr. Teplova had indeed been one of Halberd's manufactured prodigies, it looked like all she was doing was using it to live the capitalist American dream and make herself rich.

"There's nothing here," I complained aloud. Other than Checker making a run into the house to bring us coffee—he usually didn't allow liquids around his computers, but coffee was an exception—we hadn't spoken in hours. The silence hadn't *quite* been frosty. "This is *interesting,* but why would you kill someone over it? So, she was making people beautiful. So what?"

Checker sat back, pushing up his glasses to rub at his eyes. "Beauty is a form of power. Maybe someone didn't like what she was doing in a philosophical sense."

Willow Grace had implied as much. "But then, why kill her now, half a year after she stopped doing it?"

"Maybe they couldn't get to her before? Or maybe it's the reverse—maybe someone wanted the power she could give them, but she'd stopped taking new clients and said no."

"So they *killed* her?"

"Stranger things have happened." Checker waved at his screens. "I'm still decrypting the databases on the clients—it's painful going; we're only a few inches into what we got, and I don't think we managed to pull out close to everything. But a few of the names so far are, well, *fantastically* famous people. And I don't think they got there until after they were—worked on." He sounded disturbed.

"Then maybe we should be looking for one who was disgruntled.

Someone whose life didn't take off after the procedures. Beauty can't be a panacea; it's not going to magically open every door."

"But beauty plus wealth? All of these people were rich going in; otherwise, they wouldn't have been able to afford her. Yeah, it's hard to deny someone like Willow Grace has ridiculous talent, but I think you're underestimating how much looks matter in our society. And we only got a partial data haul—this beauty thing may not be all she came up with." He pointed at my computer. "For all we know, she wasn't only working on making people 'beautiful,' but she figured out how to make people look, I don't know, *trustworthy*, or sincere, or like a leader you would believe in. I have CEOs on this list, Cas. And politicians. Not just movie stars and models, although they're here too, but—"

"Wait," I said.

He paused. "What?"

It was all coming together in my head, so suddenly and strongly that I was stunned I hadn't seen it before.

Halberd combined genius with physical ability, Simon had said. Like what I could do: map mathematics onto my environment and effortlessly propel my body to match. Or like . . .

Somewhere in my memory, a Black girl touched wires together in a shower of sparks and yelled in exultation. Like—her. Or like a surgeon, a surgeon like Eva Teplova. If I took that to its logical conclusion . . .

I had been asking Simon about something else when we talked about Halberd—someone else—dammit, why couldn't I remember? I had been thinking of someone, and it hadn't been Teplova. Or her clients.

Or the *dogs*.

Oh, shit.

I jumped up and ran outside. The sky was just starting to lighten toward day. I pulled open the back door and banged into the house, Checker following me an instant later.

Pilar and Willow Grace looked up from laptops. Pilar's eyes sagged with lack of sleep, and her hair stuck up at odd angles. Willow somehow still appeared pristine.

It was disconcerting as fuck.

"What is it, Cas?" Pilar asked.

I recovered myself and pointed at Willow. "The dogs. You know where they came from."

"I don't—"

"Don't fuck around with me," I said. "That dog and its master, they were part of Teplova's research, weren't they? Beauty, trustworthiness—and fear. She figured out the mathematical aesthetics of fear. For this culture, in this time."

Pilar gasped. Willow Grace's inscrutable veneer cracked a little.

"Like you," I said. "She made that dog the same way she made you, and made those politicians—she hard-coded you all." Not just beauty. Not just riches. If she could hard-code anything into a face . . . what kind of potential would that give her? What kind of power?

The image of the man from the wellness center swam before me again, his face both changed and not. It hadn't been so different—a little older—a little harder—

Except that somehow, whatever his face was now had suffocated me with panic. Even thinking back on it, I only wanted to run or kill.

"They must have forced her," Willow Grace said. The words were hoarse, as if she had to drag them out, and her anguish was palpable. "I suspected—it was only supposed to be theoretical. Do you understand? It fascinated her, but Eva never would have done it. I know her, and she would never—they must have made her. D.J. must have made her do it."

If I had known the man on the lawn a long time ago, Teplova might have too. Someone she knew, from our joint past, whom she'd been forced to turn into a monster.

"What does he want?" I said. "What the hell would D.J. want that he's doing this?"

"Power," Checker said. It was almost a whisper. "People like Eva Teplova—people like you, Cas—think how much he could control."

So the connection to my own history *was* coincidence. Or rather, not coincidence, but selected purely by virtue of D.J.'s thirst for people he could wield as weapons. It didn't sound like he'd only been a hired gun on this one.

I didn't feel the vindication at that I would have expected.

"You lied to us," I said to Willow Grace.

She paled. "I'm sorry. I—Eva was my friend. I didn't want her to be remembered as . . . I promise, that wasn't who she was. She only liked the theory. She did the research only to see if she could, not to hurt anyone; she was *helping* people—"

"People who were rich enough," Pilar murmured, almost too low to hear.

"You think there's a bright line between helping a burn victim, or rebuilding a woman's body after cancer, and what I did," Willow said to her shortly. "I would have languished at a minor local news station forever without Eva. Why should I have stood for that? It's the same reason you wear makeup and dress well. I didn't make the world this way."

I turned away at an angle, trying not to let Willow's face cloud my thinking. Christ, she was like a fucking Renaissance painting or something. My head had started to hurt.

"Researching whether something is solvable—I get that," I declared to her. Calmly. I hadn't lost my temper again—yet. "But we need to know what the hell else you're hiding. Right now."

Pilar glanced at me and seemed to gather herself before turning back to Willow. "I didn't mean to offend you. We only want to find our friend. We're not on any crusade against Dr. Teplova's research, I promise, and we're not here to think badly of her."

"What she said," Checker added. "For the record, I think it's utter bullshit that you had to do what you did to get ahead, but I'm not going to judge you for it. Or your doctor. If you get in our way now, though—" He'd started to sound angry, but then he stumbled a little. "Just—just don't. Okay?"

I scrubbed my hands over my face. Willow Grace might be on the same side with us against Pithica, or Halberd, or whoever . . . but I'd been right all along that she'd been hiding things, secrets that could help, intel we could use. What did that mean? Fuck, I wasn't good at people. I didn't know if I wanted to demand her help or put her beautiful face through a wall.

My brain felt full of static and contradictions. The only thing I was sure of was that we needed to find Arthur.

Checker seemed to be thinking the same thing. "Cards on the table," he said. "You've gathered we have a friend missing, right? Help us find him, and we'll keep your friend's secrets. We're not interested in wrecking her reputation. We don't give a damn."

Willow paused for a moment. "Believe me. I haven't hidden anything that could help find your friend. But . . ." She sat up straighter and shut her laptop. "All right. Tell me why he was looking into us."

"He wasn't after you," Pilar assured her. "It was an unrelated case that must have connected to Dr. Teplova somehow."

"D.J.," I said. "Your friend's killer is probably our kidnapper, and could very well be after all the rest of us by now. So spill."

She narrowed her eyes at me for a moment at that, but sharply, like her brain was whirring at impossible speeds behind them. Then, without sacrificing an inch of composure, she said, "I wasn't entirely truthful earlier. I do have passwords to some parts of her file system. I don't know if they would help, but I'll share them with you."

Checker's face tightened, and his hands clenched against his jeans. We'd been at this the whole *night*.

"I apologize," Willow Grace said. "I . . . I lost my friend last night. I didn't want to do anything that would tarnish her, and the dangerous research, she was never going to use it, and I . . . I only wanted to protect her. I promise I'm not withholding anything else."

For the first time, she seemed fragile, like if she gave voice to any too-strong emotion it might shatter her.

That didn't stop me from wanting to do it myself. The enormity of the time wasted crashed down on me, wrapped in worry and screaming exhaustion.

I ordered myself to calm down. She was cooperating now. It wouldn't help Arthur for me to rage at her.

Willow Grace reopened her laptop and hit a few keys. "Eva had some confidential files. Projects like what I assume were used to make the dogs. And other research like that."

Of course, she was making it really fucking hard to let go of that anger.

Checker grabbed a tablet, presumably to follow along with whatever Willow Grace was unlocking. His jaw worked, but he didn't say anything.

"It's okay," Pilar said quickly into the tension. "We've got the info now, right? Let's not lose any more time."

Checker took a deep breath and then spoke in a surprisingly even tone. "Whoever killed Teplova was obviously after this research. If we're looking for a connection to D.J. or anyone else Arthur might have been tracking, the most likely trail is straight through what her enemies wanted her for, which means something in here. This is going to take a long time to sift through. I've got caffeine in both pill and five different liquid forms for whoever needs it; nobody sleeps till we find him."

He turned and started back outside.

I scrambled to catch up. "We should get Rio on the data mining too, now that we've got data. He's aces at it."

Checker nodded, a short, clipped motion.

"I should go back him up anyway. I can take some laptops and keep in touch."

"Fine."

"You going to be okay here?" He didn't look it.

"I know she didn't mean to, but—dammit, Cas. We lost *time* . . ."

"You want me to punch her?" I was only half kidding.

It was a mark of how upset he was that he didn't have a retort and instead only shot me a hooded glare.

"At least we know what this is now," I tried. "This doctor's powers, and what people were using them for." Human weapons, to be pointed like a missile. Like Dawna. Like me.

The apprehension sank in my gut, that Arthur's abduction might only be the tip of it all, that this was going to go deeper than any of us had assumed . . . and with manufactured fear and who knew what else ready to take us out at any step. Teplova was dead, but her creations weren't.

I'd been right about what I'd so casually tossed out as a threat to Willow Grace: They might be after us already.

"Hey," I said to Checker. "I know you'll work faster from here, but if you want us all to go over to Diego's house together, it might be safer—"

He didn't stop moving, pushing out through the back door into the twilit dawn and heading back to his computer cluster. "Is Pilar armed?"

Holy shit. Checker *hated* guns.

"Yes," I admitted. Not only did Pilar have her CZ at the hotel with her, but it turned out she'd been carrying more ammo to reload with in her trunk. I'd heartily approved, but I hadn't thought Checker would have.

"Good. We'll work from here. Like you said, it'll be faster."

"Checker—" I started.

But I didn't know what to say. We'd reached the Hole; Checker beelined inside and immediately buried himself in scrolling screens again. "Take some laptops and go, Cas. You're right, you should be with Diego and the kids, just in case. Tell Diego—"

He stopped, the movement on his monitors pausing with him. I waited.

"Tell Diego I'll fix this," he finished finally, his hands moving on the keys again.

We'll fix it, I wanted to say, but the words stuck in my throat.

thirteen

When I got to Arthur's family's house, the morning already had that sort of hazy, scorching sunlight that made everything too bright and hard to see. I squeezed into a parking spot pointing back toward the freeway—just in case—and hiked to the bungalow with my bag of laptops.

All the blinds were drawn. At Rio's direction, I was sure.

I knocked and called, "It's Cas."

Knowing Rio, he'd probably been monitoring my approach since before I was within a stone's throw of the house. The deadbolt drew back almost immediately, and he pulled the door open. "Come in, Cas."

I stepped into a tiny, crooked foyer with dark hardwood floors. The house had one of those bizarre, slightly haphazard architectures that happened when places were old enough to have survived several remodels. A hallway led in front of me at a slight angle, with stairs tucked against it to the right, and doorways popping off in three directions. Picture frames lined the walls—some holding photographs, presumably of the kids as they grew up, and some holding drawings or art projects or other displays of familial sentimentality.

It was a homey, cozy place. One that needed a lot more escape routes.

Rio led the way through the doorway to the right, which turned out to be a room in a slightly smashed *L* shape that held living room furniture in the longer part of it and a dining table back closer to the kitchen. Spread out on the table were several weapons, with a KRISS Vector half field-stripped over newspaper next to some patches and oil. I noted the Vector with approval—I loved the things; they had all the elegance and compactness of an MP5 but in .45 caliber. Speaking of, I'd have to grab some .45 from Rio for my Colt. Pilar had only had nine-mil.

Rio sat at the table and went back to cleaning his guns. "I have some security measures I would like to review with you, Cas," he said, his hands moving deftly on the cleaning rod, "but I believe it is something we should discuss without an audience."

I needed to discuss *everything* with him, from our conclusions about Teplova to the weapons and security on down, but I'd also noticed the eyes peeking through the hinges of the open kitchen door. "What's going on with them?"

"They are playing a game," Rio answered.

Both pairs of eyes got huge and then vanished. I'd recognized one of them as Tabitha already.

"I don't think they realized you knew they were there," I said to Rio. I pulled out the chair across from him and sat. "How many liabilities right now?"

"Three at the moment—the father and one son and daughter. I have been informed there are five children total, and that two more will join us today and another tomorrow."

"You can introduce yourself, you know," Diego said. I looked around. He'd come to the doorway of the cheery kitchen. "Juwon and Tabitha are home now. The twins are Matthias and Roy—they're both USC students, and they're taking summer session. They were staying over with friends last night, but I called and asked them to come home today so they could talk to you about how to stay safe. Elisa is our eldest. She's a lawyer down in Inglewood. She's on a business trip today, but she'll be back tomorrow, and she has agreed to stay here until this is over. She is not the happiest about the arrangement."

"Tomorrow?" I frowned. "You can't get her back sooner?"

Diego's lips flattened. I supposed this was what came of impending doom getting normalized in his family, but hell, even I was freaked out by what might be going down here.

"Look," I tried one more time. "Not meaning to scare you, but—screw that, I do want to scare you. We are dealing with some incredibly dangerous people. They've already committed kidnapping, murder, and bombings that could level this block, and *they targeted your ex-husband.* The smartest thing you could do for your kids until this is over is *hide.*"

Diego hesitated, and I thought I'd won him over for a second before he said softly, "We did, the first time Arthur told us to. And the next. And . . . that's no way for anyone to grow up, pulled out of your home, scared, never knowing how bad it really is."

"It's bad this time. I promise you."

"Thank you," Diego answered after a moment, and it was as polite a dismissal of my argument as anyone could have sculpted. "Thank you for being here. If I seem ungracious or unhappy, it is directed at the situation, not at you. I appreciate your time and aid."

"If that's the way you want it." I debated adding that he shouldn't blame me if the whole family was murdered in their sleep. I probably should have, but . . . even I didn't want to visualize that possibility.

Instead, I got up, leaving the bag with the laptops. "I'll have Rio give me the nickel tour and then we'll need to work. Keep the kids away if you want to spare them."

Diego grimaced. "They're teenagers, and their father is missing. They want to know what's going on."

"You won't want them to know everything that goes on." Not the way Rio and I worked. "Trust me."

We went to move past him, and Diego hesitated long enough before shifting that he managed to telegraph his unhappiness loud and clear. Christ knew what he wanted us to do about it.

The house had bits of Spanish architecture and bits of Southwest ranch and bits of "some prior owner wanted a bigger kitchen at some point and didn't think too much about it." The ground floor had the odd-shaped living/dining room, a kitchen in the back, and on the other side of the hall, a bathroom and a room set up as a bedroom.

In keeping with the mood of the house, the downstairs bedroom had originally been intended for something else; the doors were paned glass covered over in paper and a wardrobe stood in lieu of a built-in closet.

Upstairs simultaneously felt small and endless—a loft that had been expanded and then expanded again during several different architectural eras. Four bedrooms, none of which were rectangular and which varied wildly in size, some windows that were dormered and some that weren't, a funky-shaped landing at the top of the stairs, and a second bathroom that looked like it had originally been a master bath but had a door knocked in the other side now.

The downstairs bedroom had been arranged somewhat generically, and Rio had confirmed it was the guest room Diego had offered for our use. The upstairs bedrooms, on the other hand, were all shouting with personality. The disorganized mess of newspapers and notebooks and true crime novels had to be Tabitha's room; she had flashcards of California law spread out across an untidy desk, and one whole wall had been nailed over with corkboard and turned into what looked like analyzing real-life cold cases. A jury of well-loved stuffed animals oversaw the chaos from an unmade bed.

Arthur and Diego must have their hands full with her.

The largest room with two beds that was wallpapered with loud, clashing movie and music posters clearly belonged to the twins, and the smallest bedroom was a study in neatness that could rival Arthur, with alphabetically shelved books on science and Latin, a lineup of precisely spaced gadgety trinkets that included a gyroscope and a Rubik's cube, and glow-in-the-dark stars pasted to the ceiling in a scale map of the real night sky that was pretty damn exact.

This must be the boy who'd been with Tabitha downstairs. Juwon, Diego had said his name was.

The fourth bedroom was clearly Diego's, with the more restrained decorating taste of an adult and some weights and exercise equipment against one wall.

Rio noted lines of sight, distances, and possible escape venues as we went. His tone never gave away much, but when we finished the circuit and returned to the stairs, he said bluntly, "Cas, this place is not secure."

"I know," I said. Shit.

Should we pressure Diego harder? How? Haul his kids out by their hair? It wasn't like I knew the man, but he seemed barely inclined to cooperate as it was. Not to mention that we needed to be concentrating on *finding Arthur*, not wrangling recalcitrant families.

Maybe I could get Checker to talk to him. My eyes felt grainy—God, I needed some sleep, but that wasn't going to be happening for a while.

"Let's get the whole family under one roof and concentrate on the Teplova data pull," I said. I'd briefed Rio on how my night had gone in between studying the house. "If things develop, I'll force the issue with Diego."

Somehow.

As if it had heard my last statement, something in Rio's pocket beeped. He pulled out a device that looked something like a smartphone and said, "Someone approaches."

I glanced at the screen. Two gangly figures were ambling up what was unmistakably the house's front walk.

"Cameras and motion sensors?" I guessed.

"I've set up some rudimentary surveillance. It was next on my agenda to relay to you."

Sending Rio had been a good idea. I might have an edge or two over him in a direct fight, but he blasted me out of the water when it came to planning and forethought.

"The twins, I'm guessing?" I tried to recall the photos in the hallway and along the stairs.

Rio nodded—knowing him, he'd filed dossiers of all possible friendlies away in his head immediately upon arriving. With a glance around the landing, he made a compact carbine appear from somewhere underneath his duster and slid down the hall back toward Diego's bedroom at the front of the second floor. High ground in case any threat was following the kids.

I split off to go back downstairs. The twins were noisy, their keys scraping and jangling in the locks as they piled in with bags and backpacks.

"Hellooo!" one of them called from the door, making the *o* sound into a long hoot. "We hear our lives are in danger again! Such a dramatic existence for two lowly students of comedy. Oh! Hello."

The young man who was talking—a tall Black kid with dreads hanging in his eyes and a wide grin—had noticed me coming down the stairs and into view of the foyer.

"Wait, you're not one of the people trying to kill us, are you?" said the other one, a white boy with shaggy hair who was equally tall and lanky. "Because if so, you have to give us at least the dignity of wetting our pants and screaming for a few seconds."

"No, I'm here to—I'm a friend of your dad's. Arthur's," I said. The two boys might have height in common, but the numerical aspects of their physical genetic characteristics had no statistically significant overlap, so I thought it likely their twinship was a chosen one. "Matthias and Roy?"

"I'm Matthias, he's Roy," said the Black boy with the dreads.

"Or Matti, if you're friendly with him, and if you're not, it is my fraternal duty to challenge you in a duel to the death," Roy added.

"Which on your end would start and end with the aforementioned pants-wetting," Matti said.

"Truth."

"You two seem awfully cavalier," I said, before I could think better of it.

"Oh, even threats to our lives get mundane after a while," Matti said. "Plus, we're comedians. We're contractually obligated not to take anything seriously. It's in the oath."

"Don't ask us to say something funny, though," Roy added. "If you tell us to say something funny, we're contractually obligated to beat you around the head with a stick."

"Zing!"

They high-fived.

"No, I meant about your dad," I said.

Their smiles dropped to the floor and shattered.

"What about our dad?" Roy asked after a moment.

"Yeah," Matti said. "Did he call saying there's more danger? What's going on?"

Diego's voice came from behind me, in the direction of the kitchen. "Miss Russell. I'll take it from here."

I turned slightly. "You didn't tell them?"

"Papá?" Matti said uncertainly.

I ducked into the living room to start setting up the laptops. Roy and Matti crowded around Diego, asking if their dad was okay, asking questions he couldn't answer any better than I could.

But this wasn't, apparently, a house where I could escape human company. I'd barely gotten a workspace going and signed us into a secure chat session with Checker and Pilar when Tabitha came around from the kitchen and stood watching me, her eyes wide, like she wanted to say something but didn't want to interrupt. The brother who'd been with her before hovered behind her. I got a good look at him for the first time—skin a few shades darker than Tabitha's, a JPL T-shirt, and a deportment that was equal parts awkward, shy, nervous, and determined. They looked to be about the same age, or maybe Juwon was a little older, though Tabitha was taller.

I tried to ignore them and get started, but Tabitha ventured, "Ms. Russell?"

"You want me to find your dad, right?" I said. "Then go away and let me work."

"We will, in a second, but, um. We wanted to say. If we can help at all—"

"What did I tell you about 'helping'?" I said, not looking up.

"It doesn't have to be important help," piped up Juwon. "We can get you coffee, or breakfast, or run errands or—I know Tabitha makes people think otherwise, but we're actually very good at following directions. Very good."

Tabitha tossed her head. "When I *want* to be."

Her brother elbowed her.

I closed my eyes for a moment and scrubbed my hands through my hair. Food. I did need food.

"Coffee," I said. "Black and as strong as you can make it, for Rio and me both. And something high in protein." What Checker didn't know about me eating over his computers wouldn't hurt him. He might even give it a pass, considering the circumstances.

Tabitha and Juwon almost tripped over each other in their rush back into the kitchen, as if what I'd asked them for was a matter of life and death. The smell of coffee and the sizzle of breakfast frying followed a few minutes later, in between bangs and a loud argument over whether they should bother me again to find out how I wanted my eggs and whether there was a possibility I was vegetarian.

I let them get on with it and concentrated on the computer.

Checker reported that he'd finally gotten his hands on the police reports for both the bombing at my place and the smaller explosives at Arthur's office, and both, he relayed with some resignation, had sported D.J.'s signature. Apparently, even bombers who were as mercurial about their explosives materials as D.J. could be tracked through the way they crimped wires, strung components, or wrapped electrical tape—law enforcement could even match tool marks and soldering style. Taken together, it was almost as unique as a written signature.

D.J.'s involvement definitely wasn't theoretical anymore. But law enforcement had no more intelligence than we did on his whereabouts, so Teplova's more secret files were still far more promising for granting us some actual progress. Checker and Pilar had been steamrolling through the doctor's hidden research with the force of a crusade.

it's clear someone else's paws were all up in here, Checker scribbled in the chat window. *WG agrees, not ET's style at all, this is what we want. do ur thing*

The minute I started working my way down the directories, I could see exactly what he meant. In the easier parts of the system to access, Eva Teplova's style had been meticulous, bordering on strict. All her research had been dated and categorized, all her file names prefixed and suffixed according to topic and chronology, with nary a text document out of place.

The more hidden records were . . . not that. The structure was the ghost of the same system, but then it was as if someone had trampled through with a keyboard throwing a coked-out party all over her organizational tidiness.

These changes, I wrote to Checker. *All in the past six months?*

yupppppppppp, he responded.

So this was not only what D.J. and any of his cohorts had been after, but they'd worked within Eva Teplova's own computer system while they'd kept her under their thumb. Forcing her to surgically modify animals and people and then eventually murdering her.

Maybe she'd figured out how to fight back. Maybe she'd finally been about to get the upper hand, but they'd gotten to her first.

In any case, Checker was right. Our enemies had left muddy digital tracks through all of this. It was the best lead we had.

Anger against Willow Grace surged in me again. She could have put us on this path hours ago.

I shoved down the emotions and concentrated on what I knew Checker wanted from me. My math abilities made me capable of becoming a human cross-referencing machine, mentally rewriting regex on the fly as I processed the data for every new criterion. I worked sequentially, feeding in each directory and trusting my instant pattern-matching skills to do their work on the inputs. Appropriate regular expressions popped out at me from the chaos and practically yelled their usefulness. I slotted them right in and kept going.

Checker hadn't had instructions for Rio, other than, "Tell him what everyone else is doing and sic him on the data in whatever way he thinks he can be most helpful." Rio had come down to join me in the interim, and I relayed the message and pointed a laptop in his direction. I had a sneaking suspicion he wasn't looking at the Teplova data pull at all, but digging into the Halberd angle, no matter how long ago Simon had said that connection might be.

I didn't ask.

"Thanks for this," I said a little awkwardly. "Looking for one guy, I know it's not your usual beat."

"Arthur Tresting is a good man," Rio said, pronouncing the word *good* in a way that sounded abstractly philosophical. "We walk in the light of God in seeking him."

In other words, as long as this case went in the direction Rio's principles generally pointed, it made no difference to him to go along with me instead of working a different case. Six of one, half a dozen of the other.

"However, I admit to grave concern that this incident has some connection to Halberd and Pithica," Rio went on, confirming my dread. "If this doctor involved you at their behest . . . one man's life may turn out to be the smallest of our concerns."

"Yours, maybe," I said. "Not mine. And the doctor didn't involve us. She was dead when we got there."

Rio paused for a moment, then said, "There is no such thing as coincidence. Not when it comes to Pithica's operations."

"Simon said this isn't them. They made a deal with us, remember? Besides, Arthur was looking into D.J., not them." I almost repeated what I'd claimed to Checker about selection bias justifying the coincidence, but something in me didn't want to hear what Rio thought of that claim.

As it was, his hands paused on the keyboard, and he turned slightly to face me. "I have already discovered evidence that Teplova's current name is nothing more than a backstopped identity. I am attempting to discern when she first appeared in this role."

The information wasn't unexpected. But it still made me go cold.

I didn't *want* to know who Teplova was. Of course, I couldn't very well object under these circumstances. Just because I didn't think that angle was our most promising approach didn't mean it would yield nothing.

"It is possible Pithica is attempting to make a play that is far enough unconnected to them to maintain plausible deniability," Rio continued. "I have been investigating that possibility, and will continue to. But, Cas, regardless—tread lightly. We don't know yet what this doctor may have left behind, and we have already encountered three creations of hers that may be beyond what you are ordinarily prepared to fight."

"Three?" I could only think of the panic-inducers. The dogs and their master.

"The Australian you left with Simon," Rio reminded me. "The one who is so forgettable. That may not seem like a threat, but I am in agreement with you that someone made him that way."

"The Australian," I repeated, trying to drill his existence into my head. He also had to be the work of Teplova—beauty, trustworthiness, fear, and forgettability. She must have altered his face too, but why? "That's two, then. And number three?"

"This reporter you are working with, and any others like her."

I waved that one off. "She's beautiful. That doesn't seem like much of a threat either."

"Perhaps not. I wonder."

"I still seem to be able to get pissed at her just fine." Her beauty was affecting, but not mind-altering.

Or was it all part of the same spectrum? I rubbed my eyes. But no, I'd read enough of Teplova's research to feel sure Willow Grace's aesthetics were on a completely different axis, the optima chosen and pinpointed in a way that wasn't at all correlative with what the doctor had been doing in the hidden, more dangerous records. Although . . . Teplova's genius was different enough from mine—*applied* enough— that as easily as I could follow it, I didn't nearly have a handle on the leaps she'd made. How she structured her matrices, the reasoning behind the estimates that smoothed her functions, why she pinned the changes to which critical points the way she had . . .

I blinked on the man's face from the wellness center—clean-cut, military haircut, even reasonably handsome. And he had induced screaming panic in me.

Attractiveness had to be orthogonal to the rest of it.

Still, I suddenly wanted to introduce Rio to Willow Grace. But even when we knew we were talking to a full-strength telepath, he couldn't always tell when their influence was in play, could he? He was immune himself, but unless I started acting wildly out of character, would he be able to give me anything more than innuendo and suspicion? And a niggling thought joined the first—how much did I still always agree with his assessments of a situation?

In the past, I'd trusted Rio's judgment one hundred percent. I still trusted him, but I was also no longer sure that disagreeing with him would be a sign I was compromised. The time he'd pulled a gun on Pilar . . .

I didn't like to think about it.

Evidence. I had to follow the evidence. And that pointed toward Willow Grace being exactly who she said she was—a complicated, driven, and overly selfish person who was a mostly ethical newscaster and had been friends with Eva Teplova. Her motivations didn't all match ours, but her enemies were our enemies, and right now, I wasn't in a position to be choosy.

Besides, building a nearly decade-long reputation as a recognizable journalist would have been a hell of a long con. I wasn't planning to trust her with my darkest secrets, but neither was I going to waste time dissecting her. After this, she could go do whatever the hell she wanted—and if Rio decided to keep being suspicious, well, he could do it on his own time.

Tabitha and Juwon came back after half an hour, juggling a pot of hot coffee and platters with way too much food. They'd apparently solved their egg dilemma by making three different kinds, along with bacon and sausage and toast. Rio and I ate over the guns and computers while Tabitha and Juwon hovered in the entrance to the kitchen as if just waiting to be ordered to do something else.

Rio surprised me, then, by looking up at the kids. "You wish to be a resource?"

They surged forward, expressions simultaneously hopeful and terrified.

I'd brought four laptops in case we needed to run anything in parallel; Rio reached for a third one and placed it in front of them. "You can contribute to this process by finding particular publicly available information and organizing it in a way that is accessible and clear."

They nodded like their heads were about to come off. From that point on, Rio began firing off absurdly specific requests every ten minutes or so—"the Saturday train schedule between Chatsworth and LAX for May of 2009"; "a list of stores that offer delivery of grocery items to zip code 90411"; "whether the company Ocean Star

Taxi has ever released a public statement about insufficient safety standards in their vehicles."

If Rio were someone else, I might have thought he was trying to be nice by involving them, but this was *Rio*. He was simply, as he'd said, using them as an administrative resource to speed his own research.

Tabitha and Juwon quickly appropriated the fourth computer as well and applied themselves to the work with single-minded focus, only occasionally whispering consultations to each other as they completed Rio's tasks. They must have been doing a good job, because he didn't tell them to redo anything.

Diego came to the door of the kitchen and watched us for a few minutes, his arms folded, before vanishing again without a word. Tabitha and Juwon were concentrating so hard, I didn't even think they noticed. Over the next few hours, the murmur of voices reached us every so often from the kitchen, and Matti came in twice to bring us fresh pots of coffee, but he didn't say anything. The wide grin was gone, and his expression had gone drawn and flattened, dreads hanging over his eyes.

Rio's surveillance system beeped in the early afternoon.

He and I were both instantly on alert. "The last kid isn't due home till tomorrow, is she?"

"No," said Rio, at the same time Tabitha and Juwon both looked up and simultaneously made nervous noises in the negative. Rio had already reached into his pocket to pull out the security screen. I took it from him, squinting.

A man built like a bulldog was hiking up the path to the door. He was in plain clothes, but the way he moved screamed *cop*.

What the ever-living fuck.

fourteen

"POLICE. Hide the guns," I said to Rio, reaching across to slap all the laptops shut. The firearms on the table had disappeared along with Rio before I'd finished speaking. I knew without asking that he'd gone to take up an invisible defensive position.

Just in case.

Diego materialized by my elbow. "What's happening?"

"Cops. Did you call it in?"

"No. Not yet. It must have been someone else."

I hadn't expected him to, not with the warning he'd given me the night before about Arthur's former colleagues. Speaking of . . . I held up the screen.

"This guy anyone you know?"

"Yes." He didn't elaborate.

"Who?"

"His name is Sikorsky. He worked with Arthur." Diego glanced toward Tabitha and Juwon, who were still sitting wide-eyed, and Matti and Roy, who had appeared in the kitchen doorway behind them. "Kids, upstairs, now."

His voice was quiet, but it was the type of intense, urgent tone a person would obey and then wonder why later. The children scampered.

"What aren't you telling me?" I demanded as they went, keeping my voice low. "What's the deal with this guy? Excessive force? Old grudge against Arthur? Talk fast."

Someone pounded on the door so hard, the wall shook.

"I believe—I think he is a criminal," Diego said equally low. "And that Arthur knew."

Great. A dirty cop who knew Arthur had been sitting on evidence against him would have every incentive *not* to see Arthur found after such a convenient disappearance.

The thumping knock came again, rattling the picture frames on the front wall. "Open up, Rosales. LAPD."

Disappearing into the shadows along with Rio probably would've been the smartest play for me, but a strong sense of foreboding made me decide Diego could use a visible witness. It wasn't like even clean cops had a stellar record when it came to leaving them alone with brown men.

I followed Diego into the foyer. He glanced behind him up the stairs to make sure all the kids were clear before settling his hand on the lock, taking a breath, and then pulling the door open.

Sikorsky pushed inside, crowding Diego back toward the stairway. "About time, Rosales. I was this close to kicking it in, and that would be a costly fix for you, what with twenty little fosterlings or whatever you have these days." He looked around the foyer. "Where are they? Unless after Tresting's thuggery, you kicked them all out of the house."

A few muscles jumped under Diego's skin, but he didn't rise to a response.

Sikorsky shoved past us into the living room, uninvited, picking up books and knickknacks and examining them with an expression of revulsion. "Guess not. More fool you. Who the hell are you?"

He hadn't looked around, but I was pretty sure the question was directed at me. "A friend," I said. I pulled out the Cassie Wells ID. "I'm helping out."

Sikorsky swiped the fake PI license from me, read it, looked me up and down like I was a rotting piece of meat, and then tore the license in half and let the pieces flutter to the floor. "You interfere with the real cops, I'll do a lot worse than this."

The threat was so theatrical, it was hard to take him seriously. "Okay."

"What do you want?" demanded Diego in a tight voice.

Sikorsky spun back to face us, every movement that of a man who liked to literally throw his weight around. "I wasn't kidding about the tykes. I know they're here. Get them down here or I'll start dragging them to the station."

"On what grounds?" Diego said.

"On the grounds I said so, that's what," Sikorsky answered. "They're growing up, ain't they? No more getting off with wiped juvie records. Something'll stick."

Diego moved subtly so he was between Sikorsky and the path to the stairs.

"What do you want with the kids?" I said.

Sikorsky narrowed his eyes at me. Then he tossed the decorative mug he'd just picked up into the corner so it broke in two pieces and said to Diego, "Where was your youngest at approximately 3:00 p.m. yesterday?"

My skin went cold. Tabitha had visited my erstwhile office at just about that time.

"I've got witness reports," Sikorsky said, "before you lie to me."

"I think I should call a lawyer," Diego said.

"You do that, this is a thing." The words were a clear threat. "Don't make it a thing, Rosales."

Diego folded his lips together.

"Kids," shouted Sikorsky, his voice a bullhorn. "Get out here or I'm arresting your father."

Something thumped upstairs. Sikorsky grinned, his lips peeling back from coffee-stained teeth. More thumps, and Tabitha squeezed into the room behind her dad, followed by her siblings. They stood silently.

"Don't answer any questions without a lawyer," Diego said, without taking his eyes off Sikorsky. "You hear me, children? None."

"Hurtful, Rosales. I only want to talk to them." Sikorsky shoved his hands in his pockets. "Here's the deal, kids. I know one of you was at 725 Carmichael Street and then at Tresting's cute little PI office yesterday. Crime scenes, both of 'em, which you didn't report."

Nobody moved a muscle.

"You know who the first people a cop suspects is? Family. Especially family who doesn't report the crime. One of you cap your old man?"

Tabitha made a high sound and then clapped a hand against her mouth.

"You know they didn't," Diego said sharply. "What do you want?"

"Why would I know that?" Sikorsky said, the words threaded with a taunt. "A leopard don't change its stripes. But if they did have anything to do with this, I'll find out. And in the meantime, stay the fuck out of my investigation."

He spat the words.

"Leave the crimes to the cops. This is a pea-brained enough concept for everyone else in this fucking world to get, but no, the way you teach your kids is to run around hiring PIs, making trouble. So here's how this works. I smell any one of you near this case—and that includes *you* and *you*"—he pointed a blunt finger at Tabitha and then at me—"and I drop the hammer on every fucking one of you. And we all know some of you can't afford another nasty little mark."

He settled back, weight on his heels, and let his words sink in, taking the time to pull a pack of cigarettes from his shirt pocket.

"Please don't smoke in here," Diego said.

Sikorsky didn't pause, lighting up and puffing out a few breaths at the ceiling. Then he walked over to Diego and stood very close, so his cigarette ash dusted the other man's socks. "It's hard being a single parent," he said. "You can't keep track of them all the time, can you? Especially with so many of the darling little monkeys."

Diego didn't react.

"Your youngest two are still under eighteen, aren't they? It would be a shame if Child Protective Services felt the need to step in."

There was a muffled squeal and shuffle as Tabitha tried to say something and the twins held her back.

"Keep a leash on 'em," Sikorsky ordered flatly. He lumbered past them, back to the door, and then turned to stab his cigarette at the whole family. "I'll be watching. Any of you puts a toe out of line, you'll regret it."

Then he slammed the door behind him so hard that the frame rattled and one of the pictures fell off the wall.

"You—you *twitterpated imbecile!*" Tabitha shouted after him. I didn't think she knew what all of those words meant.

Juwon was crying silently, his face half-turned away as though embarrassed.

"I'm not going to let that man harm any of you," Diego said, with icy calm. He twitched his head at the twins, toward Tabitha, and went to put an arm around Juwon. "Come with me, son." The two of them left the room.

Matti knelt on the couch so he was more on eye level with Tabitha. "Hey, sis. Ain't no way that, uh, that twitterpated birdbrain will hurt this family, okay?"

"Yeah," Roy said. "I don't care if he's a cop. It's all hot air. Matti and I are 'mancipated anyway, so what's he gonna do, say you have to live with us instead of Papá? Big deal. We'd let you have ice cream every night and no curfew."

"Cops can *do* things," Tabitha said. "You know they can. And he's trying to keep Dad missing, and he's going to arrest us if we try to look, and I hate feeling so *helpless!*" She punched the arm of the couch.

The twins were probably trying to comfort her, but she was more right than they were.

"I'm not going to let Arthur stay missing," I said. I meant the words to be factual, but they came out like I wanted to crush them into gravel.

They all looked over at me.

"Sikorsky can come after me all he wants. I don't care. I'll come after him right back." The last thing I needed here was another fucking complication. If Sikorsky and his sadistic melodrama got in my way, well, I had a couple of choice solutions for that.

Rio reappeared in the room. "He is gone."

The tension in the house softened, but only slightly. Anxiety still blanketed the kids. Matti was rubbing Tabitha's back in slow circles while she avoided his eyes.

"Police can be shitty," I said to them, trying to make it a comforting declaration. "But, look. Sikorsky doesn't suspect any of you, not for real. Tabitha's right—if he really intended to throw down against your family, he could've done a lot worse. The good news is, he didn't. He's either got other suspects or he's not looking to solve the case, and I'd bet on the latter. Stay out of his way, leave it to us, and we'll bring your dad home safe."

Tabitha gave me a forced nod, her head down and her hands still closed into fists.

My mobile buzzed.

I didn't recognize the number. I took a steadying breath and picked up, trying to backtrack who knew this phone. It was the one out of Pilar's car, so unless she'd given someone the number in advance, that limited it only to—

"Ms. Wells, it's Willow," said Willow Grace's voice. "The police have taken your friends into custody."

fifteen

"WE'RE OKAY, we're okay," Pilar kept assuring me over the phone, so many times it didn't seem likely at all. "They're just investigating, right? They asked me some questions and checked my alibis, but they didn't try to railroad me or anything . . ."

"Don't be so naïve," I snapped. She had far too much faith in the system. "What about Checker?"

"He—um—he's being held. I mean, he kind of lost his temper when they said they were taking us in, because the delay and all, and—well, I think they might have suspected him already. But they're not going to have any evidence, right?"

"They *what*? How the hell is he a suspect?"

"His history with the bomb guy is on the record. He almost went to prison for something D.J. did, Cas. As an accessory. It was like almost a decade ago. I—I didn't know."

None of us had known. None of us had known because Checker hadn't said a damn word about it. Neither had Diego, and he sure as hell knew.

Now the authorities had at least two more explosive crime scenes that were both linked to Checker's business partner's disappearance. Both of them, as we ourselves had discovered, with D.J.'s signature.

Of *course* they suspected Checker. How could they not? How had Checker not realized they would? How had he not *told us*?

Someone touched my arm. Diego. He had a cell phone to his ear, and he reached out his hand for mine. I was surprised enough that I handed it to him without demanding to know why.

"Mija, what station are you at?" he asked Pilar. After listening for a moment, he said, "No, no, no. That won't happen. I'm calling Elisa. She'll send someone in her firm till she can get here. Oh—Lisie?" he said into the other phone as someone picked up. "I'll call if she needs more information," he added to Pilar, and handed the phone back to me before moving away to continue the conversation with his eldest daughter. Elisa was the lawyer, I thought I remembered.

"Cas?" Pilar said. "Are you still there?"

"Yeah." I felt numb.

"Checker didn't want us to call at all, because he didn't want anything distracting you from Arthur. Diego's right, though, that won't happen because we'll handle this legally. You and Willow Grace need to keep on with the search, and—and I do too. They haven't filed any official charges yet—they're just questioning him—Elisa will be able to protect him; I know she will. And at least he's not in danger here." She said it like she was trying to convince herself.

She didn't know Arthur had old police enemies still nursing grudges. I'd gathered from Sikorsky that most of the kids had trouble in their pasts—if Arthur had helped get Checker off the hook a decade ago, the fact that Checker had never legally become part of the family wasn't going to stop a resentful cop from throwing the book at him.

And short of breaking Checker out of prison, I couldn't think of one single thing I could do about it. Fuck.

Except—I could rescue Arthur. If we got Arthur back, safe and whole, that would go a long way toward getting Checker out of the crosshairs of the law.

Christ, it would be so much easier if I could just break into the police station and bust him out. But unlike me, Checker had a life. I wasn't sure he'd regard being rescued only to go off the grid as significantly better than prison.

I had a life, shivered the dead woman in my head.

"Cas," Rio said by my ear.

I shook myself. I couldn't tell if he'd noticed the lapse. The last thing I needed was Rio dragging me back to Simon for brain help.

"We need to focus," I said.

"What do you want us to do?" asked Pilar from the phone, reminding me I was still on the line with her.

I tried to gather my thoughts.

"You and Willow Grace come here," I said after a moment. I was guessing Checker's machines were automatically locked now, and the cops might very well be coming to execute a search warrant on the place. Without the additional computing power—or our computing expert—it didn't make sense for us to split locations.

I tried not to feel like we were deserting Checker.

I hung up the phone and turned to Rio to ask for a status report on his search, but someone tugged at my sleeve.

Fucking *Tabitha*.

"Is Checker okay?" she asked. She sounded like she was about to cry.

"Go ask—I don't know. Your dad or your sister," I said shortly, waving a hand after Diego.

Or your sister, chittered the voices in my head. Usually being a day late on my sessions with Simon wouldn't have shoved me to teeter so far on the edge. But with old memories chipping at my psyche . . .

I just needed to hold on. Long enough to get Arthur back. Then my brain could go to hell.

Tabitha still hadn't moved, staring at me with glassily anxious eyes.

"Beat it!" I yelled.

She scrambled away and vanished.

"Hey," someone said.

I turned. It was Matti, the Black twin with the dreads. "Don't talk to our sister that way," he said, poised on his toes like he wanted to fight me.

"This is all shitty," Roy said beside him. "It's shitty for all of us. But we don't stand for that sort of thing, you hear? Not ever."

I almost wanted to laugh in their faces. They were—what, *standing up* to me? What the hell kind of a thing was that?

They continued to stare at me, balanced in defiance like they expected me to take a swing at them.

Fight—I saw the man from the wellness center, with the mask of his old face, standing like a referee between me and a blurred opponent. An anticipatory grin slashed that face, and he brought his hand down between us with a shout. I felt myself surge forward—

"Cas," Rio said, blinking me back to a single reality.

"Get out," I ordered the twins. They glanced at each other, and Matti visibly swallowed, rocking back from me a few inches. "*Now*," I said.

They left.

Finally alone with Rio, I slumped into one of the dining chairs and let my head hang down.

You're never alone, sang Valarmathi, from the depths of my brain where she'd been banished. *Or you're always alone. Whichever is the greater hell.*

"Cas." Rio had pulled up a chair next to me. "Cas. Keep yourself here."

I took a deep breath. "They. Are fucking. *Overwhelming.*"

"I can keep them away, if it aids you," Rio said.

Nobody can keep them away, added the dead woman. *They'll find you wherever you go.*

This was fucked up. I could face down armies, and couldn't handle four kids and their dad without starting to crumble? I even liked children, usually. But this was . . . a lot of them. And right when I needed to have zero distractions, with Arthur still missing and kidnapped, and now Checker locked in an interrogation room and all the enemies in the shadows we still couldn't track down—

I squeezed my malfunctioning brain in a death grip and pushed myself up to standing.

"Thanks," I said to Rio. "Now, tell me where you're at. We need to get Arthur back right fucking yesterday."

Then if Valarmathi wanted to take me down with her, she could have me.

·.·˙·.·˙·.·˙·

PILAR, WILLOW Grace, Rio, and I had redoubled our efforts viciously against the four laptops on the dining table. I'd kept an eye on Rio when he met Willow, but he hadn't seemed perturbed—not that he ever did. But he hadn't said anything to me about her, which I took to mean that he agreed she was an unlikely threat.

I tried to put that all out of my head and concentrate.

Willow Grace did seem to be fully on board now. She'd made notes and lists for the rest of us regarding everyone she could think of who might have had any argument with Teplova. The list was long, and Pilar had taken over cross-referencing it against the doctor's more hidden research files. Meanwhile, I'd stopped trying to direct my search and skimmed instead, trying to let my brain relax and find those patterns it was so good at. My fingers fiddled with some of the clutter the family had left on the table as I worked—pens, notepads, a 3-D puzzle that it took me three distracted seconds to fit together—and I did my best to run the data through my head plain, with no bias, inputs seeking a natural organization.

This time, miraculously, only a few minutes after the other women had arrived and we'd all sat down, an anomaly blazed out of the data with the brightness of a wildfire.

I stiffened in my chair, zeroing in on where the pattern matching had flared with its screaming mismatch. The directory I'd just opened . . . I went back up in the file tree. Went back down.

"What is it, Cas?" Rio said.

"Something changed." My memory, sadly, was far from eidetic, but my brain had fit the directory structure into a numerical tree, and now . . . it was a different tree.

But I couldn't see how.

"Rio," I said. "Go into the directory labeled seventeen-dash-R-seven-three-N. Tell me what you see."

A second's pause as he did what I asked. "You are correct, Cas. One more file is here than previously."

"You can tell that?" Willow Grace said. She looked disturbed by our abilities. I didn't bother telling her that Rio's, at least, was human, either genetic or trained.

"Can you tell which one wasn't there before?" I said.

"I had not been through this part of the data yet, so I am unsure."

"Maybe your friend unlocked more hidden files," Willow Grace said.

"She could be right," Pilar put in. Her fingers were moving on the keyboard almost as fast as Checker's did. "Everything in this directory's marked as not being touched since months ago. Maybe one was invisible and Checker did something—he's done that a few times already. He might not even have realized."

With no way to ask him.

"Everyone on this folder," I said.

Rio found the file we sought almost immediately. "Cas, I believe this document to be real estate holdings."

I switched to the one he was looking at. He must have recognized the format in some way, because the whole thing was in code—code that shifted and broke apart before my eyes, transforming itself. I pulled up a text editor and started typing a translation as fast as I could read it.

"There," Pilar said, pointing over my shoulder. The name listed on the holding by her finger was "Dick Jizzy."

D.J. did have an obscene sense of humor, I remembered.

"I'll map the address," Pilar said, diving back to her own screen.

So it was D.J. who'd been trampling through Teplova's files. Confirmation that he was one of the people running this operation, not just a mercenary goon. The picture was starting to coalesce—somehow he had found out about Teplova's thorniest thought experiments, and he'd violently stolen their magic for himself. Along with, eventually, the doctor's life.

Until Arthur got in his way.

But a tightness in my chest eased, one I hadn't even noticed building, and new energy pushed back my fatigue—because finally, we had an actual location I could storm with a gun. A solid lead.

Or a trap. But traps could be leads too.

"This is weird," Pilar broke into my thoughts. "The address, it's coming up as a mission."

"A mission to do what?" I said.

"No, a mission, as in, the historical landmark building type. There are a whole bunch of missions around SoCal—most of them are tourist attractions. They're from when people came out here to, um, be missionaries and stuff? I think we went to one on some school trip when I was a kid."

"You're saying D.J. owns a historical landmark?" Or Teplova, or some shell corporation, depending on how D.J. had mixed things up.

"The Internet says this particular one is closed to the public," Pilar continued rapidly as she keyed up more information. "For renovations, or something, though it's not clear whether they're actually renovating it to reopen it or whether it's closed permanently. But the Internet also seems to think all the California missions are owned by either the state or the Catholic Church, so I don't know how . . ."

"Unless this isn't a site D.J. owns, only one he uses," I said. "Either with or without permission—it's not like there isn't rampant corruption in either the government *or* the Catholic Chur—"

I cut myself off with a sidelong glance at Rio.

"A sin becomes all the graver when committed by those in the ministry," he said.

"Right." I stood. "Well, we're not taking on the Church *or* the government even if it turns out one of them's involved. I'll go in, check it out, pull Arthur if he's there or find whatever clues I can if he isn't. That's it." I pointed at Rio. "Much as I'd love to have backup, you'd better stay here."

Just in case D.J. came while I was gone.

"Unless you think I'd be a liability, I'll come," Pilar said. She'd stood as well.

I squinted at her. I could use an extra gun, but . . . "I don't know how this is going to play out," I said. "D.J. might collapse the place on top of us. This could be a suicide mission."

"There's something I didn't tell you." She swallowed, and her eyes darted around to Rio before returning to me. She straightened as if bracing herself. "I told you before how I signed up for tactical training. I didn't tell you I still went. I knew I was going to quit, so I paid for it myself, but I went. And I've kept training."

"So?" I'd already seen that Pilar could acquit herself well in the field; I didn't care how she had gotten there.

"So, I kept telling myself it was just in case. Just in case something happened. Well, this is . . . this is the thing happening. This is the just in case. If I can help, I can't stay home."

I studied her for a moment. She met my gaze levelly.

"Okay," I said. "Do whatever you need to do to gear up. We head out in five."

I went to grab some ammo and food myself, but Rio followed me from the room. "Cas. Wait."

"What is it?"

Rio drew closer, glancing around to make sure we were alone for the moment. "This is too easy."

My jaw clenched. I'd had the same thought, but hadn't wanted to examine it too closely. Or to have it confirmed.

"If you're suggesting it's a trap . . ." My eyes itched with fatigue; I blinked hard. "For that sort of thing to work, D.J. would have to have known we would be looking, that we'd get the data before he blew the clinic, that we'd get the passwords from someone like Willow Grace, that we'd manage to unlock the hidden file or whatever, that I'd be able to read it, and that one of us would know D.J. well enough to recognize his prints on the name. That's . . . convoluted."

"You trust no one could have gotten into your friend's systems since we obtained the data?"

"And planted the file? Through Checker's security?" I snorted. "I suppose it's possible, but it's not the side I'd bet on."

"And you trust your friends?"

"Who?" I was genuinely confused for an instant. "Wait, you mean Checker or Pilar? They didn't plant anything."

"In my experience, people can be . . . surprising," Rio said. "There is also the reporter."

"What about her? You suspect something?"

"Nothing specific, but she is an unknown."

My head was starting to hurt. I leaned up against the wall. "You tell me how it makes any sense with the rest of what we know about her, and I'll bite. Do you have any evidence, or is this playing paranoia dartboard?"

Rio angled one shoulder up in a minute shrug. "As I said, people can be surprising. We are not privy to their thoughts, or what leverage may be held against them."

"Okay. Then let's not assume any givens." I tried to be logical instead of irritated. Just because I wasn't inclined to listen to Rio without question anymore didn't mean he was all the way wrong. "If we say it's a trap—is it for us, or to get us out of the way?"

"I will protect the family, Cas."

"I know you will, but . . ." But Elisa and Checker weren't *here.*

What were my choices, though? I sure as hell wasn't going to ignore the only lead we'd had. I desperately wished we had Checker back—he could have dug into any electronic fingerprints on the file better than Pilar or Rio. He would have been able to tell us if its sudden appearance had an innocent explanation, or if Pilar and I were about to walk right into D.J.'s hands.

"You should contact Simon," Rio suggested. "With the connection to the doctor, you may encounter more of her creations."

He didn't just mean the dogs either.

"I was thinking we'd put Simon in our ears going in." I wasn't sure it would be enough in the moment. But what would?

"A wise move," Rio agreed.

Pilar came out of the bathroom. "I'm ready whenever you are."

"Lend me a rifle," I said to Rio. "The Vector, if you can spare it. And anything you've got for explosives detection. Then let's hoof it."

If this was a trap, maybe we could spring it hard enough to get taken to wherever Arthur was anyway.

sixteen

JUST WHAT I need, I thought, as I wedged the earpiece in before driving us off into the darkening evening in Pilar's car. *Another voice in my head.*

Valarmathi snickered.

In the passenger seat beside me, Pilar was checking all her spare magazines were topped off. She'd had those in her trunk as well, apparently.

"Hey," I said to her. "We should ask Mr. Mind Reader if he knows why you were able to pull us away from things when we were attacked at the wellness center. We need every edge possible."

"I asked him already," Pilar said. "He called last night to make sure I was feeling okay, you know, after. From what I could tell him, his best guess was . . ." She took a breath. "I'd never killed anything before. Not like that. He thinks I got a wash of, of something for a minute that fought the panic. A different emotion that was strong enough to disrupt it. I don't think it's something we could replicate."

"Huh. Too bad." Simon was always telling me mind manipulation wasn't an exact science. Push here, pull there, corral a thousand variables to aim for a certain reaction and only land in the neighborhood.

People like Simon and Dawna could land in that neighborhood enough times in a row to hone down a thought to within a few neurons—metaphorically—but Teplova's hard-coding surgeries didn't seem nearly so precise. It might be worth trying to brainstorm how to disrupt their magic in some other way, if this lasted beyond tonight.

For tonight, we were stuck with Simon. I dialed and conferenced in Pilar. The phone rang a good four times before he picked up.

"What the hell took so long?" I said.

"What?" Simon sounded distracted. "Oh—I'm just . . ."

I waited for him to finish the thought, but he didn't.

"Hey," I said sharply.

"Sorry! What is it?"

"Hang on, Cas," Pilar said. "Is he okay? Simon, are you okay?"

"Yeah. Yes. I'm a bit—uh. Knackered, to tell you the truth."

He seemed a lot further gone than that. Shit.

"Well, get un-knackered," I said. "We need you. Pilar and I are both staying on this call. We're chasing down a lead on Arthur. If we run into any of Teplova's creations, we need you to talk us down. Got it?"

"In the moment?" Simon said.

"Yes, in the moment," I said. "Why, is that a problem for you?" Pilar winced at my tone.

"The continuous pushing against this . . . it's difficult. I'm becoming more impressed with this, Cas. It may be crude, but it's . . . wearing." I was about to ask him what the hell he was talking about when his tone changed. "Oh. Oh. You forgot again."

"Forgot what?" I said.

"Oscar. The man who tried to blow up your office."

"That was D.J.," I said. I turned down a winding back road that would shortcut some of the worst city congestion.

"Maybe D.J. is the mastermind, but the person who set you up is named Oscar. He arranged an appointment with you and then tried to keep you there. You knocked him down and then locked him up and asked me to come see if I could discover anything of substance from him."

Despite the exhaustion threading his words, Simon's speech was annoyingly patient.

And I did remember now.

Shit.

"The Australian," I said, to prove it. His voice was easier to latch on to than his face. What Rio and I had discussed came back to me: the ways the doctor had left her legacy on so many varied people's bodies. Or the ways she'd been forced to.

How did Oscar fit into the puzzle? Why had he been made—as some sort of covert operations test, an invisible man?

"He's Teplova's too." I filled Simon and Pilar in, now that I could remember him. "He has to be. Plastic surgery. He must have had his face changed to make him forgettable, or, I don't know, unimportant-looking."

"Holy smokes," Pilar murmured.

"Can you see it?" I asked Simon. "Can you tell what she did?"

"Plastic surgery . . . yes, it's possible. In fact, that would make a lot of sense. I'm used to people blasting their emotions at me all the time, but his face . . . it doesn't. I don't think it's that I couldn't read him if I tried, but it's more obscured. A bit, anyway."

"Maybe I should get plastic surgery," I said. "Defense against psychics."

"I don't think it would help, not if I really . . . you know. Wanted to."

"Well, have you gotten anything more out of him?" I said. "I mean non-psychically; don't get your knickers in a bunch. Has he told you anything else?"

"He has a single-minded loyalty, but I'm not sure if he remembers why anymore. Still, he's repeated it to himself so many times that it's hard for him to see past it." He cleared his throat. "I've offered to help him. If he'd let me, I think he could become more lucid."

The telepathic brand of psychiatric care. Even though I was benefitting from it, I wasn't sure I'd recommend it. At least not from Simon.

"Does he understand what you're offering?" Pilar asked quietly.

"I don't—I'm not sure," he answered.

"More importantly, if he let you in, would you then be able to find out what he knows about D.J.?" I put in.

The phone went silent. I'd gotten stuck in a jam behind a traffic light and inched the car forward impatiently, waiting. Simon finally said, "I think that would have to be his decision, Cas."

I didn't know if he meant, he wouldn't know unless Oscar shared, or he wouldn't tell me unless Oscar okayed it. But I was too tired to argue with him about a hypothetical.

"I need to remember this guy exists," I said instead. I jerked a thumb at Pilar. "You've never seen him. Do you have trouble?"

"No—at least, I don't think so. But so much has been happening that I might have—I mean, I haven't been thinking about him being there, so maybe I forgot? Wait, I'm not sure now."

"Your new job is to find out," I said. "Keep reminding me of him. Simon will double-check that you're doing it, and we'll give Rio a heads up too. I'm guessing he's immune." I supposed I could've had Simon call to keep checking in with me, but that would mean I'd have to talk to him more. And considering the way he sounded, maybe it wasn't the best idea to make him keep dividing his focus.

"I promise I *will* call if he tells me anything you can use," Simon said. "And I'll make sure I keep remembering him. I will."

"And how about now?" I said. "Are you going to be up for backing us?"

"Yes. I—yes. Yes."

The number of affirmatives was not inspiring me with confidence.

"Can you leave yourself a note and take a break?" Pilar asked.

"That might work," said Simon. "I could try something, ah, like that."

Some shuffling and muffled speech sounded from the other end of the phone, and then Simon's voice came back. "I'm going to hang up and record a video memo to myself, and a note to watch it. Then I'm going to lock myself in the bathroom. How far out are you?"

I'd mentally mapped the fastest way through the clogged streets, but we were fighting rush hour. "Fifty minutes, give or take seven."

"Good. I'll, uh, I'll take a little time to rest, then. Will you call me just before?"

I said I would, and we hung up.

My eyes were on the road, but I caught Pilar's quick glance at me and then at the floor. "*What?*" I snapped.

"I just—I know he's a telepath and all, and it's hard to trust him, but he is just trying to help," she said. "And he's been good about keeping his word not to read us, right? And to help you?"

"Yeah, well, considering how many of my problems were his fault in the first place, I'm not going to give him much credit," I growled. "I don't buy into his whole 'I erased your entire personality to save your life' justification, and if you've jumped on that bandwagon, well then, fuck you too."

Pilar was silent for a moment. Then she said, very quietly, "That was him?"

I hadn't realized she didn't know. I'd sort of assumed everyone in my life knew. Checker and Arthur had been there, and if nothing else, I would've assumed they'd told her.

But they hadn't. Apparently.

"I knew you'd lost your memory," Pilar said. "And that Simon was—helping you—but he was the one who . . . ?"

"Yeah," I said. I hadn't meant to revisit this. "He does say he did it because I was dying. Or she was dying. Whoever I used to be. But she didn't want him to, and he did it anyway." I shifted gears harder than I should have as I took us around a corner. "Dawna knocked his work apart, and now he has to see me to keep patching it up, so I don't go crazy and die again. That's it."

"My God, how have you not—" She cut herself off, but I had the distinct feeling the end of that sentence was going to be, "killed him," which was . . . uncharacteristically violent of Pilar. "I didn't know," she said instead. "I'm so sorry."

But she didn't sound pitying. She sounded angry, and not just passingly angry, but an intense, deep kind of fury I'd only seen in her once before.

"I'm over it," I said, not strictly truthfully. "We need him. I need him. And he's been behaving. Water, bridges. Don't shoot him, please."

"I won't." The promise was immediate but grim, like she gave it while contemplating all the ways she could make Simon's life hell without shooting him.

Touching of her, but also annoying. "Follow my lead," I said. "No shooting, no maiming, no conspiring with Checker to make him miserable. Don't dig it all up again."

"All right. I'll do—if you want me to. I can be civil."

She could, too. She was always civil to Rio, despite putting a hand on her weapon every time she saw him. And I knew she hadn't forgiven *him*.

. .˙. .˙. .˙.

THE MISSION was a little ways outside the urban sprawl. Between the lack of city lights and the hour, the darkness had begun pressing in on us as the road wound through dry hills.

"What's the plan?" asked Pilar, as we drew nearer.

"I take point, you watch our six," I answered. "If there are more 'dogs,' or any humans like them, Simon will just have to start talking as fast as possible."

"And if it's rigged with bombs and stuff?" Pilar said. "We might not be able to see that, will we?"

"No," I said. "It's a risk. Are you sure you want to go in?"

She touched her holster. "Yes."

I thought back to the other times D.J. and I had crossed paths, what his setups had been like. "Watch where you put your feet," I said. "This guy is in the cool-but-lazy school of thought—"

"Like Checker," Pilar said absently.

"What?"

"Oh, I just mean, I mean Checker's sort of like that, isn't he?" Pilar said. "Never mind."

Checker had never struck me as lazy, but then, the only things I'd ever seen him doing were things he was already obsessed with. I thought of him climbing the walls in police interrogation again. He'd be miserable.

Shit.

"You were saying?" Pilar prompted. "Watch where I put my feet?"

"Yeah," I said, wrenching my thoughts back onto the rails. The headlights cut through the darkness ahead of us, the barest hints of scenery flashing by on the periphery. "D.J. likes elegance, and he likes showing off. If I'm remembering right, he's the type who might even show off at the expense of efficiency, which is good for us—it gives us an extra margin of possibility to spot anything he has set. Try to step only on ground unlikely to have a pressure sensor, like asphalt and cement, if possible. And keep your eye out. If you see anything, freeze where you are until I can look at it."

"Okay," Pilar said. "Am I looking for anything specific? Would it be like in the movies, um, wires and sticks of dynamite and blinking lights?"

"Probably not the blinking lights," I said.

Except D.J. might. Of all the people in the world, he might.

I sighed. "Maybe, but probably not. And dynamite is less stable than plastic explosives, but this might have been set up as a short-term snare anyway. Plus, you saw the binary at Teplova's—I'd say it's safe to assume that was him, and he very well might have something else we've never seen before. Use your imagination, and tell me right away if you see anything."

"Got it." In the dimness of the car, I saw her press the palms of her hands against her thighs.

But if she was up for this, I wasn't going to turn her down.

I'd gotten some gear from Rio, including the KRISS Vector with a night-vision scope for the rail, a wand he said was good for registering explosive material about eighty-five percent of the time, and an independent GPS unit we were following to the mission address. Half a mile out, I pulled the e-brake and hairpinned the Yaris in a smooth one-eighty to point the other way, then took us off the shoulder onto dry grass before turning off the engine.

Pilar had slapped a hand against the dash when I started the maneuver. "I'm invoicing you for any damage to my car," she said.

"Invoice Arthur. It's his ass we're trying to rescue."

"Good plan," she answered, with only a little edge to the gallows humor.

I called Simon back as we got out, bracing myself for having him in my ear again. The phone rang. And rang.

Voicemail.

I tried again.

Voicemail.

Pilar's eyes were huge in the dark, reflecting the minimal starlight. "He's not picking up?"

Instead of answering her, I tried again.

Nothing.

Shit.

I called Rio. Within one ring, his voice came on. "Hello."

"Rio, have you heard from Simon?"

"I have not."

"We spoke to him when we left. Now he's not answering."

Rio paused. I figured he was flipping through the same options I was. "It may be what this antagonist wants, for me to leave the family," he said.

"Yeah." I rubbed my forehead. "Yeah. Stay there. Call what's-her-face. The oldest daughter. Make sure she and Checker are okay."

"I shall. I can also keep trying Simon."

"Do that. If you reach him, tell him to call, *stat*."

"Cas," Rio said. "Without Simon's aid, do you think it wise to—"

"Probably not, but do you think it's likely you'll talk me out of it?"

"Cas. We do not even know the likelihood this is a good lead."

Even if it weren't a trap for Pilar and me, even if it weren't a convenient way to get us out of the city in order to hurt someone else—I determinedly didn't think about D.J. and Checker's prior relationship—if we didn't investigate, we were back to where we'd been before. We could go through the rest of the real estate holdings, but the most logical place to start was the one where we already were.

"Have you or Willow Grace found anything else we can pursue?" I said.

"I am still looking, but no. And she has retired for the night. She attempted to go to her own home, but I deemed it unwise."

That almost made me snicker, despite the ominous feeling that every other damn thing was about to topple on us right now from all directions.

"Well, we've got to do this, then," I said. "Consider us mostly radio silent, but use your own judgment for urgency. Good luck."

"To you as well," Rio said. "Have a care, Cas, and God bless."

I hung up before checking the chamber of my borrowed Vector and muttering, "If there was ever a time, now's it."

seventeen

PILAR AND I hiked through the night at a half jog. She had her handgun drawn; I had the rifle at low ready on its sling. I'd put the phone in my pocket on vibrate, just in case Rio or Simon called.

Where the fuck was Simon? I didn't like the guy, but out of all the things I could call him, *flake* wasn't one of them. If he wasn't picking up, the most likely scenario was that something had happened to him.

But what? He was an extremely powerful telepath. There weren't many somethings that *could* happen to him.

Maybe he'd been so tired, he'd fallen asleep, and the phone hadn't woken him.

Maybe.

We hurried through the dark. The mission rose up against the washed-out stars, a shadow of negative space in the night. It commanded a good view of the surrounding land, with an empty parking lot sprawled before it and more dry, grassy hills behind. A quick scan through the night-vision scope I'd put on the Vector gave me more depth and texture to the Spanish architecture, but no actionable intel.

"For future reference," I said to Pilar, "this is the crappiest possible scenario to approach. Anyone inside has all the high ground, and we have zero advantage."

"What can we do?" She breathed the words just above a whisper.

"If we had a day to plan, we might be able to cook up a more creative approach," I said. "Come in from below or above, maybe. But we don't have a day to chase a lead that might not even be a lead."

She didn't argue the point, just nodded very quickly.

"We'll sneak in from the back," I said. "They might not be able to keep a good three-sixty view, and the hills will keep us hidden until we're closer."

Again the quick, silent nod from Pilar.

The highest point in the building's silhouette looked like it was probably some sort of bell tower. I kept half an eye up there, straining for the smallest flash of movement or reflected gleam that might indicate a sniper or a lookout. A breeze stirred the night, bringing the quiet rustle of dry grass and a whispering rattle of gravel and dust.

I briefly considered shooting into the bell tower. If nothing else, it would bring out whatever response to a threat this place had.

But if there was even the slightest chance Arthur was in here . . .

D.J.'s explosive defense systems might be wholly devastating. I wasn't about to risk it.

"Could there be, like . . . motion detectors or something?" Pilar whispered. "That we might trip?"

Or infrared. There were a thousand ways this could go wrong we wouldn't see coming.

"Yes," I said.

We didn't converse anymore. I led the way swiftly across the open space behind the mission, rifle raised with one eye on the scope. We ducked onto the tile of a roofed outside hallway, Spanish arches framing the night between square pillars. I held up a fist to Pilar as we reached the first open archway leading inside. It had no door within it, only pitch blackness beckoning us.

Fortunately, I had the rifle scope. I'd dialed in on the fly and the flat green-and-black monochrome played across a worn, empty interior. Flaking plaster, cracking walls.

No people. No bombs. No Arthur.

I played the sensor wand across the doorway and our immediate surroundings. No sign of explosives.

Trusting Pilar would follow, I slid into the darkness.

Inside, the only sounds were my own breathing and Pilar's, and our footsteps against the loose debris of the flooring. I bore in mind my own warning to Pilar about trying not to step where there might be a trigger or tripwire, but it wasn't always possible. I did keep the wand out and running, but it stayed dark.

The remains of the mission flashed out of the black at me through the scope. Church pews. Crosses. Decorative recesses that had probably once held religious iconography. The night-vision scope gave it all the same eerie greenness.

We paced out the entire ground floor within minutes. Nothing.

The only place left was the tower.

Here, a heavy wooden door blocked our way, but the wand gave no sign of explosives, and it was unbarred. I had Pilar stand back as I pushed it open, just in case.

The bell tower had a square cross section, and a spiral staircase crawled up in short, straight flights against the walls. In the center hung a thick, heavy rope, so long, it coiled on the floor. I scanned the underside of the stairs, but nothing struck me as peculiar or out of place.

I motioned Pilar to stay against the wall, where we'd have a smaller chance of being spotted by anyone peering down through the center of the staircase from above. Letting the sensor wand and my raised rifle lead the way, I put a cautious foot on the first wooden step.

It creaked slightly. Nothing exploded.

By six steps up, I had the additional concern of how much the steps were sagging under us. The mission was closed for restoration, after all—how much did it need? I kept my weight near the wall and tried to keep up approximated force calculations to make sure Pilar would be all right behind me. She was sidling up with her back to the stone, her handgun covering the way we'd come.

We were halfway up the third shallow flight when the top of the staircase erupted into a fireball that seared my retinas.

Debris rained down, black silhouettes of wood and stone backlit momentarily by the brightness. I'd barely started to react when another explosion took out the stairs just below the top. Then another.

Then another. A domino of fireworks dissolving the stairway from the top down in a brilliant chain of sound and light.

Distance over rate equaled time before the explosions reached us and the stairs went out from under us. Distance over rate equaled time before we could get down off the stairs, before we could jump without breaking something.

Time-sub-two exceeded time-sub-one by a split second that might as well have been an infinity.

I reached for Pilar, swinging around so I half-tackled her on the way to leaping off the stairs. I threw my whole body weight against the arm I had around her, shouting, "*Jump!*" in her ear as I took us over the edge.

Fortunately, she reacted fast enough to help push us off. In the brief moment when we left the floor behind, the steps behind us destroyed themselves with a concussion that smacked us across the back with the strength of a two-by-four.

The heavy bell rope hit me in the face, and I latched on to it with the hand that wasn't clenched up around Pilar. I had one moment of jarring pain in my hand and tendons as the change in momentum tried to wrench them apart, and then gravity yanked down, and I was dropping Pilar.

I couldn't keep a grip on her, not with a bad one-armed hold when I was only dangling by clenched fingers with the other. I tried to whip a foot around to help support her, but my body's momentum was swinging in the wrong direction. Tooth-jarring *clangs* sounded from above us and the bell rope jerked in my hand. At the same time I lost Pilar completely, the bottom of the staircase went up in a spectacular fountain of flame below us.

But the instant's delay had given Pilar the reaction window she needed to let go of her gun and get her own hands around the rope. She slid a good six inches before she got her feet around too, probably taking all the skin off her palms, but then she clung. Her gun clattered on the floor below us in the echoing silence.

By that time, I'd used my free hand to pull my Colt and aim it upward, as the rifle was dangling off the wrong side of my neck. But though afterimages of the explosions flickered in my vision, the dimness above us was quiet and inert.

Only the stairs had gone, in very controlled explosions that had left charred shadows against the stone but had touched nothing else.

"Slide down if you need to," I called softly to Pilar.

"I'm okay," she answered.

I started up the rope. Pilar's weight below me kept it taut, so I climbed by clenching my boots on either side and skidding my hand up slide by slide, the other hand keeping my gun above us. Pilar swung below me, shimmying up more conventionally, but she made it up behind me without slowing. She *had* been training.

As I came past the lip of the landing at the top of the bell tower, right under the clapper of the huge bell, I tried to rotate and sight my pistol everywhere at once. But the top of the tower was a maze of timbers and dark, and my vision still had afterimages dancing in it.

"Hang tight," I said. "I'm going to jump." Without Pilar below me, I would have had to climb out and over the bell itself, but with the rope held taut with tension, I had the leverage to leap off.

I landed lightly on dusty boards. The starlight filtering into the top of the bell tower showed some sort of restoration had been begun, but it had clearly been given up many months ago. I slid a board off some makeshift scaffolding and across the opening in the floor where Pilar dangled. It took her some effort to disengage herself from the rope and climb onto the board—her hands were shaking slightly, and dark with blood from when she'd caught the rope—but she managed, and she crawled down the makeshift bridge to join me on the floor. "Thanks."

"Anytime," I said. I handed her my Colt and raised the Vector again.

I pointed a finger below us and then at the closest of the arching, open-air windows into the night. *Keep an eye on anywhere someone might be approaching while I look around,* I was telling her.

She got it. I put my eye to the scope and began picking my way through the forest of timbers and scaffolding.

A third of the way around, the green-black outlines swept across a form lying limp on the floor, back against the outside wall behind a ripped, half-draped tarp.

A human form.

"*Arthur*," I said.

eighteen

ARTHUR DIDN'T respond. Unconscious. He had to be unconscious.

I didn't let myself consider any other possibility.

The stupid sensor wand hadn't helped us on the stairs, but it had been looped to my belt and I reflexively had it held out in front of me as I hastened over. Two feet from Arthur, it lit up like a Christmas tree.

I stopped short. "We've got more kaboom over here."

"Is he all right?" Pilar hadn't left her post by the window.

I didn't answer.

I ran the night-vision scope over him. Rough rope knotted itself far more times than necessary around his wrists and ankles. A blindfold covered half his face, and what looked like blood crusted the cloth.

It was too dark to see, but I had the sudden visceral certainty someone had worked him over. Thoroughly.

Fuck. Focus.

It took some careful examination, but I finally made out the wires stringing behind and around him. I tracked their configuration warily with my eyes as I edged closer.

"I'm going to disarm this," I said aloud. I didn't want to admit that I said it more for my own benefit than for Pilar's.

Considering the stairs hadn't brought any defenders down on us, I dropped the rifle to dangle from its sling and pulled out an LED flashlight. Better to see what I was doing than try to fight the slim chance anyone watching wouldn't know we'd survived.

I stepped around Arthur with care, forcing myself to ignore his injuries. I did let my fingers brush his throat—a pulse fluttered against them under the warmth of living skin. My legs almost went liquid with relief, but I forcibly ignored all that too.

I played the flashlight carefully along the wires, following the logic of the device. Trigger, detonation, explosion, lined up in unfailing conditional progression. But . . .

I ran it backward. Explosion, and before that the detonation, and before that the trigger. I ran it forward again, then back, then forward.

What the hell?

"This is put together wrong," I said. As I said it, I was positive.

"What do you mean?" Pilar's voice carried across to me, wired with tension.

"It's active, but it's not set," I said. "There's no way it can go off. Well, not from moving him away from it, at least."

"Are you sure?"

"Yeah," I said. "I'm sure."

But I stood for a moment longer, because this didn't make *sense*. I was missing something.

And I'd missed something on the stairs too. My mind rewound, backfilled, and I knew what it was.

"Cas?" Pilar ventured.

I shook myself. Get out, then analyze.

Unless all the missing pieces were hiding what would kill us . . .

But that didn't make sense either.

"Come here. I'm going to need your help," I ordered Pilar, and suiting actions to words, I knelt and pulled my knife. I worked as delicately as I could, cutting the ropes minimally to unwind them from Arthur's hands and feet. Next came the wires and duct tape, peeling them gingerly from bruises and crusted blood.

"How are we going to get him down?" Pilar asked in a hushed voice.

"Gently," I answered. "He's probably got—internal injuries, and—" I had to pause to concentrate on what I was doing for a moment. "He's going to need a hospital. We'll have to figure out what to tell the police; we can probably give them this place, and say you found him—we'll make up how—and get Checker cleared—"

"Cas." Pilar put a hand on my shoulder. "Is anything else here going to go off?"

"No. Not unless there's something we missed. We can take him out of here. I'm sure." And then I'd figure out why the hell we *could*.

"Then why don't we call the ambulance now?" Pilar asked gently. "If we're telling the cops we found him here, and he's this injured— Cas, there are no more stairs."

I knew that. But we'd be able to rig it so he was tied onto me, or lower him by . . .

Fuck. Pilar was right. I was good, but EMS would be better.

My hands hesitated, hovering, already sticky with what was probably Arthur's blood, and I didn't want to think about that—"They'll want to call the bomb squad. They'll see all this and delay."

"We could just move him closer to the middle. So it's clear they can take him out."

"Right. Right." And come to that, if I wanted to, I could take the rest of the explosives out of here instead of Arthur.

Because of course I had to disappear if police and EMS were coming. They'd have questions, questions I wasn't good enough at lying to answer, not when I was the center of scrutiny like we would be here.

Pilar read my mind. "Help me move him," she said. "Then you go; I'll make the call."

She didn't mean to hurt me by it. It was what she knew I'd want, what I *did* want.

Arthur had kept all the most important parts of his life from me for exactly this reason. I was the type of person who would leave him bleeding and unconscious in enemy territory so I could hide my face from the cops.

I found another loose scaffolding board and pulled it down so we could carefully shift Arthur onto it, then carefully lift him toward the hole in the floor, one of us on each end.

"Don't wait," I said, with a harshness that scraped my throat.

"Make the call now." Even if response times were fast, I could be faster. No reason to delay. I handed Pilar back the burner phone we'd originally pulled from her car.

"I'll ride with him to the hospital," she said. "Don't worry about us."

"Call," I answered.

While Pilar calmly answered the 911 dispatcher's questions, I slipped through the rest of the top of the bell tower, running the wand over everything, but I found no more explosives. At least, I p-equals-eighty-five-percent found no explosives every place I looked.

I bundled up the active device very carefully, making sure none of the wires touched, and took my Colt back from Pilar. After all, I was more than skilled enough to throw her CZ back up to her from the bottom, and the Colt wasn't registered to her, and . . . *cops*.

The dispatcher had stopped asking questions by then, but apparently told her to stay on the line. We nodded to each other silently.

Then I ran lightly back over our board bridge and swung down onto the rope to slide to the ground.

·.·˙·.·˙·.·˙

I RAN hard back to Pilar's car. None of this made *sense*.

Rio had told me it felt too easy. Too contrived, the intelligence we'd stumbled across that had led us here. Then we'd encountered no defenses until the stairs, and . . .

The sequence kept replaying itself in my head. The flashes blowing the steps off their brackets, out of the wall, collapsing each flight from the top down.

If the steps had blown out from underneath us, we'd probably have fallen and broken our legs, maybe suffered some burns and internal bleeding, but not died.

But the stairs hadn't blown from beneath us. They'd given us warning by starting at the top.

Who *did* that? Who set up their triggering mechanism so its victims had *warning*?

If we'd turned and run toward the bottom, we'd still have been injured, but not too badly. Broken bones, perhaps. I knew how to fall, so I may have been able to land with no more than some bruises and jarring. Heck, maybe I even would have been able to help Pilar land gently enough too.

But the point was, even for normal people, the explosion of the stairs hadn't been meant to kill us.

And the unconnected bomb that was now cradled carefully under my arm had *definitely* not been meant to kill us.

Also, now that I thought about it—I wasn't great at taking note of my environment, not like Arthur was, but nothing pointed to him having been beaten in the bell tower. There'd been no blood on the floor. No sign in the dust that a human being had been thrashing under the timbers. None of the strong scents I associated with human suffering.

The conclusion was inescapable. Arthur had been placed in the bell tower for us to find; the building had been rigged sloppily so he would *appear* hard to get to; and whoever had placed him there had wanted us to succeed in rescuing him without knowing it was all a setup.

Which left two possibilities. The first one was that D.J. had begun feeling remorse—maybe he hadn't known he'd been working against an old friend, and the revelation had spurred him to release Arthur in a fit of magnanimity toward his prior connections. The second possibility was that D.J. had wanted to get some number of us away from LA for reasons of his own.

I wasn't betting on the remorse.

I reached Pilar's car and placed the bomb carefully in the front seat. Then I flattened the accelerator so fast, the Yaris spit dirt and gravel behind me, and floored it back toward LA, pushing the car's tachometer into the red zone. I realized too late that I'd left my only phone with Pilar and had no way to warn Rio anything might be going down.

But I had a good first guess of who D.J.'s target might be. If he no longer cared about killing Arthur because he had someone else in mind, if he'd then used Arthur to lure Pilar and me and possibly Rio if he was lucky out of Los Angeles, if he'd been the one to attack Simon somehow—the one person among us it made sense for him to be targeting was the one he'd known the longest.

The person who used to be his friend.

The people you love can always hurt you more than anyone else, a sad voice said in my head.

nineteen

I REMEMBERED which station Checker had been taken to. Forty minutes later, my single-minded fury brought me swinging in to a hard stop in front of it.

A quick hiccup of relief as I registered it as intact. No flames. No half-destroyed walls or screaming, crying people. The parking lot was quiet around me, the black-and-white squad cars orderly beetles in the dark.

Everything was calm.

It was only then that I realized I didn't know quite what to do.

I still vibrated with the sense of some imminent danger. But if I wasn't pulling Checker out of a burning building . . . then what?

Did I even know he was still here? It was the middle of the night. If he'd been released, he would have gone straight to Diego's house, where Rio was, but if not . . . I was foggy on police procedure. If they were still holding him without charging him—and they'd have to do anything official during daylight hours, wouldn't they?—he'd probably still be here at the station. Unless they moved people around for other reasons.

I punched a hand against the dash. This was exactly the time I needed someone like Checker—to *find out where Checker was*.

However, I did know someone who might not have Checker's particular skills, but was pretty damned good at acquiring information. I just needed a way to reach him.

I got out of Pilar's car and took a walk toward the shopping center on the corner. Not many people were about at this time of night, but the grocery store was a twenty-four-hour one, with the odd customer hustling in and out with their head down. Ten minutes later, I had pickpocketed a cell phone within hailing distance of a police station while leaving a bomb in the front seat of the Yaris I had parked in front of it.

I'd started hurrying back with my prize when something moved in my peripheral vision.

Without thinking, without considering, my Colt whipped out of my belt and I pulled the trigger without even registering what was behind my sights. The white fire of the gunshots rent the night, engulfing every thought.

Glass shattered and alarms pealed in echo. My brain finally caught up with my hands after the third shot and—*what the fuck had I just done*—

The large front window of the grocery store had come crashing down. Screams echoed from inside.

I managed to pry my grip looser on the gun and wrench my finger away from the trigger, and I ran, hunched into a stumble, until I hit the relative safety of a nearby alleyway. Sirens already wailed down the street. The grocery store wouldn't have long response times, not with a police station practically next door.

I cradled the Colt to my chest, my hands shaking . . . and panic chewing around the edges of my vision.

The same panic that had incapacitated me at the wellness center.

Oh, fuck. Oh, *fuck*.

The shadow I'd seen out of the corner of my eye . . . I was a good enough shot that if I'd been aiming at him, he'd be dead. But I'd only managed to kill a building's display window.

I'd targeted a reflection.

The man from the wellness center had been *behind me*.

I twisted suddenly, frantically, trying to see along all axes at once. But if the smallest gleam of the man's face in dim glass had caused me to lose all control—what could I do? How the hell could I hope to fight someone like that if I saw him before I had a chance to fire?

Fight. Run. Kill.

You make me proud, Vala, said the memory of the man in my head.

Oh, Jesus Christ. Who was this guy?

And he was *here*—I was right, Checker was in danger—

I pushed myself away from the alley wall. It felt like it took much more effort than Newton's Third Law dictated. Then I shoved my gun back in my belt, under my jacket, which felt like it took even more effort. But I had to circle around to get eyes on the police station. If this man had come to attack, the police wouldn't be able to do anything against him—but then, I wasn't sure I could either . . .

My feet managed a staggered wobble around the next block until I could circle back the way I had come. Fortunately I'd managed to hang on to the phone somehow. I disabled the GPS—it would still be trackable, but with more difficulty—and tried Simon's number first.

Still no answer.

A horrible foreboding closed its jaws around me.

I could see the police station by then. It wasn't quiet anymore, uniforms shouting to one another as a pair took off toward the shopping center. I stayed enough in the shadows not to draw attention, anxiety clawing its way out of my skin, and dialed with fingers that didn't want to obey me.

Pick up, pick up, pick up—

"Hello," Rio answered blandly.

I hadn't realized how much I needed to hear his unruffled greeting. Everyone at Diego's house was safe, at least. I tried to breathe through the residual fear the way Simon had told us.

"It's Cas," I managed after a beat too long. "Is everything okay there?"

"There is no sign of any new danger. What did you learn from your mission?"

My mission to the mission. I struggled to cut through the static in my brain. "We found Arthur . . . Pilar is getting him to the hospital."

"I am aware. She called Mr. Rosales with an update."

Of course she had. Because Pilar was not me, and remembered to tell his family he had been found, and was alive.

"Rio, I—"

"Cas, it strikes me that allowing your friend Mr. Tresting's rescue was not the aim of this exercise."

"I know. I just saw the—the man, one of Teplova's—"

"Where are you?" he asked immediately.

"You need to stay with Arthur's family," I snapped back. "Don't even think about leaving them. Rio, I'm at the police station. The one where Checker was—can you tell me if he's still here? D.J. was a friend of his, if he sent . . ."

I couldn't finish the thought.

"A moment," Rio said.

The thirty seconds it took him to look up the information felt like an eternity. My hand that wasn't holding the phone clenched and unclenched.

"He is still being held in the same precinct," Rio confirmed. "Cas, if this man is there to attack your friend—"

"I'll destroy him."

"Cas, it appears you are still feeling the effects of having glimpsed him. Your frame of mind may not be best suited to a rescue."

"Only because Simon won't answer his goddamn phone."

"He may have a situation of his own. Cas, there was an incident reported at the building where you left Simon and Oscar. The police were dispatched. I have as yet not been able to reach Simon."

Oh. Oh, no. "What kind of incident?"

"Reports vary thus far, but they believe it to have been an explosive device."

Of course it fucking was.

Maybe this wasn't just about Checker, then. Maybe D.J. had also wanted to rescue—fuck, Rio had just said—Oscar, right. Fuck, I had to remember him.

But only Simon had been with Oscar. For that, the rest of us wouldn't have needed to be spread thin and lured away.

"I do not yet have intelligence on whether Simon or Oscar was a casualty of the explosion, or whether it even occurred in the apartment in which you left them," Rio continued. "But if not, it seems an unlikely coincidence. The police are on scene now."

"I can't leave here," I said.

But even if I camped out watching all night . . . whatever role the monstrous, altered man played, he hadn't been D.J.'s go-to assassination method. Nightmares of ticking timers danced in my mind's eye.

I could watch every second from now on and never see a deadly blast coming. Not if it had been planted while I was conveniently out of the way.

"Rio, how can I tell if something explosive has been left here at the station, before I drove in? The sensors don't pick up everything."

"It is impossible to be certain, but I usually find a combination of technology, close observation, and prior knowledge can suffice to warn me of explosives."

I only had the first one. I could trade places with Rio—he might have a better chance against one of Teplova's villains too—but that left the station unprotected for far too long while I drove to Diego's house and then Rio drove back. And I sure as hell wasn't going to leave Diego and the kids without a guardian.

"I could break him out," I said. "If it's a choice between getting him in deep shit with the law and getting him blown to tiny bits—"

"Might I suggest that it would be better for your friend's situation if the police move him to an unexpected location instead?"

That would at least give us a clean slate on the explosives danger. "But why would they . . ."

I got it even as Rio spoke. "I am capable of calling in a credible bomb threat. It may take some little time, but it will be taken seriously."

My eyes strayed to Pilar's Yaris, still parked in front of the station. "I may be able to speed that up," I said. "Make it more credible. So to speak."

twenty

THERE'S A certain finesse in setting a bomb you don't actually want to go off and hurt anyone. While trying not to be seen. At a police station.

Fortunately, it was the middle of the night, and I was very good at not being seen. Unfortunately, my hands still wanted to shake at odd moments from my encounter with the man who had panic for a face. And I couldn't help twitching to look over my shoulders constantly, twisting around and up above me and behind me to scan the dark.

Not to mention the station was a lot more awake than it had been before my little dustup with a building down the street. *Dammit.*

After a few harried minutes ducking around patrols and casing the station, I found a large electrical junction box in the back of the building. Big enough for me to tear apart and pack the device in behind a rat's nest of wires. The theoretical yield of the explosives wasn't high—enough to have immolated a lone person, presumably to fake that Arthur had been in danger—but not much more. And since I didn't only want the bomb squad to cordon off an area but to evacuate the whole station with all due haste, I needed to make it seem like it could be bigger, or had a good likelihood of causing a fire.

My working efficiency ratio had dropped precipitously from my usual, with every useful output trawling through molasses. I tried to loosen the junction box wires carefully and make sure not to disrupt the station's power flow anywhere, but my fingers were still twitchy enough that I was fairly sure I didn't even succeed. Hopefully I hadn't done much more than make the lights flicker. I kept an eye on the back door of the station just in case, while I twisted everything together and made sure the triggering mechanism would be hard to tease out.

The actual device I kept as hidden as possible. The K-9 dogs would be able to smell it once Rio tipped the station off, and I wanted the disarming process to take as long as humanly possible.

I finished and pressed my palms against my jacket. They were sweating. Jesus. I hadn't made any mistakes, had I? If this bomb actually went off and killed a cop . . .

I followed the logic train of what I had done one more time. No. I was sure. I wasn't going to hurt anybody.

With this one device for verification, Rio could probably imply there were a lot more threats on the premises. I closed the junction box, called Rio to give him the details, and then dropped back into Pilar's Yaris to pull away while he did the threatening part. I kept eyes on all my mirrors, but glimpsed no whispers of a frightening shadow.

I was starting to doubt having seen him again in the first place. But no, the way my whole body was still shuddering, not to mention every thought jumping like it was on a hot griddle—that was proof enough.

I looped in the opposite direction from the grocery store I'd shot up and parked in a bank lot a block down, where I still had a good view of the station. If I'd been in a better state of mind, it would have been funny how fast and brilliantly everything lit up a few minutes later. As if we had whacked a hornet's nest that had been quietly minding its own business, the activity multiplied until the whole street in front buzzed with flashing lights and people in uniform. In short order, prisoners began filing out between watchful officers.

Yes. It was working.

Checker was easy to spot in his chair—I hadn't thought of it till I saw him, but I was relieved they'd let him move under his own power, though his progress was stilted enough that I could tell he was probably cuffed to the frame. He sat between two uniforms in the parking lot for a long damn time, many minutes after all the other prisoners had been carted away, until I wanted to scream, because *my* bomb wasn't going to go off but if D.J. had left anything, it would take everyone out sooner before later . . .

Finally a lift van pulled up and swallowed Checker and his escorts. Cursing the ADA under my breath while almost blacking out with relief, I followed them.

·.·˙·.·˙·.·˙·.

MY FIRM intention was to stay glued to the new precinct until Checker was released. It couldn't be too long, could it? Now that Arthur was safe, as soon as we got some daylight, the wheels of justice could grind right on in our favor.

This station was bigger, and I suspected it was handling the bomb threat investigation at its neighbor as well as taking in its prisoners, because the place was hopping. Uniforms teemed in and out long after the evacuation would've been settled, bright floodlights turning the surrounding plaza to near daylight. This place was also on a much more open corner, giving me almost no cover to lurk in from the Yaris. I had to keep swapping locations to avoid the officers crawling all over the plaza spotting me as a possible threat.

On the plus side, I didn't think there was any way D.J. would brave all that to set a new bomb. We'd saved Checker from one danger, at least.

But every time I had to duck around and change watch positions, the fear spiked in me again. I didn't catch any indication of the man who had caused it, but it didn't seem to be dribbling off with the hours either. By the fifth time I moved the car, my paranoia made the world seesaw enough that I scraped Pilar's right side mirror off on an alley wall—with a good helping of paint—before I got control of myself.

I breathed through gritted teeth and considered calling Rio or Pilar again, just to have an anchor to reality in my ear.

I'd swapped out phones by stealing another one and had been keeping up with them most of the night. Arthur had made it to the hospital and was in surgery—my throat closed when Pilar said those words, even though, of course he was in surgery; how could he not be? She hadn't had any other news.

Meanwhile, according to Rio, Elisa had arrived back in town to help Checker and had been chewing the midnight phone lines to get him released as soon as Pilar had called them with the news we'd found Arthur. Once our bomb threat went through, she'd climbed the walls at Diego's place until it was plausible she might have found out about her client-slash-foster-brother being moved without hearing it from the people who'd set the bomb, and then she'd whisked off saying something about protecting his disability rights in transport situations.

The person I really needed to talk to was Simon. But nobody had heard from him, and his phone was still ringing out to voicemail. Rio related to me that the police report from the building I'd left him in had noted no known casualties, and the cause was still categorized as unknown, but the crime scene was definitely listed as what had been my apartment.

"Cas, there could be important information to be gleaned from the scene," Rio said to me over the phone, making me regret calling again. "I feel I should also remind you that you depend on Simon for your continued mental well-being."

I hated being reminded of that.

"The likelihood of someone successfully attacking your friend through such heightened police security is much lower," Rio continued. "The best calculation is to proceed with this investigation. There is little more you can do by waiting."

I didn't like to admit that I saw his logic. The police station was on its highest alert, and swelling at the seams with people carrying guns. If they reacted like I did, any attack by our mystery assailant would be met with enough blind crossfire that he'd probably die in the attempt.

The same way Pilar and I had killed the dog. It might incapacitate the whole station, but he wouldn't get to Checker. Neither would D.J.

I still didn't feel right leaving. I couldn't do for Checker what Elisa could, pushing for his legal release, but at the very least, I could be his well-armed guardian angel . . .

A harsh tap on the window. I jumped and nearly went for my gun before I registered the imposing navy-blue lines and visored cap of an officer, the butt end of a flashlight importantly ordering me to roll down my window.

Oh, crap. I dropped the phone and groped for the keys to get the window down, trying like hell not to look like I'd just been on the verge of drawing on a member of the force.

"What's your business here?" the cop demanded. Not quite hostile, but with an authority that left no room for error.

"Uh—" I found the phone in my lap and grabbed for it. "I was making a call."

The cop's hand twitched on his holster at my sudden movement. Christ, I was not good at this. His flashlight beacon swept the other side of the car, across the dangling side mirror.

"Ma'am, have you been drinking?"

"No," I answered truthfully, and then blurted, "It's been like that for a while."

Pilar was going to kill me.

"License and registration."

"But I'm not—" I bit my lip and rethought the wisdom of that argument. *Cops can do things*, Tabitha had said. She wasn't wrong. I could get out of obeying, but only in ways that defeated the whole purpose of not breaking Checker out of custody.

Be cool, Cas.

I fumbled in my pocket for a forged driver's license and then leaned across to Pilar's glove compartment. She was law abiding. The thing would be registered.

I handed the paperwork through to the officer, trying not to look guilty. Where the hell did a normal person put their eyes?

He stared at the documents for far longer than I was comfortable with. "This isn't your car, Ms. Dhar?"

"No, it's my friend's. I'm, uh, I'm borrowing it."

"We don't want people loitering out here. Move along."

"Right, okay."

"And get that mirror fixed."

He handed everything back to me. I took it, trying not to let my hands shake. Under the officer's too-bright flashlight, I started the Yaris and managed to turn sedately out of the alley and down the street without sideswiping it again.

I glanced in my rearview. The officer was still watching. I carefully turned the corner with exaggerated slowness and a gentle moderate curvature, just tight enough not to veer into any other lane.

Fuck, I was less and less in shape to help Checker anyway. Rio was right—I needed to figure out what was going on with Simon, and preferably drag him along with me until I was functionally able to fight back. Besides, Rio and Pilar had both reminded me about Oscar, again, and we still didn't know how he was mixed up in this. Best case scenario was that we figured out exactly where D.J. was and stopped *him*—I was sick of playing games.

I hoped Simon wasn't injured, or dead, or in some other serious trouble I was trying very hard to care about. Reluctantly, I texted Rio with my plans and drove back toward where I'd left Simon.

And Oscar. Shit. *Remember!*

I had to pay more attention to my driving than usual to keep it from going erratic. I kept seeing phantom cars following mine, but every time I slowed, they sped past. The game theory played strangely and woozily through my head, every other car an irrational player. By the time I reached the apartment building where Simon and Oscar had been, my skin was crawling off me. I pathetically hoped I'd find Simon in short order so he could set me right.

Whatever explosion had occurred in my flat apparently hadn't been big enough for the street to be blocked off, and any police had left the scene. I parked down the block and got out. The light was edging toward predawn, still too dark to see clearly but graying softly around the edges.

The man lurched up in front of me so fast, it was as if he'd blinked out of nowhere.

Even through the too-familiar curtain of black static dropping over my senses, I should have been faster. But I was going on two days without sleep, plus a full night spent sliding against the edge of terror. My legs buckled while I groped for my gun.

I still got it out inhumanly fast, but the instant's stumble gave the man his window. He came at me like a freight train, his limbs taking the most brutal distance to efficiency. Even as I tried to push through the grasping fear and dodge away or defend, some ghostly echo doubled our fight, his moves an instruction, a demonstration of an optimum assignment of variables.

The twist of memory lasted barely a moment. The man's shin splintered into my knee and his fist snapped my head around against brick. Flashbulbs went off in my vision. My gun clattered away.

The panic howled up inside me, drowning out any other input. Somewhere in me, I was aware that the man had wrapped his face with a scarf, but it barely dented the horror clogging my senses. My fight-or-flight instinct shorted out my brain until I was frozen. The man hit me again, and I saw the explosion of kinetic energy coming but registered it too slowly, the physical quantities washing over me with such certain accelerations—and then the blow landed, and I tasted blood.

The wall was the only thing holding me up. I scratched at it like a plea to help me stand. Or run. Or fight.

The man grabbed my shoulders and slammed me back. My head ricocheted like a rag doll's. I tried to look anywhere but at him, but the shape of him filled everything, everywhere, a cracked mirror reflecting nightmare in all directions.

"*Help*," he hissed. "Help . . . me . . ."

My head was filled with wasps, buzzing out into my tunneled vision until I thought I would burst apart. With one last scrap of coherence, I levered up one leg and rocketed it into him.

He staggered back. I slid down the wall, my hands clawing at my head. Blood swamped my eyes and nose, and I couldn't tell if it was that or the panic that suffocated me.

The man shrieked, a long, unearthly baying of pain and fury. A knife flashed silver into his hand, and he lunged. His hand slashed across between us.

Against his own face.

We were so close that the wet spray smacked my skin. I tore at the wall again as if I could burrow through it in horror. The man slashed himself again, and again, the scarf hanging mangled with shreds of skin. Blood sheeted down, soaking the cloth and dribbling down his chest like it was a painter's smock.

He threw back his head and yelled once more, an inarticulate keen.

I yelled back, my hands throwing themselves up over my head. My body had hit the street at some point. I curled against the wall, every muscle knotted in a rictus of pain and fear.

"I help *you!*" the man raved at me. "I help you—I help *you!*"

He backed away from me, stumbling into the street.

A car nosed around the corner.

Everything happened in seconds. The driver saw the apparition in the middle of the roadway and swerved. A terrific crash echoed over the street as the car went headfirst into the nearest storefront. The driver staggered out, screaming, and tried to run.

The man screamed back and pounced after him, flinging the driver's body like it was a wet rag. The skeleton outline of a human being smacked hard into the asphalt, its angles all wrong and bent backward along far too many axes.

My attacker bawled at the sky again and then ran, bounding into the early morning shadows and out of sight.

I lay on the pavement and tried to breathe. My lungs pulsed and seized like I needed to cry or scream.

Get off the road—out of sight—

Anyone who lived on this street had likely cowered under their beds at the sounds outside, but even in a neighborhood like this, someone might have called the authorities . . . especially with this not being the only report of the night . . .

The frenzy the man had sparked still eclipsed my brain. It was all I could do to unclench a hand and scrape it against the sidewalk, dragging myself in something that wasn't a crawl. I fell on something hard and realized it was my gun.

I peeled myself up the steps and into the building. Sweat drenched my clothes and made my skin slick. My knee and head throbbed in time to the blood crusting over my nose and left eye.

I sat in the dingy stairwell for a long time, struggling, every muscle and joint trying to shove opposite every other one.

Sirens came eventually. I pressed myself into the cobweb-choked space beneath the stairs. The desperate thought floated that I hoped I hadn't left an obvious blood trail, but I didn't have the wherewithal to check. Fortunately, the police mostly stayed outside, though a few did tromp up to the crime scene that had been my apartment, then back down. Probably checking for a connection.

There was one. It was me.

Eventually, the sirens wailed away. Doubtless taking the dead driver with them. Sprawled and mangled on the street, all because he'd been in the wrong place in the wrong second.

He'd been a young guy. Maybe early twenties. Maybe not even that.

In minutes or hours or a thousand years or an eternity, I dragged myself out and up the steps. My body was uncooperative flesh, welded into dead weight beyond reason. Continuing waves of dread wracked me and brought me into shivering cold sweats.

I found the doorway to my apartment through a fog, drawn by the beacon of crisscrossing crime scene tape. The door was missing.

I rolled under the tape and inside.

After seeing the police come and go, I wasn't even sure what I expected here. But my brain was sparking with little but desperate intuition. I needed to find Simon—he could help—he had been here.

My eyes rolled in their sockets, desperate to make sense out of what they saw. The mess in the apartment wasn't large. The explosives had only held a big enough boom to blow apart whatever barricading Rio had put on the door.

Blow it all apart—from the inside.

The conclusion came too slow and after far too long. The bits of twisted-up items from my emergency supplies strewn across the stove. The shredded, burned plastic on the floor, suggesting some sort of controlled gas pressure explosion made in a food container. The shock wave and blast pattern sluggishly sketched themselves out for me, every number coming stubborn and difficult, until a wobbly half picture centered itself just inside where the door had been.

The Australian hadn't been rescued. He had *escaped*.

Someone groaned.

I twitched toward the bathroom, groping for my gun. Had I left the Colt on the pavement outside? No, here it was—but my hand wouldn't close on it, my tendons stretching the joints into unreal talons.

The flimsy bathroom door was shut, but it had been partially shredded by shrapnel from the explosion, a large chunk of the lower half missing.

"Cas . . ." a voice croaked.

It wasn't relief that grabbed me by the throat—I was too far gone for that. More like a driving need. With a herculean heave of my remaining energy and sanity, I hauled myself at the bathroom door, shoved it open, and fell inside.

On the floor, pupils dilated and bleeding copiously from a head wound, was Simon.

twenty-one

"Cas," Simon said. He reached out and gripped my arm.

Aren't we a pair, drifted through the haze of my mind.

Then the haze lifted, sloughed off like a skin I had shed and left behind. I rolled up to sitting, pulling away from Simon. I felt like myself—alert, whip-fast, and capable of instant momentum calculations. Like I had just had a cleansing shower for my brain, with everything settled back the way it should be.

I blinked at Simon and scrabbled backward, my heels hitting rubble. "Holy shit. What did you do?"

"I'm sorry . . ." he murmured. "I didn't mean, I just wanted you to . . . feel better . . ."

Black suspicion reared in me at the wrongness of it. Simon had just reached in and—*fixed me*—with no warning, no permission, no effort on my own part—

But what was wrong with that? I did feel better now, didn't I? Everything set back in its proper place.

I had to . . . do something, tell people, I had learned something . . .

A man slashed at his own face. But dimly, like a reflection of a reflection that had been dulled by years.

And Simon was hurt. I needed to take care of him. Everything else could wait.

I managed to help him up and over to the apartment's threadbare sofa, where I set to work cleaning his scalp wound and brought over the medical kit I'd had stored here. The injury didn't seem deep, but he was worryingly woozy.

Well. *Worrying* if he was the sort of person I'd worry about . . .

I blinked.

"Cassandra," he murmured.

My fingers became gentler as they carded away the black curls of his hair. No matter what I thought of him, I didn't like to see him hurt. It made me feel protective of him in a way I never had before.

His hand shot up and locked around my wrist.

"What is it? Did that hurt?" I tried to soften my touch.

"I'm sorry," he gasped. "Cas—I'm trying to stop—" His eyes went in and out of focus. A tear slid down the side of his nose, leaving a trail in the dust and sweat.

"Stop what?" I said. "Lie still. You almost certainly have a concussion."

"Cas . . ."

My senses fuzzed for a moment, like I was seeing two of him, like I was living two identical moments, but in one I was tender and concerned and in the other turning away in frantic urgency.

The world snapped back into clarity, settling on *concerned*.

"What happened?" I asked. "Can you tell me?"

He shut his eyes. Even though he was lying still, his body was strained, his fist locked in the ratty blanket across the cushions. "I didn't think anyone could hurt me," he said.

He sounded like a lost little boy.

Well, I'd hurt him before, I recalled with some embarrassment. If you counted punching him when I'd really wanted to kill him.

I was abashed at the memory. I had been so naïve.

Hurt people . . . I had been worried, a few minutes ago. About somebody being hurt. Who? It probably didn't matter. My stolen phone buzzed, but I ignored it.

"I'm sorry," I said to Simon, dabbing antiseptic as lightly as possible. It had to sting. "I've never said that before, have I? I've treated you pretty awfully, and I know you were only trying to help. I'm sorry."

He gulped in a breath like he wanted to choke on it. "No, you're not."

"Hey. I am too. Can we get a new start? On the right foot this time."

Why did my knee ache? I scratched at my face and was surprised when my nails came away bloody.

My phone buzzed again. Irritated, I silenced it.

"Cas." Simon took another ragged breath, and his shoulders convulsed like he was holding in a sob. "Oh, God, Cas, I—you're going to kill me. I'm sorry. I'm sorry. I'm trying to stop. I'm sorry—"

"Don't be stupid. I'm telling you *I'm* sorry now." I re-sanitized the mystery blood off my hands with alcohol wipes and dug through the first aid kit for the right kind of bandages. "Now, can you tell me what happened? Memory loss can be normal with concussions, so just tell me what you do remember."

This time his sob sounded halfway like a laugh.

He really did seem to be having trouble with his memory, but at least part of that was some muddled mindfuck regarding the Australian, whom I had barely remembered until Simon brought him up again. He also kept repeating that he'd never thought anyone could hurt him.

"I don't think anyone did hurt you," I said. "Not intentionally. The blast damage is centered with its target as the front door, but some of the shrapnel became projectiles. Whizz bam. You were standing in the wrong place."

"I thought it was wrong . . ." he started, but seemed to lose the thread.

Someone else had been in the wrong place too. A man without a face slammed a boy into the ground, and it flashed through me like something out of a nightmare.

I shuddered. Bad dreams best forgotten.

"No, *don't*," Simon said. "Cas, this isn't, it isn't right. You have to get away from me."

"I'm not going anywhere," I said. "And this wasn't your fault. The

Australian must've learned a few tricks from D.J. Do you remember anything else?"

He seemed to struggle for a moment.

"I remember—police. For a long time. But I didn't want them to talk to me—or notice me—it would be so complicated. And I knew you would be coming, Cassandra, I knew . . ." His eyes went out of focus again.

"I'll always come," I said. "I promise." What the hell had taken me so long this time, anyway?

No matter. Whatever it was, it wasn't as important as being here.

I finished dressing his scalp wound and got up to dig out some canned soup to heat for us. A dull headache had started behind my own eyes. I tried as hard as I could to pinch it out, or, failing that, ignore it, but it spread until it melded with a bruise on the back of my head I didn't remember getting.

I didn't have bowls, but I brought the pot back to Simon, regretful I didn't have anything better.

"Cas." Simon had mustered a bit of energy, but he closed his eyes again, and blocked my hand when I attempted to spoon-feed him. "Cas, I'm not going to let—please go."

I barked a laugh. "I said no. No way. You're injured. You absolutely need someone with you."

"Then get Rio."

"Why?" My headache shaded itself a little worse, but I was still perfectly capable of taking care of him. And he needed someone to do that right now.

He needed someone, and I wanted to be that someone. Forever.

He pushed himself up to sitting and faced away, his back a wall shutting me out. Something shivered in my head, a bleak rejection, a rattling unease.

"Because I don't want you here," Simon answered me thickly. "Now. Get Rio. Please."

I still didn't want to leave him. But he kept insisting, over and over, pushing and pleading. My emotions spiked in strange cycles, half insulted, half confusion. I proposed taking him with me back to Diego's house, but he shut that down too, saying he didn't want to be around anyone right now, but especially me.

That stung.

"Send Rio," he repeated, and I reluctantly agreed.

It took walking away in the outside air and a good five minutes of Rio unraveling my strange, concerned behavior over the phone before my headache spiked along with an absolute fury at Simon, concussion be damned.

Fucking *telepaths.*

I sat down hard on the bumper to Pilar's Yaris. Rio's voice was still in my ear, but I didn't hear it. I didn't care that Simon hadn't been in control, that it hadn't been his fault. The thought of his mind slithering into mine made the back of my throat close. The way I had fawned over him—for an instant, I had deliriously opposite fantasies of stabbing his pathetic face through the eye. He wanted me to love him? So much his deepest and most unfettered desires would *force* me?

"Cas," Rio was saying. "Cas, speak to me. You said you saw Teplova's changed man again."

"If Simon didn't yank it all out of my head—"

"How long ago? I may be able to track him."

I glanced at my watch. Cold sweat prickled when I saw it was midmorning. I'd fought the man before the sun came up. How much time had I wasted as Simon's nursemaiding pet?

"It's been almost five hours," I said to Rio, anger and helplessness strangling the words.

"Unfortunate. It is unlikely I will be able to pick up his trail again."

"He asked for my help." It was one of the only things I could remember. "Like he was begging. He said *help me.*"

"Then perhaps he wishes to escape his master. That could be to our advantage."

"Maybe . . ." He'd done more than ask for help. Bits and pieces of the encounter scattered themselves incoherently, like beads off a broken string. The image of him slashing himself . . . he'd hidden his face and then mutilated himself in front of me, and it had barely dented whatever Teplova's haunting alterations had been. At most, a desperate sliver that had let me fling the limpest of defenses. "I don't think he was very coherent."

Or sympathetic. Even setting aside whatever piece of him now pressed every fear center in my brain, he hadn't started with polite entreaties, I remembered that much. The popping throb in my right knee attested to it, as did the bloody nose, split lip, and deep bruise on the back of my skull.

And the body of the young man he'd murdered for daring to be afraid.

I remembered what Simon had said about Oscar. *The mind is a malleable thing, Cas. What would happen to a person's mind if nobody could ever see them?*

What would happen to a person's mind if nobody could ever cease to fear them?

But the question was academic. Whoever this man had been, whatever forces had brutalized him—it didn't change what he was now. A dangerous killer.

"He said something else." I couldn't remember. Why couldn't I remember? "He told me something, something about where he was going . . ."

I squeezed my thoughts like I wanted to wring them out. Simon couldn't have snatched the whole encounter from me. I had to be able to recall more—

As if I'd wrenched it out of the depths, I saw myself and the same man sitting at a table, a chess board discarded to the side next to empty glasses and crumpled napkins.

"They didn't tell us what this was," he said sadly, with the warmth of someone who's imbibed to just on the other side of openness. "They asked me to come train people. I didn't know what they were doing. I want you to know that."

My mouth moved, responding to him. "I'm not bothered."

"I know. But I am."

I felt my shoulders shrug, harshly, carelessly. "They gave us a gift. Some people weren't strong enough for it. That isn't on you."

The skin around his eyes tightened, like he wanted to argue the point, but then he changed his mind. "I don't regret meeting any of you. That's not what I mean, you know."

I laughed. "As they say, you're one of the good ones."

He shook his head. "You were children. You still are. I should have . . . There's no excuse for any of us."

My hip hit the ground so hard, I lost my grip on the phone. I'd fallen off Pilar's bumper into the street.

"I remember," I said aloud. I scrambled for the phone. "Rio, I remember. They—we—we called him Coach. He was a—he trained us, he designed how we . . ." Who was *we*? I grasped for it and it slipped away. "He was more than a trainer. He was like a—a parent, or a big brother, or something—"

"Cas," Rio said urgently. "You must stop. You know how this could damage you—"

I screamed, thrashing on a pallet, delirium making the room spin. "I'm not weak, I'm not weak, I'm not weak!"

Coach turned to someone in the shadows. "This is the same as the others. You have to get her out of here."

"I will," said Simon's voice.

"He said he was going to help *me*." The moment crashed back with terrible clarity. "Rio, I think he was following me. From the police station—maybe even from the mission, if he knew what D.J.'s plans were and picked me up there. He must have recognized me at the wellness center, and he wanted my help, and when I didn't say yes, he said *he* was going to . . ."

The body of the young driver broken on the street crossed my vision again.

"I don't know what he means by that." I was almost babbling, a frightened pleading. "I don't know what he's going to do." If I didn't give him what he wanted, what lengths would that drive him to? What would he do if Checker or Pilar or Arthur—or someone like Tabitha—happened to be standing next to me at the wrong moment?

I saw the man—Coach—again, gripping me by the shoulders and look-ing into my eyes. "Go," he said. "Good luck."

And I turned and followed Rio.

"Oh, God," I said. "Rio, he was . . . he was my friend, wasn't he?"

twenty-two

"I RECALL the person you speak of, and I believe you did consider him so, yes," Rio answered. "Now I strongly suggest you cease this attempt at discovering more."

"He was my friend . . ." And now he wanted my help.

Just as Arthur had needed my help. I'd sworn I'd break apart the world to find him, struggling so hard to claim that identity for myself. Promising myself I wouldn't fail my friends as Willow Grace had failed hers.

I wasn't a very good person, by almost any metric. I wasn't even Rio, with his impressive consistency, no matter how many repugnant acts he still allowed himself. But recently, I'd begun to cling to the idea of the people in my life who mattered to me. To the promise that I could protect them.

Now I wasn't even sure if Arthur and Checker thought that way about me in return—maybe they never had. And the sudden remembered emotion about the person I'd called Coach . . .

It cratered into a desperate obligation. A need to prove myself in some way I couldn't even define.

"Maybe I could help him," I said recklessly. "Teplova's surgeries, they're just math. I can figure out what she did. I could find someone to undo it." I wasn't at all certain about any of that. But if Coach had any chance, it was probably me.

As long as he didn't kill me before I could try.

Voices hummed dissonantly in the back of my brain. Rio was

right, I was shaking everything loose, destabilizing my own coherence just when I needed to be able to think.

Too late, too late, Valarmathi mocked me.

"D.J. must have forced Teplova to make him into that. As a, as an experiment," I plowed on. "Nobody would choose this. Nobody." And once done, I could think of a dozen ways such a victim could be controlled, from dangling the prospect of changing them back to being the sole person who didn't run in fear. D.J. must have figured out some way to interact with his own creations.

The horror lanced through me of Teplova at that operating table, threatened into putting a knife to someone she considered a close companion. Distorting his face and body into something people would react to like a monster in the dark.

"I am pessimistic a rescue in this case is possible," Rio said. "Even if you could transform him back to his prior form, someone like him may never be able to return fully from such an experience. He is a serious threat right now, Cas."

"You're suggesting we put him down, then?" I demanded. "Shoot him in the head and be done with it?"

"There may not be a choice in the matter."

I pushed myself up aggressively and swung around into the car. "I'll *make* it a choice. We take down D.J., we rescue Coach, and we make sure everyone's safe. That's the new plan."

Arthur and the others would back me up on that. They saw the value in never letting go of a person's humanity, even if Rio didn't. Even if I wasn't so sure either. They'd take my side.

Assuming Coach didn't kill any of *them* first either.

．．∵．．∵．．∵．

THE SPECTER of Coach's promise to *help* pressed me to urgency. What did he know about me? Who might he hurt, in a state of mind that had been so forcibly wrenched from reality?

He wasn't like that before, a sneaking defense spoke up. I flashed on his hands wrapping mine with tape, handing me a bottle of water, giving me a mock salute before I ran and ran and ran faster than anyone could catch me.

Christ, if this kept up, I was going to crash the car. I consciously did the full fluid dynamics equations of threading through LA's weekday morning traffic, even if I didn't need to, and tried to conjecture what Coach's next move might be.

Rio had relayed that the whole family—sans Elisa, who was at the police station with Checker—were now at the hospital where Arthur was. If Coach came after them for some reason, Rio would keep them safe. And if I could get back to Checker before he was released, I could watch over him and then everybody else too while Rio headed back to Simon. Then we'd work on taking down D.J. and saving the people he'd destroyed.

I should have been more worried about leaving Simon alone with a head injury and a killer out there who used to know him. The vindictive part of me muttered that it would serve him right if he was the one Coach came after.

I allowed myself a brief and malicious imagining that Simon's murder might be how Coach chose to "help" me . . . not that I *really* wanted him to.

But I'd been in such a haze about helping Simon that for hours I hadn't kept up with any of the people who actually mattered to me. I checked my phone as I drove, hoping it would help keep me balanced against whatever fissures I'd started cracking open in my own head. Rio had called six times throughout the morning, Pilar four. Eventually Pilar had segued into sending texts, half of which were worried and the other half of which were updates. Arthur was now out of surgery and reported stable, something Rio apparently hadn't felt was important enough to pass on. The doctors weren't letting anyone in to see him yet, but all the kids had trooped down to sit around the waiting room and be ready to descend the moment their dad was allowed visitors.

I sent Pilar back a few texts of my own—I didn't feel like enduring her well-intentioned concern over the phone. The screen immediately lit up with replies, the first with delight that I was okay, the second an acknowledgment of my warning about the possible danger from Coach and my directive to stay near Rio, and the third and fourth another update. She told me they'd just been with Arthur, who'd been torn up something awful (her words) but all things considered was doing really well, and according to the doctors, should recover without trouble as long as he didn't strain himself. She concluded the message by telling me two detectives were in with him now, so Checker should definitely be out *soonest*, with a smiley face.

I tried to remember why I liked Pilar again. Oh, yeah. She was good with a gun.

Also because she sent another text a few minutes later saying, Oh and remember Oscar! Who has run away, so maybe you don't want to remember him.

No. Running away made me want to remember him more. But he'd have to wait.

I ran six red lights and cut through four gas stations to get to the police station faster. The last thing I needed was Checker and Elisa heading out of there unprotected with who knew what waiting. The streets wavered in front of me in the midday heat, and I couldn't tell if it was exhaustion or anxiety or my own attempt at fucking up my brain.

My fatigue had trenched bone-deep by the time I finally made it. Now that it was daylight, I slid into the station's parking lot like a regular upstanding citizen and got out. No more updates from Pilar, and it had been thirty-seven minutes since her text that the detectives were interviewing Arthur. That *had* to be enough time for them to finish and make a phone call, didn't it?

I swung toward the front doors of the station, fully intending to walk through and demand . . .

I stood foolishly by the door to Pilar's car. After two years, I didn't know Checker's last name.

But what would demanding do for him anyway? I kept forgetting I couldn't punch the cops into acquiescing to me. They were either already releasing him, or they weren't. Yelling at them would only make them look more closely at me, which was not a situation I wanted to provoke. Hell, being at a police station in the first place was like voluntarily giving myself dental surgery—Checker better be grateful.

There did exist a person whose yelling was supposed to work, though. I texted Pilar for Elisa's number.

When I called Elisa, it hit voicemail. But Pilar's message had been a name card including her surname as well as her number, which gave me a different idea.

I marched into the police station, trying to ignore the cameras while at the same time keep nervous eyes in all directions. "I'm looking for Elisa Carpintero," I said to the uniform behind the desk near the entrance. "She's my lawyer."

The uniform tried to be as unhelpful as possible, but I finally got her to pass on a message and sent Tabitha's name as my own. Even after acquiescing, she shot me a poisonous look and said something about "no funny business, today of all days."

Come to think of it, a lot of the cops around here seemed jumpy, their eyes flicking over their shoulders and their hands to their holsters, even inside the station. Was that all because of my little harmless bomb?

Whoops.

I sat down to wait on one of the benches against the wall and covered my own hooded watchfulness by fiddling with my phone. I was still using one of the stolen ones from the night before; I hadn't been coherent enough to exchange it for a burner from the apartment where I'd left Simon. Simon and . . . a vague itch made me check the messages from Pilar again.

Oscar. Right. Fuck. The guy who had tried to blow up my office, and was now in the wind.

"You must be Cas Russell."

I whipped to my feet, probably too combatively for a police station, but managed to stop there. A young, heavyset Hispanic woman with an aggressive posture had come around the corner. She folded her arms and stared down at me in a way that reminded me eerily of Diego. Like father, like daughter, apparently.

"Elisa, I'm guessing," I said. "Where's Checker?"

"Still in holding. Do you have anything new?"

I didn't waste time. "I think someone might be after him. Possibly more than one someone." Both his old friend and mine. "You need to get him out of here. Detectives have already been in interviewing Arthur—can you expedite this?"

She nodded, but a frown appeared between her eyes. "I've gathered that's a concern. But if he's in danger, he might be safer in custody for the moment."

"No. He isn't. Trust me." Mostly because I'd have no guarantee of getting in there to protect him. "Get him out."

"Noted. I'll go continue making them all hate me, then. Squeaky wheels." And with no more pleasantries, she strode off the way she had come.

I decided I liked Elisa. I took a steadying breath and forced myself to sit back down.

The bright sunlight outside the glass front doors winked through the shadows of people flickering back and forth. Every one of them felt like a threat. It was all I could do not to keep a hand on the grip of my Colt.

Christ, I was tired. Or the cops' jumpiness was rubbing off on me.

But my appreciation for Elisa was tripled when she and Checker came out together half an hour later, with no handcuffs this time.

I shot up off the bench. Checker looked awful. He clearly hadn't slept much either—deep shadows gouged themselves under his eyes, and his hair stuck up in all directions. But he had a little bit of a smile and energy to his movements, and I surmised Elisa had told him about Arthur being found alive and not permanently harmed.

Finally, something that had gone right.

"Hey," he said to me, but led the way out into the sunlight before further conversation. I couldn't blame him.

I did make sure to step a little way in front of him as we got outside, though. Just to be safe.

"Are you two going to join them at the hospital?" Elisa asked.

"Yeah," Checker answered for both of us without checking. "Lise, are you sure . . . ?"

"I'll see you," Elisa answered smoothly, with a friendly prod to his shoulder. "Keep out of jail this time, sport. It was nice to meet you, Ms. Russell," she added to me, before heading out into the parking lot to her car.

I realized too late that I probably should have told her to ride with us. I was reacting to everything too slow. At least she was the much lower profile target—trying to keep track of this many people was shit.

But Checker was out of jail, and Arthur was safe, and I could be happy about that for now. For just a moment, I wanted to live in this bubble of relief and not think about old acquaintances snatching at either my consciousness or my commitments.

If they would let me.

"You all good?" I asked Checker.

"Now I am." He frowned and pointed at my face. "Are *you* okay?"

I touched my swollen cheek and the crust of blood across my nose and split lip. I probably should have cleaned that off before going into the station. "I'm fine. Long story."

"Catch me up on the way to Arthur?"

"Yeah."

I walked with him back to Pilar's car, and we piled in. As I drove, I began outlining for Checker everything that had gone down since he'd been taken into custody, including the mounting evidence of the doctor's powers and D.J.'s increasingly clear fingerprints behind it all. "I'm thinking this has gotten personal for him," I said. "And that he's after you—probably backtracked to find you after they made Arthur. Before that, he had turned Teplova into his own personal Frankenstein-making machine."

"Frankenstein was the doctor," Checker murmured.

"What?"

"Frankenstein was the name of the doctor, not the monster."

Coach wasn't a monster, I thought. I hadn't gotten to talking about him yet. I almost didn't want to. Checker needed to know, but I wasn't eager to gouge into that weakness in my psyche, or to admit I wanted to save someone who'd been so actively targeting us.

"Teplova was D.J.'s own personal Frankenstein, then," I said impatiently. "Whatever. My point is, just because we found Arthur, I don't think that means D.J. is finished with us. We need to track him down and stop him. Will you be able to get into the police systems and see if the bomb squad found any other explosives at the first precinct?"

"You mean other than the bomb you set?" His mouth twitched. "I'm honored. I've never had someone commit terrorism on my behalf before."

"It wasn't terrorism," I said. "Just, you know. Incentive. Can you do it?"

"Yeah."

He didn't sound altogether enthusiastic, though, and when I cast another sidelong glance at him, he was looking down at his lap, toying with the hem of his shirt.

"Look, I'm sorry your old friend turned out to be a homicidal kidnapper who mutilates people for his own amusement," I said. "But we have to figure this out."

He sucked in a breath and bit at a nail, gazing out the window now. "Is it wrong that . . ."

"What?"

"Never mind." He sniffed and scrubbed at his face. "I almost hope he's—like maybe someone from Pithica planted all this in his head or something. Wondering if there's still some chance this isn't his fault. But then I think back and . . . I think that's wishful thinking."

"Why psychically brainwash someone when you can just pay them," I agreed sardonically. "Besides, Simon's pretty sure Pithica isn't even part of this."

Checker hissed out a breath. "I know. But even if it's all him, doing this, even though it probably is, I just keep thinking . . . if he'd had . . . It's complicated."

How dare he. Here I'd been teetering on the brink of a guilt spiral about wanting to help *Coach*, and Checker wanted to wax blithely nostalgic about the person who had orchestrated everything? After his old friend had tortured mine into becoming someone Rio wanted me to shoot on sight?

Coach's situation was the one that was *complicated*. D.J. had made his choice—not just one but a thousand choices, descending to more hellish abuses with every branching. And now Checker was usurping this role from me, begging to shield *his* friend—even when being delicate about such a villain would come at the expense of not only Coach, but every single one of Checker's *other* friends who'd been in the line of fire since this began?

And he hadn't even hesitated over it. Like we were nothing.

The deep moat of anger at both him *and* Arthur that had been swelling up inside me threatened to overflow and burn us both. I'd spent all night strung out worrying about Checker, and his only concern was the guy who had almost killed me half a dozen times while I'd been trying to fix this whole mess. It was like he didn't even see me. Same as with Arthur. I was an old reliable tool, a convenient missile to point at whatever they needed killing.

We were always weapons, shivered Valarmathi. *We knew that.*

I slammed her away. "It's not complicated," I said to Checker. "In fact, it's really goddamn simple."

"No, it is. For me. He has good—I still have—he was my *best friend,* Cas."

I'd called Checker that, maybe, in the tentative, insecure recesses of my mind. I was glad now I'd never said it aloud.

"Well, now he's your worst enemy and probably out to kill you. And we're going to end his merry little reign of terror over your friends and family and give him a taste of his own fucking medicine." My guilty fury stabbed deeper, overturning every ugly fungus of emotion, and I hit the words meaning for them to be cruel. "Do you not realize that Arthur almost died? Tabitha and Pilar almost died. I almost died! You picked a murdering sociopath for a friend, and now it's time to buck up and face the consequences—"

"That's rich, coming from you."

My face stung like he'd slapped me, and I hit the brake so hard, the Yaris's tires lost static friction for an instant.

It wasn't like Checker hadn't ever made jabs at my tendencies toward amorality. But usually, there was more humor. And usually, he wasn't equating me with a murderous bomber who had abducted Arthur.

Or maybe he was talking about my friendship with Rio. I wasn't sure if that was better or worse. The image of Coach flashed across my mind again too, hurling the driver to the pavement as if in a toddler's tantrum, and everything I'd been so apprehensive to broach to Checker sat trapped on the back of my tongue.

We should have left him in jail to rot, Valarmathi whispered helpfully. I didn't push back against her quite so hard this time.

"If that's the way you feel," I said to him. "You want to make your own way back? Because I can arrange that."

"Look, I just mean . . . people are complicated," Checker pleaded again. "D.J., you've only seen one piece of him. What our friendship meant to me—I can't deny that, no matter what else he's done. I *won't* deny it. Besides, the person he became—that could have been me."

"Yeah, because I can really imagine you blowing people up."

"For God's sake!" He twisted in the passenger seat to pin me with a hard-eyed stare, and I was glad I had the excuse of driving to keep my eyes determinedly on the road. "Come on, Cas. You don't think I can effectively ruin people's lives? *Very* effectively? You don't think I could utterly destroy someone's livelihood and family and reputation if I wanted to, drive them to—to suicide, or worse? We *live* online now!"

"*Could* and *would* are two different—"

"And I'd like to say I've never even contemplated going there," he bulldozed right over me. "But there was a time when—there's this temptation, when you feel like nobody in the world gives a damn, when the whole system's been shitting on you, and you think, *fuck it, I'm smarter than all of them*—when taking that power starts to seem like *justice.* Like the natural, logical conclusion of the meritocracy everyone tells you life is supposed to be. And part of that whole craptastically messed-up headspace is not seeing other people as fully, equally human, because you can't do that shit to other people if you think of them as—as having dreams and laughing at jokes and worrying about their families and just trying to muddle through this goddamn life the same way you are."

My jaw clenched. I'd never heard Checker voice any of this.

"It's so *easy* to live there, in that simple-minded place, and deny that real life is actually really fucking complicated," he went on. "And D.J. and I . . . I think we reinforced it in each other. Mock the stupid people, you know? Show them who's boss."

"So, what happened to you?" I said.

"Arthur," Checker said simply. "And Diego. I'd be a completely different person if not for them. I'd be—I don't want to know what I'd be."

"And what, you want to do that for D.J.?" I bit my tongue hard before I voiced my opinion that D.J. was beyond help. "I've never believed in redemption," I said instead.

"Well, you're goddamn lucky your friends do."

He'd definitely been talking about me earlier. We finished the drive in tense silence.

twenty-three

WE MADE it to the hospital—after what felt like an eternity—and I immediately tagged out Rio, who'd been standing sentry outside Arthur's room.

"I have another apartment with an intact door about a twenty-minute drive from the old one," I told him. "You can move Simon there. Get him back on his feet and . . ." Fuck, there was something they had to do, wasn't there?

"We shall attempt to track down Oscar."

"Yes," I said. "That. Do that." Right now, he might be our best lead on finding D.J. and ending all this.

Rio nodded at me and left. Jesus, Simon was like radioactive waste right now, leaking stray thoughts all over the place. Thank Christ Rio would be able to handle it.

The whole family plus Pilar was inside the room visiting with Arthur, and Checker had beelined in right away without a word to me. I neither felt like I fit in with their whole big happy family nor particularly wanted to talk to Arthur at the moment—now that he was safe, I was still *really fucking pissed* at him—so I slouched in a plastic chair in the hallway next to Diego.

Who was also not visiting with Arthur.

"How are you, Miss Russell?" he asked courteously.

"Just peachy." Abandoned by my so-called friends, obligated to a man who was likely too far gone to help, under threat by a power-hungry egomaniac bomber and officially past fifty hours without sleep. I sighed. "You can call me Cas, you know."

He nodded, and we sat for a while. Christ, I wondered if the kids were determined to spend all day fawning. Not that I had anything better to do than be stuck here as a guard dog. Unless it was attack the mountain of digging that needed to be done to track down D.J., or maybe get three minutes in a reasonably secure place where I could close my eyes . . . I catalogued all the hospital exits seven times over and distance over human running speed equaled time to get everyone out, then added error margins for the kids tripping over one another or freezing like fearful deer.

Fortunately, I had a lot of ammunition in my pockets. I wondered what Diego would think of me then—I'd probably be putting my life on the line for his kids, so he'd better fucking thank me.

I broke the silence far more out of a pissy itch to be nosy than any desire to make small talk.

"So, what happened between you and Arthur?"

He didn't say anything for long enough that I knew he was annoyed with me for asking. Finally he said, "A marriage license and then a divorce lawyer."

I thought about making a joke about a mathematician's answer, but I didn't think he'd get it.

"And how did you meet Arthur and Charles?" Diego asked with almost too-careful politeness.

"A case." I didn't elaborate. I wondered what he'd think if I added the part about taking down a global network of telepaths.

We were saved from continued screaming awkwardness when Arthur's door opened and Willow Grace slipped out. I hadn't realized she was still here—but of course, Rio wouldn't have allowed her to leave. She'd changed to a man's button-down and a loose ankle-length skirt that had to be Tabitha's. I couldn't imagine many people in the Rosales house had clothes that would come close to fitting her, but she'd belted the ensemble in a way that made it look like a fashion statement.

She glanced around and took in the fact that Rio had left. "Seems like this is a family affair," she said to Diego and me. "I'm glad you found your friend. If you need to reach me, you have my number."

I stood. "Wait—"

She halted. "I thought you said that once you accomplished your rescue, this would be done."

Except it was obvious this had all been a setup. Except we still hadn't found the people responsible. Except . . .

"Call me anytime," said Willow Grace, after a moment's pause. "Looking more deeply into this is likely a fool's venture, but if you do, it would be better to coordinate. You can imagine I have quite a bit at stake in finding out more about Eva's killers."

Diego stood too. "Thank you for your assistance, Miss Grace. We'll be in touch."

"Hey," I said. "Wait—it's for your safety too—"

But Willow Grace nodded to us and strode off, and Diego actually put a hand on my arm. "You found Arthur. You can't keep the poor woman locked down on your say-so."

Rio would have kept her here. He would have called it a standard precaution. But I wasn't Rio . . .

You aren't you either, a ghostly voice reminded me.

"I appreciate your desire to protect my family," Diego said. "I continue to appreciate it. But the urgent situation is over. We have to go back to our lives sometime."

That was about as idiotic a statement as I'd ever heard. But Diego did have a point; there was only so long we could keep Willow Grace from leaving before we either had to tie her down or she called the police on us.

My head had a slight buzzing in it, like a fly had decided to zoom around inside my skull. I shook myself. Maybe I should call Rio back and—what?

You decided a long time ago you didn't want to be what Rio is. Maybe it was fine to let her go home.

God, I needed some sleep.

Willow Grace had left Arthur's door open slightly. I went over and called, "You two. Out here, now," at Checker and Pilar. The kids were all crowded around too closely for me to see Arthur, which was just as well.

"What is it, Cas?" Pilar asked, closing the door behind them. Her eyes widened at the sight of me. "Are you all right?"

"It looks worse than it is. We need to plan." I did a quick count in my head. "Wait a second, shouldn't Elisa have gotten here by now?"

"She's not coming," Checker answered.

It registered, then, what his cryptic half conversation with Elisa down at the station had meant. The grating frustration I'd been feeling at all of them ballooned up inside me—*people were going to get hurt* and it was going to be my fault and nobody was telling me *shit* and why were there *so damn many of them* to protect—

"Does nobody in this group think about personal safety except me and Rio?" I burst out. "The reason I am *sitting here* is that someone very dangerous is after *something* from us, and *we don't know what that is yet*!"

Diego winced. Checker tried to shush me and glanced over his shoulder at the closed door to Arthur's room.

Screw them all. I should quit and go pass out for a week.

I pointed at Diego. "Call your daughter right this second and get her down here. Wait, better yet, let's all get out of here." We couldn't work in the hospital. "Scratch Elisa. Go find a doctor and see what the earliest Arthur can go back to your place is, AMA if necessary, as long as it won't be dangerous. We can call Dr. Washington to help if we need to."

Diego stared stupidly at me, then exchanged a glance with Checker before walking off.

"I'll come with you," Pilar said hastily, and followed.

Checker waved after them. "It is his house."

"So?" Diego was the one who'd been refusing to go somewhere safer from the beginning. If he didn't want to put up with some coziness, that was his fault.

"What I mean is, you just volunteered him to have his ex-husband convalesce in his guest room," Checker explained impatiently. "There might be, you know, some awkwardness there."

"Well, too bad," I said. "If Arthur was worried about me causing awkwardness, maybe he should've told me his family fucking existed in the first place."

"And would you even have noticed if he had?" Checker's words had real bite to them. Even more than in the car. "For someone who doesn't respect boundaries, it's not like you ever show much actual interest in our lives. You know the only reason you care now? Because you're bitter we didn't tell you, that's why."

I opened my mouth and tried to say that wasn't true. But some sort of heavy emotion sat hard on my throat, and the words wouldn't come.

Checker scrubbed a hand across his face, and the aggression went out of him. "Cas, I'm—what I mean is—"

"You said what you meant."

"No, I mean yes, but—"

"As soon as we get back, I need you to get all the forensic reports on Arthur's kidnapping so we can start going through them. Okay?"

"Right. Okay." He put a hand on Arthur's door, but stopped.

"What?" I said, my tone going as ugly as his had been.

But his breath hitched, and he turned his face away.

Oh. Oh, Jesus.

I *sucked* at this stuff.

"Arthur is . . . God," Checker whispered to the door. "He got so messed up. And all because—I'm the one who . . ."

"You didn't mean for this to happen," I tried.

"But it's still my fault, isn't it? He's really hurt. I didn't believe—I never thought he'd—" He swiped at his nose with the back of one hand.

I didn't think "he" meant Arthur anymore. "We're all fucked in the head about some things," I said.

I'm not crazy; I'm just a new species, Valarmathi added helpfully.

Checker took a breath and resettled himself. He still wasn't looking up, but he reached out and touched my hand. "You found him. Thank you. And I . . . I'm sorry. I wish I could've been more help."

"It's okay," I said. "I'm pretty sure you didn't plan to get taken to jail."

He choked out a laugh, and his hand tightened on my wrist for a second. "You should come in. He was asking for you."

"Seven's a crowd. Later." I meant it to sound light. I wasn't sure I managed.

Checker looked like he wanted to say something else, but instead, he just gave my hand another squeeze and went back into Arthur's room.

I leaned against the wall next to the door, alone in the hallway.

twenty-four

GETTING EVERYONE back to the Rosales house was a caravan of chaos, and I didn't relax until we were safely behind both closed doors and Rio's security system. Fortunately, everyone else was almost as sacked out as I was, and were being docile about it instead of following my short-fused example. They obeyed my orders without pushback, and then Diego took over to sort everyone into rooms and sleeping space.

Arthur got the downstairs guest room so he could have dark and quiet. Elisa was to bunk in with Tabitha, and Diego pulled out a sofa bed in the living room for anyone else who needed to sleep—I caught him looking at Checker as he offered it. I wasn't the only one who'd been up for more than fifty hours.

I claimed the other couch with Rio's security monitor next to me. It was the best strategic location if my alarm clock turned out to be someone trying to bust in.

Pilar said she'd been catnapping, but her usual chipperness was starting to look worn around the edges too. With minimal prodding from Diego, she agreed to borrow some pajamas and collapse, but before she did, she made up a schedule so Arthur would never be without someone sitting with him, just in case he woke up and needed something. I was of the opinion that it was serious overkill considering how determined the kids were to spend every second hovering, but I wasn't about to get into an argument with her about it.

I did notice she put me on the spreadsheet but left Diego and Elisa off.

So some hours later found me slightly better rested and having finally washed my face, and on a laptop by Arthur's bedside while most of the household continued sleeping. I'd left the light off and the blinds drawn, working only by the glow of the screen. Before claiming a spot on the sofa bed with Pilar, Checker had gotten me copies of all the police data regarding Arthur's kidnapping to start on, and I was slowly slogging through it.

It felt horribly voyeuristic reading both the notes on Checker's interrogations and the interview Arthur had given the police. Even through the filter of impersonal police observation, Checker's desperation and fear were plain. Trapped in custody, with no way to keep looking for Arthur, no means of getting news—I was grateful Elisa had descended on him; I'd started to get a sense he might have been on the verge of saying something stupid in the hopes of getting officially arraigned and released on bail before it was too late for him to help Arthur.

I had to stop reading a few times and switch to something else.

But attacking Teplova's research again was almost as depressing. Now that I didn't only want to follow her methods, but figure out how to reverse them, her science proved far more daunting. The files didn't seem to have any templates or records of the individual surgeries she'd done, making a simple inversion out of the question.

I remembered again how Coach had tried to disfigure his face himself, and shivered. If changes like that were statistically insignificant against the weight of Teplova's alterations . . . what if it wasn't reversible?

I pulled up footage of Willow Grace to try to find a frame of reference for her surgeries, but the oldest I found still had her current face. I kept the volume muted and watched her newscasting for a few minutes anyway. She was good—her bearing was so confident, I wanted to believe what she was saying without even hearing the words.

She was also slightly different. The bones below the flawless skin of the woman I'd met sloped just inside the lines of the one on the news report—she must've had some additional work done since. She was also shorter in reality, but I figured that was probably heels, not bone deletion. I tried to at least figure out where the most recent modifications might fit into Teplova's algorithms, but could figure out no statistical justification for them.

Frustrated, I flipped to reading the police report on the interview with Arthur. At least that read more clinically than Checker's interrogation, but I was also sure he hadn't told the police close to everything. I'd have to re-interview him myself.

I got the chance when Arthur stirred toward the end of my shift. His eyes cracked open. "Russell?"

"Yeah," I said.

"Hey."

I didn't answer. I was glad he was all right, but not in any mood to simper.

"Water?" he whispered.

I found the water bottle next to his bed and stuck it within reach.

"Thank you," he said, after managing a few sips.

"No problem."

"Not talking about the water."

"Well, don't thank me for the rescue either. They let you go."

"Pilar, she said something . . ." He shifted and grimaced in pain. "Catch me up?"

"You catch me up first." I didn't want him falling asleep again before I got some intel. "This isn't over. Give me whatever you remember."

"Yeah. Okay." The words were weak, but he didn't seem as out of it anymore. "Did it for the cops, I think it helped. Don't remember much about when . . . I guess it was Friday. Got bashed in the head. Don't think I saw who, though."

"We think we know who." Small favors D.J. had taken a break from the explosives obsession. "I'm glad he opted for blunt force trauma for once in his life."

"We sure it was D.J.?" It looked like Arthur's features tried to tighten into a frown, but then he found it too painful. "Couldn't see, they had me blind through all of it, but the cat who had me the whole time—thought it was a woman."

He'd said as much in the police interview, but I'd sort of assumed he was just trying to get the heat off Checker. "D.J.'s got a pretty high voice," I said, digging back in my memory. "You ever meet him in person?"

"No. And I was tracking his sig on the bombs. Right, makes sense."

"It's not just him, though. He's got some seriously supercharged people under his thumb." I gave him a brief paraphrase of what Teplova's surgical magic was capable of, leaving out the more personal connections to me. For now. I could tell him when he could stay awake for more than twenty seconds.

"Shit," Arthur said, his face going slack.

"And he hasn't been shy about the explosives either," I continued. "He broke out the bombs on your office after kidnapping you, by the way. And on mine."

"Oh, Lord. Russell, I'm sorry—I'm so sorry—" He covered his face with both hands.

"Not your fault." I was much more pissed at him for other things.

"Yes. 'S my fault. I'm sorry, so sorry, they kept—kept pushing me to say who I'd been working with, who else might know. I swore it was only me, said I was alone in it, the truth, but they—they were going to dig, go after—I knew they'd find your name on my voice-mail message anyway. I got this mad crazy hope . . ."

He'd given me away knowing D.J. and his cohorts would come after me. First, because he'd known I'd be easy to find anyway, but second, because he'd clung to the possibility that out of everyone, I would beat them, I would survive, I would outsmart them and turn around and come track him down.

Arthur had used me to protect Checker and Pilar, the people who actually worked with him. He'd used me to protect his family, for just that little bit longer.

"I'm sorry, Russell. I'm so sorry . . ." He was weeping now, into his hands.

Instead of adding to my resentment, the revelation made something inside me fold open like an unraveling flower. Arthur did trust me. In some ways.

In at least one way.

"I did get out," I said. "You were right." It had been mostly luck, but I decided not to add that. Or to reveal Tabitha had almost been blown up along with me. "It was a good call."

"Shouldn't've said—shouldn't've said anything—"

"And who's the person with the most clear-cut employee connection to you? Pilar, right? If D.J. was going after people who'd worked with you, she would've been the first one he found. Send bad guys to me instead of Pilar any day."

He didn't answer. I wasn't sure he heard me.

I sighed. "Keep going. I want to know how D.J. got control of the doctor. How did you find her?"

"The doctor . . ."

"Teplova. You had her business card, and you asked Sonya about a mathematical formula for beauty. You're the one who led us to her."

"Oh," he said. "Didn't think that was going to pan out, to be honest. Potential client of hers was going to meet her about six months ago . . . bridge went out, he had to turn around, clinic closed before he could ever reschedule. Official conclusion on the bridge was accidental construction explosion . . . but the case didn't close for a while because preliminaries had a bunch of signature matches to D.J.'s devices. Thought it was worth a look." He coughed weakly. "This sounded weird enough for a check, but there'd been so many false leads . . . hadn't found much yet . . ."

So he'd only been at the beginning of chasing down that thread. We knew more than he did at this point about Teplova—and about what D.J. had been doing with her research.

Damn.

"Okay, go back to what happened when they had you. D.J. threatened you, threatened the people you worked with, tried to find out who else might know what you'd been investigating—what else?"

"The person who—D.J., I guess," Arthur said. "He rambled a lot. I think there's some plan. To . . . bomb a lot of places. All at the same time."

Holy shit. That definitely hadn't been in the police interview. "What? Why? Is someone paying him?"

He started coughing again, a longer fit this time. I handed him the water, but it still took some time for it to calm down. I wondered if I should worry about straining him.

But hell, he was a grown adult. He could say if he got too tired. And more bombings? Shit, he should have led with that.

"No, I don't think it's someone else's dime. Think it's more . . . personal in some way. He wasn't being real coherent, but he sounded angry. Like this was about fixing something. Don't know what."

"Keep thinking, maybe more will come back to you," I said. "In the meantime, what kinds of places are we talking? There's no way to stop random terrorism, but high-profile targets will have security—"

"Yeah. I hope so. It was—now I'm thinking about it, the ranting was mostly about US-based stuff, I think. Not real specific, but I remember some things about the Hill and Washington. Big ticket places, some sort of higher cause . . . dunno, maybe it was just talk."

That frankly surprised me. And didn't match the impression I'd had of D.J., but then, it wasn't like I knew the guy. And if he'd been talking explosions, it couldn't be anyone else.

"Should tell the cops, right?" Arthur murmured. "Wasn't sure . . . but now that Checker's out . . ."

"Don't even think about telling the cops this," I said. "You do that, they're hauling us all in for questioning, and nobody's getting out this time."

"Someone's gotta stop him, Russell."

"Then we'll do it." We were on the case anyway. We could add preventing a few high-profile assassinations to protecting Checker and the kids and tracking down D.J. and saving Coach and . . . fuck me.

"Might only be so much we can do," objected Arthur. "Russell . . . might be this is best to pass on to the law."

"We're not going to hang our own out to dry just to take a bullet for some politicians," I said. "That's not happening."

"But if we can't find him—could be we won't have a choice, you know? I was on his tail for so many months, and nada. We can give it a day or so and see if we've got some progress, but after that . . ."

Arthur and his fucking *conscience*. And today, in particular, after all the secrets, after his kidnapping, after everything, the constant moral harping crawled under my skin like parasitic worms, chewing me from the inside out. Tell the cops? They'd re-arrest Checker in the first heartbeat, and probably Tabitha, and *definitely* me—good luck to them there. Then they'd put a bullet in Coach and odds-on end up chasing their tails trying to find D.J. until he set off whatever whole anarchist movement he was gunning for anyway.

That was what you got for calling police. I didn't know why I'd ever listened to Arthur.

"You wanna tell the cops, I'm disappearing," I said harshly. I clenched my teeth together, swallowing back bitterness. "You want to know who's been keeping your whole damn family safe? Me and Rio. If you want to actually find out what's going on here, let us handle it."

His face was still creased, and I expected him to balk again. But after a moment of thought, he nodded. "Take a day; we can revisit tomorrow if you're not finding anything."

We weren't going to revisit shit, but by a couple of days from now, I was determined to have D.J.'s head on a pike anyway. "What else did you overhear?"

"Dunno. It's all scattered—think maybe it was nothing I was meant to be able to catch, or there's no way she'd—he—no way he'd have let me live, right? He kept me pretty loopy after trying to get me to say what I knew about him, who else I'd told, all that sort."

He was starting to ramble.

"All right. Tell me about where you were being held."

"Don't think it's the place you found me. Real quiet. No traffic sounds, wooden floors, smelled like bleach. They had me under when they brought me both in and out, though. And just the one person almost the whole time, D.J., I guess it was. Thought I heard other footsteps a few times, but no voices. Except there was an Aussie guy in at one point, real brief."

We knew who that was anyway, didn't we? We did. We definitely did. I'd check my notes.

"I have to go call Rio," I said. "He needs to be updated on all this. I'll be right back."

"Wait. Russell."

I stopped in the process of shutting the laptop. "Yeah?"

"You seem . . . I dunno. We okay?"

I'd thought he'd be too out of it to notice.

I debated just brushing him off—we had more important things to worry about—but . . . I was so *angry* with him. I'd been holding on to it this whole time, white-knuckling my resentment and fury to shove it under everything that had needed to be done to get him back.

"You've probably figured out I met your kids," I said slowly.

"Oh."

"Yes, *oh*. And Diego."

His face went carefully neutral. "He's a good man."

Star-crossed lovers, *Jesus*. "Yeah, I gathered. You want to tell me more?"

He pressed his lips together. "Can't say I do."

"Were you ever going to tell me about them?"

He was so long responding that I thought he was going to wuss out and pretend to have fallen asleep. But he finally said, very softly, "No."

Something inside me went heavy and leaden.

"Russell, you gotta understand," he whispered. "It's my family. The life you—your life, the people you associate with—you're a dangerous person to know. If you met my kids, got to know them . . . doesn't matter how much I like working with you. No matter what it costs, I got to keep my kids out of harm's way."

I hadn't expected him to try to defend it. I'd expected . . . I didn't know.

"Sure. Makes perfect sense," I said, the syllables like knives. "'Cause you live such a safe and risk-free existence."

"Don't think it doesn't keep me up nights, wondering if some scum criminal will come after my family one day in revenge. But I got to do the good I can. And my life doesn't hold a candle to yours, sweetheart. Ninety percent of my cases are normal folk running into a string of bad luck, not mob bosses or arms dealers or other . . . questionable folk. Not to mention, I got a license and a social security card and a California driver's license—"

"Is that what this is about? Just because I choose not to have the government spying on my every move—"

"No, that's not even the point!" He was still rasping, but his voice was gaining strength. "All I'm saying is, you choose to live a dangerous life. And I'm going to do everything in my power to have as wide a moat between that kind of danger and my own flesh and blood as I possibly can. That's it."

"Flesh and blood? I thought all your kids were adopted," I said snidely.

"You are way out of line," Arthur said, so quietly I almost couldn't hear him. "Get out."

It was coming up on Roy's turn to play nursemaid anyway. I took my computer and left.

twenty-five

I GOT Roy from upstairs, then looked at the time, said screw it, and woke up Checker and Pilar.

"'S morning?" Pilar mumbled sleepily.

"No," I said. "Not even close."

I prodded them into the kitchen and then got Rio on speaker-phone.

"We have a problem," I announced to them.

"Which one?" Checker asked through a yawn.

"A new one." I relayed to them everything Arthur had said about possible political bombings. "We're too connected to this. If we don't figure it out before the cops do, we're the first ones they're going to drop the hammer on. Not to mention that Arthur's already lied to them."

I didn't mention Arthur's oh-so-sanctimonious deadline. But that wasn't far from my mind either.

"Fuck," Checker said with feeling, and scrubbed his hands over his face. "This makes a scary amount of sense. D.J. was always . . . you know the type, 'it's all too corrupt, we've got to burn it down to fix it.'"

"That's a pretty popular attitude with a lot of people these days," Pilar said unhappily.

"I wouldn't have thought even he would . . . but the way he's been *building* people now, that all fits in too," Checker said. "If he's that angry, he must think he can make his own country out of the ashes or something. Complete with all these altered people who can keep him in control . . ."

"This supports my suspicions that a more complicated manipulation is present here," Rio put in. "Regardless of whether this explosives expert you have been tracking is responsible for most of it."

No. I didn't want to believe that. This was bad enough if it was only headed by D.J. on a power kick, using the doctor's Halberd-granted skills for his own ends. Creating an army out of either willing allies or coerced victims, a custom-designed arsenal of undeniable people . . .

"You still think Pithica might be involved," I said slowly to Rio. "You think Dawna's somewhere in this pulling all these puppet strings."

"I believe we must proceed with caution. I have been following up multiple avenues to support or repudiate their involvement. Simon has a severe concussion and is suffering short-term memory loss, but we are also attempting to construct a more whole picture of who Oscar was and whom he might have been connected to."

I stopped myself from saying *who?* just in time not to feel ridiculous. Oscar. Who was missing, but before that he had talked to Simon for a long time.

"If this is them, what do they want?" Pilar asked nervously. "And why would they have taken Arthur and then let him go?"

"So they can still claim they're holding up their end of their little détente with us?" I guessed. "Or maybe they wanted to feed him false intel and have us believe it. Or maybe they wanted us to stop looking for him. Or they might be *planning* on us realizing they let him go and predicting what we'll do next now—with them it's Russian nesting dolls all the way down."

"Cas," Rio said. "Be careful whom you involve in further investigation. You know Pithica's methods."

"Right." Fortunately, most everyone had been in the same vicinity with me since we'd gotten Arthur back, which meant they probably weren't compromised by telepathic brainwashing. Unless Pithica had been playing an even longer game than we thought . . .

This was why I *fucking hated psychics.*

"What *is* our next move?" Checker asked. "I can work the Oscar angle too, from a distance. What else?"

"There has been an incident at the police station we threatened last night," Rio said. "Cas, I believe it to be connected to the man you used to know."

Oh, God.

Hey, I think you broke a world record, said the Coach in my memory, laughing. *Too bad we can never tell anyone.*

I pushed my head against my hands.

"Cas?" Checker said.

He had every right to be angry with me. I'd yelled at him and Arthur from the mount of my self-righteousness for not telling me anything, and then I had done the same thing right back at them. It didn't quite hit me until that moment how much I'd been pushing off any discussion of how any of this intersected with my past, shoving it down the line from the very first time I'd suspected it at the wellness center and lied to Pilar. I'd told myself I was sharing the necessary bits, but other than Rio, I'd only let go the barest minimum. Halberd. An objective history for a talented doctor. Nothing to do with me.

Even though it had everything to do with me.

But Checker didn't sound angry. He sounded worried.

"What happened?" I asked Rio thickly.

"News stories are relaying it as a massacre, although I think that term is incorrect. More like a notably tightly grouped serial killing."

Checker pulled a laptop toward him and hit a few keys. "Oh, geez," he said, going pale. "This has to do with us?"

"What is it?" Pilar asked. Checker pushed the screen so that she and I could both see.

The images seared themselves into my retinas. Body after body. Mangled against the pavement, limbs too acute, skulls flattened beyond the volume necessary to hold a human brain.

Most of them in well-creased navy-blue uniforms.

"Officer Massacre," read the headlines. "Twelve Police Killed in the Streets Surrounding Valley Bureau Station After Bomb Threat Prompts Evacuation."

Just like the driver in the street. After he'd promised to *help* me.

Coach had seen me setting that bomb. Somewhere in his mind, he thought I wanted them all dead.

So he'd killed them.

Because of me.

This was why the cops at the other station had been so spooked. A monster in the shadows targeting them, picking them off one by one all morning while I'd been in with Simon. I remembered how strenuously I'd double-checked everything when I'd set the damn bomb, making extra sure no one would be hurt by it.

Twelve people. Dead.

What if he didn't stop there? What the hell was he going to do next?

"Cas," Checker said. He touched my arm. "You know who did this?"

"He was my friend," I said to the tabletop. "D.J. made him like the dogs. And now he . . ." I couldn't finish.

"He was . . . your friend?" Pilar repeated hesitantly.

"Not really mine, I guess. From before. But I remember . . ." I cleared my throat. "I don't remember a lot. But enough. I remember that he was important. To me."

"The current hypothesis is that he was likewise a friend of the doctor calling herself Eva Teplova," Rio said blandly. "And as such, a victim of experimentation once she was subjugated. It may not have taken long after that for people's reactions to him to drive him into such an altered state. Cas, I reiterate my opinion that it may not be possible to rescue him, and unraveling more of your connection to him would compromise you in any case. A better approach would be to see if he can lead you to his master."

I tried to answer, to say something about how of course that was all logical, or maybe argue that I still wanted to try for some miracle cure. Or to shout at Rio, because murdering twelve unoffending people in cold blood might just be an average Sunday for him, but it was about six bridges too far for me, and I didn't want to be reminded that I accepted him doing it either, and was there so little moral span between me and an act like this that Rio expected me not to react to it?

"We can try to track this dude down," Checker said to the phone. "We'll be in touch." He reached over and hung it up. Then took one of my hands and grasped it. "Hey. Cas. We're here for you, all right? Tell us what you want us to do."

Only hours ago, I'd railed at Checker in the car for wanting to be sympathetic to his own old friend. And now here he was, taking my hand and offering his help.

I wanted to save Coach. I also wanted to put a bullet in D.J.'s head while I did it.

Maybe that made me every kind of hypocrite.

"I don't know if he's even affiliated with D.J. anymore," I murmured. "Or if he just went off on his own." To try to please *me*.

"We still might get something by looking," Pilar said. "If D.J. made him . . ." She gulped. "That's as bad as setting a bomb in a place already. Like, making someone who sparks that kind of fear everywhere he goes, and now killing—it's like it's made to terrify folks."

"Oh, God." Checker's head dropped, and he murmured the words to the table. "It's a perfect, classic means of political repression. Fear-mongering 101. The first step to oppressing people is to make them scared—then you don't even have to take over. They invite you in."

It fit. It all fit.

If that was the case . . . maybe D.J. hadn't even intended to be able to control Coach. Just counted on him to twist people to panic, and if he eventually became the monster he'd been cast as, then that was an anarchic bonus.

I pushed up from my chair and grabbed back my phone. "I need to use the bathroom."

They let me go. I slipped around the corner and out into the hall only to run straight into a pajama-clad Tabitha.

"Jesus! Don't do that to me." I shoved my Colt back into my belt from where I'd drawn it halfway out, my nerves ping-ponging back from adrenaline.

Tabitha straightened from where she'd clearly been eavesdropping, looking slightly abashed. "Sorry."

"You heard all that, huh?" I said.

"Yeah. But it's okay. I'm not scared."

"You should be," I said.

I made to move past her, but she kept staring at me, and hopped a little from one foot to the other.

"Can I help you with something?" I asked.

"You are really cool," she blurted.

Of anything I would have expected her to say, that ranked about dead fucking last. "I'm *what?*"

Tabitha hunched her shoulders. "I really admire you. You're so—fearless. I want to be like that."

God help me, she thought I was a role model.

"Kid, I don't think your dad would be—" I tried.

"Papá is too overprotective! He thinks I'm going to—"

"I was talking about Arthur."

"Oh." She thought on that long enough for me to start down the hallway, but then came and dogged my heels. "Dad does tell me all the time how dangerous his work is. Like, so many times. But I don't care. I think I might want to be a private investigator too. And he does say I have good instincts about people."

If she thought I was *cool,* I heartily disagreed with that assessment.

"Bully for you," I said.

She ran around to my other side so she could face me. "For example. Willow Grace. Something's not right about her."

I'd left the kitchen desperate for a minute alone, and I'd been half a second from snapping at Tabitha hard enough to make her run back to the safety of her true crime books. But that statement gave me pause. She'd said it with defiance, like she was expecting to have to defend it.

"We wouldn't have found your dad without her, you know," I said.

"I know! I can't explain it. I keep feeling like I should trust her, but then my gut tells me not to."

"Oh, your *gut.*" Tabitha's face fell, enough that I regretted the sarcasm despite myself. Christ, I was not in the right state of mind to be coddling a child right now. "Look, kid," I amended. "You can't rely on gut feeling, okay? You need evidence."

"Dad says we should always listen to our gut," Tabitha said. "He says it's our subconscious telling us things."

"It is. It's our subconscious telling us probabilities based on our priors. That's all. You met Willow when she was aggressively lying to us, so of course your priors make your subconscious distrust her." The reporter had proven herself since then, though. Of everything I was worried about at the moment, Willow Grace didn't even make the list.

"I think it's more than that." Tabitha bridled up like she was about to launch into an argument, but she took in my expression and faltered. "You said I need evidence. If I get some, will you look at it?"

"Sure. Fine," I said. "Now go away."

I needed to get back on a computer myself and look for evidence— real, solid, relevant evidence that would lead us leapfrogging forward and solve every question mark. Instead, I passed the door to the washroom and sank down against the wall in the foyer.

You'll never make it, Valarmathi assured me cheerfully. *I didn't.*

What would we be able to find now that we hadn't when we were so full-throatedly tearing after Arthur? Even with all of Teplova's files, we'd been hitting dead ends until the lucky break that now seemed no more than a devious setup by someone who could predict our moves too well. That certainly fit Rio's Pithica hypothesis. Checker might be able to track down Coach now that he knew what to look for, but even if he did . . .

The thought of finding more bodies made me want to throw up. Left for me on the street like proud gifts, the way a cat might trot home with the corpse of a small animal as if such a trophy would impress its human keepers. Coach was killing people, thinking it would get me to help him, and even if we found him, I didn't know how I could get him to stop. Let alone how to communicate that I wanted so badly to be on his side . . . because the instant I saw him, I'd fly into the same confused panic as everyone else he met.

I'd probably try to kill him. I didn't think it unlikely he'd try to kill me back this time.

There had to be some creative answer. I indulged myself for a moment in wondering if we could pull off some feat of capture that meant we weren't drawn into his sphere of blackout terror. Or using Simon somehow, once he was better.

If we didn't have less than zero time to track down D.J. and protect ourselves. If every hour that passed didn't mean Coach was out there stalking and mangling another human being. If we had all the luxury and resources to plan how to reach a too-charitable hand after one man.

Rio would have said something about numerical good. I'd already rejected that in trying to move earth and sky to get back Arthur.

Hands—reaching for me, through the cracks in my brain, Valarmathi and Coach and a thousand others, each grasping for too many pieces of me . . .

My breathing stuttered. I just had to hold out a little longer. People were depending on me.

"Hey, Cas."

Checker had come out of the kitchen. He came over and pushed out of his chair, swinging down to scoot against the wall next to me.

We sat together for a minute.

Tiny veins of rawness and insecurity whispered to ask how Checker really felt about me, if, after all this was over, he'd step back. Realize that he no longer had to sit in sympathy with someone like me. Shut me out to protect himself.

I wanted to make them all safe. But once this was over, once this case had resolved after shattering every boundary they'd erected to keep me at such a careful distance . . . We couldn't come back from that. Nothing could go back to how it was, and I didn't know what decisions they'd all make after we were out of danger, what lines they'd draw when they had space to think about it.

I wanted to make them all safe, and once I did, I might lose them all.

"Is it better if Pilar and I do the legwork on this?" Checker asked quietly. "There's still plenty of Teplova's data we could put you on."

"That's all dead ends." And I didn't want to be cut out of the search for Coach. "It might help if I can remember more. About him or Teplova. I haven't really—I haven't pushed it yet."

"Will that . . . hurt you?"

I shrugged harshly and meant yes. The smallest beginnings of it had made me start to wobble into an unstable orbit; I knew what more would do.

But some childish piece of me still wanted to prove something by trying. If I couldn't control whether I still had friends at the end of this, the least I could do was justify to myself that I hadn't walked away. Part of it was pettiness, a vindication that I was willing to put my life in front of theirs beyond logical reason . . . even as an ugly truthfulness knew that sort of extremum couldn't make up for failing a friendship in every other way.

But another part of it was desperation. Because if I couldn't at least do *this,* protecting Arthur and Diego and their family, and Checker and Pilar, and rescuing *one* man who used to mean something to me . . . what did that say about me?

"Do you think—I don't know if you'd be comfortable with this, but do you think maybe Simon could help you pull things out safely?"

"Can't," I said. "He's still leaking his brain all over the place . . ."

I stopped.

Simon was leaking his brain all over the place.

It wasn't Rio we needed over there after all. How had I not thought of this? I stiffened and yanked out my phone.

"Cas, what is it?" Checker tried, but I held up a finger to him, punching the numbers to dial.

"Do you have something new?" Rio asked by way of greeting.

The impulsive anticipation made my thoughts scatter. I should have rehearsed what I was going to say. Especially as I'd never been good at lying to Rio.

"N—maybe. Actually, change of plans," I invented rapidly. If Rio cottoned on to what I was thinking, he'd never let me do it in a million years. "I need you to come back to the house. Nobody's in danger, but we've got a . . . situation you could help with. I think it might lead somewhere."

He was instantly on alert. "What did you find?"

"It's a little hard to explain," I hedged. "When can you get here?"

"Cas," Rio said slowly. "Did you by any chance look over the Lazarus data?"

Oh. Shit.

It was a code question. My lying was making me sound so uncharacteristic that he was trying to figure out if I was suddenly calling under duress.

I toyed with giving the affirmative response as a cover, since that would easily explain everything. But that also might mean Rio would crash into the house guns blazing, and that was probably more dangerous than I should trifle with.

"No," I said. "I'm fine. Everyone's fine. I'm just—" I thought of a good excuse, and kind of hated myself for using it. "My brain's not doing great, and things are stressful. I'd talk to . . . well, you know who, except I can't right now. I'm sorta barely hanging on—it's going to be better if you take over follow-up here. Unless you really think you're close to getting something out of Simon."

"I see," said Rio. "In that case, I shall be with you shortly."

Apparently explaining my bad lies with something I would be stressed enough to lie badly about was enough, then.

Are you sure it was all a lie? Valarmathi asked sweetly, from where she lolled in the back of my head.

Shut up, I told her, and she laughed.

Rio was still on the line—I could hear his voice, slightly muffled, talking to Simon. I confirmed with him that he'd be leaving Simon there—he was still too much of a danger to other people, after all— and we hung up.

I hoped he wouldn't be too pissed at me when he figured out what I was actually up to.

"Cas?" Checker caught my arm. "What you just said to Rio—are you really—is everything okay?"

"Everything's great!" A new and almost reckless energy was

flooding into me. I knew exactly what I could do to break through and get us just what we needed. "Simon was talking to Oscar forever, right? He probably picked up some things he's not telling us because he judged it 'immoral' that he knows them. Well, that's not good enough anymore. For once in his life, I'm going to make him use his telepathy for us."

It was fantastically amusing watching Checker's face as it dawned on him what I was about to try.

Rio would be at Diego's house soon to protect the rest of them. And I'd be on the trail of D.J. and whoever else was behind all this, Halberd or Pithica or whatever shadowy villains wanted to use them to blow the whole country up so they could build their own better version on top of it. All it would take was turning the tables on one morally dubious mind-leaking psychic.

If Checker called any objections after me, I didn't hear them.

My face bent into a feral grin as I slipped out onto the midnight streets and then tore away from the Rosales house. We could get the information to break through this stalemate and rout all our enemies. I would see it happen. And if we could take D.J. down with a one-two punch, then maybe, just maybe, I could take a breath and find a way to get through to Coach.

Of course, Rio and Simon would most emphatically not be on board with this plan. But it served Simon right for everything he had done to me that morning, because I was going to do the same fucking thing back to him. And as for Rio . . .

Well. Faking remorse was a lot easier than asking permission.

twenty-six

WHEN I busted into the apartment, Simon lurched up from the bed. I caught a wash of panic that sent me scrambling for the door before he saw it was me.

"Cassandra—Cas! I'm sorry—"

His emotions whipped me around so fast, I reeled. I no longer wanted to run; I wanted to stay and sit with him, comfort him until he felt better . . .

I beat at the urge with an effort.

"Cas, I'm still not—you have to go. Why are you *here*?"

No point in hiding, not when Simon had no control anyway. I thought about it loud and clear.

"What? No!" he cried, and tried to bolt.

Before he could realize what I was doing and think at me to stop it, I slammed the door and kicked the key out underneath it. This door locked from both sides—I'd still be able to break out, but it would take more effort. Hopefully enough that Simon's leaking brain wouldn't *force* me to do it.

"I'm trying not to *force* you to do anything!" He sounded panicked. But at least I didn't have a strong urge to break the door down. Yet.

He did try for the window. I did my best to get in front of him, but he didn't want me to, and I started doubting it really was a good idea to try to push him into answering my questions about Oscar anyway. I sat down hard on the bed while he tried and failed to get the window to open.

"We're six stories up in this place, anyway," I pointed out. "Are you really going to commit suicide to avoid me?"

No, he wasn't.

"Hey, this is super convenient," I said.

"Cas, please. Don't." His eyes darted around like a cornered animal's. Guilt and sympathy washed through me. How could I be so cruel as to force him to do the one thing he tried so hard to avoid?

How could I do the same thing *to* him that I despised his ability to do to others?

"I'm not reading your mind." Even as I said it, Simon's certainty on the matter convinced me I was wrong. This *was* the same thing as mind reading, involuntarily, forcefully. And I would be committing this crime against him, the same crime I would have wrung his neck for deliberately doing to me.

"You did do it to me," I said. "Oh, wait, you didn't just read my mind. You fucking erased it."

He buried his face in his hands, and his grief flooded me with such force, I stopped breathing.

I saw through his eyes. Saw myself. Was overwhelmed by the magnitude of the connection he felt . . . for me. Or her. Valarmathi.

Saw him reaching for her, his vision blurring with tears, her frantic begging tearing apart his soul until he had nothing left.

It had killed him to save her. He almost couldn't bear it, still, every time he remembered, every time he saw me. But the one thing he truly could not have borne was burying her.

"We've been through this," I gritted out. "You're incredibly self-involved with regard to erasing me, I *get* it." I found the kernel of my anger. It helped me struggle back against him.

He turned to the wall, pressed against it as if he could disappear through it. "I can't help what I feel."

"Then maybe you should do some work on yourself, shouldn't you? Now. Let's think about Oscar."

He tried not to. But I flashed on him talking to the guy, carefully, gently, drawing out voluntary admissions in that Australian accent.

He asked where, who, how. Oscar's face betrayed images he hadn't put into words: a barn, a ranch house, more of the do—

I fell off the bed.

"Cas!" Simon rushed to me. "Cas, remember, you can move outside the fear. Talk to me, Cas."

Maybe it was all his unfiltered reassurances and worry *pushing* at me in person, but leaving the panic behind was easier this time. "You saw the dogs," I gasped. "The rest of them. He—what, he takes care of them? Feeds them?"

Jesus, how many were there? And had D.J. made more *people* like them—like Coach?

More flashes from Oscar. It jarred us both. The dogs snapped and snarled, and this time, I saw glimpses of Coach too, in the same place, a chaotic tangle of mindless fright. Simon's hand on my shoulder gripped me so hard, it went painful.

"You're affected by them too?" I said.

"I have to—like with Oscar, I have to convince myself out of it. I don't know if in person . . ."

"Well, we're going to find out," I said.

"What? No, Cas, that's not a—you shouldn't—I won't—"

He was right. It wasn't a good plan. I struggled against the certainty, but fortunately, I could set the battle aside for a moment while I concentrated on asking more about Oscar. Simon didn't want me to, which made it terribly hard even to order my thoughts enough to ask anything else, but since *he* was thinking about not wanting *me* to ask, he was necessarily thinking about Oscar anyway, no matter how hard he tried not to.

"Ha," I gasped. "Again, convenient!"

I was immediately ashamed for mocking him. The poor guy had a head injury, and I was using it to *read his mind*.

But as much as Simon's imposed guilt made me slump in mortification, the thoughts he was trying *not* to have about what he'd accidentally gleaned from Oscar washed through my consciousness as well. The ranch. How long it took the man to slog there from Los

Angeles. The stars wheeling above. The line of mountains on the horizon.

How it felt, going there—everything was always wrong these days, but here was worse, here was always such a fog, high, high as a kite, the drugs, the drugs she said would let him be near, and they did. The dogs wouldn't attack him anyway; they didn't see him; nobody saw him; nobody saw nobody saw nobody saw alone alone alone—

"*Ow!*" I cried, grabbing at my head.

Simon had smashed his own into the wall.

He staggered, blind with the pain. All thoughts of Oscar had fled.

I hadn't seen D.J. or anyone else. But I had enough. It had to be enough.

I pressed a groaning Simon onto the bed a lot more gently than I ordinarily would have and resisted the urge to sit ministering to him. I did check his vitals and the dressing on his bandages. As far as I could tell, he wasn't in immediate danger, and his own head injury was muddling through my consciousness so clearly, I thought I could tell how bad the concussion actually was.

Huh.

I was also keenly disappointed in myself.

Or he was. In me.

"Sorry," I said, not sure whether I meant it this time.

I did sit with him for a few minutes after that. He needed rest; his thoughts eventually started to become more disorganized as he drifted, and I managed to rouse myself to go to the computer Rio had left. I opened a chat session with Checker.

Is Rio there? I asked.

Checker's reply came back immediately: *cas!*

And one second later: *he's been trying 2 reach u*

After another second: *how did it go? r u ok?*

I made sure Rio wasn't watching over his shoulder and then explained what I'd seen. *Can you help me pinpoint this place?* I asked.

We put our brains together. I gathered Rio was not happy—at least, if Checker's *i think he might be furious at u but its rly hard to tell w him and i'm not putting my neck on that block sry* was anything to go by.

But Rio had at least done what I predicted and stayed at the Rosales house to ensure the family wouldn't go unprotected just because *I* decided to do something foolhardy.

Foolhardy and unethical.

With Checker's help, forty minutes later, we'd pinpointed the ranch in Oscar's memories. Time to reach it gave us a radius from the city, and I'd been able to estimate the distance to the mountains and also to a line of light that had indicated a highway. A blurred memory of the sky showed the angle to the North Star, so we had approximate latitude.

And once we were down to scanning satellite imagery, the three-dimensional shapes of the buildings easily converted to a two-dimensional bird's-eye in my head, and there was the ranch.

Excellent, I wrote to Checker. *We found where the dogs are kept. Or bred. Or . . . something.*

and whats yr plan??? u aren't going r u???

Of course I am, I typed back.

??? !!!

Checker's chat responses didn't always get the benefit of words.

Simon's going too, I said. Though he didn't know it yet. *If we run into anything mind-warping, he'll just have to talk both of us down.*

V BAD IDEA CAS

Bombers and killers coming after us and a lot of other people, I reminded him. *Plus possibly psychics behind it all. Do you have a better plan? If not, bye.*

And I shut the laptop. A text popped up on my phone, but it was only more punctuation marks.

But this was good. This was perfect. This was a risk I could take, a good risk, the *right* risk. One I could win. And be the person who shielded everyone else.

Simon groaned.

"Wakey wakey," I said. "How's the head? Are you still out of control? Because if so, I'll wait. We're going on a field trip."

Usually Simon's unintentional telepathy didn't come with words attached, but this time I caught the virulent *Fuck you, Cas.*

That was uncharacteristic of him. He must be very, very mad at me.

twenty-seven

HAVING SOME backup who wasn't Simon along might have been nice, especially given his head wound. But I was sure Rio was still pissed, plus I needed him where he was.

I thought about calling Pilar. But a twinge of risk assessment reminded me how many probabilities here were still question marks. Checker wasn't out of line in objecting—this was dangerous, and impulsive, and I didn't know what we'd find. But dangerous and impulsive were where I lived. And Pilar could be one of the people I did it to protect.

That was the way things should be.

Besides, bringing Pilar might have strained Simon's focus too far. I was already a bit worried about that with only two of us. Simon had tried to refuse to go at first—but after a little more rest, he'd wrestled back enough of his control that his refusal didn't have any more weight than making me second-guess myself. I pushed it away and told him that if he wasn't coming, I'd be going in alone. As whacked as it was that he felt so strongly about not seeing me hurt—*I'm not her, I'm not her, I'm not* fucking *her*—the leverage was certainly handy.

"Screw you, Cas," Simon said unhappily, aloud this time.

But he agreed—unwillingly, unenthusiastically, warily, but he came—and we managed to head off in the wee hours of the morning. The perfect time for breaking and entering. I drove, again having appropriated Pilar's car, and Simon hunched in the passenger seat.

It was a clear night, and the stars imprinted on me through the windshield like they had in Oscar's memories, leaving the taste of his mind in my mouth.

"That's what you get for taking someone's thoughts by force," muttered Simon.

He was one to talk. "I think it's great that when you *don't* read people, you still happen to know so much about them."

"I try to respect people's secrets."

I snorted. "Oh, hey, I bet you knew too, didn't you?"

"Knew what?"

"Don't give me that."

Simon cleared his throat. "I didn't—he didn't—Arthur never told me. I've never met his family. But I couldn't not know, it's too important to him. I could see it every time he—"

"Thought so." It was almost funny. Checker knew, Pilar knew, Rio knew, *Simon* knew—the only person Arthur had prevented from knowing about his family by not telling me was me.

At least I knew where I stood. It was sort of freeing.

Simon heaved a sigh. "What are you planning to do when we get there?"

"Look for clues." I wasn't sure whether to expect that we'd actually run into Oscar or Coach—or D.J.—at the ranch. I'd had the sense in Oscar's memories that he was going to the place only to take care of the animals. I'd felt his desolation.

His loneliness.

I shivered. As angry and uncomfortable as my current friendships were, going through life with nobody ever knowing I existed . . .

"Cas," said Simon. "I don't like what you did to me just now."

"Here are some tats to go with those tits. Do you even know how many hours you kept me in your *thrall* yesterday morning?"

He sucked in a breath. "You know I didn't mean to. Maybe I could have done better, but . . . God, Cas, you meant to do this. You—you planned it. It was violent and it was wrong and you did it on purpose."

His voice was shaking, low and intense, and it only renewed my disgust for him. After how he had contorted and violated my entire life—the *gall* of it. "Say those words back to yourself."

"What I did to you years ago was awful. Maybe unforgiveable. I'm not denying it. But does that mean—"

"Yes," I said.

He stared out the window.

"Are you going to quote some fun little aphorism here?" I said. "Something like two wrongs not making a right, or an eye for an eye making the whole world blind?"

"No," he said. "You weren't doing it for revenge. It might have been better if you were."

I had a chilling premonition of how he was going to finish.

"If you had been trying to get back at me, that would be one thing, but . . . you were doing it because you had an opportunity, and because . . . because I'm not a human being to you. Don't try to deny it," he added hollowly. "I could see it."

I swallowed. Checker's words from the car came back to me, about only being able to take clever advantage of people when one didn't think of them as fully, equally human.

"Maybe you handed in that card when you killed me," I said.

"Maybe." He dipped his head, interlacing his fingers in his lap. "I'm not asking you to forgive me, Cas. I wouldn't. But I don't think it means I can't tell you—this was wrong. This was really, really wrong, and I'm asking you, please—please don't do it again."

I shrugged uncomfortably. "Hey, look. We're here."

I flicked off the car headlights and nosed up outside the lane into the ranch. An old, creaking sign with illegible writing swung over the gate.

And lights were on down in the buildings. We could see them from the main road.

Simon saw it too. "Someone's here," he said. "Cas, are you sure about this?"

Someone here . . . I didn't know whether to consider that a stroke of good fortune or bad. Could it be D.J.? I hoped so; I could level him right now. Oscar? We'd take him back with Simon's help. Coach?

Having Simon with me at least gave us the best odds possible.

And if we encountered anyone from Pithica, as Rio suspected?

Well, Simon would just have to step up to that too. This was too good an opportunity to waste. Besides, one of the things I hated, *hated* about Pithica's people was the way they made me feel helpless. Like I couldn't make any move if they *might* be there to counter me . . . it made me want to boil into a hurricane of rage, show them I could be a goddamn threat. I wasn't going to become a mewling coward around them. I had Simon, and I could place my bets on him and take a chance for a win.

"Yeah," I said. "I'm sure."

I checked my weapons—my Colt and the Vector I still had from the venture to rescue Arthur. Then I backed up the car so it wouldn't be visible to anyone peeling out of the ranch, and we got out.

"If we run into any of Teplova's people, or the dogs, your job is to start talking very fast," I said. "If we run into Dawna or someone like her, you've got the lead. Otherwise, don't distract me."

"Cas, I can't guarantee I'm going to be . . . strong enough. Especially if—"

"We'll try not to face anyone directly," I conceded. "But you're the only telepath we've got, and I'm not passing on a shot like this."

I broke into a jog, and he swallowed any other doubtful protests to hurry after me.

The layout here was burned into my brain from Oscar's memories. We were coming in at an angle to the lane, and we would hit the barn and outbuildings before the ranch house itself. Right now, the buildings were only shapes in the dark, but lights shone from between the barn and the ranch house—outside halogens of some sort. A large cube truck partially blocked our view of what the activity was.

But as we got closer, shouts and barks echoed through the night.

Barking. And growling.

My skin crawled, already anticipating the rabid fear.

I held up a hand to halt Simon as we approached the first of the outbuildings, and tried to listen without getting distracted, even as the all-too-familiar feeling began tugging at me to cringe into a hole and quiver. I hoped Simon didn't see my shaky relief when I realized what was happening—although, of course he did, the bastard.

"They're loading up the animals for transport," I said. "It's unlikely to be anyone from Pithica, then. Just people drugged up enough not to be affected. That means we can take them and interrogate them." Oscar's memories had revealed how anyone handling the dogs got close—take something mind-altering enough to make yourself unable to be properly afraid, and apparently that did the trick.

Of course, it also meant whoever was down there would not be the most cooperative.

I glanced back at Simon. He gave me a rapid nod. I took a second look at his face and tried to ignore how glassy his eyes were, how shallow his breath was.

I'd bullied him into this, but he'd have told me if he wasn't up for it, wouldn't he?

"I'm okay," he said, as if he could feel my doubts. "I—I think it's a bad idea, but—I'm okay. I think."

Unless his judgment was impaired . . .

But I had to make the call. If he wasn't fighting telepathic humans, only the dogs—that would be okay, right? He could handle that.

"Here's what we'll do," I said. "Whenever they're done loading or unloading or whatever they're doing—they have to drive out of here. I'll take them down as they come up the lane. The dogs will have to be shut up at that point." They'd be locked either back in the barn or in the truck itself, if they happened to be the cargo.

Fuck, depending on how many dogs they were transporting—what were they planning with them? No, we definitely had to go in now.

Simon nodded again and wrapped his arms around himself. We waited in the dark.

We were still too far away to hear the shouts, but I thought I counted two voices. Two humans. That was fine. That was easy.

Simon had started fidgeting.

"Quit it," I whispered. "I'm trying to concentrate."

Doors slammed across the yard. They must be getting set to go. We wanted to take them alive, I reminded myself. For questioning. Even if it was D.J. himself, interrogation would be smartest. I'd give them to Rio this time and damn the consequences.

The lights changed as someone turned half of them off. A human voice hollered. The sound of chains rattling. A dog barked, apart from the rest of the clamor, echoing against its surroundings. Not all the animals were shut up yet.

The human voices raised in pitch, shouting in concern.

The dog barked louder. Threatening.

"How good are these animals at being actual guard dogs?" Simon whispered.

My hand tightened on the rifle. "What are you saying? Is it sensing us?"

"I don't know; I can't read dogs—"

But the human voices rose to a shout, and I didn't need Simon clawing at my arm to hear their raw panic. Something was going wrong, something scaring them—and I might not be able to read dogs either, but sounds pinpointed location instantly for me, the growling roar breaking free and leaping in our direction—

The noise crescendoed, breaking for our position. One of the dogs.

Charging us.

In a split second it would round into view and attack. No time to think about the consequences: I snapped my eyes shut, raised the Vector, and stepped around the corner.

The snarling burst out and magnified, the position zeroing. I pulled the trigger in one smooth motion while Simon began a rapid mantra behind me, something about fear and self-control. The rifle clapped in my hands, and the snarls that had roared toward us cut off with a thump.

Someone shouted again. The truck engine roared to life just as the cacophony of a thousand more animals clawed into the night.

No. Not a thousand animals. Seventeen. Six in the truck and eight in the barn and three who weren't anywhere yet, between the truck and the barn, and now loose, loose and leaping to attack us. Wheels skidded on gravel, and my ears couldn't keep up with the changing variables anymore—it was open my eyes or be devoured alive.

The panic took hold before the colors and shapes even registered in my vision.

I screamed my attack and starbursts went off in front of my eyes—
the rifle, I was firing the rifle, and I emptied the magazine in seconds. Someone shouted at me, but someone else was shouting up
ahead, and everything was chaos and noise and light.

Monsters. Monsters everywhere.

I shot them and kicked and snarled and brought my elbow back
into someone who tried to grab me from behind. A roar filled my
senses and something grew bright and huge in my vision, but that
wasn't the threat, the threat was in front of me, the threat was claws
and fur and teeth—

"*Cas!*" someone yelled, and tackled me. I hit the ground, and my
mouth filled with dirt and grass. A vehicle thundered by my face close
enough for the dust to spit in my eyes, and a human voice screamed.

I raked at the ground, trying to find the rifle, to reload and bring
it up again. It clicked and misfired, clogged with dirt. Still prone, I
pawed for the handgun I knew I had.

"Cas, Cas, you can do this, think—"

Shaking words, hands on my shoulder. My senses vibrated like an
earthquake had hit.

"Cas, that's it—that's—" The trembling voice cut off in another
scream. My gun came up and dispatched the monster bearing down
on us, but this time, I saw it more clearly, its outlines more animal
than demon.

Begone, witches! Begone! wailed a voice in my head, the dead woman
rearing up out of the recesses as if to devour the chaos. My brain
compressed like it was in a vise.

"Cas! Come back to me—come back here. You need to stay
with me!"

Wiiiiiiiiiiiiiitches!

"*Cas!*"

I struggled back to the night and the tearing pain in my arm and
the scents of blood and smoke. I had to do something. Had to get to
the people.

No time had passed. I was still half-lying on the hard, sandy
ground. The truck was still in range, roaring up the lane. The spiky

shape of an automatic weaved from the driver's window and went off in a wild spray as the truck lurched.

Over our heads. Over our heads.

I had much better aim than that. I raised my pistol.

I didn't see the man who leapt up in front of me, running, yelling in the wake of the truck. I literally did not see him, as if my brain had edited him out of the picture.

"Cas, no!"

A hand shoved my gun off line the instant I pulled the trigger, taking my shot far astray, into the night.

The truck lurched one more time, and the automatic sprayed again, much lower this time.

I grabbed Simon and rolled us into a hedge. I barely saw the shape of the invisible man jerk like a puppet as the automatic fire caught him, as his invisibility deleted him from the vision of his own side in the very same way it had deleted him from mine.

This is what we deserve! Valarmathi howled. *Burn us all!*

twenty-eight

SIMON WASN'T moving.

His limbs sprawled limply, both legs bent at impossible angles, blood, so much blood, and the white gleam of bone.

My hands stumbled to staunch the bleeding, to find a pulse, but the furred corpses pushed in on my consciousness from all directions. Simon had made them less than hellhounds, but Simon wasn't here anymore, couldn't tell me they were only fairy stories constructed by a malicious villain.

I groped for his thoughts, his emotions, his pain, and found nothing.

A pulse stuttered against my fingers. Barely.

The dead shapes in my peripheral vision began to rise back up as ghosts, into ominous shadows of pestilence and war. I had to get out of here.

I got my arm under Simon and hauled. One of his broken legs caught on a shrub and wobbled grotesquely. I tried to get a better hold on him, to lift him, but my foot buckled under me.

My heart ramped faster, more adrenaline leaking into my bloodstream. I tried to keep my eyes on Simon, on Simon, but murdered nightmares punched through the edges.

I stumbled and almost fell, and squeezed my eyes shut. Run, I needed to run.

No. *Fight.*

My hand tightened on the hard grip of my Colt.

My other hand was fisted in Simon's clothes. I focused on the roughness of the fabric. The heat from his body, still living, still living. *Get him out. Get out.*

Somehow, I managed to begin dragging us, unseeing, across dried grass and ridged, uneven ground. My mind extrapolated the curve beneath my feet, guiding my stumbling steps. But aberrations in the curve's assumed smoothness kept pushing up and tripping me, catching at my boots and making our progress a jagged stumble in the dark.

I didn't open my eyes until we'd gotten back to the road.

Simon's skin had gone so pale and waxen, he was an inert dummy, texture stretched over misaligned bones in an attempt at a human form.

Heartbeat, still a heartbeat. I had nothing to splint the bones with. Tore my jacket at the seams to bind the worst of the bleeding and tourniquet him. Groped for a phone, he needed a hospital—but mine was gone, dropped or lost. Simon had a burner in his pocket, but its face was cracked and dark.

I pressed his wrist again—then harder. The weak tap of a heartbeat was gone. His chest wasn't moving.

Fuck. No. I pressed my hands against his sternum, the dimensions of his ribcage building themselves for me faster than thought. The success rate of CPR was somewhere in the single digits, but that was when people who weren't me did it.

Compress, the force waves radiating downward, the impact rippling through the flesh, pressing the blood into circulation. Exactly the pressure to beat the heart by hand, pushing oxygen to his brain, pushing his body into functioning. Compress again. Again. Again. Fast and rhythmic, exactly in time, exactly consistent, a scrupulous substitute, until the flesh fluttered back against my hands, and I pressed one more time before laying my hand flat across his chest to feel.

The beats pushed back small and labored, and I'd broken two ribs, but his heart was working again.

The distant hum of an engine rose in my hearing. A vehicle. I leapt up, and my foot almost went out from under me—*fucking stupid ankle, it's a sprain, it's just a sprain.* I pushed at the ground, willing myself upright, and staggered out into the street.

The silhouette of a semi cab rose behind headlights, taller and taller, and then brakes squealed as it skidded and swerved. The rest of the truck fishhooked around in slow motion, almost going over onto its side as the cab ran off the road and up against the brush.

"What the *fuck*, get out of the road!" the driver screamed at me.

I limped up to the driver's window. "There's a man dying right there, on the side of the road. Call 911."

The man's hands had gone up, even though I wasn't pointing a weapon at him. He was a large, mustached fellow, burly and dark. "What? There's what?"

"A man. Dying," I said. "Call the fucking ambulance."

He slapped at his pockets. "I don't have a cell phone, man!"

Who the *fuck* didn't have a cell phone?

The man had started babbling. "I don't got it, man, I don't got one! I'm sorry!"

"You have a radio!" I yelled in his face. "Use it, *now*!"

He couldn't obey fast enough. Even without drawing on him, I'd scared him so badly, he fumbled with the handset before sending out the call.

I'd lost the rifle somewhere, but my Colt was still on me. I left it tucked away for now and limped back to Simon.

He was still breathing, but barely, only the slightest stirring of air. I guarded his condition until sirens wailed on the horizon and the red lights washed toward us in waves, and then I slipped back to the car. I pulled away just as they arrived, the bulk of the semi still blocking the street and hiding my departure from view.

.·.·.·.·.

I HAD to pull over to do a rudimentary job of tending to my own injuries. My right arm throbbed—laceration, tearing, puncture wounds—a dog bite. And the sprained ankle. Cuts, bruises, abrasions. On top of the deep bruising to my knee and head from—had it been only a day ago?

Nothing that wouldn't heal. Nothing I couldn't wrap tightly and function on.

I kept feeling again the spooky silence of Simon's unconsciousness. No pushing, no unintentional projections of his thoughts or emotions. Just . . . absence.

It would be bad for me if he died. As Simon himself had said, Valarmathi leaking through my brain amounted to a chronic mental condition that I didn't have another stable solution for.

Would I care, otherwise, if he died? I should. I had violated his mind and then dragged him along and he had—he had saved my life—

My memory flashed on images I hadn't understood at the time— the cube truck, roaring toward us, my whole consciousness consumed and paralyzed. Simon tackling me out of the way. The crack of bone as he screamed.

I slumped in the driver's seat. I should regret how injured he'd gotten, I thought. I should feel grateful for his help, sick that it had gotten him so hurt.

I should want him not to die. Be fighting against guilt.

If Simon died, I'd wake up the next day and start trying to track down another way of staying sane. If Simon died . . .

I did feel guilty. I felt guilty about how little compunction I felt. He might have just died *saving* me, and I still didn't . . .

Would a better person forgive him now? Would a better person mourn him as a fellow human being, even if she didn't forgive him?

Would a better person consider that no matter what he'd done, he wasn't a piece of nothing to be used and discarded as I just had?

All those messy lines that never felt visible until after I'd crossed them. And sometimes not even then.

I thought of Arthur. I'd used him as my conscience for years now, trying to live up to his standards, and it had never been as easy as making the decision—it had instead been a constant struggle, a morass of self-doubt and getting sucked backward again after every time I did manage to meet with his approval. And in the end, it hadn't merited me the least bit of real trust.

But I didn't want his approval anymore. I wanted his friendship.

And I didn't want to be him. I wanted to find my own standards—if I could figure out what those were. The fear lurked that my friends might break with me over whatever I chose . . . but better they walked away from me than I refused to go to the mat for them.

I reached the Rosales house in the muted cool of early morning, the time just after sunrise when quiet still blanketed the streets. When I opened the door, Rio was sitting in a chair he had dragged into the foyer, a rifle across his lap.

"Hello, Cas."

I shut the door and leaned against it. "We got attacked," I said baldly. "Simon's in the hospital."

"I see."

"There might still be evidence or—or something there, but I can't go back with the dogs there, even the ones I—" The ones I'd killed would still leave me mewling and rocking in blanked-out terror without Simon along. Even his presence had barely kept me lucid against that many of them. "Can you go and follow up, see if you can find anything? I'm assuming the dogs won't affect you, and I'm betting they'll be torching the place any minute to hide their tracks. Or blowing it up, what with D.J. involved."

"I'm sorry, Cas. I won't be doing that."

The air suddenly went heavy. "What's—what's going on?"

"You used Simon's injury to take his thoughts."

I swallowed.

Deciding to steal Simon's memory already seemed like such a long time ago. It had felt so clever. An ingenious cheat.

One I'd known I had to hide from Rio.

I didn't know how to answer, but Rio saw the truth anyway.

"You deceived me to accomplish this," he said. "You knew I would not agree with such methods."

I licked my lips, tried to speak. Rio—I'd seen what *he'd* done to people when trying to get information. Or even just to get his way—people shot, stabbed, carved up and flayed alive; there was a *reason* Checker and Arthur and Pilar didn't want Rio around—heck, only months ago he'd threatened Checker's life and then broken Pilar's arm, and I'd had to extract the promise from him not to go after them again, ever, them or their families, not that I'd known at the time about Arthur's, but the point was I'd had to make Rio give me that promise because it had been *necessary*. Malcolm's body splayed in front of me again, his face half gone, killed by Rio to get to me.

"I know you think any sort of—of mind control—I know you think it's unethical," I got out. "But it's not like Simon's innocent; you *know* he's not—"

"And that does not make what you did right."

I was having some trouble standing. I pressed my hand against the doorknob to keep myself upright. "But you . . . Rio, *you* . . ."

He stood. "I would not aid someone like myself in an endeavor either."

Less than an hour ago, I'd sat in the car hoping I could choose a morality my friends could live with. Never, in my entire remembered lifespan, would I have predicted *Rio* would be the one to walk out on me.

"Cas," Rio said. "I have no wish for harm to come to you, nor to your friends. But I cannot continue with nor condone your choices here. We must part ways on this."

"But you keep saying—this could be Pithica," I got out desperately. "And this could be a lead. Don't you want—"

"I shall follow my own leads," Rio said. "Ones that were obtained by other methods. If it means a longer process, so be it."

Other methods. Like torturing or massacring people. That was okay, but mind reading wasn't. The gospel according to Rio.

"Be well, Cas, and repent," Rio said to me. "I would prefer to see you again soon."

He moved toward me. I lurched out of the way so he could let himself out the front door, and he was gone.

A laugh wanted to strangle me. Rio had seen me kill *so many* people—Rio had *helped* me kill so many people. But I read the mind of one morally ambiguous psychic, and he decided my methods had turned an ethical shade he could not abide. I wanted to race after him, to tear into him as a hypocrite, but I wasn't even sure if he was one. The world had turned upside down.

I couldn't even tell if he was angry with me or just gracefully bowing out. Who knew, I might walk into my next session with Simon and find Rio waiting for me there, just like always, his presence a comforting monitor so Simon didn't do anything to me unasked.

Assuming Simon lived.

I'd lost Rio, I'd lost Simon, and we'd lost Oscar and all the evidence at the ranch. I still had a friend out there who needed me . . . or at least the shape of one. Plus, a bomber to find and possible psychics out to get us, nine people to protect, and with Arthur down, only one person with even basic capability in helping me defend them.

I briefly considered waking everyone and telling them to pack. But how securely would I need to plan to take us off the grid? It wouldn't be as simple as just giving them a cash apartment anymore, would it? Not if Rio was right about Pithica. Plus, Rio had put a healthy dose of security on this house—at this point, without Rio's help, transit might be more dangerous than staying put. What if Dawna had people watching, waiting for us to try to leave?

Or—maybe worse—what if Coach had stalked me here somehow, and was outside right now, skulking in the shadows? Usually I picked up people on my tail, but somewhere between the fatigue and mental fog, I'd failed to make him when he'd followed me the day before.

Rio had left the handheld for the security system on the foyer table. I picked it up and checked. Everything was humming along smoothly, and I was so exhausted that the thought of trying to move *nine people* en masse right now sheered into me with the impossibility of a glacier.

"Cas? Is that you?" Pilar poked her head in from Arthur's room, and her face changed as she took in my appearance. "Oh my God! What happened?"

"We failed." I gritted my teeth and forced myself to stand more upright. "Does Diego have a first aid kit?"

"He does. I can get it." She glanced down at the bandaging wrapping her own palms as she came out and shut Arthur's door quietly behind her. "I heard, um, what Rio just said. Is he—gone?"

"Yeah." I didn't want to talk about it. "Is everything okay here?"

"No problems. It's been quiet. Not everyone's awake yet; I was on Arthur duty." She paused, then started to say something twice before plunging on with it. "Just so you know—I would have gone with you. I know Arthur's out of danger now, but your other friend still needs you. I would have said yes."

A transitive property of friendship. Pilar was too kindhearted for her own good.

If I'd asked . . . would she be dead? Or would the extra gun mean we would have been able to stave off disaster?

"Was there any sign of him?" she asked softly.

"No." Unless he had been the person in the truck. I'd never gotten a clear look. "Checker and Simon both thought this was a bad idea."

Pilar squished her shoulders in something like a shrug. "So was going into the mission without Simon's help, but it meant we got Arthur back and to a hospital fast enough that he's okay. You're the sort of person who . . . when the iron's hot, you always just go and jump on it, you know? But most of the time it works, so who am I to say we'll get burned? Besides, we're all going cross-eyed waiting for the other shoe to drop. I get why you pushed it."

She was the only one, then.

"I don't think I made us safer." The confession slipped out, resonating in the early hour and Rio's absence.

She looked like she wanted to say something comforting, but she couldn't deny the truth of it. And with my failure at the ranch, what else did we have to try? The ranch gave us another real estate listing, and Checker could start hacking through the Internet jungle to try to make another opening for us . . . but aside from the file that had baited us to the mission, D.J. had thus far been a ghost.

And Rio had been the one looking into the Pithica angle. Rio and Simon.

Maybe that was still the right track. Teplova and Oscar and Coach, and a history we didn't have all the parts to yet, and how they'd intersected with the explosives expert who had so viciously warped all their lives. I might have answers too, somewhere inside me—

Mocking laughter reverberated against the insides of my skull. If I dug into my own memories, I'd take myself off the gameboard right when I was trying to stand in front of nine people who mattered to me. But if I didn't . . .

Wait. Besides Rio and Simon, there was one other person who'd dug a frightening amount into Halberd and Pithica. Who'd discovered enough of what they were to be scared, and had given air cover to one of their supernatural graduates. And who hadn't shared nearly enough of what she knew.

Some wriggling discomfort wrapped itself in Tabitha's voice— *Something's not right about her.* I told myself it was only the looming prospect of confronting my own history.

"Come on, let's get you that first aid kit," Pilar's voice cut in gently.

"Good," I said. "And then we need to get Willow Grace back in here."

"Oh." Pilar blinked at me. "Cas, she's already here."

twenty-nine

"SHE IS?" Something sat strangely with me about that, unsettling and undefined. "Did Rio call her back in?"

"No, though he wasn't happy about us letting her go home," Pilar answered. "Said something about 'insufficient vigilance' or something. But no, she contacted us. When Checker told her we were still working the case, she offered to come back and help."

Willow Grace did have her own reasons for continuing to investigate. D.J. had murdered her friend, after all. Maybe she had known Coach too . . . it would be worth asking her about . . .

I let Pilar lead me into the living room and sit me down. I registered hushed voices in the kitchen and the clink of people getting a quiet breakfast—most of the household seemed to be up despite the early hour. I supposed that made sense, considering we'd all come back exhausted in the middle of the afternoon yesterday. The only person in the living room was Juwon, who was curled up on the other couch, absorbed in a tome of a book that was bigger than his head, and was so engrossed he didn't even look up when we came in.

Pilar disappeared into the kitchen briefly. The voices picked up for a tick before she returned with a first aid kit and some towels, followed by Checker with a laptop.

"Oh, geez, Cas," Checker said, his eyes sweeping up and down my various injuries. "I take it, uh, things didn't go well."

"Oscar's dead. Simon's in the hospital." I hoped. Assuming he'd made it there. "You've kept working here?"

"Yeah. Nothing to write home about. The police didn't find any other explosives at the station, other than the bomb you set. The ranch is owned by a shell corporation, but I'm trying to track it back. And an arson report just hit the wires for that address, but I'm guessing it's less 'fire' and more 'incendiary device.'"

Exactly as predicted. Rio wouldn't have made it in time anyway, then. I tried to feel mollified by that and failed. "How about any connection to Halberd or Pithica? Where's Willow Grace?"

"She said she needed to go take a call," Checker said. "It was just a minute ago. She should be back in soon. Don't worry, I told her to stay close to the house."

I left off digging through the first aid kit to glance at the security screen. Sure enough, Willow's statuesque figure paced against the back wall of the house, her phone to her ear. Good. In a second I'd get her back in here and nail her down on everything she knew.

"We haven't, uh, really been driving hard on looking into the Pithica thing," Checker went on. "I didn't know if we wanted to . . . antagonize them. Unless we're sure. Because of the deal you've got."

Christ, I didn't know either. If they *weren't* involved and they caught wind of us preparing to move against them . . . I had no doubt Dawna was still watching. The instant they had any excuse, they'd move to crush us. And with Rio gone . . .

But Willow could give us information without tipping them off. We'd see what she had and go from there.

"I've also been researching the place you found Arthur," Checker continued, while I worked on wrapping my ankle. "As far as I can make out, neither D.J. nor Teplova has any connection to the people who own or administer it. I'd say the weird file that led us there was just a list of out-of-the-way places deserted enough for them to make use of, but the rest of it didn't fit—it's all random places like office buildings and parking garages."

"Dummy addresses," I muttered.

"Yeah. I don't know . . . Rio mentioned about how you and he thought it was, um, not on the level."

"It was too easy." I thought back. "That file just appeared. *While* we were looking."

"I figured maybe you'd done something to unlock more stuff," Pilar said to Checker. "But we couldn't ask you at the time."

"Huh?" Checker turned to her. "No, I didn't do anything."

"Wait, you're saying whoever planted it had to have done it in real time?" I said. "Not beforehand in some sort of long con?"

"No, I mean yes, it would have to be—hang on, this is really important." His fingers had started going on the laptop keys, and he spoke while engrossed in the screen. "This is a big deal. Tell me exactly what happened."

Pilar and I exchanged a glance. "We were looking at the directory," I said. "The file wasn't there, and then it was."

"You're sure?"

"Rio and I both were." The creepy feeling I'd missed something vital started to crawl over me. "How could that happen?"

"There's only one way. Someone put it there and backdated it. Someone who knew we were looking and had access."

I started to feel sick. "That's a very short list."

"Oh, crap," said Checker. "What if it's one of us? We know what Pithica can do. What if one of us did it and didn't even know?"

"Simon," I said. "We need Simon here . . ."

But he was in a hospital somewhere. Thanks to me.

"We can figure this out." I glanced over at Juwon and kept my voice low—the last thing we needed was a panicked family. "Simon probably would have been able to tell if I'd been messed with. He's seen me since then. And it can't be you, unless the cops gave you access to a computer."

"Can't be Arthur," Checker picked up the thread. "Or Rio. That leaves . . ."

"Me," Pilar said, lowering her eyes.

"Or Diego," I pointed out. "Or any of the kids except Elisa. She wasn't here either."

Six people whom we no longer knew we could trust.

"Should I . . ." Pilar started hesitantly.

Something caught at my mind. Something obvious. A number that was unequal. "We're missing someone," I cut her off. "We had nine people in the house at the time, and we've only counted eight of them."

Checker's face knotted up as he thought back through as well. "Simon wasn't here, right? And you just said Elisa wasn't. And I wasn't."

Pilar counted on her fingers. "Me, Diego, Tabitha, Juwon, Roy, and Matti. Plus you and Rio, Cas. That's eight. Right?"

I glanced around the long living/dining room as if it would spark my memory. Juwon was still across from us reading his book. I could hear the twins and Diego in the kitchen. We'd counted all of them. Who else?

Then my gaze hit the security monitor next to me, and it was as if I were seeing double.

"Willow Grace." My mouth shaped the syllables, but they were barely audible.

"Oh, right," Checker said. "Well, it wouldn't have been her . . ." He frowned.

But Willow Grace could have been influenced by a telepath like anyone else, couldn't she?

Then why was it a grinding cognitive dissonance in my head to believe she might have been? If Pilar or Diego or Tabitha had been brainwashed by a psychic, that wouldn't be their fault, I could accept that . . . hell, Pithica had told Arthur to point a gun at me before and he had.

But Willow Grace was trustworthy. We'd checked her background. We knew—

That doesn't matter when it comes to psychics! You know it doesn't matter!

"Why do we . . ." I said slowly. It was a struggle to push sound into speech.

Why do we trust her?

The only person who didn't was Rio, and I'd been writing his concerns off as the paranoia of someone who didn't trust anyone.

And Simon hadn't met her.

Willow Grace had lied to us from the beginning, and I'd let her off easy and with mild irritation, instead of nailing her to the wall and interrogating her. She'd delayed us in finding Arthur, and Checker and Pilar had been upset, but they should have taken her head off. Diego had easily convinced me to let her walk out and go home. Somehow, Tabitha had maintained some doubts—precocious, naïve Tabitha—and I'd brushed off her gut feeling too.

Telepathy isn't an exact science, Simon had reminded me over and over again.

"She can't be Pithica, right?" Checker asked, sounding freaked. He craned his neck around, as if he could see through the walls to where Willow Grace stood outside. "If she were, we wouldn't—we wouldn't *know*, would we?"

I got what he meant. The simple fact that we had begun to doubt her—if she were Pithica, I didn't think we'd have been able to start suspecting her on our own, even as difficult as it seemed to be. I'd never been able to figure out myself whether someone from Pithica was psychically influencing me, not without Rio's help.

Unless . . . what if there were levels of skill? What if she just wasn't as strong? *Something* had sure as hell been influencing me—

Just like with Oscar.

"Hard-coding," I whispered. Oscar was forgettable, and so I forgot him; Coach and the dogs were terrifying, and so I panicked; and Willow Grace was . . . I'd thought she was only beautiful. But she was more.

I'd dismissed her allure as not having the mathematical capability to be mind-warping. It hadn't even occurred to me that Teplova might have worked on her in a separate way, for another purpose. That one set of surgeries didn't preclude another.

Because I'd trusted Willow Grace before it could.

She was perfectly positioned too. She graced everyone's televisions, telling people to trust her, making them feel safe . . . becoming a goddess in their minds. Hell, Pilar and Checker and almost everyone else had already seen her on the screen before meeting her. They would have been doubly primed to believe everything good about her. I'd suspected her, a little—but I'd kept rationalizing that away until it was gone, so smoothly it had felt like the natural course of logic. Tabitha probably would have relented too, eventually, but she'd been alert enough to question and to bring it to me, and I'd—I'd dismissed her utterly.

"Oh, fuck. Oh, *fuck*," said Checker softly.

"Check what she's been doing since she's been here," I said to him. "Which computer has she been using?"

He nodded rapidly and moved over to the dining room table. Pilar and I followed.

I took the security screen with me, clenched tightly in one fist, keeping half an eye on it. What should I do? Should I try to incapacitate her? What if . . . what if her face worked well enough that I couldn't?

"Go lock her out," I said to Pilar.

She slipped off to the hallway. A moment later the screen's security settings confirmed that all doors and windows were secured.

"Hey guys!" Matti poked his head in from the kitchen. "There are plans afoot in here for making waffles. Anyone want in?"

Roy jostled up beside him. "Don't worry, we two dashing gentlemen shall not be the primary architects of said waffles, we know our culinary limits. We shall be kitchen minions only—"

"We're working," I said. I'd grabbed a new phone out of the piles of equipment around the table and was dialing Rio.

It rang out and disconnected.

Damn. Damn. *Damn.*

If I'd just discussed Rio's concerns with him, instead of nodding and then ignoring—if I'd been more open with Simon, kept him up-to-the-minute on everything we were doing—

If Willow Grace was working against us, if she had planted that file . . . the file had led us *to* Arthur. Why? False information? What Arthur had said about the planned bombings . . .

A door slammed upstairs, making us all jump and look up. "Be that way, then!" Tabitha's voice cried. "Dad almost *died,* and you still can't get over your stupid grudge!"

Someone tried to respond—Elisa, though I couldn't make out the words. But a door opened and slammed again, and the conversation cut off.

"Well, that was awkward," Roy said. He and Matti were still hovering in the doorway to the kitchen. "Welcome to the Casa Rosales, where all the women are fierce, all the men are good-looking, and all the children have above-average felony records."

"Do *you* know what Dad did?" Juwon asked almost aggressively. He'd stood and come over, thumping his book down on the table.

It took me a minute to realize he was talking to me. I'd barely been listening to the argument upstairs—something about Arthur. "What?"

"When he stopped being a police officer. And when he left—" He bit down on the unsaid *us.* "No one is willing to tell us. We only know it's bad."

I hadn't even known that much. Checker's bare-bones retelling had implied only that some big event had gone down, but not that Arthur had been at fault somehow.

Either way, I didn't have time for this. "I don't know," I said. "Try Checker later—"

"He definitely knows," said Juwon. "He won't tell me either." He glanced pointedly over at where Checker was head-down in a laptop, grabbed his book, and stalked sulkily out of the room.

"Tabitha'll figure it all out eventually," Matti put in. "She actually started calling Dad's old colleagues once. And newspapers. Papá stopped her—"

"Well, not so much stopped her as got all devastated and begged her not to—" Roy added.

"Sorry, this family is like a sappy documentary," Matti said. "I give you the tragic story of five hard-luck cases, too old and too delinquent for anyone to take pity on—well except Tabitha, she got in as a baby. But the rest of us were all sordid tales of petty larceny, poor choices, jazz, and liquor . . ."

Footsteps sounded on the stairs, and then another thump. Christ, this family was noisy. I ignored the twins' continued prattling and scrolled through the handheld again. Then frowned.

The back door was unlocked.

What . . .

Pilar had just locked it—Willow Grace still paced outside—

Where *was* Pilar?

I squinted at the screen.

Dread suddenly clogged my senses. No. *No.*

Verification took only seconds. I made a few precise measurements with my eyes, the rustle of leaves through time, the exact position of the almost motionless clouds, the angle of Willow's face against the scenery as she paced, and ran the recording backward.

The security footage—*Rio's* security system—how—

"Get everybody down here," I yelled at the twins, dashing back over to Checker. "Everyone, you hear? Where I can have eyes on them!"

They tripped over themselves, scrambling to obey and shouting their siblings' names.

"What is it?" Checker's head came up from the computer, his eyes darting everywhere at once.

"Get us into the back end of the security system, *now*. Someone looped it. I need to get outside."

"Sure, give me two—"

The screen on his laptop fritzed, brown and green pixelating across it.

Checker yelled and began hitting keys in a frenzy.

"What happened?" I'd drawn my Colt.

"I don't know yet—"

Diego burst into the room. "Can someone please tell me what's going on?"

"No time," I snapped, and pushed past him. He sucked in a hard breath when he saw my gun and fell back out of the way.

I raced to the back door.

Pilar was on her hands and knees in the vestibule, trying to stand.

"Cas," she gasped. "I'm sorry . . ."

I stayed low, reached for the doorknob, and in one move pulled it open and twisted through.

The backyard was empty.

I slid through the wild garden and did the quickest perimeter check of my life. No sign of Willow Grace.

But the door had been unlocked . . . and she'd attacked Pilar . . .

Could she be in the house somewhere?

I dashed back inside. The twins were falling into the living room, followed by Juwon and Elisa. Diego had sat Pilar down on the couch and was insisting on examining her head.

"Has anyone seen Tabitha?" Matti asked. "She's not upstairs anymore—"

Diego straightened in alarm.

"Locate her phone *now*," I ordered Checker.

"Right, *fuck*—someone hand me another computer—"

Footsteps hurried through the small house, every voice calling Tabitha's name. Matti had his cell against his ear and was dialing her repeatedly, but I didn't hear it ringing anywhere in the house. I started my own quick walkthrough, clearing each room, eyes scanning for either Tabitha or Willow Grace.

Willow Grace would've looped the security system for a reason . . . she'd *been here* for a reason . . .

"Cas!" Checker hollered.

His urgency made my throat clench so hard it hurt, and I vaulted across the foyer and pushed past Diego to come to his shoulder. Everyone else crowded in after me.

"What is it?" I said.

"I can't—" He glanced behind me at all the watching faces— Tabitha's family, his family. "Tabitha's cell, it's not pinging. The only way that's possible is . . ."

"The battery's been taken out," I said.

"Could it just be off?" Roy asked.

"Most phones I can still get a fix even when they're off," Checker said. "And Tabitha just switched to an old TREX phone because hers was waterlogged, which I'd definitely be able to track."

"Tabitha, she'd know that," Matti babbled. "She'd pull the battery, then, wouldn't she, if she was sneaking out and didn't want us to find her . . ."

"Ping Willow Grace's," I said to Checker.

After a tense and silent few seconds, he said, "Can't find her either."

"She took her." I felt numb.

Diego cursed in Spanish.

"I'll go wake Dad," Roy said, and slipped out of the room.

"What do we do?" Juwon asked. "The police won't help; we know the police won't help—"

"We're better than the police," I said. I tried to straighten my thoughts, to concentrate. "We *will* find Tabitha. She told me . . ." She'd told me she was suspicious. Said she had a gut feeling, that she wanted to look for evidence. "Something was making Tabitha suspect Willow Grace. Maybe she was digging into her on her own, and she found something the rest of us missed."

Matti let out a strangled laugh. "She said she suspected something? Duh, man, then of course she was still digging. She's *Tabitha*."

"I'll search her room," Juwon declared. "Maybe she left notes, or there'll be something on her computer." He disappeared.

"Hey. Talk to me." Arthur's voice.

I froze. I couldn't bear to look at him.

I'd been the one here watching, I'd thought I was as good as Rio—my fault, and his daughter—

"I'm going to finish clearing the house," I said. "Everyone stay here while I secure it." And then we'd find her. We would . . .

Something tickled my skin, tugging at my thermoreceptors.

"Wait," Diego said. "I don't understand. Please—you're saying this woman—"

"Stop talking," I said.

Diego stopped.

I lifted a hand, brushing it through the air. A temperature differential lined up for me, isoclines climbing and ever so slightly warming the side of my body closest to the stairs, and the bottom dropped out of my stomach.

"Everyone out of the house," I cried. "*Now!*"

thirty

THE FAMILY began scrambling in confusion. I pushed past them and raced through the foyer, swinging around to a door that had to be a closet beneath the stairs. It was a lot hotter here. A *lot* hotter. And I could smell something—

I pulled a sleeve over my hand and wrenched the door open.

The heat bowled me backward. A red nest of flames had already subsumed the closet, making the door a portal to a hell dimension, one that must have been devoured by some sort of chemical fuel. And in the middle of it all, its pill-shaped silhouette seeming to writhe in the heat, was . . .

A tank.

I knew what it was without knowing. *Liquid to gas expansion—radius of destruction, devastation, scorched earth, nothing left—*

Gallons per minute from the kitchen faucet versus volume and BTUs, upper bound on capacity of indoor fire extinguishers, there was no way to put this out, no way to prevent—

"*Go!*" I screamed, dashing back into the foyer. "Get to a vehicle, *go!*"

Checker and Pilar and Arthur were already doing a good job at hustling everyone, but Diego tried to push back toward the stairs. "Juwon—"

"I'll get him! *Go!*"

I vaguely heard Arthur reassuring Diego as they went, as I flew up the stairs. I shouted Juwon's name and some combination of the ruckus caused him to come hurrying out of Tabitha's room to freeze at the top of the stairs. I barreled up at him, swung an arm around his body, and vaulted over the railing. He yelled and flailed, but there was no time to explain.

We landed hard in the foyer. My bad ankle shrieked as the compression maxed out my torn ligaments, and I nearly fell against Juwon as I took us diving toward the door.

Everyone else had cleared. I hauled a quieting Juwon to the driveway, where, thank Christ, the Rosales minivan was already running. They'd squeezed into two rows of back seats that didn't fit nearly everybody, and left the driver's seat for me.

I practically threw Arthur's son into the back and pressed the gas before I was sure they'd all gotten the door shut. The van shot forward, and someone behind me squealed as I slewed it onto the street.

"D.J.?" Arthur asked faintly. He was in the front passenger seat, crutch leaning across him, and his face was sweaty and gray.

I knew what he was asking. *What kind of threat is this?*

"I think so." But Willow Grace must have been the one to sneak the materials in.

After Rio had left. When no one had been keeping a sharp enough eye on her.

"The neighbors . . ." Arthur whispered.

"Maybe," I said. Bounds for the released energy, shock front, blast wave, all folded through my head—this was going to be big. "Call it in if you want to."

Crouched between seats behind us, Diego had his phone out before I'd finished the sentence. I hadn't realized he could hear us.

"*911, what is your emergency?*" I heard from his phone, and the house blew up.

We were only halfway down the block. Debris slammed into the van like they had been fired from a cannon. One of the back tires blew amid screams and yells from the back. I wrestled with the steering wheel to keep us upright.

"Oh, Lord," moaned Arthur.

Someone in the back seat started sobbing.

The operator on the other side of Diego's call was talking urgently. "There was a bomb in my house," Diego said into the phone, with remarkable articulateness. "3191 McFadden Hill. I think you will need to send the fire department."

"You're sure . . . Tabitha . . . ?" Arthur wheezed at me.

"I'm sure," I said quickly, even though—how could we be? We hadn't finished checking every closet, under every bed. But it was unlikely she had been hiding somewhere in the house, and I pushed the possibility out of my head. "We have to get you all somewhere Willow Grace and D.J. can't find you," I said. "I have—"

A car cut me off, an unmarked one but with red flashing from its roof. I locked up the wheels into a sideways skid to avoid broadsiding it. The rim from the blown tire dragged against the asphalt in a thumping staccato, catching the back end of the van and almost tipping us again.

"Go or stay!" I yelled. "Talk to me!"

"Go," said Arthur.

"What? No, no!" cried Diego. "That will only lead to more trouble—"

"Someone's trying to kill us. *Go,*" Arthur said.

The wheels spun and then caught, lurching back into static friction. I rocketed us forward to swerve around the cop car. As we hauled past, I glimpsed Sikorsky's face scowling behind the glass.

He'd been staking out the house. Jesus.

Sikorsky tried to pull around to pursue us just as two black-and-whites came around the corner. I accelerated toward them, the van kicking back at me.

"Stop!" yelled Diego. "*You're* going to get us killed!"

"Arthur!" I barked. The variables in a car chase branched and compared in my head. Too many people who weren't me who didn't have seat belts. A minivan with an awful center of gravity that was already severely damaged. The last time I'd been in a car chase, I'd ended it with a nasty concussion, even without all those other variables—

"Stop," Arthur mumbled, and I took the van half into another skid, bleeding momentum until we jolted to a halt between the three police vehicles.

Fuck.

If I was fast, I could probably disappear—slip to the side, roll under one of the cop cars. But I was one hundred percent sure Sikorsky had seen me driving.

There was no crime here. We were victims. *Victims.* Right?

Officers leapt out behind open doors, aiming handguns, yelling, screaming so they overlapped each other with no clear meaning. Arthur immediately lowered the window and thrust his hands out, yelling back about children, there were children here.

A jumble of chaos followed. Even if I couldn't take advantage of it to escape, once out of the van, I was close enough to the edge of the road that I used the bedlam to cover me as I kicked both my sidearm and my long knife into a sewer before straightening with my hands raised.

Ordinarily I would have winced over willfully damaging my Colt. Today, right now, it barely registered.

The police swarmed us and patted us down. Pilar was carrying legally, though her gun did make the cops jump and yell and keep the business ends of their service weapons on us for an unsettlingly long time. Sikorsky patted me down more roughly than necessary, sneering, his breath hot on my face.

I clenched my teeth and let him paw at me. We had to get through this, get out of here, find Tabitha . . .

Elisa was pale and shaking, but she was also trying to speak reasonably to the police. The other three kids were in hysterics. Sikorsky's partner kept trying to interview them, but all she was getting was that there had been a bomb in their house, which everybody already knew.

Down the block, flames leapt merrily from the remains of the Rosales yard. The blaze had begun spreading to the lots next door, and neighbors wailed and cried and ran and milled on the street. Fire sirens wailed closer.

"Where's the youngest hooligan?" Sikorsky demanded, swiveling his head across us. "The girl. Where is she?"

Apprehension somersaulted into my throat, but Diego answered without missing a beat. "At her friend's," he said immediately, at the same time Arthur said, "Friend's house."

They glanced at each other.

"What friend?" Sikorsky was poised with his pen over his pad.

Diego shook his head. "No. We'll go. My children just lost their home. I will not stand for them being subject to any more of your harassment."

Sikorsky and his partner both stopped dead. Sikorsky began to swell like a reddening balloon.

Diego's face flickered in fearful recognition. "Please," he back-tracked. "I didn't mean—"

"Are you accusing an officer of the law, sir?" the partner demanded.

Diego tried to raise his hands in a gesture of surrender, but she got in his face and shoved him in the chest, and Roy broke ranks to surge forward yelling. His twin and Elisa both tried to grab at him, but not fast enough to stop two of the uniforms from pushing in and shoving Roy against the side of the van.

Diego dove to try to put himself between the cops and his son.

I wanted to scream at him—if we wanted to run we should have *run*. The heavy inevitability of *police* meant we knew exactly how stupid it was to challenge them, and now all I could do, the only thing I could do, was keep my hands in the fucking air and my eyes in all directions to make sure none of the cops went for their guns again. I flashed on nightmare images of trigger-happy officers gunning down Diego or Arthur—of course, Arthur had tried to lunge forward too, with Pilar only just holding him back, because apparently it was a paternal axiom to *be stupid* when a cop went at one of your sons.

The scuffle lasted less than thirty brutal seconds. And ended exactly as predicted, with the younger three kids backed against the van crying, Elisa trying to argue loudly and fruitlessly, and Diego facedown on the hood with Sikorsky cuffing his wrists.

"That's it, Rosales. You are under arrest."

The kids screamed at him. I thought I heard something about due process from Juwon. But Sikorsky cut it all off by giving Diego's head a vicious shove.

His face hit metal hard. The kids went as silent as if their throats had been cut.

Down the street, the fire trucks had arrived. Firefighters unreeled hose and barked orders. Neighbors moaned and cried. A hellish backdrop to our little drama.

"What charge, Detective?" Elisa asked coldly.

"What charge?" Sikorsky snarled at her. "Pick one. Child endangerment, resisting arrest, assault on a police officer, *terrorism*—even a dressed-up mouthpiece like you won't be able to pry him out of this one."

"Frank," Arthur called to Sikorsky. Checker had joined Pilar in holding him back, though Arthur wasn't really trying anymore. It was probably a good thing he was still too injured to walk. "Frank, if this is about you and me, don't go taking it out on them—take me in if you want to; don't—"

Sikorsky drilled Arthur with a stare and started reading Diego his rights while manhandling him toward one of the black-and-whites.

The partner tried to get statements from the rest of us, then. Juwon and the twins were distraught on the level of incoherence. Elisa made a clipped, contentless response and then immediately called a car to take her down to the station to meet Diego. Arthur, Pilar, Checker, and I managed to give brief, consistent accounts that implied we knew nothing and had only spotted something suspicious, prompting our run for safety, and then had missed the police lights at first in our panic. The partner let us go with stern warnings to stay where we could be contacted easily.

I used the Cassie Wells IDs with her again. She looked at the two halves of the PI license and then back up at me, unamused.

"Your partner objected to it being in one piece," I said, as neutrally as I knew how, and she handed it back to me without changing her expression.

By the time they let us leave, a lot more cop cars jigsawed the street. The firefighters had mostly put out the blaze, and were now hiking through a street flooded with water and crisscrossed with hoses.

The barest black bones of the Rosales house stuck up from the ruins.

thirty-one

WE PILED into the van and lurched past the roadblocks being set up on the corner. "I'll give you an address to go to ground at. Try to lose any tails," I said to Arthur. If Pithica was behind this, it wouldn't be enough. Everything was triage right now, fractured and bleeding. "Checker and I will work on getting you all IDs out of the country—you take the van—"

"Russell, I can't . . ." Arthur's inflection bent with pain. "I got to—can't just sit. Not when . . ."

"You have three other kids who need protecting," I said.

Four if we could get Elisa to join them in hiding, though with Diego needing a lawyer now, I rated that as only slightly more likely than impossible.

Until D.J. came after them too. Shit, shit.

If they were all about to disappear anyway, maybe we should just break Diego out. That'd make this a one-way trip. But that might be what was happening anyway.

"Can't just do nothing," Arthur whispered.

"You *will* be doing something. For them. Leave Tabitha to us."

Arthur didn't answer. His face had gone closed and hard.

I had to pull over and see what I could do about the van's tire. I swung into a nearby park and obscured us between a line of trees and a span of tennis courts and baseball diamonds. The hour was still early enough that they lay flat and empty.

My ankle and knee both flared when I jumped down onto the

pavement, but I determinedly ignored them and hiked around to the back of the van to hunt for a spare. Before I could open up the back, my eyes snagged on the snarls of wood and metal stabbed deep into the panels of the vehicle. House bones made shrapnel. If those had hit a window . . .

"Russell."

Arthur had gotten down out of the passenger side and was limping back to confront me, leaning on his crutch with one arm and the side of the van with the other.

I hauled open the rear hatch and started searching for a jack kit. The cargo area behind the seats was piled in semi-ordered detritus— umbrellas, blankets, reusable grocery bags. I pushed things aside and found a side panel with the tools. Pilar twisted from the back seat as if she were about to offer to help, but I waved her off and busied myself with cranking the spare tire down out of the van's undercarriage.

"Russell," Arthur said again, a little louder. It sounded like it took every ounce of energy he had.

"Give all your phones to me," I said to him mechanically. "I'll have Checker forward them to VOIP in case the cops call."

He grunted. "Matti and Roy and Juwon, they can go. I'm gonna find my daughter."

The twins had started to glance around from the back too, shifting to overhear. I rolled the spare around, away from their watching eyes, and began jacking the car viciously.

"How long are you able to stay awake right now?" I said to Arthur. "Twenty minutes, tops?"

I wasn't looking up at him. But I could feel his eyes on me, angrier than I'd ever known him, searing into my back.

No father would want to be benched when his daughter was missing, but especially not someone like Arthur. The crack private investigator who would brave hell and high water for *any* victim wasn't going to be able to help his own kid.

But he had to accept reality. For Tabitha's sake. And I was going to have to make him.

"You're dead weight right now," I said. "You've got almost no mobility, and you're hopped up on drugs. If we have to move fast, you're going to get yourself killed. Tabitha's best chance is if you stay out of the fucking way."

Even if we put Arthur on a computer, I was betting he couldn't type more than ten words per minute. I was going to maximize our chances of getting Tabitha back alive, and if I had to sacrifice Arthur's sensitivities in the process, so be it.

I told myself that was the reason I bit the words at him as harshly as possible. And I told myself the same old flash of hurt was irrelevant, and not why I was saying any of it at all.

"Dad still might see something you don't," said a defiant voice.

I glanced up from wrenching at the last of the lug nuts. Juwon had slipped out of the van to come up next to his father, his face puffy and streaked with tears. The twins had climbed around and poked their heads out behind him.

Arthur tried to turn and say something back, but he hunched in pain. All three of the kids leapt to support him.

I stood to face them. "We can keep a phone line open. But be realistic. You shouldn't even be out of the hospital."

He wouldn't look at me.

Since the house, I'd been mostly running on auto. The numbness let me function. If I let myself stop and think . . . but now a darkness twisted below it, the oily smear of everything I'd felt toward Arthur since all this began.

"Arthur," I said, and I tasted the ache of it on my tongue. "Do you trust me?"

To go to any lengths, never rest, sacrifice anything, until I either found Tabitha alive or proved I never would? To know this was a one-way function, and that I would find his daughter—his precocious, headstrong, too-smart-for-her-own-good daughter—unless I literally died trying? Whatever else he thought of me, did Arthur at least believe that?

. His face creased, a deep pain I was sure wasn't physical. Tears slid down and over his jaw. And then he turned his eyes on me at last.

"You were there, Russell. You were there when she got taken. You didn't stop it."

My joints stopped working. Everything in me went dead. The accusation shattered at my feet, the shards lethally sharp.

I couldn't speak. The silence swelled and cracked, fissuring every tie with Arthur I'd thought I had.

Into that silence, from off to the right, a keening yell wailed at the sky.

I had one narrow instant before it barreled directly at us, when I heard before I saw and managed to slam my eyes shut. I tried to shout a warning, but it was too late.

A cacophony erupted, inarticulate voices, cries and yells and thuds. I kept my eyes glued shut. Sound localization in space wasn't a difficult computation—it only depended on two ears, two points of input from which all other points can be mapped, as long as those points are off the axis between them . . .

It helped when everyone was screaming.

I turned my head in a rapid twitch to cover every angle, and the scene snapped into place. Arthur collapsing on top of Juwon—he must have tackled him, his panic risking every re-injury to block his nearest child from danger. The twins spiraling behind them, falling to the asphalt, and Pilar, spinning up at the open rear hatch from the back seat of the van.

And Coach. A hundred and ten degrees around from me. Closing fast.

Even with my eyes closed, the memory of him staggered me. I reeled against the bumper of the van, banging my swollen knee, the one Coach had bruised and nearly broken. The shape of him yanked at every neuron, clambering over itself to drag me down.

And strung through it, other memories—Coach and I laughing in the dark, doubled over in giggles as we raced back from a well-executed prank. Coach making a dubious face at what he'd just challenged me to do, and telling me he was pretty sure it was impossible, and I looked and measured and ran a thousand scenarios in a second and smiled.

Coach looking at a stopwatch and shaking my hand. Telling me he was proud of me.

Gunfire roared out over my head. Pilar, shooting from the back seat, but wildly, the heat and concussion so close, they stung my cheek.

I pressed my hearing past the gunfire that threatened to eclipse it. The audio outputs whizzed and bounced, almost an extra point-seven milliseconds between one ear and the other, here shadowed by the diameter of my head, here making a ratio between the direct signal and the reverberation off the van. Coach's path arced around, smooth and intentional and deadly. In nine-tenths of a second, he was going to reach us.

No. Not us. Arthur. His velocity vector stabbed directly to where Arthur's and Juwon's cries overlapped, not deviating, not slowing.

Arthur who I'd just been arguing with. Arthur and the kids, who'd been confronting me. Antagonistically. Aggressively. As if they were my enemies.

Just like the cops Coach had thought I wanted dead.

I could have tried to reach him first. Hack through the strands of induced fear and the memory of another person's life. Fight blind and try to incapacitate him. He was a brutally efficient fighter, but still no match for me—not usually. Not when my brain wasn't so slick, it was squirting out of my grasp.

My ankle buckled under me, and I flashed on Coach again, finding me in the dark, and I was shaking so hard, every muscle vibrating apart, and I knew what this was. *"Don't tell them,"* I whispered, the words tasting of weakness. He bent under my arm and helped brace me upright, and his steady grip around my shoulders was built of wry challenges and kept promises.

Less than half a second until he reached Arthur.

I shot my hand up and palmed Pilar's weapon away from her. She'd been almost on target. Adjusting took no time at all.

The gunshot seemed to ring out louder than any of the others.

thirty-two

SCREAMING. Crying.

The continued anguish around me seemed to reflect every atom in my body. I kept my eyes closed, my hip against the rear of the van holding me up, Pilar's CZ limp in my hand.

"Cas? Cas! Shit—"

Checker's voice. He'd still been inside the van—"Don't look!" I yelled.

"I'm not! I'm not, I'm not looking . . ."

I pushed myself to action. Gunfire and screams—the population within the radius to hear, chances were good someone had called it in. I had to clean up. Get the tire on . . .

I turned my back on what I'd just done, opened my eyes, and stuck Pilar's gun in my belt to paw through the back of the Rosales minivan for the blankets I'd seen there. Large picnic blanket. A tarp under it. I grabbed some bungies from under the seats too. Pilar was slumped over the seatbacks, mewling slightly, her hands clawing at the fabric so hard, her fingernails were bloody.

"Checker," I called. "Find out if we can reach Simon, right now."

Then, with my armload of coverage, I shut my eyes again and stepped over to where I'd murdered the man who used to be my friend.

He sprawled less than two meters from Arthur. The probable position flashed against my eyelids like an afterimage, and I draped the picnic blanket, then the tarp. Something in me curdled away from touching him, but I had to tuck in the edges and loop the bungies around by feel.

My hand ran into something hard at one point. A phone. I slipped it out and into my pocket. Robbing the dead.

I didn't even know how effective masking his body like this would be, and I didn't want to test it, but I also couldn't leave it here. I got my hands underneath and dragged him to the van, then rolled the body inside, wedging it to fit behind the seats and then shoving the rear hatch closed. I took a second before I did to push Pilar back over onto the rear seats, where she curled on her side, making small noises in her throat.

Coach's blood would soak into the blankets and umbrellas and carpeting until the stain would never scorch away. A final, humiliating tomb, crammed into a vehicle on the run like he'd been nothing. A nobody I had cut down like a rabid animal.

"Cas, I think I got—I think I found Simon," came Checker's voice, high and reedy. "San Fernando Memorial, as a John Doe, but the rest of it fits. He's in the ICU—I don't think we can reach him . . ."

"Hold on."

I rolled each of the twins into a fireman's carry and hauled them inside, then more carefully tried to move Arthur. He seemed mostly catatonic. I couldn't tell if he'd torn open his injuries or not. I supported his spine as well as I could and got him back into the front seat.

Juwon had been curled crying beneath him. But when I went back to get him, he staggered up and back, beating at me with his hands. "What happened? Oh my God, oh my God, what happened, what happened!"

"Wait," I cried. "You're okay?"

His elbows were scraped and bleeding from where he'd hit the pavement, and the side of his face was pebbled in red also. But he wasn't comatose in residual panic like the others.

Arthur had tackled him down before he'd seen.

"Get in!" I commanded. "Right now. Checker, get him in there!"

I hauled the spare tire onto the hub, tightened it down, kicked a layer of dust over the blood on the asphalt and then shoved the old wheel and tools into the back after Juwon, who had cowered in next to Checker.

Four minutes and thirteen seconds after I'd pulled the trigger and killed the man I meant to save, we rolled back onto the street and sedately joined the flow of traffic.

Juwon hadn't gotten into a proper seat. Checker had his arm around him, and Juwon stayed shivering against his foster brother, hitching away from Matti and Roy when they rolled and moaned on the floor.

"Hey. Juwon."

He twitched and turned red and frightened eyes up to me in the rearview mirror.

"You're going to have to take the van," I said. None of this changed the fact that the whole family had been targeted, that I needed to send them somewhere safe. Safer. "We'll follow for a few minutes to make sure nobody's behind you. I'll give you a warehouse address where you can drive it right in, and then you're to *stay there*. Take care of your brothers and your dad, don't leave for any reason, and under no circumstances look in the back unless you want to end up like they are. Got it?"

"I—I can't—" He was hyperventilating. "I can't, I can't do it—"

"Yes, you can. Checker, tell him he can."

"No, I mean I *can't*," Juwon sobbed. "I don't have, I don't have a driver's license. I failed the test . . ."

"But you know how, right?"

He jerked his head in a nod.

"You can't get stopped anyway. Nothing in this car will be explainable to the police, do you understand? Do not take risks, do not crash."

"Cas," Checker broke in.

I let him take over. He was better at being comforting even under normal circumstances.

We're not normal, Valarmathi said in my head sadly. And she said it again—proudly—to Coach, a long time ago, gleefully celebrating how many sigmas off the mean we were. He smiled tolerantly and let her high-five him.

I flexed my own hand against the steering wheel. *Push the memories away, bury them back down,* the logical part of my brain reminded me, but the mantra lacked any teeth. *Don't be stupid, if you don't stop, it'll start taking you back over, you'll crash the van, you'll fail, you'll fail Tabitha, like at the ranch with Simon . . .*

What did it matter? I'd failed Coach—in the final, ultimate fashion. He deserved to have someone remember him. A bastardized wake in my head was a pale mockery of the rescue I'd sworn up and down I would make possible for him.

Arthur wheezed in the seat next to me, a plaintive, pleading sound layered on every breath.

Arthur. I'd just been trying to promise him too. To vow I'd save Tabitha, that if anyone had a chance, if *she* had a chance, I would make it reality. That he could trust me.

Right before I shot the other person I'd wanted to save.

I'd done it without even trying for any other way. I'd opted for the probability of one against Arthur's body broken and dying, even when it meant pulling the trigger on a man who hadn't deserved to die either.

He hadn't deserved any of it.

Part of me had been so stunned and bitter that Arthur didn't believe in me to get Tabitha back. But he'd been right. I'd been at the house, and I hadn't stopped Willow Grace. I hadn't saved Tabitha then, and I couldn't promise I could save her now.

Rio might have been able to. Rio might have blocked it all— Willow Grace hadn't taken a single step until he left, and then she'd jumped to action within minutes. Which meant I was to blame again, so many chains back, because if I hadn't driven Rio away, he would have been present to stop her.

Rio. His absence ached all over again, a black hole of negative space. Like the support I'd been leaning all my weight against had turned out to be nothing but shadow and air.

I'd tried his number again while I was driving. Several times.

Once I hit Van Nuys, I pulled into a sparsely populated parking garage attached to an ancient apartment building, one without cameras where we could be hidden from watching eyes. The rusted signs proclaimed parking for residents only. I kept an eye out for an older-model car that would allow for easy pickings and slid the van into the space next to it—I needed to hotwire transport for me and Checker.

And Pilar.

It was unkind of me to take her with us, in the state she was in. If we couldn't reach Simon ourselves, or if we had to leave her somewhere because she'd gone comatose . . .

But if we could reach Simon . . . I needed her.

I heard Tabitha telling me again about her *gut,* and my own clenched. Checker wasn't a combatant. Without Rio, without Arthur, without Simon—if I didn't have Pilar, I had nobody else to ask.

Checker had gotten my safe house address from me while we drove, and I'd heard him carefully writing down paper directions for Juwon to avoid the trackability of a GPS. I came around the side of the van to heave Matti and Roy more comfortably into the back seats and buckle them in. Roy clawed at me, his hands fisting against my shirt. I pried them off. The pulse beating against his wrist was alarmingly high.

How long could they stay in this state before it did permanent physiological damage?

I also collected all of their phones, and I stuck them in my pockets where they jostled up against Coach's.

He'd had a phone. Odd. I'd levered it out while driving, while Rio wasn't picking up, and run my eyes over it. It was dead, the battery completely drained. An artifact from his past life, before he became a violence-driven victim? Or from his current one? Who had been able to call him? Was there someone he had talked to, as he slipped into his damaged reality, held down and drowned by the world's reactions to him?

I wondered if he'd been able to speak to people still. At the end, even hearing him had triggered enough sense memory to start warping my reactions.

Checker was helping Juwon install himself in the driver's seat and gently reminding him how to adjust his mirrors and what everything did. Juwon wasn't actually shorter than I was, but somehow he looked so small there, a terrified mouse thrust into a throne of towering responsibility.

I passed him Pilar's burner.

"Checker's going to give you a phone number to keep calling," I said. "When you do, don't give any information, but keep asking to talk to a John Doe who will answer to the name of Simon. He'll be able to help. Until then, keep Arthur and your brothers hydrated. Okay? You'll find food and water and blankets in crates in the warehouse I'm sending you to. There's also several firearms and ammunition—"

Juwon jerked.

"You don't have to touch them," I said. I glanced across at Arthur. "Checker, give him Dr. Washington's number too. This is a doctor Arthur's used in the past. She's very discreet. If absolutely necessary, if Arthur needs it, you can tell her where you are. Nobody else. Do you understand?"

He'd started crying again, but silently, the tears leaking down his face like a tap had been left on. In answer to my question, his head quivered in a rapid shake that didn't stop.

I almost knew how he felt.

I let Checker finish giving him the details, transferred Pilar to the car I was stealing, and checked over Arthur's wounds as well as I could. But I was no doctor. Not like Teplova.

Her applied skills had somehow been so many worlds away from my realm and everything I could control. How was that possible? Mathematics underpinned everything. I had followed the intricacies of how she'd made Willow beautiful, and the theory had all been so perfectly understandable, a well-fitted jigsaw puzzle of ingenious creativity. But I'd missed everything important.

And in practice, the more I saw of her creations, the more her choices eluded me. The confluence of equations, the local and absolute extrema that served as her fulcrums, the web of reinforcing and refining with each new technique to build that theory into usefulness—I had the creeping, desperate premonition that it might be fundamentally beyond me.

Just because I understood circuit theory didn't mean I had the first idea of how to build a mobile phone. I'd failed to save Coach, but . . . I didn't even know if I could have.

I went over and jacked the sedan to life, then once the engine turned over I slumped in the driver's seat waiting for Checker. The door to the van slammed with a dull finality, locking Juwon and his family inside. Checker came over and swung into the passenger side next to me, pulling apart his chair with practiced smoothness to pass into the back next to Pilar, who was curled in the fetal position against one of the doors.

"How is she?" he asked.

I didn't know any better than he did.

"Hey." He prodded my shoulder and pointed. Juwon was backing up in fits and starts. He took a stuttering turn and then managed to creep out toward the street. "We're following for a second, right?" Checker asked.

I'd said we were. It was smart. I'd be able to spot any tails from back here, for sure.

None of it seemed to matter. D.J., Willow Grace, Pithica—whoever wanted us dead, they'd been a dozen moves ahead before we'd ever realized we were playing. Willow Grace could have planted a tracker on the minivan. Juwon might have been brainwashed by Pithica. D.J. might have figured out Dr. Washington was a known acquaintance of Arthur, and already staked her out . . .

What was the *point*? What did they want? They'd jerked us around for days, kidnapping Arthur and letting him go, only to try blowing up him and his whole family. They'd had Willow Grace embedded with us from the beginning, only for her to help us find Arthur and then kidnap Tabitha a day later. Nothing we'd done seemed to have made a damn bit of difference.

"My house is clear. So far," Checker said. He must have been looking at his security system on his phone. "I need to stop there.

Get some equipment, and—" His words squeezed off, and his hand stuttered in the air, waving off an end to the sentence. "If you think it's safe enough for me to work from the Hole, even better."

Willow Grace knew about Checker's place. She knew about all of us.

I followed Juwon for long enough to be sure I was the only one behind him. He was an awful driver, creeping up to lights and hesitating and swerving into any lane changes, but at least he didn't seem inclined to speed. Rush hour was beginning to seep out of LA's over-clogged pores, which would either help him out by keeping traffic to a crawl or become a trial by fire.

Either way, we couldn't help him. I peeled off and headed toward Checker's place.

"There has to be something about Willow Grace." Checker spoke rapidly and tightly, engrossed in his phone. "Something, some way we can—use that—we could go to her house, her work place, call everyone she knows . . ."

She'd taken Tabitha over an hour ago now. An hour was enough time to hide the body of one sixteen-year-old child.

Four minutes had been long enough for me to get Coach's body off the street.

"Cas! Cas, are you listening to me?"

I pulled into his driveway and jolted to a stop. My hands felt like clay on the steering wheel.

"Cas, snap out of it! We need to find Tabitha—"

"Arthur was right," I said, so hollowly it sounded like a stranger. "I don't know if I can save her."

Checker twisted in the passenger seat, grabbing onto my shoulder roughly. "Stop it!" He shook me. "This is not the time to go blue screen of death on me—Cas! You are the most arrogant person I've ever met and—" He swiped at his face with the back of one hand and seemed to gulp back a sob. "I *need you*. Tabitha needs you, Arthur—I can't do this by myself! I need you to be your cocky, smug son-of-a-bitch self right now and tell me if anyone can do this, it's you, of course it's you, and we're going to get her back or literally die trying, because *that's what we do.* Otherwise we might as well just call the police, and if they arrest all the rest of us, then fuck it, because we weren't doing her any good anyway."

By the end of it, he was quaking, every breath heaving like he was about to shake apart at the seams.

He'd been so strong for Juwon. I hadn't put it together that this was probably the worst day of his life.

Checker's phone went off in his hand. He jumped and almost dropped it, then glanced at the screen. "It's—it's an unknown number . . ."

It could be a ransom call. Oh, God, please let it be a ransom call. *Let her be alive.*

"Answer it."

Checker swiped his fingers rapidly on the touchscreen, changing some settings before he wet his lips and hit the button to pick up the call on speaker. "H—hello?"

"*Charles,*" breathed the person on the other end. "I *got* you."

thirty-three

THE WORDS came through some sort of synthesizer, disguising the voice. But it was no less gloating for that.

Checker jerked in his seat. He opened his mouth, but no sound came out.

"You don't remember me? After all the hijinks we got up to together, I'm hurt. I'll never forget the time we trolled all those *serious* wannabe actors in North Hollywood—"

"D.J.," Checker whispered.

"The one and only!" sang the disguised voice. "I have your friend's daughter. Or would you say your sister? I don't want her, though. I want you."

"Don't hurt her. Please don't hurt her," said Checker.

"I only blew her up a *little*," the person said. "Oh, she'll be fine, don't shit your trousers. As long as you come, that is. Come meet me, right now, the same place we used to do RC racing—and I won't even tell you to come alone. Bring your whole ridiculous little posse."

The line went dead.

"I have to go," Checker said. "I have to go, we have to go, of course we have to go—"

"Wait." My brain was dragging itself out of its sludge and suddenly processing very fast. *Very* fast, dredging up memory, running every algorithmic comparison I could find . . .

"No," Checker cried. "We have to—to figure out what we, and we have to go, he'll kill her—"

"*Wait*," I repeated. *Wrong, wrong, wrong*, sang the algorithms in my head, spitting out high-probability mismatches. "Wait. This is going to sound—I don't even know. But I'm not sure that was D.J."

"You—*what?*"

I'd only met D.J. briefly before . . .

"Were you recording?" The way he'd adjusted things before picking up, I had a suspicion. Checker was security-conscious to a fault. He nodded and quickly tapped at the screen to play the phone conversation again, the voices coming tinnily from the speaker.

I was sure this time.

"The cadence is off," I said. "The voice is disguised, but the sinusoidal features of the intonation—there's a vanishingly low probability this is the same person."

"But then who . . . ?" said Checker. "What—*why*—"

"I don't know. Do you have anyone else in your past who'd want to kill you and everyone you care about?"

He inhaled sharply and looked away.

I hadn't meant the question as a dig. But we didn't have time to dwell on it—because whoever had called us had just made a very big mistake.

Either they didn't know what I could do, or they'd underestimated it.

I told you it was a gift, murmured Valarmathi.

A fragile bubble of hope wobbled up in me. Our enemy wasn't infallible. They'd made a mistake, and they didn't know what I could do, and oh, fuck, maybe this gave us a chance after all. I hadn't been able to save Coach, but like Checker had said . . . that didn't mean we couldn't make this one last desperate dive after Tabitha.

It wasn't about proving myself to anybody. Not anymore. It wasn't about me at all.

"Get on your computers," I said. I dug in my pocket and tossed him Coach's phone. "See what you can do with that too. I'll get Pilar inside and then join you."

"Cas, he said—he said to come now; what if—"

I pointed at the streets. "It's rush hour. That gives us a magically expandable amount of time to prepare. Let's not waste it."

. . ˙ . . ˙ . . ˙.

I HURRIED in getting Pilar into the house. Whoever had called us . . .

They didn't know about my abilities, or they never would have risked it. Which meant they didn't know about my connection to Halberd. Or Teplova. Or Coach.

Which meant . . . *they weren't Pithica.* Dawna knew exactly who I was and what I could do.

The screaming relief of that conclusion made me want to sit on the floor and weep. If this wasn't Pithica, if the connection to Halberd and my past was only the coincidence of selection bias as I'd first tried to insist . . . Tabitha might have a chance after all.

But what did it mean that it hadn't been *D.J.?* The person had talked to Checker like they'd known him, assuming the detail about trolling actors or whatever was accurate. So D.J. still had to be involved here somewhere, didn't he? After all, it had been Arthur's investigation that led him to stumble into all this in the first place . . .

Unless we'd had it all wrong.

I laid Pilar on Checker's couch and tried to make sure she wasn't about to chew off her own limbs. "Cas," she whispered plaintively. "Cas—I, I, I . . ."

"Stay there," I said. "Sorry."

Then I dashed out to the Hole and burst in the door. "Assumptions off the table. If D.J. *isn't* involved here, what does that mean?"

Checker straightened toward me, his eyes wide and owl-like. "He still has to be, right?"

The signature matches in the explosives, the obscene real estate listing, the voice on the phone—

"Someone is sure trying very hard to convince us of that," I answered.

"No, I still think he is," Checker said. "I'm looking at this cell phone—you got this from the guy who—?"

I nodded curtly, gesturing him on.

"There are only a couple of contacts on here. One tracks back to Eva Teplova. And one is . . . it's totally anonymous, but I'm finding it all over the dark web, and the context . . . Cas, it does make me think it's D.J. I think—I think your guy had his phone number."

That brought me up short.

But everything was fitting together just a little bit wrong. Like we'd built a whole system with one contradictory axiom.

"We do know there's *some* explosives expert involved here . . ." I thought for a second. "Call the number."

"Are you sure? If I keep searching it, maybe I can find—"

"Yeah. Call it. I want to see who picks up."

Checker's face cleared as he got it. "I'll keep us muted unless you give me the word. Are you ready?"

I leaned on the desktop over his shoulder. "Go."

He dialed through the computer, every keystroke like a falling hailstone.

A phone rang on the other end. Once. Twice. Three times.

Four times.

A rustle as someone picked up.

"Hello? You've got *me!*" sang a merry voice on the other end. "What can I do you for?"

I recognized the high, singsong cadence instantly as D.J.'s, the amplitudes falling out into matching cycles and patterns. I pointed at the speakers. "That's D.J. That's him."

Checker had gone white. "What the hell is going on? I don't understand. Why have someone impersonate him instead of just . . ."

"Hello? Hello? Hello?" crowed D.J. over the speakers. "Is this a prank call? Because I fucking love pranks. They turn me on something wicked."

"Unmute it," I said. "I want to talk to him."

Checker didn't seem able to hit the button. I reached over and did it for him.

"I'm up for phone sex, but you do have to pay me," D.J. was chattering on. "Nothing's free in life, yanno."

I took a deep breath. If D.J. was behind everything, he already knew what I was about to tell him. If he wasn't . . .

"I'm here with an old friend of yours," I said, and nudged Checker in the arm.

"Hey," Checker said faintly, after a second.

So much emotion was packed into that one syllable it sounded alien. But D.J. went dead quiet. And then he screamed.

Or—I thought he was screaming. It must have been more like a squeal of excitement. "*Charles!* Oh my coke-addled gods. How the fuck are you?"

"Not . . . great," Checker managed. "D.J., we need to know . . ."

"You need something from me? How marvelous. How absolutely *spiffing.* Oh hey, look, you're on a fancy computer connection too! Go modern tech."

A video window filled the screen.

D.J. looked exactly like my vague recollection of him: short and rotund, with very dark skin and long braided dreads. His appearance didn't immediately parse as male or female, and I'd gotten the sense that was intentional.

It might only help if he saw Checker was who he said he was. I enabled our own side of the video link, and the little inset window popped up with Checker's and my tense, shadowed faces. We both looked like hell.

"Well, well, well. It truly is Charles the Good," D.J. said. "The crip look works for you. I heard he did that, by the way. What a fucker. Wait, I know you too!" He poked at the screen on his end, which made his finger go off camera and jar the whole thing.

"Yeah," I said. "You've tried to blow me up."

"That's most people I meet, sweetcheeks. I tried to blow Charles up, too, back in the day. That was a laugh, wasn't it, Charles?"

I squinted at the screen. "I thought you two used to be friends."

"He didn't mean to," Checker said in a low voice. "But 'laugh' isn't what I would call it, no. D.J., someone is . . . did you . . ."

"What can you tell us about a whole mess of recent bombings in Los Angeles that all seem to have your signature?" I said.

"That bomb squads are idiots?" D.J. said brightly. "I've only done one here lately. Okay, two. All those alphabet soup agent-faces must have a major crush on me—"

"Then someone is going to pretty great lengths to frame you," I cut in.

"Frame me?" D.J. looked genuinely surprised. "Charles, what on earth did you get yourself into? Don't go trying to replace me with a lesser model."

Checker glanced up at me, questioning, and I nodded him on. "There's . . . there's someone here in LA pretending to be you," he said. Under the desktop, his hands were clenching each other very tightly. "They've been attacking everyone I know. And now they've kidnapped my friend's daughter and we have to, *I* have to, get her back, but we don't know who, or where, or—or why. But they called me pretending to be you, and on the bombs—if that wasn't you either, then somehow they're copying how you do that too."

"Aaaa, that little motherfucking douchenozzle!" D.J. cried. "Thinking she can *impersonate* me? And kidnapping? She must die. She must have her head removed posthaste so the rats can fuck her throat-parts."

I had absolutely no idea whether he was kidding or not. The probability fell out straight down the middle.

But only one piece of what he'd said mattered.

"You know who it is," I said. "You know who's got our friend—"

"But should I tell you? Oh, fuck it, I'm too lazy for games. It's fucking Fifer. Or whatever she's calling herself now."

"Is that a pseudonym, then?" I asked.

"Who knows?"

"She knows your methods," Checker said. "She knows . . . things about you. Me."

"Because I taught her everything!" D.J. said. "For reals, the bomb squad is being an idiot on the sig thing; her sig matches mine because she learned from the best. She was my protégé. My apprentice. The font into which I poured all my—oh, not like that, Charles, I can see your mind splashing around in the gutter, but I'm still saving myself for you." He winked.

As far as I could tell, Checker was *not* thinking about sex for probably the first time since I'd known him. "Are you saying—" The words drew out of him like a forced extraction. "Is this about—is she out to get *me*?"

"Oh, yes," D.J. said. "She's ever so jealous of what you and I had together. She's obsessed with you. She built a shrine to stabbing the eyes out of your photographs! Get your head outta your ass, Charles, not everything is about you."

Checker had gone stone-white. He started coughing like he was choking on his own breath.

D.J. crowed in delight. "Did you believe me? You've gotten so gullible in your old age! Or you just have an ego the size of God's butt, but we knew that already."

I wanted to shake him through the camera. A name, a name was a start, but D.J. clearly knew a lot more. "Why is she out to get us, then?" I demanded. "If it's not about you two, then what the hell does she want from us?"

"You? I have no idea. Are you someone important? She's got some fucktastic shitbrained mission now, thinks the US of A needs to be burned to the ground and rebuilt or some shit. Clean slate, she calls it, destroy the establishment and all that, it's too corrupt and worm-eaten from the inside. She's gonna try for it too, says things are just too fucked up to solve otherwise." He didn't sound particularly bothered.

What Arthur had said. Targeting people in government.

"I wonder where she got that idea," Checker said bitterly.

"Are you trying to blame me? Charles, I'm hurt. And here she tried to blow me up with my own powder magazine for saying no! I get no love."

"So, she's not working for you," I put in.

"Nobody *works for* me," D.J. said with distaste. "I'm *independent*. 'Sides which, I just told you. We had that nice little blowup a while back."

"Literally," I couldn't help muttering.

"It was only a few hundred kilos of TNT," D.J. said. "I tried to shortwick her in return, but it only blew her up a little." He made a face so serious, it was comical. "She's a royal fucking nutcase, Charles. You oughta be careful."

"I take it she got that from you too," I snapped before I could think about it. I was willing to bet I was more fucked in the head than either of them, and it wasn't making *me* go around kidnapping sixteen-year-old girls.

But D.J. only giggled. "We did get along, for a while. Every so often, I still poke at her, but I'm really fucking lazy—didn't know she was going around pretending to be yours truly, though." He considered us for a moment and seemed to make a decision. "I was just here in your town pestering her, as it happens. A little pick-me-up between jobs, test some new toys, make her mad as a hornet. How funny that you ended up after her too."

Not really—Arthur had been after D.J. when he'd stumbled across Fifer's trail. Everything was finally beginning to fit together.

Then I connected. "The binary explosive," I said. "At the wellness center. That was you."

"You were there? Delightful!" D.J. threw his hands wide. "First time I'd given that a go. I give it five stars, two thumbs up, and a blowjob."

"You were mocking her for the assassination of Teplova." I remembered thinking how messy that murder had struck me. Not with the terrifying completeness D.J. had rendered on the buildings. Two different bombers, that was why. *SLOPPY,* the sky writing had said—D.J.'s jeering message for Fifer before he showed her how it was done.

"We need to know everything you know," I overrode D.J.'s snickering. "Whoever this Fifer person could be working with, any other information you have."

He snorted another laugh. "Fifer? Work *with* people? Her ass is far too cray for that. And I told you, she thinks she knows best anyway. I pity the dude or dudette who tries to work *with* her—they're probably dead."

Like Teplova was dead. And Oscar. But then what about Willow Grace . . . ?

And it hit me.

Willow Grace.

Willow Grace.

Willow Grace, the famous news anchor, whose background was pristine. But Willow Grace, with her perfect features, who had gone under Dr. Teplova's knife to get them, those perfect features that had differed very slightly from the online footage I'd seen of her. Willow Grace who'd changed her whole life six months ago to seclude herself away, supposedly on a sabbatical from her far more public life.

Willow Grace . . . who, as of six months ago, *was not Willow Grace at all.*

She was Fifer. An imposter. Taking a famous news anchor's place, a news anchor who'd had a history of secret surgeries herself, surgeries that could then be copied. The real Willow Grace likely dead and at the bottom of a lake by Fifer's hand.

And now Fifer had Tabitha. She had Tabitha.

"She changed her face," I said. "She changed her face to be a famous news anchor, so . . ." She wanted access, access for her bombings . . . "Checker, find out where Willow Grace has been issued a press pass in the last six months."

Checker started typing, fast, his face pale and dazed.

"She kidnapped Arthur to see what he knew," I continued, feeling it all out aloud. "To see if he was investigating her plan. Tried to kill me in case I was looking into her too. But then . . . it turned out Arthur didn't know anything, not about her, and once she saw that *we* wouldn't stop digging until we found him—that's when she gave him back to us." We'd known it was too easy. Once we'd flat-out told Willow Grace we'd stop investigating once we found Arthur, she'd directed us practically straight there. She'd grabbed her old mentor D.J. as a convenient scapegoat only after I'd given away that we suspected him, and then she'd planted a file she knew we'd find.

Though she hadn't known how easily we'd crack it, or that it would therefore arouse our suspicions. And she hadn't counted on Tabitha.

"Tabitha kept on thinking something was up with her," I said. "She was looking, she must have found something . . ." Had she caught Willow Grace setting the bomb? Disabling the security system? Leaving the house? Had Fifer decided to take Tabitha as she'd taken Arthur, to find out how much she knew and who she had told?

Please let her have been taken. We'd never heard Tabitha's voice on the phone call.

We hadn't given up the investigation like we'd told Willow Grace we would. And Arthur had overheard more than she'd known, the exact plan Fifer had been trying to prevent us from finding out. Not only that, but we had Teplova's files now, and we hadn't stopped digging into them.

I remembered then my guesses about how Teplova's clients could be used. How they might be molded into an army.

And Fifer—she wouldn't even have to do any molding, I realized. The hard-coded powers worked on anyone from regular folk to people like Simon; they'd definitely work on one another. Whatever politicians and other powerful people had been Teplova's clients, they were primed into a ready-made force of impossible people, and Fifer not only knew who they were but could make them follow her just by smiling at them.

Fifer hadn't only killed Dr. Teplova to protect herself after getting her new features. She'd committed the murder to *take over.*

Had she known about the power Teplova had bestowed on Willow Grace's flesh and bones before forcing the doctor to make the same copy on her own? She must have. Any position or press credentials had been a side benefit to worming her way onto the top of Teplova's pyramid, all with a face that couldn't be refused.

And we, the people with a partial client list, who wouldn't stop looking under all the virtual rocks—we would have been the only people who knew enough to stop her. The only people who had a chance of recognizing her army for what it was.

She had stolen prestige and a frightening ability with explosives. Add who knew how many brainwashed superpowered minions who wielded their own power . . . if she thought the country needed to be taken down a peg, she could drop us into anarchy as easily as pushing a button, playing the sides of both terrorist and authority to her own predetermined tune. It wasn't a perfectly coordinated plan, but it didn't need to be—any sloppiness could be papered over by raw power.

Until we got in her way.

Apparently, as soon as that seemed at all likely, she'd aborted subtlety and decided to put the kibosh on all of us before we discovered the truth. D.J. wasn't kidding about what kind of person she was. If she'd decided the same about Tabitha . . .

But Tabitha had been researching on her own, and very well might have found something solid revealing Fifer's true goals. Fifer had to be worried about that, had to want to interrogate her.

Had to have kept her alive. I wouldn't allow myself to entertain alternatives.

"Glad you got all that mumbly-jiggero figured out," D.J. broke into my stunned thoughts. "Good luck being on her hit list. It was nice knowing you."

Checker spun back to the screen. "You have to help us. You're here in LA, right? You've been tracking her, you know her—you *have* to help us. You have to!"

"What?" D.J. said. "No, I don't! Don't get me wrong, I will heartily agree to blowing shit up for money, or if I'm mad, or if it's fun enough, but going up against Fifer? No, thank you. I'd rather relax by the surf and build more orgasmic little toys."

"Then you *should* help us!" Checker argued. "What do you think is going to happen if this Fifer person gets her way? It's going to be chaos! Where do you think you'll get your advanced devices then?"

"Oh, the old evil versus oblivion argument," D.J. said. "Oldie but a goodie. 'Come on, D.J., you live in the world too!' But you should remember, Charles, I'm really fucking lazy." He leaned back and studied his nails. "Besides, she probably won't be able to do it. She's a fucking slob. Somebody'll catch her. Too bad it won't be in time for the little kitten you're trying to save."

D.J. didn't know she had access to a whole supernatural army of power. People who could grab her coup for her and then run her empire with the hand of a vise, one the people never even noticed as the faces on their television sets soothed and controlled them.

But we had one last shot, because Checker was right—her old mentor's help might be just what we needed to blindside her.

"If it's money you want, fine," I said. "Name your price."

"What'd I just say? There's no pile of green in the world that would be worth plopping myself into *this* bucket of diarrhea tentacles. I taught the kid, remember? She may be sloppy, but harmless, she is not. I like my fleshy parts attached to me, not in bitty bits."

"But you already tried to stop her," Checker said. "Isn't that why you're here? And now you know she's impersonating you. Don't tell me you're going to let her get away with that!"

"I dunno. Am I?"

Checker's eyes narrowed. "You want something. You already would've hung up otherwise. The girl this Fifer has, she's—she's like my sister, okay? Tell me what you want, and I'll do it. Anything." His jaw bunched. "Do you want me to beg you? I'll beg."

"Oh, *tempting*! But no. There you go again, Charles, thinking everything is about you." D.J. turned his face up to me. "But *you,* you are fascinating. I've been thinking about you. In my *dreams.* Who are you, for realsies?"

A subject I didn't want to talk about with anyone, up to and including myself.

It's okay, Vala, said Coach's voice in my ear. *I know who I am.*

I cleared my throat. "I'm nobody."

"Oh, we both know that's not true. Did you really solve the P versus NP thing?"

"No. You've been misinformed." Technically true. I hadn't solved it. I didn't even know if it really had been solved.

D.J. laughed and wagged a finger at me. "Aaaa, you're such a shithead. I can see why he likes you. Hey, Charles, should she join our cabal?"

Checker opened his mouth, closed it, and then acted like he hadn't heard the question.

"Spit it out," I said to D.J. "You may not care about this girl's life, but *we do*. What do you want?"

D.J. flexed his fingers against each other and stretched. "I like to build shit," he said. "Come to my labs. You're some sort of mathematical professor genius. Promise to give me some new shiny, and you've got yourself a deal."

"You want me to help you build new bombs?"

"I get so *bored*," D.J. whined.

"No," Checker cut in. "No. We're not doing that."

"Wasn't asking you, darling," D.J. said. "Don't fuss your pretty heads; I'm not saying I want you to help me *use* them. I'll take all the responsibility and stick it up my own ass."

"Yes," I said.

"No!" said Checker.

"Glee!" cried D.J., and literally clapped his hands. "Where do you want my gracious self?"

"We're in the Valley," I answered. "Are you close?"

"Oh, good, just a shake of a lamb's tail. I'll come meet you straight off, soon's I disarm a few fuses. Message me where." The video blinked off.

Sudden silence in the garage.

"We can't do this," Checker said into it. "Arthur wouldn't want—"

"Arthur would want us to do exactly this and never tell him about it," I said. "So that's what we're going to do."

I refused to see D.J.'s aid as anything other than a massive stroke of good fortune. We'd make a plan by the time he got here, and then I'd be able to take him with me after Fifer. She'd have her bombs, but I'd have a bomb expert.

One even better than she was. One who could predict how she would move.

"Don't force me to make this argument, Cas, please don't," Checker begged. "I—it's Tabitha, I know it's Tabitha, but—" His hands had curled into desperate fists. "You're promising new bomb tech to someone who has no compunction about *using it on people*. That's so far over the line it's, it's not even in the same hemisphere. We'll figure out something else; we'll offer him something else—"

"Is this guilt?" I said. "You helped him before so you swore never to do it again?"

He flushed. "Don't go there. That's not what this is."

"No? Because D.J. doesn't seem all that different from me." Checker had told me so himself, in the heat of anger, but I could own that truth. "And you seem to be able to help me out all the time without having the arrogance to say you're responsible for anything I do."

Checker's mouth flattened. "Nothing I've ever helped D.J. with—or you, for that matter—was ever about hurting people. Ever. You've seen what he's like now. There's no room for—there's no justification for this; I can't—"

"*You* can't," I said. I was calm. "You've spent too long around Arthur and Diego. You keep thinking of me like you, someone who just hasn't been *saved*. But maybe it's time you faced that I'm not." I was coming to a realization—a hard one, but one that was giving me back my equilibrium, my direction. Maybe I wasn't the person I wanted Arthur to see. Maybe he'd been right about me all along.

But that meant I could do this for him when people like Checker couldn't.

D.J. wasn't the worst person I'd ever worked with, not by a long shot. And maybe it was time for me to start shaking out my own morality and see exactly how my friends would react. Either they'd come to terms with it . . . or they'd leave.

"Arthur already knows what I am," I said. "That's clear now. And you know what? I . . . it's okay. I can figure out how to live with that. But if I'm willing to do the things I'm willing to do, what does it say if I suddenly won't when it's Tabitha's life? Because that's something *I* can't do. If you want D.J. to be more judicious with his dynamite, take it up with him when this is over."

I'd already shown how far I would go. When I shot Coach to protect Arthur.

Checker opened his mouth to argue back. But at that moment, his security system pinged.

Our attention snapped over.

"Oh, no—Cas—" Checker hurried to blank all his computer screens. "Oh, no, this is bad—"

The screens for the outside security cameras showed the burly form of Detective Sikorsky striding up the walk.

thirty-four

"SHIT," CHECKER said. "Shit, shit, shit—"

We shouldn't have come back to Checker's place, I thought numbly.

No way to take out a cop without consequences. And no way to run without Sikorsky seeing us.

"My security's recording," Checker said in a whisper. "But we can't let him—Cas, if he does anything, we can't fight this after the fact, we can't let him delay us, not with Tabitha . . ."

I saw what Checker was driving at. Sikorsky didn't have his partner with him. Or any uniforms. Which meant he wasn't here with an on-the-books arrest warrant. That made this simultaneously easier and more dangerous—I might be able to take a dirty cop out of play even without the threat of Checker's recording, but it also meant he wasn't going to be playing by the rules of the law.

And, like Checker had said, we had to deal with this *fast*.

"Steady," I said out of the corner of my mouth. "Follow my lead."

Sikorsky bypassed the house—either he'd glimpsed movement through the garage's window or he remembered from when he'd dragged Checker in before. A meaty knock thumped through the Hole.

"I know you're in there," he called. "Open up."

I moved forward and tugged open the door.

Sikorsky barged in and gazed around with a smirk. He ran a finger across the top of one of Checker's machines as though checking for nonexistent dust, then rubbed his finger and thumb together.

"You rats," he said. His tone was deliberately careless, conversational.

"Did you find the person who blew up Diego's house?" I said.

"Oh, I know who." He sneered at Checker behind me. "Always an attention seeker, weren't you?"

Checker didn't reply.

"Where's your partner?" I asked.

"I sent 'er home. I told her she looked *tired*. She agreed."

So he was unquestionably here to do something off the books, and his partner was turning a blind eye. And he wanted us to know it. Checker's gaze flickered to me for a second, but he said nothing.

"And as for you, *Wells*," Sikorsky continued, "or should I say . . . Dhar."

Dhar—it took me too long to remember that was the name on the license I'd given the uniform who'd told me off for loitering. A day ago. It seemed like a century.

And if that cop had taken note . . . oh, fuck, there'd been a lot going on that night. My bomb. The evacuation. The murders of twelve police officers who were investigating it.

Sikorsky was watching my reaction closely. I tried to stop my face from twitching.

"See, I don't think you're our killer," Sikorsky went on, still casual. "You don't got enough heft. But you know something. And as for that bombing dance, we all know you're buddies with a right little terrorist." He flicked a hand at Checker. "And if you're conspiring about all that, well, let me tell you, none of my colleagues are going to cry if you turn up missing. Or missing some teeth. They'll line up to testify I was at the fucking movies."

With Sikorsky's obvious grudge against Arthur and Diego, plus the implications of his corruption—it had never occurred to me that he might actually be a good investigator. But he was dead-on.

I'd set the bomb. I knew everything about the killings.

"And now," Sikorsky went on, "just now, we got a tip. Did you know that?"

Both of us stayed quiet. Sikorsky slammed a fist into the computer tower he'd just been fondling, and Checker flinched.

"*I asked you a question*," Sikorsky bellowed.

"We didn't know," I said.

"It's a solid one. Real classy lady, and she might do some investigatin' but she knows when to let the police handle things. And she's heard all these whisperings on more bombings, a whole criminal plot."

"Willow Grace." I said it without thinking, my stomach going leaden. Fuck, she was still ahead of us. Now tipping off the police— what had she told them?

Sikorsky loomed over me, practically vibrating with rage. "Everything you say just digs you deeper. Some pissant judge might say we still don't have enough, but I say this is terrorism, and that every fucking one of you should be in Gitmo. And in Gitmo, there are no rules."

His hand went for his service weapon.

It was the moment I'd been waiting for. The visual that would slam-dunk Checker's recording, just in case we needed it.

I lashed out to strike him just below the elbow and transfer a nice wad of kinetic energy to the nerves in his forearm. His hand jerked and dropped his weapon, which I brought up a foot to meet. I gave the Glock a pop like it was a hacky sack, and it sprang in the air and rotated, so I caught it pointing right at Sikorsky's face.

"Why do you cops always have such bad taste in weapons?" I couldn't help saying. "This is a toy, not a gun."

Sikorsky had started to lurch toward me, but he aborted the move just as abruptly when the business end of his own firearm popped up right in front of him. His little deep-set eyes flicked around, assessing the situation, searching for a way to regain the upper hand. He wasn't panicking, not yet, but his face was creeping over red with anger.

"What were you going to do?" I said. "Pistol whip us until we gave you something?"

"Oh, you've done it now." Spittle limned the edge of Sikorsky's mouth. "Put the motherfucking gun on the ground or I will end your motherfucking ass right here."

"Look, we're honestly not the people who—" I tried.

"Drop the fucking gun!"

He lunged at me. He executed the move fairly well, trying to trap me between him and the long desktop and tangle up my arm before I could shoot him. But I slipped my center of gravity just off where he needed it to be, and his lunge did nothing but take him wildly off balance. He crashed into Checker's machines and hit the floor without any help from me.

But he didn't stay down. Some part of me had to respect him—he thought we were terrorists out to blow up the world, or at least involved with someone who was, and due process wasn't letting him torture information out of us, so he was going dark to do it. And now he probably believed this was a last stand and that I was going to shoot him with his own gun, but he wouldn't stop fighting.

He threw himself back up at me, but the instant before I kicked him in the head, his limbs jerked and he went down with an unearthly yell.

Keeping the gun on Sikorsky, I followed the leads of the Taser back to Checker, who was holding the device in a white-knuckled grip. "I thought you didn't—" I started.

"I don't like guns. Fifty thousand volts is totally okay."

The flatness he said it with belied any humor.

I bent down and searched a twitching, groaning Sikorsky, found a cell phone, and tossed it to Checker. "See if anyone's going to come looking for him."

"What are you—what are we going to do? He's a *cop*—"

"We are going to worry about this after we find Tabitha, that's what we're going to do." And if we didn't find her . . . if we didn't, nothing would matter anymore. "I'll secure him until then."

I zip-tied Sikorsky's hands in front of him and forced him up and into the house at gunpoint, where I shoved him down on Checker's bed and used more zip ties and some plastic rope to thoroughly hogtie him to it. By that time, he'd recovered himself enough to holler and snarl at me. I stuffed some socks in his mouth and gagged him.

"The irony is, we're actually the good guys on this one," I told him while I secured the knots. "We're trying to stop your bomber."

He glowered at me.

I made sure to use enough redundancy that he had no nontrivial chance of escape and left him in Checker's bedroom, wedging the door shut so Pilar wouldn't go wandering in. She was in mostly the same state, though she'd ended up on the floor, hugging one of the legs of the coffee table. I satisfied myself that she was still breathing—there wasn't much more I could do, not until we reached Simon—and went back outside.

"We've got all day," Checker said rapidly as soon as I came back into the Hole. "Probably till morning even. He told his partner he'd check in by the end of his shift, which I can totally fake. And he already texted his wife that he'd be home late if at all, to which she didn't even reply, likely because his text and GPS history are a patch-work quilt of being as irresponsible as humanly possible, lucky us."

"Are you sure?" I said.

"Of course I'm not sure, Cas! This could backfire on us in a thousand and five ways! For fuck's sake, I am trying to keep it together when my sister is missing and a police detective is being held hostage in my *house*—"

"I'll handle him," I said. "Tonight. As soon as we get Tabitha back."

The blood drained out of Checker's face. "You mean by turning him in, right? You're not going to—"

"No." Coach's victims splashed themselves across my vision again, and I felt a little sick. "No. It's not—practical. Cop murders draw out more cops, and his grudge against all of you is a known thing, and—" I took a breath. "We're not killing him. But it's not the smartest play to turn him in either. That would mean getting tangled in an IA inves-tigation, and that recording's not the best for us even if it buries him."

Checker swallowed. "What's your plan, then?"

"I told you, I'll handle him. But I might need your money-laundering skills."

"How did you—I never—"

"Come on, give me some credit," I said. "Remember how we *met*? I'm capable of adding two and two."

"Oh. Uh." He rolled his lips together. "Do you think Willow Grace was trying to send the police after us?"

I started to say *of course,* but then stopped. If Willow Grace had wanted the whole LAPD on Checker's doorstep, she could have engineered it. Her background as a reporter would have given her any credibility her face hadn't conferred. If that had been her aim, she could have told them *anything,* could have claimed fear of her life or national security, and she would have been taken seriously.

Instead, we'd only gotten one rogue cop . . .

Horror dawned, exploding in my hindbrain.

"Oh, *shit*"—I'd thought of this, but everything had been moving too fast—"Checker, get us security footage of the station Diego and Elisa are at. Right now!"

He keyed it up faster than I'd ever seen him move at a monitor. I leaned to look over his shoulder.

The screen showed security footage of a police precinct. Presumably also the station Sikorsky worked at. And with the unmistakable form of Willow Grace strolling through the halls.

"What do we do?" Checker said, his voice going high and scared. "She was there, she was just there—"

Willow Grace wanted to kill us. She wanted to kill us, and we had footage of her poking around the station, right where Diego and Elisa were, where we couldn't protect them, couldn't fight back, couldn't do a goddamn thing to stop her.

Checker's security system pinged. We both jerked around to look.

D.J. was coming up the walk, a huge mountain backpack on his back and a spring in his step like he didn't have a care in the world.

thirty-five

I HURRIED out of the Hole and went to meet the amoral bomber who'd tried to kill me more times than I really felt comfortable with.

"D.J., over here. Quickly."

He turned. Or rather, he bounced around to face me on the balls of his feet like he was executing a dance move. "Hi! Hi, you! Oh, delightful. Top-shelf fucking peachy to see you again. How you been?"

"Not dead yet." I grabbed him by the backpack and dragged him with me into the garage so he had to scurry to keep up.

"You're so serious. Lighten the fuck up. Literally if you want to; I have a lighter and some very volatile—"

He stopped. We'd gotten to the doorway.

Inside, Checker had gone so still that I doubted my senses for a moment.

D.J. immediately became more hyperactive than usual, rolling his weight back and forth and looking a thousand directions at once without ever meeting the gaze Checker had fixed on him.

"Charles," he said finally. "Nice digs you got. You sure you're a hundred percent on the level now? You know you can tell me. I'm an angel of discretion."

"It turns out I have related skill sets. Legal ones." The comeback was brittle.

D.J. guffawed and started to say something back, but I interrupted, "We've got a new problem. Your buddy Fifer has been casing the police station two more of our friends are at right now."

"Right, right, deadlines, I can dig it," D.J. said, swinging down his backpack and twirling around a chair to drop into it. "Give me the scoop."

Checker brought up the footage. "We think she went in pretending to have a tip. About her own plans, believe it or not . . ."

I rubbed my forehead. "I could call in a bomb threat again, try to push another evacuation. But I'm not sure if they'd take it seriously." Would Willow Grace have hidden things too cunningly to find? Should we plant another fake to make sure the cops would evacuate? I wasn't as good as Rio at being convincingly menacing over the phone—not to mention that we didn't have *time* for this. Tabitha's seconds ticked down almost audibly in my head.

"And it would only be a delay tactic," Checker said miserably. "She's going to go after them wherever they get moved."

Which would keep us scrambling to protect people.

"Here's the video of what she did to—our friend's house," Checker added. "Our police stalkers were nice enough to give us dash cam footage."

Sikorsky was good for something, then. The sequence played out in silent black and white on the monitor: the front of the Rosales home, still and quiet, then our frantic exodus, and then . . .

I hadn't seen the explosion happen while we were fleeing. The entire house went up in an all-consuming fireball that filled the screen and mushroomed more than fifty feet into the sky. Large chunks of unidentifiable debris cannoned in all directions. The viewpoint shook and then wheeled into blurred scenery as Sikorsky and his partner took off.

I swallowed. Checker had stopped watching.

But D.J. squealed like Christmas had come early. "Oh my God, she BLEVE'd your ass!" he crowed. "This is amazing! I love a good BLEVE. They're so *dramatic*."

"What the hell is a blevy?" I said.

"Boiling liquid expanding vapor explosion," D.J. enthused very fast. "Ya get the gas so pressurized, it goes liquid, and then you clog the release valves and get it hot enough with a nice little fire until the whole shebang gets pee-vee-equals-en-ar-*tee'd*."

He noticed me staring.

"What? Dollie, I build bombs. Of course I know all the science shit."

"Do you think she could do that at the station?" Checker interrupted. "Sneak things in the same way? It didn't take her long; at the house she only had minutes—"

"Play it again!" D.J.'s grin filled up his whole face.

Checker obeyed.

"What are you looking for?" I asked.

"Oh, nothing. Just appreciating the beauty of a well-executed pressure explosion. Fifer does get it right once in a while—"

Checker stabbed the keyboard so viciously, it probably hurt his hand, and the screen blanked.

I thought of the twins' music posters, Tabitha's crime novels and stuffed animals, Juwon's science puzzles and Latin. All gone in less than a heartbeat.

"You people are so fucking *sensitive*," D.J. whined. "All right, all right. You can stop a BLEVE by either popping the release valves or putting out the fire. They're not all that useful in real life other than to look cool, 'cause there ain't no good failsafe. Way too easy to make sure they don't go if you find 'em in advance."

Like Rio would have, if he had been there.

"So yeah, I don't think she's setting up a BLEVE," D.J. went on. "She'd need to haul a tank in, for one, and you got her going in and out empty-handed. Easiest way to ice someone in prison is to slip a nice lil' fellow inmate a shiv and a promise, but Fifer, she's got an ego. Likes doing things her own self." He cocked his head and watched the police station footage for another second. "Nah, I don't think she's setting anything. I think she's casing the joint."

"For later?" I said. "Are you sure?"

"Yeah, yeah, sure I'm sure. She's coming back with something, no question."

"She doesn't have her invisible friend anymore," Checker said. "She probably used to use him to set things. Like at your place, Cas."

"What invisible friend?" D.J. said.

"His name was Oscar," I answered. "Asian Australian, not alto-gether with it. Someone you know?"

"Oh, Oscar Lee?" D.J. said. "The washed-up med student? Gotta be. God, what a whiny bitch that guy was. I suggested she kill him, or at the very least break up with him, but she dug being worshipped. I mentioned the ego, right?"

"Wait, they were a couple?" Checker asked. "How—"

D.J. waved a hand. "Yes, yes, of course you're asking yourselves why she was in some insipid hetero relationship when she could've been hitting on me, but this dude would do literally anything for her. She'd test that sometimes when she was drunk—blew half his face off once and he still stuck with her."

"Not anymore," I muttered.

Oscar's history got more horrific the more I learned about it. I couldn't recall his face terribly well, but I didn't think he'd had obvi-ous scarring—that wouldn't be *forgettable*. Which implied all sorts of things. He'd apparently been with Fifer before she'd decided to go after Teplova's outfit—and then maybe Fifer had told him she'd repair the damage and instead made him disappear. If no one else could ever know he existed, he'd worship her forever, with no other option unless he wanted to fade from the world completely.

I pushed aside my disgusted pity for another time.

"So, if she doesn't have the person who helped her set things, what's her plan?" I said. "And more importantly, how do we stop it?"

"Fifer's about six thousand percent more psycho than I am," D.J. said blithely. "But if it were me . . ."

Checker muttered something under his breath. D.J. flicked his shoulder and then went on as if there had been no interruption.

"If it were *me*, I'd blow something next door or down the street. The cops all run to help, chaos galore, and she can sneak in with a nice little boom stick and whack your pals. Kill a few other pris-oners along with 'em, and it might not even be obvious who she wanted out of the way, though I'm guessing that ship sailed with the BLEVE."

"We could stake out the station . . ." Checker suggested.

I checked my watch. Thirty-three minutes since Fifer had called. We might have a little more breathing room since she'd so recently been down at the station rather than waiting for us in person, but not much.

"We're going to need to split up," I said.

"You on one team, D.J. on the other," Checker added. "You're the only two who'd have a shot at disarming things."

"I'll go after Tabitha," I said. "You two head down to the station."

"With any luck, she's still going to be hanging around the station now, and it'll give you a window for a rescue," Checker pointed out. "We can keep updating you if we get a bead on her. Fifer is claiming she's got Tabitha at the Barberry Canyon bridge."

"And whether she's there in person or not, I'm guessing the biggest things to worry about are going to be bombs or more of the dogs," I said. Or their human counterparts. Depending on who Fifer had made—or could co-opt.

Crap. I'd momentarily thought having D.J. along would give me an edge. Not only on the explosives—as much as I could leverage theory and logic and place my bets that way, I didn't have his expertise—but also in throwing Fifer off her game, predicting her next steps. Without a wild card like him, and without someone like Simon . . .

Fifer was baiting us in with Tabitha, but her setup would be designed to kill us all before we got her hostage out. I would have put money on it. But we were running out of time to come up with anything better than dashing after Tabitha headlong.

The sudden breakthrough of information had made me so sure we could come up with something better—some way of coming at her weak points, taking advantage of what we now knew . . .

"Did you say Barberry Canyon?" D.J. asked. He cocked his head at us. "During the day? You guys know this is a trap, right?"

"Of course it's a trap," I said. "But our friend—"

"No, I mean, like, sure she's probably rigged the whole bridge to do something spectacular, but the kid you're after won't be there. Remember, Charles? We used to goof off there all the time at night, but—"

"But during the day it's actually a busy area," Checker said breathlessly. "You're right, and there are hikers in the canyon too. She can't have Tabitha there. Or any dogs, or anyone else—people would see."

"Bridges make great traps," D.J. said cheerfully. "They blow real nice, and you can wait till someone's right in the middle so there's no scurrying out. Shit crackers, she's probably going to blame me for blowing it, huh?"

"Or me," Checker said bitterly. "And she's not going to worry about how many bystanders it takes down either. The first major hit in her big fearmongering plan. But, Cas, if Tabitha isn't there—"

"Wait." I pointed at him. "You said it, earlier, when we realized Willow Grace was bad news. Fifer's impersonating someone famous. To avoid making people suspicious, she would be having to *impersonate* her, right? I don't care how detailed her 'sabbatical to write a book' cover story was, she'd still need to keep it looking like Willow Grace was alive and kicking."

Checker sucked in a breath. "You think she's using Willow Grace's house. The real Willow Grace's house."

I nodded, and he spun back to his computers like he'd been shot from a cannon.

"If there are multiple options, find somewhere the correct radius from the ranch for her to bring the dogs there and come back to blow it up when the police reports say she did," I said.

"Got it," Checker said. "She's got some Malibu mansion—oh my God, what a cliché."

"Right distance?"

"Right distance," he confirmed. "With a little extra time for her to get the dogs installed wherever she wanted them and then make a return trip."

"What are these dogs you're talking about?" D.J. asked curiously.

What about the dogs, indeed. I still had no strategy against them. "What's the latest on Simon's condition?" I asked Checker.

He shook his head grimly, pulling something up on one of his machines. "Last medical notation I'm getting is . . . okay, it seems like he's stable now. But still in the ICU. Uh, looking at this—it looks pretty bad, but—I don't know; I'm not a doctor. I did tell Juwon to call us as soon as he got through, and no word from him yet. From this, I'm not optimistic they're passing in any calls."

"Okay." I rolled things around in my head. If I couldn't take Simon with me, either in person or on the phone . . . but with telepathy on our side, there still had to be a way we could use it. "Can he talk at all?"

"I can show you his charts, but . . . I'm not a doctor?" Checker repeated.

Neither was I.

"It still makes sense to try him," I declared. "I can go in person; the hospital's not a big detour. That way I can take Pilar too, see if he can set her right." And then see if there was any way he could either help us in advance or talk us through. "Checker, do you have another phone for me to leave with him, if he can talk?"

He opened a drawer and tossed me a new burner. "I'm sending Willow Grace's address to it right now. And the hospital address."

Perfect. The chance of getting some backup in the form of Pilar made stopping at Simon's bedside doubly worth it, and a hospital wouldn't be an unsafe place to leave her if Simon wasn't communicable.

And if he wasn't . . . Oscar's memories washed through me again, his drug-addled brain purposely high and reckless.

"There *is* a plan B," I said. "If Simon can't back us up. We know how Oscar and Fifer were able to approach the things."

"*Cas,*" Checker said.

"We might not know exactly what they were using, but I have contacts I can ask for something similar," I plowed on. "I'm guessing it would be something like PCP. That won't addict after one use." Even if it did, withdrawal would have been a small price to pay to give Tabitha a chance.

"PCP won't addict you after eight uses," D.J. said brightly. "Or has it been nine?"

"Wait. Think this through. Drugs are a huge risk," Checker protested. "PCP might work to make you feel invulnerable to the dogs, but it also *fucks you up*. You could end up killing yourself. Or Tabitha.

Or just tanking the goddamn mission, which would, oh, right, *also kill Tabitha—*"

"Keep your shirt on," I said. "I have a lot of experience with drugs, remember?"

"Depressants," Checker pointed out. "And not ever when you're on a job and there are people depending on you. You have absolutely no experience with that!"

What did you take?

My medicine.

The crack of bone against flesh, the sharp snap of moves so fast they couldn't be countered.

"You don't know everything about me," I said to Checker. Coldly.

He pulled away from me, his face closing up like I'd threatened him.

Fuck. Fuck "chronic illnesses" and their interference with my fucking life. I took a breath and did something I'd never purposely done before—acknowledged it. "Sorry. I've got some brain leakage happening."

"Is it . . ." Checker licked his lips. "Are you okay for this?"

"Yeah. I am," I said honestly. "It's just . . . moments."

"Nobody interesting is sane, dollface," D.J. put in. "You're in good company, right, Charles?"

Christ save me from *D.J.'s* help. "Where were we?"

"I was telling you I thought drugs were an incredibly risky plan," Checker said. "Which I still think is true, but . . ." He shut his eyes a moment. "It's all we've got, isn't it? Just, Cas—be careful, okay?"

"Careful is for suckers," D.J. piped up. But at least it rescued me from having to answer.

"That's the plan, then," I said. "I'll go to Simon, failing that, find some injectable courage, and head to the mansion. You two sit on the station and either dismantle whatever Fifer leaves or get the cops on it. They can pull the bomb squad in if you can pinpoint a device."

D.J. snorted. "I wouldn't trust the bomb squad to take apart one of Fifer's shebangs. She may be sloppy, but she did learn from the best, and trust me, I taught her how to derail a bomb squad."

"Look, all we need is for the prisoners to get moved," I said to him. "That's all. If you can't keep the rest of the station from going up, so be it. You keep our people safe, you've held up your end of the deal."

A slow smile spread across D.J.'s face. "See? I knew I liked you!"

"No, we do care," Checker said. "We *definitely* care if other people get hurt. But . . . our first priority is Diego and Elisa. Just, you know, don't ignore everyone else."

"Sure! It'll be like old times!" D.J. yelped. He grabbed his backpack of equipment and scampered out of the garage.

Checker shuddered slightly and then followed.

thirty-six

San Fernando Memorial Hospital was a big, boxy institutional place. I slipped in to steal a wheelchair for Pilar and then walked us straight into the intensive care unit, trying to act as though we belonged there. Pilar had gone quiet, and when she grabbed a bit at my sleeve, her hands didn't seem to be closing right. Her skin was clammy, her hair plastered across her face.

Simon had a private room. When we first came in, my eyes had trouble finding him on the bed—his body was so buried behind blankets and traction equipment and an oxygen mask. Tubes crisscrossed the room, machines beeping in the corner, and the sterile dryness of the air sucked everything raw.

I had a moment of trepidation, wondering if this had been a fool's errand. Then his head turned slightly, and a weak hand burrowed up to pull at the mask. He must have sensed our presence somehow.

I nudged Pilar closer to the side of the bed.

I didn't know what to say. I didn't want him to see how little I'd been thinking of him since I left him with the ambulance. How I never even checked to see if he'd lived, not until we needed him.

He'd see it anyway, I knew.

I brought Pilar up right to the side of the bed, close enough that he twitched a hand over to cover hers loosely. I pulled up a chair next to her. "Can you help her?"

His hand pressed gently, quivering against her skin. Her head lolled up, her eyes coming into focus on his face.

They stayed that way for fourteen long seconds, while I shifted in the chair, waiting. Then Simon's eyelids fluttered and his hand slid down.

Pilar slumped in the wheelchair, her eyes closed. I reached over and touched her wrist. Her pulse had slowed to something only a little above normal.

"Hey," I said.

She opened her eyes. "Cas? Wh—where are we?"

Her voice sounded hoarse, as if she'd been screaming.

"The hospital," I said. "I think Simon just fixed you."

She moved as if to get up from the wheelchair, then sagged back down. "I don't, I don't feel very fixed . . ."

She probably wasn't, not all the way. At least, assuming Simon hadn't flung his powers against her accidentally—like he had at me the day before—and stolen her whole memory of the incident. I realized too late that I should have been worried about him ensnaring us in an unintentional psychic morass, but whatever his new injuries, he seemed to have control of his brain.

I could tell by how embarrassingly uncharitable I felt toward him.

"You've been in a state of panic for hours now," I said to Pilar. "It probably took something out of you."

She gave a little nod, her face going greenish.

"If you need to be sick, I can find you a bedpan or something."

She seemed to swallow it back down, and then croaked, "Tabitha?"

"I'm asking you this time," I said quietly. "Are you in?"

Without any hesitation, she twitched her head in a nod. "Just, um. Let me . . ."

I reached back into my belt and retrieved her CZ, keeping Sikorsky's Glock for myself. "Here. Get yourself together."

She took the gun and holstered it, managing it on the second try.

I turned back to Simon.

His eyes were still slitted open, following me and Pilar.

I wanted to tell him I was glad he was okay, but he would see the lie in it.

Cas, just tell me what else you need. The words projected themselves wearily at me.

"Uh. We're . . . Tabitha got taken. Arthur's daughter. We think we know where she is, but we need to . . ."

He shifted his head slightly, his eyelids fluttering again as if he were having trouble keeping them open. Then he lifted his hand toward me in the smallest motion.

It was a clear invitation.

Fuck. He was too weak to talk.

I'd said I would do anything.

I took a deep breath and reached for his hand, concentrating on his face, trying to bring the whole mess of a situation to the forefront of my mind: Willow Grace and Tabitha, and Elisa and Diego in danger, and Pilar and I had to go in but there would be no way we could get past the fucking dogs, or if she had any other people like Coach . . .

Coach.

Simon's hand tightened on mine, his fingernails digging into my skin. With an effort, I wrestled back the wave of guilt and self-recrimination and failure and grief. Killing the man I'd barely known in this life.

"Sorry," I said, and I actually meant it.

Simon had begun twitching like he was about to seize, but then he rode through it. I refocused on the problem—the dogs, we knew she had more, they'd probably been her first experiments, and they'd been moved from the ranch. We thought we knew where. We'd never get past them.

Simon read my microexpressions and the pressure of my hand and the movement of my eyes and the twitch of my second eyelash, or whatever constituted his powers, and his chin dipped slightly. *I understand.*

Can you—I don't know. Brainwash us? Hypnotize us somehow, in advance, so that we won't be afraid of them? I thought the words as clearly as I could, in English.

No.

Annoyance from him—because of course he would have done that before, if it were possible. It wasn't. At least, there was no way he could think of to pinpoint it; the dogs were designed to push our fear centers.

Frustration roughed through my thoughts, along with a push for him to help us, to brainstorm, that there *must* be something he could do. Unfair, and I knew it, but he had goddamn superpowers and so did I. We had to be able to figure something out.

I caught something then, from Simon. Despite how rudely I was asking, he *was* trying to think of a way to help us, something he could do, and . . .

"What do you mean, it's too specific?" I said aloud.

It's too specific. I could . . . but it's too dangerous. Bad idea. Bad idea . . .

"You're breaking up," I said. I felt my own thoughts poking at him—*what? What? What? What is it?*

He sighed, the smallest breath through dry lips. *Another way . . .*

But I'd picked it up by that time. "Fear," I breathed. "You can take our fear."

Cas, it's too dangerous. Fear is useful. You need it. Without fear, who knows what you would do?

"I'd win," I said.

You could kill yourself. Just by not being afraid enough of death.

"Cas?" ventured Pilar. She'd managed to stand, her hand shaky on the back of my chair.

"He can make us immune to fear," I said. "But not only of the dogs. All of our fear. We wouldn't be afraid of anything."

"Maybe that's good, huh?" She made a small, slightly hysterical sound. "I could use a little less fear."

Tell her! barked Simon.

"I'm telling her," I snapped. "He says it's too dangerous. That we need our fear. Without it, we might do something stupid and die."

I felt Simon's mental irritation at my description.

But Pilar nodded slowly. "I see. With our fear, though . . . would we have any chance at all? Against those things?" She swallowed. "I don't—I don't ever want to go through that again, Cas."

I didn't either.

"He can reverse it, right?" she asked.

Bad. Idea, Simon thought at me again, but I got the confirmation.

"Yes, he can reverse it," I said to Pilar.

"Then, uh, is there any other—do we have a better choice?"

Let me think . . . pleaded Simon.

We could always shoot ourselves up with PCP, I said to him. *Wouldn't be afraid of anything then either, and slightly more damaging to the brain.*

From his mental reaction, Simon could clearly tell that was the actual Plan B. I caught a wash of exasperation and anger.

It's one or the other, I informed him. *This is what we've got.*

I looked at him. He looked at me.

"It's the best option, isn't it?" I said aloud.

The ghost of a growl from him. I snapped at him before I could stop myself: *This isn't something I want either, you know—letting you in my head. She's sixteen, Simon.*

He could be annoyed with me all he wanted. We both had to put Tabitha first.

Simon's thoughts sighed at me, and I got a resigned feeling of acquiescence.

"What do we do?" Pilar asked.

Cas. You first.

I followed Simon's mental directions to scoot my chair closer and lean forward. My wariness spiked, as it always did when I was around him, when I was about to allow him access to my mind. It was an irrational fear—Simon was powerful enough for me not even to know he was affecting me. But I couldn't shake it.

Until now, I supposed. After this, I wouldn't be afraid of anything.

Simon's fingers closed around my hand. *Focus on me,* he directed in my head. *Focus on me . . .*

I did. His eyes were fever-bright. They fastened on mine, held me close like they were my one safe harbor in the universe.

Relax. The order intoned through me. *Relax. You're not afraid.*

"I'm not afraid," I whispered.

My mental landscape flattened, expanded, wavered into a trance-like state.

I can do anything, I thought. *I'm not afraid.*

You're not afraid.

I'm not afraid . . .

Worry, concern, apprehension, fear—they one and all receded and washed away from me, as if I were rising out of a lake and shedding streams of emotion behind me, forgotten.

I'm not afraid.

I'm not afraid.

I'm not afraid. I am powerful.

I can do anything, and win.

I caught Simon's quick, sharp spike of apprehension. Not about me—toward me.

I blinked and sat up. "Wait, seriously? I'm not going to try to become a world dictator."

In fact, I felt mostly the same. Maybe slightly more narcissistic. But Pilar shot me a quick, slightly nervous glance too, and stepped back from where she'd been leaning on my chair again.

"Oh, come on," I said. "You two really think it was *fear* that kept me from going on a rampage?"

Pilar opened her mouth and then shut it again. "I think I should ask you to do me now before *Cas* scares the daylights out of me," she said to Simon.

I stood so she could take my place at his bedside. "I can't tell if you're joking."

"Me neither." She sat.

The process took a lot longer than it felt like it had with me—and I usually had a good sense of time. Ordinarily the discrepancy would have made me squirrelly, but now I shrugged and acknowledged it as fact. Pilar went tense for a few minutes and then began to sway slightly; when she stilled and blinked her eyes, she seemed to come back to herself.

"Are we done?" she asked.

I didn't hear Simon's assent, but he must have told her yes mentally with a twitch or a glance. Pilar stood.

"I'm ready," she said. She was a lot more relaxed than she'd been a few minutes ago. Her eyes were clear.

"So you are," I said.

Be careful, I thought I heard from Simon, but it was mixed with so much regret and fatalism that I couldn't be sure of the meaning.

We'd walk straight through the dogs, and if Fifer threw anything else at us, well, we'd handle that too. Including her. *PCP fucks you up,* Checker had said, and he was right—even odds Fifer was going to be going into this standoff hopped up and reckless.

Thanks to Simon, we'd be able to be just as reckless. Hopefully, it would be enough.

thirty-seven

I LEFT the second phone with Simon anyway, even though he wouldn't be able to talk to us over it. Instead, I told him to call the number Juwon was at, the moment he could be any help over a phone line.

The pressure and guilt he felt at his inability to do more—it brushed faintly against me, and a few moments ago it might have mirrored my own powerlessness. But now, the concern that had been chewing at me about Arthur and the twins, about Checker and D.J. and Diego and Elisa—it had all simply dropped away. Everyone else would either be fine or they wouldn't. It no longer weighed on me.

Our only job was Tabitha, and we would succeed.

I had become used to Pilar grabbing the dash or the door every other minute whenever I was driving. This time, she calmly finished some crackers and apple juice she'd picked up from a hospital vending machine and then sat with her hands in her lap. She did wear her seat belt, but I supposed that was logic or habit rather than fear. Personally, I didn't think my driving differed markedly without being afraid, but I also wasn't worried about getting stopped by the cops. If flashing lights appeared on our tail, we would deal with them. That was all.

We wound our way out to Malibu, and I parked just down the street from the real Willow Grace's luxury home, the streets curvy and shaded enough here to give us good cover. Checker had been sending us regular updates via text:

AT STA

WG GONE

WAITING

STILL NO

WAITNG

NOT BACK

NOT HERE

NOPE

NADA

"It would help us out if we wait until Checker and D.J. see her back at the station, wouldn't it?" Pilar said. Her voice was steady.

"Probably." If they had eyes on her, it would be a good bet on the house being clear. "On the other hand, we don't know if she's actually going after Diego and Elisa right now. She might have been casing the place so she could go back after she deals with us."

"She might be at the place she told you to go for Tabitha too," Pilar added. I'd filled her in on the way over. "If she thinks we're going to fall for her trap."

"Or she might be here." I shrugged. None of the possibilities seemed particularly prohibitive. "Go now?"

"Why not?"

We got out of the car. I pulled Sikorsky's gun. A Glock in nine-millimeter was the worst of all possible worlds as far as I was concerned, but if something needed a bullet put in it, it would do.

Pilar's legs buckled a little when she stood. "I'm okay," she said.

Her muscles must still be a little fried. I thought of Arthur and Matti and Roy. Simon had been deep enough in my head that I was sure he'd picked up on their condition, but until he could whisper over a phone, there wasn't much he'd be able to do. Juwon would have to take care of them.

I wasn't worried.

We crested the hill on the edge of the property. Willow Grace's house was a sweeping indulgence in extravagance, complete with a high wall of gleaming white stone that swooped around its perimeter.

She would have a security system, of course, but I wasn't worried about that either.

Willow Grace did have a security system—or rather, her bomb-making doppelgänger did, not only cameras but tripwires and laser mounts that led back to real wires and kabooms. I evaded or disabled them all, giving Pilar a heads-up behind me.

It all felt markedly easy. I wouldn't have thought I was usually nervous while busting into places like this, but maybe I was. Maybe it kept me on my toes. This was all so—boring.

We snuck through groves of orange trees and past an honest-to-God infinity pool. And came face-to-face with one of the dogs.

At least, I assumed it was. To my senses, it just looked like . . . a dog.

Granted, a very large dog, who was not at all happy to see us, its fur spiking up across its back in an aggressive crest as it bared very sharp-looking teeth. But otherwise, just a dog. Not a particularly ugly or vicious-looking dog either.

Its golden eyes gleamed in the darkness. It growled at us. We stared back at it.

"I kinda don't want to kill them," Pilar said in a whisper. "Now that they're just . . . dogs. I like dogs."

I wasn't so fond of them, but there was also no reason to waste the ammunition if the thing wasn't going to attack us.

We stared at it for another few seconds. It started to dip its head, and then its torn ears flattened against its head and it crouched with a whine.

"Oh, poor thing," Pilar said. "It probably never sees anyone who isn't scared to death of it. Do you, champ?" She lowered her gun, stepped forward, and reached out to scratch the dog behind its ears.

It twitched and whined again, but didn't snap at her hand. Almost as if it didn't dare.

"No, you're not keeping him," I said.

We ran into two more of the animals on the way to the main house. They reacted in much the same way, starting with a growl and then slinking back into the trees and bushes when we didn't seem afraid.

"We could start a TV show," Pilar said. "A new kind of dog whispering."

I was sure Simon would *love* that idea.

The mansion was large enough to have balconies and wings. It expanded above us like a ship at full sail, pale and stately against the sky. We climbed onto a bleached wooden deck and approached a side door, where I found and cut the wire for the alarm and then found and cut the wire for the booby trap.

We went inside.

The rooms were large, empty, and slovenly in the manner of someone who wasn't living in her own space. Greasy pizza boxes and old Chinese food cartons tipped against one another on the first coffee table we passed, with past food spills staining the carpet uncleaned. Clothes and electronics paraphernalia draped the wide-open spaces haphazardly or collected in corners. Fifer must be a fan of cheap beer—cans showed up crumpled on every surface, old half-full ones leaving rings on mahogany tables or the grand piano.

One small, empty room that didn't seem to have much defined purpose now had blood-crusted ropes thrown against the wall and dark stains soaking the hardwood. Someone had tried to clean them, but not very well. *Real quiet. Wooden floors, smelled like bleach,* Arthur had said.

I shut the door and didn't share my suspicions with Pilar.

The other oddity was a solarium—it looked like it was about to become a full-on operating theater, with an operating table, equipment, and tools all sort of stacked and jumbled together in a way that probably wasn't sanitary. None of it seemed to have been put to use here yet, though.

Pilar and I finished canvassing the front half of the ground floor and stepped up a shallow flight of stairs toward the back. My phone vibrated in my pocket.

It was Checker. I picked up one-handed, still stepping forward cautiously gun-first and keeping my voice low. "Hello?"

"She's there! Fifer's there, where you are, I mean she probably is—she's not here at least—Cas, we got it wrong. D.J. was wrong about what she would do—" I could tell he was typing as he talked; his voice had the distracted quality it did when he was at a computer, and the clack of keys was audible in the background. "She hit us already. She wasn't casing the station, she set it and left, she's done here. And we found her device but—but that's not important. What's important is that if she's not here, there's a good chance she went back to the house; she could be waiting for you—"

"Okay," I said. "Thanks."

"Right. Okay." A moment of dead air as Checker waited for me to hang up and I didn't. "Cas? I called you in time, right? Is everything okay?"

"So far," I said. He thought he'd catch us early enough to deliver a warning. Oh, well. I stepped through the next doorway, more of my attention on my front sight than the conversation. "Stop panicking. We're fine. And it sounds like you found the bomb where you are, so you're good too. Just get D.J. on it."

"We did! We snuck him in and—he's working on it now and he says not to alert the bomb squad because they'll blow it, but he says she did a good job for once and he's not sure if he can do it in time, and Elisa and I, we have to get Diego out of here, everyone out if we can, because we don't know if he'll even be able to—and Elisa won't leave either—"

"You have a plan?" I said.

"Break him out," Checker said.

"Okay. Good."

He sucked in a breath. "Diego's going to kill me. He . . . but better that than dead. Cas. If you have a sec . . . this got complicated, and what I'm about to do, there's a chance it will—the power grid is—I have to be here at the station, and D.J. says there's a chance what we're about to do is going to set it off."

"Okay," I said again. "How much of a chance?"

"I don't know. But if, if Elisa and Diego and I, if we don't—just in case, can you take a message? For Arthur." He paused. "Tell him they forgave him."

"Did they?"

"No. Just tell him. And him and the twins and Juwon and Tabitha, tell them—tell them I love them, please." His voice wobbled.

"Sure."

"Cas, it's—it's been a good time, hasn't it? We've had a good run."

I didn't know why I asked the question, then. I shouldn't have even been taking attention from our walkthrough to keep talking to him, especially not with the new intelligence that Fifer was probably somewhere on the premises. But the doubt had been lurking, chewing at the back of my mind, and maybe I knew I wouldn't have had the courage to voice it if I hadn't been dead to all my fear. "Hey, Checker. Honest answer. Would we still be friends if you didn't think I could be saved?"

He made a choking sound. "What? You can't ask me that."

"Why not?"

"You just can't. And when you figure out the reason, you'll know why."

The way he was talking, I wondered if that would be the last thing Checker would ever say to me.

"I gotta go, Cas. Take care, okay? Don't go in if it's—get Tabitha, find her, but stay safe. Please."

"I have to go too," I said. "See you on the other side."

"I hope so," he said, and hung up.

"That was Checker?" Pilar said.

"Yeah. They got fucked."

She digested this. "They have a plan?"

I shrugged. "I think so."

"Good." She pointed. "Cas, what's that?"

I followed her gaze. A bookshelf had been shifted to the side on runners, and behind it, a metal door as thick as a vault's stood open.

I tracked back where we'd been in my head. We were somewhere around the middle of the sprawling floor plan, I reckoned. It could be a large safe, but the opening looked more like a darkened hallway, and I thought safe *room* was more likely.

"For disasters or home invasions," I said. "And it looks like someone's inviting us in."

I stepped carefully into the darkened entrance, snapping up an LED flashlight under my gun hand to flash around. The white light showed only smooth, bare walls.

"It goes deeper," I said. "Fancy safe room." Some rich people had panic rooms they could live in for days or weeks, especially in case of natural disaster. Since in California that usually meant earthquake, this one would be sure to be reinforced in every dimension—my brain ran the calculations disinterestedly, seismic amplitudes spiking at resonant frequencies, shear forces that would have to be rebuffed by solidity and minimum thicknesses.

Pilar had out a keychain flashlight of her own, and she angled to cover behind us as we stepped down the short corridor. After a few meters, it opened up into a bunkroom. Aside from the bunks, the side of the room was stacked in neat organization with containers of emergency rations, bags of water, clothes and blankets, gas masks, medicines, sanitation supplies, and everything else a rich person might plausibly need in case of apocalypse.

Or, almost everything. If I'd been designing a safe room, I'd have a lot more gasoline and ammunition in it. But people like the real Willow Grace probably didn't buy into guns being more important than food.

"I don't like this," Pilar murmured. "Cas, if this is a safe room meant to keep people from getting in, doesn't that also mean it would be hard to get ou—"

The lights came on in a blaze of brilliance. At the same time, the door behind us clanged shut with the resounding finality of reinforced steel.

"—out," Pilar finished in a resigned tone.

Well, shit.

A loud, obnoxious ticking rose in the silence following her statement.

"Cas—"

I didn't bother to answer, hurrying through the one door left, which led to a second reinforced room built against the short hallway. This one had originally been for surveillance and communication, with large monitors tiling one wall. Emergency communications gear had been wired into a desktop, but now it had all been pried open and scattered, a sprawling tangle of electrical and fiberoptic spaghetti. And the monitors—half the screens were dark, presumably the feeds I had cut on our way into the mansion, but the other half . . .

The other half showed black-and-white surveillance footage from somewhere that wasn't the mansion. On one screen was Checker, in a dark room frantically clattering at a keyboard, a flashlight rolling on the desktop beside him. On a second, a prison cell, Diego sitting on the cot, leaning against the wall in exhaustion. Other screens flashed on the lobby or hallways of the police station, and I caught Elisa's form walking and talking with a detective who seemed to be listening more rationally than Sikorsky had. And a final one showed a close-up of a complicated device somewhere in a basement, wires and lights cheerfully spelling out fourteen minutes left, and D.J.'s face bending close with a deranged grin.

Counters in the corners of all the monitors showed the same number.

"Give me your phone; I'll call them," Pilar said.

"No. Wait." I turned, widening my survey of the room. Against every wall was stacked one more addition: metal canisters wired together in disturbingly familiar ways, and an LED timer of our own flashing down through 26:04.

"No cell signals," I said to Pilar. "It could set something off."

She glanced around at the reinforced walls. "Probably no bars anyway."

"We can't help them. We have to trust D.J." I turned my back on the monitors. "But I can disarm this."

I started following the wires back the same way I had been throughout our whole walk into the mansion, using the same if-A-then-B logical trees. This was fine. I could do it. Disarm Fifer's last-ditch attempt at entrapping us, ignore the psychological warfare she had thrown in with the feeds of our friends, and then figure out how to break out of the safe room and keep hunting for Tabitha.

I cut the first wire.

"Cas!" shouted Pilar.

I spun back around. The countdowns on the monitors had suddenly accelerated. Twelve minutes. Eleven. D.J. flailed in black-and-white silence on his monitor, clearly cursing a blue streak while his LED numbers plummeted. I whipped back to the wires I still held—backtracked to where they connected—I thought I knew what was going on here—

I slashed the flat of my knife down both wire ends to strip them and in one twist sealed them back together. On the monitors, the countdown threatening Checker, D.J., Diego, and Elisa slowed again.

"We can't—without . . ." said Pilar. "How bad of a boom will this make? Is there anywhere in here we could protect ourselves?" She looked around the room, then toward me hopefully.

I used my knife to pry up one corner of one of the canisters, very carefully. The explosive was some sort of white powder—I didn't know how I might identify it, but I was guessing something on the level of military-grade explosives. TNT, RDX, maybe PETN . . . maybe a combination . . . I charted out the mass and explosive yields, the thermodynamic work that would become flame and death, the Friedlander waveform that would make the air into a bludgeon, refracting and diffracting around the surfaces in the room and through our fragile human bodies.

My best estimates were that there would be nothing left of anything in the safe room once this went off. On the plus side, the walls were reinforced enough that the explosion would likely stay contained in here. Probably why Fifer had planned it this way.

"We wouldn't even be smears on the wall," I answered Pilar.

She made a face. "Gotcha."

I focused back on the wiring. Translated again to the logic of conditional statements. If this worked the way I thought it might . . .

I followed a different wire back, pulled out my knife, and cut it, ignoring Pilar's yelp of, "Wait, Cas, what—"

Our timer jumped down by five minutes, and the one on D.J.'s bomb simultaneously jumped up by five. He exclaimed in surprise and then mimed kissing the thing.

"Fifer does like her games," I said.

"We can give them more time," breathed Pilar. "If we're going to die anyway . . . not that, I mean, I don't want to, but . . . what can we do?"

"We're not giving up on Tabitha," I said. "Self-sacrificing shit is all well and good, but not today. If we die, she dies."

"But if we can't disable the bomb without killing our friends—" Her face went slack in shock and horror. "Cas, you're not thinking of—are you? Tell me you aren't!"

I almost laughed at her. "No, Pilar, Simon taking our fear away did not make me suddenly willing to kill Checker or Arthur's *other* daughter."

"Oh," Pilar said. "Okay. Well, good. Then . . . what are we going to do?"

"We," I answered, "are going to set off this bomb."

Not having any fear might not make me a murderer, but it sure did make me rash.

thirty-eight

I TASKED Pilar with finding me something heavy and metal, and with delicate precision started cataloguing the logic of Fifer's bomb. The wires disappeared into the air vents in the walls, whatever system they were rigged into inaccessible to me. I wished I had enough leeway to experiment and figure out exactly what all the functions were—when I did X, what Y fell out on D.J. and Checker's end— but gathering data might have gobbled one or both of our remaining clocks. So I had two simpler goals: set off the whole mess as early as possible and transfer all remaining time to D.J., and somehow introduce a *tiny* bit of delay so that some of it went before the rest.

Pilar came back from the bunkroom with a heavy metal flashlight. "Will this do?"

"Perfect." I'd started counting down infallibly in my head, but I checked the two timers to make sure nothing had changed. D.J.'s clock was back above fourteen, ours at 19:28.

If possible, I wanted to give them at least fifteen of those minutes.

I didn't bother to remind myself the germ of an idea in my head might not even be possible. The flashlight would tell me. I took the heavy metal cylinder from Pilar and began tapping it along the walls of the safe room.

Sound waves echoed back at me, dully telegraphing the solidity of steel and concrete, the oscillations drawing out the perfect, invisible acoustic picture. Pristine and uncracked. No weak points.

I kept going, letting the sound graph out an X-ray of the walls for me. I tapped across first the surveillance room, then into the bunk-room, all the while both timers ticking down in my head.

Nothing. The place was tight as a drum.

If I'd been capable, I might have started feeling nervous.

"What about the ceiling?" Pilar asked.

I looked up. Difficult. First to direct a charge up there, and then to rig ourselves somehow to catapult out. Alone I could have done it, maybe . . .

I cut off that line of thought before I started questioning the balance of Pilar's life versus Tabitha's. "I haven't tried the floor yet," I said instead.

Not that I was optimistic. An earthquake safe room would probably be built right against the ground, even if this mansion was fancy enough to support the rare beast of a Southern California basement under other rooms.

But when I struck the floor near the back wall of the bunk room, the *thunk* of a new acoustic skeleton was the sweetest sound I'd ever heard.

"Here." I tapped more, listening for the echo through solid and then a blessedly close boundary, sounding across the patch of floor and drawing out the outline in my head. We'd have almost no margin for error. A small slice against the wall—barely big enough for one human to stand on, let alone two—was admitting to some miniscule overlap with empty space below it. Empty space, and a floor telling us it was just unreinforced enough for a shaped charge to bust through, given how everywhere else it sat firmly against unyielding earth.

Of course, I had no idea what was underneath. It might be no more than a vent of a crawl space. If so, we were fucked.

Oh well.

Nine and a half minutes, said D.J.'s clock in my head. We could still give him another ten.

"I need you to do exactly as I say," I said to Pilar. I didn't bother telling her the unknown variables still might kill us. Either we'd survive, or she'd die not knowing the difference. "Pull the bottom mattress off the bunks, and push the bed frames away from the wall a few feet."

While she did that, I scanned my eyes over the rest of the contents of the room. The casings from the broken communications equipment were passable, but some of the metal canisters the emergency rations were in would work even better. I dumped them out and banged the metal hard against the wall to deform it, angles playing out in my head and the theatrical ticking omnipresent in the background.

"What can I do now?" asked Pilar.

"Stand there." I pointed, then went to the other room and very, very carefully tugged out one of the canisters of explosive material. The wiring would only let it move so far, but I yanked one of the useless radio wires from the tangle, pulled my knife, and spliced the new wire in before slicing through the old one in one move. I was smooth enough that the ominous clocks backgrounding me on every monitor kept ticking down at the exact same speed, one second at a time.

"Your job is going to be to shoot the detonator on this," I said to Pilar, explaining as I moved, lifting my chosen canister carefully over to sit on the exposed springs of the bunk frame. "I'm jury-rigging a shaped charge, which means directing the explosives in a way that they concentrate a bunch of metal into a projectile and punch it through. This is going to take the floor out from under us, so be prepared."

I finished setting the canister in my bent-up shaped metal and aimed it at Pilar's feet, materials charting themselves with estimates and error margins through my consciousness. I didn't know the exact explosives yield of what we were dealing with here, which made this worse than foolhardy, especially given how many variables the physics of shaped charges had . . . but I could make some good guesses. And, well, if it didn't work, I wouldn't exactly be able to regret it.

"If we set off the one, though—won't the bomb read that as a disconnection?" Pilar asked.

"That's why I'm going to set off the rest of it before it realizes what we did." My aim was more than good enough to hit the right wire from through the doorway and across the room. Hopefully the bomb would give all our remaining time to D.J. and Checker as it went up in flaming glory, give D.J. enough time to finish disarming or Checker enough minutes to get Diego and the others out. Or both.

Not that an extra ten minutes was a lot of time. But it was all I could control.

I finished positioning my device at what I estimated was the optimal stand-off distance for punch through. Then I tilted the mattress up against the bed frame, giving Pilar and me a tiny bit of shielding from the main bomb. It wouldn't do much. My timing was going to have to be exact to the millisecond—too soon and I'd destroy us, too late and I'd kill everyone at the police station when our bomb sensed we'd tampered.

I ducked behind the mattress next to Pilar and leaned forward to tap my makeshift shaped charge right at the back. "See this? That's the detonator. You have to target exactly there. If you hit the explosives, it probably won't do anything." Depending on how reckless Fifer was. Most military-grade explosives were too stable to go off when hit by small arms fire, but who knew. "Got it?"

"Got it," Pilar said, readying her stance. She was still a little less firm than usual, but I didn't worry about her accuracy. The detonator might be about the width of a pencil, but if she couldn't hit a target only few feet in front of her, we had bigger problems.

I cast one last glance over the scene. "Back up more," I said to Pilar. "Unless you want the front half of your left foot torn off."

She pressed herself farther back against the wall and reset her gun hand. I crammed myself in next to her, practically standing on her feet.

Ten minutes and twenty-two seconds left for us.

"On my mark." The sequence played itself out in my mind. Detonation, the explosive punch through the floor. I would fire as we fell, and the whole safe room would go up in flames and concussion as we descended away from it.

Hopefully.

I settled the pad of my finger against the trigger. *"Now."*

Pilar fired.

I'd forgotten about protecting our hearing. A clap of pure thunder sucked all the air from around us, over us, under us, taking me off my feet—or was it the floor disappearing from beneath me?

The world was suspended in dust and flame and noise, the air made hard and spinning us where and how it would. Even my senses couldn't keep up. I desperately flailed against the concussion with my gun hand, lining up with where I had been—I thought—was I already too late?—while the rest of me fell away into oblivion, and I managed to squeeze back the trigger of the Glock.

I felt the sear trip and the grip bucked in my hand, so I was pretty sure I had fired. I didn't have a chance for a second try. Everything was falling, flattening, darkening.

Then the main explosion roared out at us like the fires of hell.

thirty-nine

I MUST have blacked out for an instant, the shock wave jellying my brain in its skull. I had the vaguest impression of the mattress disintegrating in fire before our eyes, and then blackness.

Gravity saved us.

Mathematically, our plunge must have lasted less than a second, but that split second lasted an eternity, a forever of being hopelessly out of control. I fell hard against Pilar, and metal and debris fell hard on me.

I lay for a moment, stunned. My internal organs felt like they'd been put through a blender, but every time I tried to evaluate the damage, it was like my neurons shorted out on me. Gradually, I realized that it wasn't actually all that dark in here—the lighting was a dim ambiance, but the explosion from above was still imprinted on my retinas, shrouding my surroundings with its afterimage.

I hoped I'd set it off in time. I hoped Checker and the others weren't dead.

I hoped, even if I'd given them that extra time, that they could use it, and weren't all just going to die anyway after their counter ran out.

I put those thoughts out of my head and tried to get up. It was hard. I had to push a lot of heavy things off me, and my joints didn't seem to want to respond. My bad ankle had turned to mush, and it almost went out completely before it decided it could support me, flaring up my leg in pain.

Someone made a small sound like a wounded bird, then coughed.

"Pilar?" I tracked back with my eyes. I'd been half on top of her, but she seemed to be trying to get up too now. Her skin and hair were so shrouded with a coating of dust and debris that she looked like a ghost—one who'd been put through a woodchipper. I doubted I was in any better shape.

"I lost my gun," she mumbled.

Mine was still in my hand. I dredged enough numbers to extrapolate where her CZ must have fallen, and shuffled over to retrieve it for her. By the time I pressed it into her hand, she'd managed a hunched half stand.

"Are you injured?" I said.

"My—my knee. I'm fine."

She clearly wasn't, but I let it pass.

"I don't think . . . I want to do that . . . again, though," she got out. "Where are we?"

I took a better look myself. We'd dropped out against a back wall made of brick, in the tiny piece of overlap with the destroyed safe room above. Expanding before us in the other direction now was the perfect encapsulation of a wealthy mansion: rack upon rack of smoky glass bottles, all labeled with long French and Italian names. A wine cellar.

"Come on," I said. "There must be a way back up to the house. If Fifer realizes what we . . ."

A movement in the dimness at the other side of the cellar. My gun hand came up, slower than it should have, my eyes taking a moment to focus. Pilar straightened behind me with the help of the wall, her CZ wavering.

Tabitha pushed out from the wine racks to one side. Literally pushed out, with Willow Grace—or rather, Fifer—behind her, shoving her in front. Tabitha's hands were cuffed, and her eyes rolled at us, chewing at the gag that had been stuffed in her mouth.

But she was alive. She was alive.

Fifer stopped. She was in ripped jeans and a T-shirt now, a startling difference from the imitation of Willow Grace's fashion sense, and it somehow made her look about fifteen years younger. Slung across her body was a canvas messenger bag, and she flipped back the flap on it aggressively, staring us down.

I knew what she had in the bag before she opened it. Fifer only had one weapon of choice, and the dead man's switch she was squeezing in one hand would have given it away even before I saw the wires and another goddamn LED timer, this one showing less than eight minutes left.

If I shot her, we were all dead.

I did remember to double-check that not pulling the trigger was a rational decision. I could still feel the pull of wanting to agree with whatever Fifer wanted, the hard-coded aesthetics pushing at my consciousness. It wasn't like going up against an actual psychic—now that I *knew*, I could center myself, see her for what she was. Not to mention that Tabitha, cuffed and gagged, eclipsed any other shadow of instinct or influence. But I also had a disturbing amount of doubt about what might happen if Fifer turned on the charm and begged for forgiveness.

Maybe it was fortunate that she didn't seem the least bit interested in either releasing Tabitha or admitting to her mistakes.

"You are so *freaking* annoying!" she sneered at me, her mouth twisting in her beautiful face.

"I try." I edged forward a little. "So, what's your plan? Blow yourself up along with us?"

"Stop," she said. "Stop *right there* or the girl gets it."

I stopped.

She scrunched her nose at me for a second. Then she giggled. It was disturbingly unlike her Willow Grace impersonation, her whole posture squashing up.

"I can't believe you got through all my traps," she said. "Are you proud of that? And are you proud of finally figuring out I was against you the whole time? Took you long enough. I was there right under your *nose*. You fell for my pretty face, didn't you?"

"Not anymore," I said.

"Too bad. But you see, the thing about having a hostage is, you're still going to do whatever I want. Dance to my little tune." She gave Tabitha a shake.

"The thing about having a hostage is," I echoed, "that's leverage you can only use once. You kill Tabitha, and we kill you."

"But then she'd be dead, and so will you. Which means I win."

She wasn't wrong.

"Now we have a good old-fashioned standoff," Fifer continued. She spoke almost cheerfully, and her voice had changed markedly, lilting up to what I assumed was closer to her natural accent. "I want you all dead, and you want your lives and the girl. I don't see a compromise, do you?"

"Why don't you just lock us all down here? Us and Tabitha?" Pilar suggested from behind me.

Smart. Fifer might think she could starve us to death—or give us alcohol poisoning, whichever came first—whereas Pilar had faith I'd be able to get us out once we were left alone.

But Fifer wasn't having it. "Nice try. Especially now that I've seen this one's freaky skills." She jerked her chin at me. "She's probably how you all ducked my BLEVE, isn't she? Such a waste. Now I have to redo all that work killing all of you."

"Why kill us at all?" I countered. "I honestly don't care about your little plan to muck with American politics. Let us go, and you can go do whatever the fuck idiotic thing you want."

Her face clouded. "I'm not doing this because I want to! But I'm not going to feel so helpless anymore. They're all rotten, rotten to the core, all bought and paid for by the fucking special interests and the one percent. They don't even see the rest of us, you know. They dance around in their fancy schools and fancy clubs and then do such shitty, awful things, and they won't ever even realize how fucking horrible they are. But I can stop it. I *will* stop it!"

"I said I don't care," I said. "The FBI or whoever can catch you. Just give us Tabitha and let us go."

"Hey," spoke up Pilar softly. "I get it. It can be really frustrating, right? You try to vote or donate money or go to protests, and it doesn't ever seem to mean anything. It feels like—it feels like abuse, doesn't it, but you can't even walk out or call anyone to stop them. But someone like you—who knows how to do what you do—you figure you can actually do something, right?"

Fifer narrowed her eyes. "Don't try to act like you get me."

"Okay," Pilar said.

"This country needs to get burned to the ground and restarted. It's too far gone."

"Okay," Pilar said again.

"So you're going to use terrorism to create mass panic, and then swoop in with all Teplova's people in the wake of it," I cut in. "I hate to break it to you, but I'm really not sure that'll make anything *better*."

"I'm going to do way more than that." Fifer gave Tabitha another little shake. "You think a few bombings were all I had planned? I'm going to make the whole world turn on one another. Parents killing their own children, lover against lover—"

"Oh, like you and Oscar?" I said.

"*You* killed him, not me!" she screamed at me. "It was your fault. I have to find a new doctor now, and all because *you* distracted me so I wouldn't see him!"

"Or you didn't see him because you made him almost entirely invisible." I almost added a crack about how if she needed a doctor so badly, she'd made a hell of a mistake by killing Teplova, but then I connected what she'd said.

Find a new doctor.

She'd killed Teplova. And D.J. had mentioned Oscar Lee being a medical school dropout. Oscar, who'd been willing to do anything for Fifer.

We'd assumed Teplova had given Oscar and Fifer their new features, and we'd probably been correct about that part. But we'd also assumed Teplova had been the one who'd created the dogs, and been forced to operate on Coach, and that, I suddenly realized, meant it would not have made a lick of sense for Fifer to kill her.

"Oscar learned Teplova's techniques," I said. "He was becoming your surgeon. You're planning to make . . ."

Oh God.

Fifer had an arm around Tabitha's throat now. "Yeah. You see now, don't you? I'm going to take this cute little girl and make her into a monster. She's so adorable, isn't she? And I'm going to cut her open and make her seem so vicious, her own family will scream at the sight. That is, if they don't try to kill her first." Her face bent back into a grin. "Or maybe you'll be the one to kill her. That would endear you to Daddy, now, wouldn't it?"

Fifer had already started experimenting on humans. She'd started with Coach, but he'd only been the first.

She wanted to make a lot more people into creatures everyone would hate and fear and tear apart. And she wanted to start with Tabitha.

Probably the only reason Tabitha hadn't already been sliced and diced was Oscar's death. But Fifer had all the files of Dr. Teplova's data, all the math of her techniques. As soon as she could find a new doctor to bribe, blackmail, or threaten into doing the surgeries . . .

"This was going to be step two," Fifer sneered at me. "But I had to move it all up, because of *you*."

"Yeah," I said slowly. "I'm irritating that way." The game pieces were rearranging themselves in my head. "You know, I could still force you to kill us all. Right here."

"You won't. You wouldn't sacrifice the girl. Besides, you always think you can *win*."

Not always. But I did now, considering Simon's magic.

Fifer glanced down at her bomb, which was counting down through four minutes.

"I've decided," she declared. "I'm not going to kill you—yet. I'm just going to leave, and you're going to let me, because you still think you can save her later. I bet you'd even let me carve her up, thinking there's still time. We have a compromise!" She started dragging Tabitha backward, toward the other end of the basement. I'd blinked away enough dust and grime now that I could see the stone steps at the other end.

"You're wrong." If she took Tabitha out of here, we'd never find her again. Or, if we found her, we'd be just as likely to kill her. I wasn't going to let her become Coach—Coach who I hadn't been able to rescue, who'd been so permanently warped . . . who'd died by my own hand.

Fifer was wrong. I didn't think I could save Tabitha later. I didn't think so at all.

"This ends here, today," I said. "I'll shoot you first."

"You're bluffing," Fifer spat past Tabitha's shoulder, not stopping.

"Maybe," I called back, pivoting to keep her in my sights. "But you want a compromise? I've got one."

That piqued her interest. She paused.

When I had her attention, I lowered the Glock and then slowly crouched to place it on the floor before straightening, hands raised. Her bomb readout flashed 3:19. If I could run it out . . . force her to stop it . . . change one variable . . .

"I'll give you a trade," I said. "Take me in her place."

"Cas!" gasped Pilar from behind me. I ignored her.

"Take me," I said again. "I'm a much better monster. I'm very hard to kill."

"I could take you anyway," Fifer said. "I could take you *both*."

"No, you couldn't."

Fifer paused, then broke into her biggest grin yet, her beautiful face in a beautiful grin. "I would get more mileage out of you. But what if you're just trying to get close to me to kill me?"

"Oh, I am," I said. "But there's always the chance I'll fail."

If I did fail . . .

It should have scared me, to think about being twisted into a crea-ture who would drive everyone away from me, who would inspire only panic or hatred, fleeing or bullets. The connections I'd been chasing so hard, all burned like flash paper as if they'd never been. Trapped alone in a skin no human should ever have, one that would drive me into a violent unreality. Would it be Arthur who killed me, eventually?

But today I wasn't scared. I was only sad.

Fifer seemed to read my mind. "You're already a monster," she said. "Poor widdle beastie. Trying so hard to be human, when all anybody else sees is your scales and teeth."

"Do you want me?" I said. "I'm making you my offer. You can take me. Let Pilar and Tabitha go."

Her eyes glittered.

I was too good at math not to know that I might be handing her the winning cards—not just over me, but over all of us. Without the danger I represented, would she really allow Pilar and Tabitha to walk out of here? The best I could hope for was that it would alter some inputs. Give the two of them the slimmest of chances.

That was okay with me today.

Hands still in the air, I took a step forward. Then another. I didn't need to look again at the bomb to know we were at less than two minutes. "If you're all about chaos, I promise I can cause it."

"You won't have a choice," she said. "Frankenstein's creation, King Kong . . . we tell the story over and over, how the creature that is feared and shunned will turn and shit on humanity. It's inevitable."

"You'll make the trade, then."

Fifer twisted with the hand clenched on the dead man's switch to dig around in the messenger bag holding her bomb. She came up with something and tossed it at me. It clattered to the smooth hardwood floor of the wine cellar and rolled to a stop at my feet, against the debris from the ceiling.

A syringe.

"It's a sedative," Fifer said. "You'll wake up, though you're not going to want to at that point. My own personal monster!" She giggled again and also dug out a pair of handcuffs, which she flung my way with a finger. "Punch the drugs into a muscle. Then cuff yourself up."

I crouched, keeping tabs on Pilar out of the corner of my eye. She still had her CZ aimed at Fifer in a one-handed grip, the other hand braced against the wall. Shit, she better not be so busted up that she wouldn't be able to get Tabitha out.

Probabilities bayed at me, pessimistic, but I didn't allow myself to consider them. Instead, I picked up the syringe and stuck the needle into my upper arm, through my clothes. Pushed the plunger.

The sedative felt cold going in.

If it was a sedative. If she hadn't just poisoned me.

I still wasn't afraid.

Willow Grace's eyes narrowed greedily as she watched me. "Go on now. Cuffs, and then come stand in front of me. Can't have cute little Pilar shooting me, and we're all out of time."

She waved the dead man's switch at me. Fifty-four seconds.

I reached out to retrieve the cuffs and slid the metal over my wrists. *Click, click click, click.* The sedative was already affecting my movements, making my fingers heavy.

"Now, come block your friend's line of fire," Willow Grace instructed. "Easy now. Not too close."

I stumped forward between Pilar and Willow Grace. The latter pulled Tabitha a few steps to the side and cuffed her to one of the wine racks, then drew a stubby little revolver with her free hand and trained it on me. The bomb was counting down past twenty seconds; Fifer stepped away from Arthur's daughter, moved toward the stairs, and manipulated something one-handed on the device that made the LED clock click off.

Good, I thought. *One threat down.*

Though it wasn't like Fifer couldn't toss another device down once she got us out of the basement. Pilar might only have seconds. It was all I could give. It would have to be enough.

"This is a good compromise," Fifer said, back in her taunting singsong, her hand steady with the revolver aimed right between my eyes. "Now keep coming. Nice and slow. Try anything and I'll shoot you."

I believed her. I muzzily added reaction time and movements, subtracted, and concluded that I could not jump her. She was keeping me too far away, and had arranged us so I was exactly in Pilar's line of fire—I could drop to the ground, but the data showed Willow Grace's reaction time as faster than Pilar's. She'd be able to shoot Pilar before Pilar could shoot her.

I still wasn't afraid. I knew all the data and I wasn't afraid.

Fifer groped a foot behind her for the steps, never taking her eyes off me. I drew in line with Tabitha, whose face strained toward me, her chest heaving. *If she keeps hyperventilating into that gag, she'll faint,* I thought.

Eh. It wouldn't make much difference.

Fifer started creeping up the stairs backward, determined not to let me close enough to disarm her. She'd been more careful than she needed to be—the drugs were making my vision weave, as if the world were a painting being washed away by a rainstorm.

"Come on now," she said. "Just a little more."

Then she'd have me, unconscious, and have Pilar and Tabitha injured and bound in a basement, where she'd probably try to kill them or lock them up to experiment on.

This hadn't been a very good plan. Why had I thought it was a good plan?

I stumbled as I hit the bottom of the steps, but caught myself. I didn't want to know what Fifer would do if I collapsed before she got me upstairs. I rocked on my feet, determined to stay upright, and found the first step.

Overbalanced a little. Rocked again, farther than the first time.

Pilar's gun went off.

The report echoed off the basement walls and flattened my senses, and the drugs made me clumsily slow. Fifer was snapping back and falling before I managed to hurl myself to the side, at Tabitha, because if Willow Grace managed to get her gun up—I couldn't see where she'd been hit—

She did try. Pilar shot her again, just as I crashed into Tabitha in a tangle of elbows and brought the whole wine rack smashing to the ground. Glass shattered everywhere, shards peppering my skin among the cold splash of liquid. I tried to focus my wobbly vision back over at Willow Grace, but by then, she'd stopped moving.

I pushed myself to sitting and attempted to check over Tabitha. She was soaked in red, but the cloying scent of fermentation filled my nostrils, and I was pretty sure that was all wine. I'd been trying to wedge myself against her to make sure she didn't get more than bruises from the fall—the breaking bottles had probably nicked her with the same tiny cuts they had me, but she was squirming against her bonds like an eel now, so she was probably okay.

I slid the broken spar of the wine rack out of her handcuffs and helped her sit up, in the direction that faced away from Willow Grace's corpse. My fingers were thick sausages, but I managed to tug the gag out of her mouth.

She spat out the cloth and coughed a little, then took a deep breath, her eyes fixed on me in something unnervingly like worship.

"Don't you dare say 'cool,'" I said.

She blinked at me a few times. Then she said, "Wow."

Maybe Arthur had a point, keeping me away from her.

"Pilar," I slurred, my eyes tracking over to find her. "Find the damn handcuff key and get over here."

Pilar was standing over by Willow Grace, staring down at her. At what was left of her. Now she turned toward us, her gun dangling from her hand at her side. "Cas."

"Yeah," I said. "Good shot. Now come and . . . undo the . . ." My tongue had gone thick too. "I think I'm gonna pass out in a sec."

"Cas, I—your ear."

"M'what?"

"I nicked your ear. I shot you."

I pushed my cuffed hands against the side of my head. They came away bloody. I couldn't feel it.

"That wasn't . . . I didn't know if I could make that shot," Pilar said. "I took it anyway."

"Okay," I said.

"I took it anyway, with you standing there." Pilar still hadn't taken a step toward us. "I might have shot you. Easily. Cas, I—I wasn't good enough to do it and I knew it and I knew there was a good chance I'd kill you, but I still wasn't *scared*."

"P'lar," I said. I meant to tell her to have her fucking crisis later, but instead, I passed out.

forty

I HALF-WOKE getting dragged out of the mansion by a limping, staggering Pilar, my arm slung over her shoulders, and Tabitha bending awkwardly to try to support me from the other side. Both of them were huffing hard, and I had the distinct feeling they'd dropped me several times already, but I wasn't in any position to complain.

When I woke up all the way, I was slumped in the front seat of the car we'd taken to the mansion. The day had cycled through until the sun was low in the sky, and Pilar was driving, with a phone to her ear. It would have been uncharacteristically unsafe of her if traffic had been moving the least bit, but it wasn't. At all.

Or maybe she just wasn't afraid of crashing.

"He's sure?" she was saying. "He's absolutely sure? . . . Yeah. Yeah, she's—gone. I'm bringing Cas and Tabitha back, but the roads are clogged . . . well, thank you very much for that, then. When is it coming back on? . . . Okay. No, I can't, and Cas is out of it . . . Oh, yeah, I'm pretty sure she's fine, just drugged . . . I don't know. I was going to refer that question to, um. All of you."

I must have moved, then, because her eyes tracked to me. "Oh, she's awake. Cas, Checker wants to know if there's a plan for the, um. Crime scene." She glanced toward the back seat, and I craned my head around to see a sleeping Tabitha.

Checker was alive, then. Which meant they were probably all alive. My mind wandered around the information. *That's good*, I thought. *Good.*

I'd lost the thread of what was happening. Pilar had asked something. Right. I managed to circle back to it and pondered Checker's question. Fifer had made sure Willow Grace's mansion wouldn't be stumbled into by anyone, so we had a little breathing room . . . I could come do a cleanup job tomorrow. Maybe Rio or D.J. would help.

In a perfect world, Pilar and Tabitha could report this whole thing to the authorities truthfully—mostly—and trust they'd be cleared, but I didn't think any of us had faith in this being a perfect world. The two of them might be mostly law-abiding, but they'd follow my lead.

That was to say, they'd follow my lead or I'd make them.

"Don't worry about it. I'll take care of it," I said, and I was almost sure I saw Pilar's shoulders relax slightly.

Almost sure. Maybe not. She seemed pretty calm.

"Their side went okay, then?" I dredged myself up to ask. I had the distinct feeling I should have been a lot more concerned about that. LED counters danced through my memory. Even if I'd given them the ten extra minutes, that hadn't been a lot of time for D.J. to finish.

But Checker at least was alive. That was good.

"Yes. They got it done. With a little collateral damage." Pilar glanced wryly around at the jammed streets. The power was out, I suddenly realized, the traffic lights swinging dark. That would knee-cap LA for hours.

"Checker knocked out the power? And D.J. got all the bombs?"

"Yup. They got Diego out and dismantled all Fifer's devices, and everyone's okay. He says."

So they'd gone through with pulling Diego just in case, simultaneously with disarming the police station. Smart.

"Good," I mumbled. "Yeah. That's good." There would be a few more loose ends tomorrow, in addition to making sure nothing from the Malibu mansion would connect back to Pilar or Tabitha. Sikorsky was still a loose end, for one, and also double-checking Arthur's family was permanently safe from any vengeance Fifer might have tried to reach out with from beyond the grave. And we should probably call someone in about possible explosives set to blow on the Barberry Canyon bridge.

But that could all wait. I leaned against the coolness of the window and let myself drift back to sleep.

· .· ˙. .·˙. .·.

THE POWER didn't come back until after nightfall, just as we managed to creep back into the city. Traffic was snarled into such a Gordian knot that even having the lights and gas stations back didn't improve our top speed much for the last leg in to Checker's house in Van Nuys.

Checker had taken Diego and Elisa to the same safe house Arthur and the other kids were at. And, after hearing that Fifer was no longer a threat, Checker, Juwon, and Dr. Washington hatched a plan to hack through the crowded streets and get Arthur and the twins down to San Fernando Memorial. Visiting hours were over, but they'd managed to sneak the three of them in to see Simon anyway.

Checker reported with concern that even after Simon's treatment, they were in much worse states than Pilar had been, after that many hours crushed under the adrenaline of their own panic responses. But Dr. Washington was monitoring them back at the safe house, and she hoped they'd be able to sleep it off.

My own first order of business once we got back was to deal with Sikorsky. I told Pilar to escort a sleepy Tabitha into the Hole so I could go and take care of the cop still zip-tied to Checker's bed.

"You have what I need?" I asked Checker as we got Tabitha bundled inside. I hefted a briefcase I'd had Pilar stop for on the way. I'd also picked up a new Colt for myself at the same storage unit.

He tossed me a flash drive. "Just finished."

"Whazgoinon?" Tabitha murmured.

"Criminal activity," I said. "Go back to sleep."

Pilar shot me a look that would have melted iron and said, "Nothing's going on, sweetie. Sleep, okay?"

I got everything else I needed, left them to it, and headed into the house.

Sikorsky started growling at me through the sock gag as soon as I hit the light. He flailed against his bonds, his face going red and then darkening almost to purple. The stench in the room suggested he hadn't had a very comfortable day.

I hopped up to crouch on the desk with my briefcase, took aim with the 1911 I'd just retrieved, and shot seven times in rapid succession. The shell casings *pinged* off Checker's bookshelves.

Sikorsky squealed against the socks, but I was already done. The zip ties and ropes popped free, and his flailing suddenly let his limbs go wild. He whipped up and spat out the gag.

"You—!"

I kept my Colt in his face. One bullet left, and I only needed one. "Hi there," I said. "The bomber's been taken care of. Like I said we would."

He quieted and studied me, his face going back to close to its normal color. Now that he was free, he was far less unnerved than I would have expected. He might've been a good cop, once upon a time.

"You aren't a PI, are you?" he said.

"No," I answered.

"You gonna kill me?"

"Not yet."

That did make him twitch.

"I don't need to kill you anyway," I said. "We have you on video, threatening to torture us. Now, we could turn you in, but that sounds like a lot of bother for everyone involved. So instead, I'm here to offer you a lot of money. I hear you like that sort of thing. Don't get shirty about me saying so; I'm the same way."

I patted the briefcase next to me, then pulled out his service Glock, which Pilar had been thoughtful enough to retrieve at the mansion. I stuck it on top of the briefcase, empty and with the slide locked open. I'd given Pilar the nine-mil for her CZ.

"Some cash, but that's the smallest bit, and hard to use too much of it without suspicion. Especially given your . . . history. So, there's a flash drive right inside with the information for a bank account that has a lot more. Perfectly laundered."

His brow furrowed, his eyes going squinty. The funds had come from me, but I hoped he didn't draw the connection of how I knew someone with expertise in how to launder money that effectively. I kind of suspected Checker had been one of the best money launderers around, before he'd reformed and all.

"I'm a business person," I continued to Sikorsky, hopping off the desk. "It's worth it to me to pay you in order to keep from having to deal with the cops hassling my friends. So, here's how it's going to work. Forget you arrested Rosales. Stop looking for reasons to push him and his kids around. Take the money. We'll keep that juicy little recording to ourselves, and you'll keep living."

He studied me for a moment longer. Then he pushed himself up off the bed, came over, picked up the briefcase, and holstered his empty gun.

I didn't blame him. It was a good deal. And hey, for all I knew, he was happy for an excuse to get out of an arrest as illegitimate as Diego's had been.

.·´·.·´·.·´·.

PILAR AND I probably should have gone to see Simon right when we got back. But we were so busy, and I disliked being around Simon so viscerally, that we put it off. I suppose we just weren't worried about it.

To the others, I made the excuse that he wasn't well enough to have us constantly tromping in so he could fix us. Which had the benefit of being true.

But Rio appeared the next afternoon at Willow Grace's mansion, after I arrived with a car full of tarp and bleach and D.J. in tow. D.J. had immediately scampered off to go bomb hunting, and I ran into Rio on the curving walk by the infinity pool, where he greeted me with, "Simon telephoned. You must return to him as soon as possible."

"Sure, whatever," I said. "Once I'm done here."

"Cas. I am given to understand this is serious."

Apparently Simon's first phone call had been checking up on me with Rio, then. I tried not to resent that. As for Rio . . .

We stood staring at each other. I'd left a message to ask if he'd help with cleanup here, and he hadn't called back.

"I don't . . ." I rubbed at my eyes. "My brain's a little wonked right now on purpose, as you seem to know, and it's not like I've had a lot of time to think about it, but . . . I don't know, Rio. I don't know." I swallowed. "Maybe what I did to Simon was wrong. Maybe it was—maybe it was really wrong. Or maybe it wasn't. I have to think about it, and . . . I want the answer to be mine. Okay? Not yours or Arthur's or anyone else's."

He studied me for a moment longer. Then he cocked his head slightly and said, quite softly, "Perhaps that is for the best."

"What is? Me reading Simon's mind to stop Fifer, or insisting on having my own moral compass?"

He didn't answer, just paused a hairsbreadth longer and lifted a hand slightly toward the mansion. "I believe you requested my aid?"

I chalked up the conversation as the most I could have hoped for and told him I'd appreciate the help.

D.J. went through the premises like a whirlwind, declared he'd made all the explosives inert, and then carted them off for his own personal collection, leaving us to do the actual cleanup. It went mostly as expected—Rio had an amount of experience in this sort of thing that even I was squeamish thinking about. To my surprise, he also volunteered to take the dogs off the premises.

"You're not going to kill them, are you?" Pilar said, her mouth folding downward disapprovingly. I wondered if she'd be that aggressive with him normally.

But Rio answered her, apparently unruffled. "No. I know of places that would see their value and give them purpose. They will be treated well."

He wouldn't say more than that, but Pilar reluctantly let it go. It wasn't like the rest of us would have had any idea what to do with the poor creatures.

The rest of the cleanup went smoothly, albeit with one unexpected surprise in the pool house—where we found the real Willow Grace. She was still alive, if not very coherent at first, and exactly as beautiful as Fifer had been. Even with the burns and blood and starvation and filth. I wasn't sure how that was possible.

"Well," Rio said, "that makes this job easier," and went back outside, leaving me to deal with a very out-of-it news reporter.

He was right—having a living Willow Grace would make this all much simpler, as it meant no one would be looking for a corpse.

As I might have suspected if I'd thought about it, the real Willow Grace turned out to have a personality eerily similar to the façade her kidnapper had worn. From what she eventually pulled herself together enough to tell me, Fifer had kept her alive specifically to keep getting information, mannerisms, and anything else she needed to make sure the mimicry was complete. Fifer had successfully taken her out of circulation with the fake "sabbatical to write a book" story—although it turned out as part of her detention, Willow Grace really *had* been forced to write the book—but had also needed to keep up her imitation with anyone she happened to meet, and it had kept Willow Grace alive.

Willow Grace had the same forthright selfishness and oddly admirable self-righteousness Fifer's impression had presented. She insisted on staying in her house instead of seeing anyone for medical treatment, and after she'd showered and cleaned herself up somewhat, she sank onto a couch in one of her many rooms, saying all she wanted was to have her place back when we had finished.

When we questioned her about Teplova's methods, she denied knowledge of anything other than being a client, and said she hadn't suspected her surgeon of any dubious background either. And though she admitted to having met Coach peripherally, my inquiries aiming toward Halberd or Pithica only prompted confusion. She claimed that in reality, she'd met Eva Teplova only after the latter had moved to LA and set up her practice.

It all made me a little suspicious—was Fifer forward-thinking enough to have realized on her own that she could turn Teplova's client list into a conveniently valuable asset? And Willow Grace's face might be as good at making me believe her as her twin's had been . . . I made a mental note to talk to Rio about it in depth. And to actually listen to him this time.

But if we *could* believe her, that meant Teplova's changed people were all still out there, but separate. Powerful in their own roles, more than they should have been, but not being harnessed together to take down countries.

Small favors.

At least we had a partial client list. I'd have Checker set up some kind of system to keep an eye on them.

And when I started to drill Willow Grace about what to tell the authorities, to my surprise she agreed immediately to burying most of the events.

"You aren't tempted to write another book?" I said.

"Not at the expense of my career. This one would have to be post-humous," she said. "Warning every single place I've been in the prior six months of a possible attack may already end me."

I'd passed on Fifer's motive when we'd shared information—after all, Willow Grace was the person best-suited to making sure none of Fifer's devices had already found their way into a dangerous position. "What do you mean?" I said. "With your connections, you'll be taken seriously."

She leaned her head back and closed her eyes. Her wet hair framed a bruised face that was skeletal with lost weight, and she was the very definition of fragile loveliness. "I'm not worried about being taken seriously. But some people will want to spin this to make me responsible, and I'll need to spin them back."

Despite her grim trepidation, I didn't envy those people.

.·.·.·.·.

RIO INSISTED on driving me back to Simon's hospital as soon as we were done at Willow Grace's.

Despite Rio walking me in, I hesitated at the door to the room, my hand hovering near the handle. "I've been thinking," I said.

Rio lifted an eyebrow.

"Maybe I should go see Professor Halliday, before I let Simon put everything back."

I got both eyebrows now.

"You don't understand," I said. "She wants me to do math with her. She's been bugging me about it since I've known her. I can't, not like she wants, but . . ."

I'd always shut down her requests entirely before. Because I was afraid.

Because I knew I'd run up against that mental block, the one that always stopped me, the missing parts of myself. Because I didn't want to limp along as the slow second fiddle, the one only filling in the gaps in Sonya's breakthroughs.

Better not to try than to be that, right?

Except now . . . well, maybe it would only be a shadow of what I should be able to do, but it would be something. Something real, something I could be proud of, a thing that *meant something* instead of just money or kicking people in the head all the time. Something that wasn't only about cash or bullets.

"Would it be so bad?" I said softly. "Not to fear anything?"

Not to fear Valarmathi cackling in the back of my head, waiting to tear down my sanity? Not to fear Simon's fingers trawling through my memories as if he owned them? Not to fear that I was only one footstep away from fucking up and becoming the same sort of monster Fifer had wanted to twist me into?

To be someone who could have friends without teetering on a knife point, and maybe do some math, and discover some small things that would make the world more knowledgeable rather than bloodier?

"Cas," Rio said. He reached out and put a hand on my shoulder, the pressure light. "You can inquire with Simon. But he tells me remaining in such a state would be very dangerous."

"I'm not afraid," I said, conscious of the irony.

He let his hand drop. "I will not force you, Cas. But I would request of you that you let Simon repair this."

It had always been hard for me to go against Rio. I sighed and reached for the door again. "I do listen to you, you know."

"I am aware," Rio said. I wasn't looking toward him anymore, but for some reason, the words sounded remote, resigned, as if he wanted to pry them out of their truthfulness but had no leverage to try.

forty-one

SIMON MANAGED to fix up both Pilar and me in short order, but after that, his health was too bad for him to bug me for brain sessions for a couple of weeks. This was both good and bad, considering I hated but needed them.

Valarmathi chittered in the background. Now that I was about to be out of work again, the chittering got even louder, throwing my thoughts sideways if I ever started to relax.

Every time I thought of Coach, it got worse. Sometimes until I felt on the verge of free fall. But I didn't want to forget him either. Rio had helped me disappear the Rosales' minivan and all its contents, and in the end I'd stood out in the desert tending a chemically heightened pyre, the lone mourner at the funeral that deleted him from the world.

I wondered if he'd had any family. I couldn't remember if it was something I'd ever known.

I could try asking Simon. I doubted he'd tell me, even if he had the answers.

Coach had joined Simon in my dreams now. Their faces snapped clear even where others were a blurred mass. Simon and Coach, and also Eva Teplova, young and brash with her too-intelligent scalpels. Sometimes, they slipped and slid into my waking reality as well, imaginary friends who'd forgotten to stay in their place.

"Hopefully I won't collapse in the gutter again," I said to Pilar, only half-jokingly. She and I were cleaning up Arthur's office, which had just been cleared by the police. Pilar was still on crutches, but she'd taken on the herculean task of putting all the filing to rights. Meanwhile, I was keeping her company by installing and restocking a new gun safe, which was definitely the easier half of the work.

"You could stay with me," Pilar said absently.

"What?"

Her head came up from the folder she was buried in, sweaty hair falling across her eyes. "Just, you know. In case. Arthur and Checker don't have guest rooms, but my roommate just moved back home, so I've got the space if you want." When I didn't say anything, she added, "It's up to you, but I won't hover, I promise."

It was mildly appealing to think that if I blacked out again before Simon was back on his feet, someone would find me.

"I come with a lot of alcohol and guns," I said. "That okay?"

"As long as you don't get me arrested."

"I promise," I said. "I'm really good at bribing cops."

She rolled her eyes.

I almost cracked a joke about her own good aim, then, but a thought gave me pause. "Hey," I said instead. "Are you good? Fifer was the first time you . . ."

She put down the file she was working on. "You're asking if I'm okay? No. Probably not. I don't know." She let out the smallest edge of a hysterical laugh. "I think I'm still in shock about it. I feel like I should find a good therapist, but I don't know how to talk about it without getting thrown in prison. So."

"Yeah," I said. "I'd recommend mine, but I heard he did something inappropriate to a previous patient."

That got a slightly more genuine laugh out of her. But then she sobered. "Cas, I've been meaning to . . . I shot you." She met my eyes, and hers were large and troubled. "I could have killed you."

"But you didn't," I said.

"I wasn't afraid. I knew there was a chance, a *bad* chance, but I saw that the shot was there, and—I wasn't afraid I was wrong."

"You weren't wrong," I said.

"That's . . . there's something really disturbing about that."

"That you weren't afraid?"

"That I did everything wrong, and it was right."

.·´·.·´·.·´.

PILAR WASN'T the only one feeling raw about the fallout. I was over at Checker's tying up some more loose ends when D.J. dropped in so we could see him off. He'd messaged after our sweep of the mansion to proclaim zealously that he'd taken care of cleaning off the bridge for us too, but that was the last we'd heard from him.

From the slack expression on Checker's face when D.J. burst into the Hole, I could tell he hadn't been expecting it. Probably hadn't ever expected to see D.J. again.

"Don't forget, Little Miss Logic Fingers," D.J. said, waving at me. "We had a deal, right? You're gonna come give me some sweet-ass tech."

"We have a deal," I confirmed. "I'll come hold up my end. Once things get settled here." And once Simon got my brain oiled so it didn't keep trying to stutter off the rails. At least temporarily.

"Oh, goody!" D.J. gave me a double thumbs-up. "By the by, you seem like a trustworthy sort, but if you stiff me on this, I will leave presents for all your friends. Except Charles." He reached over and poked Checker in the shoulder. "Don't be a stranger, yeah, Charles? Drop a dude a phone call every now and again. Oh, and stop making faces at me, I'm totally kidding about blowing up your buddies. I need to teach you to have a sense of humor again."

"Have you ever considered . . ." Checker cleared his throat.

"Words, Charles. Use your words."

Checker kept starting to say something before trailing off, and I had the sudden awkward desire to fade into the background.

"If you—I could help you," he finally managed to get out. "Will you consider it? You could—you could go straight."

"Like you?" D.J. cawed a laugh. "So, I only blow shit up if it's white hat? Ha!"

Checker blushed. "Mostly straight, then."

"Just like your sex life." D.J. tweaked his nose.

Checker batted him away. "I'm serious. We could—"

"*We!* You and your little *team*. Adorable." He stretched. "Remember what all we used to talk about, Charles? Taking over the world?"

Checker licked his lips, suddenly tense. "Yeah?"

"I don't care anymore. Too much work, you know? I just wanna blow shit up. Like, a lot of shit. *All* the shit."

Checker might have let out a choke or a laugh. I wasn't sure.

"I'm gonna find more people who'll hire me to do that," D.J. said.

"You know you almost killed me, right? That day." It might have been the light, but Checker's eyes were gleaming. "You almost killed both Arthur and me. And you almost killed Arthur again last year— the only reason you *didn't* is because he remembered how we got out of it the first time."

"No harm, no foul, right?" D.J. answered brightly.

"And you've almost killed Cas, and a ton of other people," Checker continued inexorably. "And, uh—there's also lots of people you *have* killed and—that doesn't give you pause? At all?"

"You ol' softie," D.J. said, with that same stubborn cheer. "Besides, she kills lots of people too!" He gestured to me, still rocking back and forth on the balls of his feet. "You get on her about it?"

When Checker didn't immediately have a comeback, D.J. pivoted and raised a hand to me. "High five. Killing people!"

I kind of suspected Checker would frown on it if I participated, so I shook my head.

"Aw, monkeyballs." D.J. stretched his mouth into an exaggerated clown face of a frown. "I'm so underappreciated. Well, I've got a plane to catch. I'll see you goofs later."

He bounced to the door, then stopped, turned, and came back to Checker. "Hey. Charles."

"Yeah?"

"I wouldn't've blown the building. If I'd known what Baxter'd done to you."

"I know."

"Woulda capped him myself for it, if he hadn't gone and got

himself Witsecced." D.J's voice had gotten softer, more serious than I'd heard from him before. "Me and Ting came back for you, but by that time you'd gone fucking State."

"I didn't turn State," Checker said. "I got probation. A friend, um, called in some favors. And a really good lawyer."

D.J. stared for a second, then laughed. "You make friends *fast*, man." He waggled his eyebrows.

The corner of Checker's mouth turned up. "Get your mind out of the gutter."

"Sure, I'll climb back into the sewer with you." D.J. rocked back and forth on his feet for another beat, and his tone went almost hesitant. "Uh. So. You okay now and shit?"

"Yeah," Checker said. "I'm okay. And shit."

"Cool, cool," D.J. said, his former bounce coming back. "That's good, man. It was good seeing ya." He gave Checker another friendly poke and turned to leave. "Oh, and, Charles—don't try to save me, okay? It's bad for your health."

The door to the garage swung shut behind him.

Checker turned back to the screen he'd been working at, but then he waved his hands vaguely, said something about getting a snack, and headed out of the Hole and toward his house.

I stood in indecision for a moment and then followed.

I found Checker snack-less on his couch, flipping channels, and sat down next to him.

"Did you need something?" he said, eyes on the television.

"No," I answered. "I'm trying. Um. To do that thing."

He muted the TV and turned to regard me as though I might be hazardous waste. "What . . . thing?"

"Where I, uh. Show interest." I cleared my throat. "Is this awkward? This feels very awkward."

Checker burst out laughing. He laughed so hard and so long, I thought he would suffocate himself. I wasn't sure whether to be relieved or embarrassed.

"Cas," he said finally, taking off his glasses to wipe his eyes. "Only you."

Only me what? I thought.

But he didn't seem inclined to elaborate. Instead, he leaned back and looked up at the ceiling. He picked up a rubber squeeze ball from the end table and started tossing it up and catching it, over and over. "I didn't expect this," he said. Throw, catch. Throw, catch. "I have so much unresolved from back then, not just D.J. And after we ran across him again, I spent so long obsessing . . . and then he just, just walks into my life and back out again? Casual as you please?" Throw, catch. Throw, catch. "I don't even know what to think. If I should want him caught. If he's unredeemable. If he's . . . I don't know. I mean, he's going around *blowing up buildings*—that's, that's wrong, right?" He started laughing again, this time a little hysterically. "I feel like someone set a magnet on my moral compass."

I felt very inadequate to this conversation. But I supposed sitting for a tick and listening . . . well, it was the least I could do. For a friend.

Checker sniffed a little. "Even though all of you ended up okay, what he's done—it's logically equivalent to killing you and Tabitha and Arthur, isn't it?"

"By that logic, every drunk driver is morally equivalent to a murderer," I said.

"Some people *do* think drunk driving is morally equivalent to murder."

"Are you one of them?" I asked.

Checker threw the ball another few times and didn't answer me. "He was like family, you know?" he said instead. "It's hard to make that tie mean nothing. And I think part of me—I think it doesn't want to. As scared as I got thinking about him—I, I built him up into this monster in my head, and instead, he's just . . . the same stupid kid, and I don't know if that's better or worse, because he's *killing* people, not even people who are his enemies or something but just random people, and he's utterly okay with it, and I don't know if I should hate him, or if it's horrible for me not to hate him, or if—and Diego . . ."

"What about Diego?" Diego and the kids had been getting their lives mostly back to normal, as far as I had been told.

Checker sighed, and his voice went a bit small and croaky. "He's furious with me."

"Why?"

"I'm not supposed to do this sort of thing."

"What sort of thing?"

"The sort of thing where I shut down the entire police force of Los Angeles to get his arrest record wiped and then am an accessory to bribing the arresting officer into not reinstating it. After having a calm discussion with *you* about that arresting officer and why we shouldn't *kill him*. That sort of thing."

"Oh," I said.

"And between that, and D.J. . . ." He scrubbed his fingers across his face again, knocking his glasses askew. "What kind of standing do I have to judge anybody anyhow?"

I didn't know what to say. "You and Diego, um. Are you two gonna be okay?"

He blew out a breath. "He'll forgive me eventually—I mean, it's Diego. Doesn't mean I don't feel guilty as hell. In one night, I threw out everything he ever tried to teach me."

"Well, if you could go back, would you do it again?" I said.

"Fuck, yes. In a heartbeat."

We didn't find out till later, but it turned out Diego was so mad about what we'd done that he tried to go into the police station as an honest man and turn himself in. But Sikorsky denied the arrest, saying it had only been a pickup for questioning and Diego was confused.

From what Checker didn't say, I half-suspected that result made the hurt in their relationship harder to repair, but Checker still claimed to have no regrets.

Or maybe he had regrets, he just still wouldn't change anything. That made sense to me.

forty-two

FOR THE first few weeks following our rescue of Tabitha, I saw a fair bit of Pilar and Checker and not much of anyone else. I heard the filtered gossip: Diego had found a temporary rental house for the family a few neighborhoods over from their old one, Arthur had moved back to his own place to convalesce, Tabitha was begging for my phone number. I satisfied myself that they'd all ended up alive and mostly unharmed and put off the rest, spending my days on Pilar's couch drinking whiskey and eating the catering leftovers she brought home for her fridge. Sometimes Checker came over while she was at work and insisted on watching the worst movies we could find together on her television.

Simon called when he was well enough to talk, and I went over to the hospital for our sessions. I was slipping enough by the first one that I almost asked Checker to drive me. It turned out I should have; when Simon saw me, he chewed me out for being foolhardy enough to take the wheel of a car with Valarmathi creeping in on all corners of my senses.

So we were back to him taking unreasonable interest in my safety and me hating on him for it. Business as usual.

But after I sat by his hospital bed and got talked through two hours of sealing my previous life back into her box, Simon stopped me from leaving right away. "Wait," he said. "Please. There's something else I need to speak to you about."

I hoped he wasn't about to bring up what had happened between us. I still hadn't sorted out my own thoughts on the matter.

But instead, he said, "I've been reading through Dr. Teplova's research."

I sat back down. He must've gotten it from Checker; I hadn't known. "What'd you find?"

"I think we were right that she was originally from Halberd."

"Okay," I said slowly. "What does that mean for us?"

"This is—" He scrunched his face a bit, scratching at the back of his neck. "I talked to Rio about this too. He agrees with me that it's too much of a coincidence."

I frowned. I hadn't seen Rio since the cleanup at Willow Grace's— I'd called him asking to meet for a fuller debrief, and he'd picked up but said he was busy and would call me when he was free. I'd taken him at his word. It gnawed at me a little that he'd found the time to talk to Simon.

I pushed the feeling aside. "What's too big of a coincidence?"

"You. Getting pulled into fighting something that came out of Halberd."

A sudden coldness crept up my spine, like I was being watched.

"It was a lot of degrees of separation away, though," I tried to rationalize. "We figured that Fifer found Teplova as someone to motivate her own ends, and Arthur stumbled onto her because of the way she was imitating D.J. . . ."

"Who was *Checker's old friend*," Simon finished. "Cas, what are the chances of that?"

"Do you mean literally? Because the number of variables—"

"Cas, where did you get D.J.'s phone number?"

"What?"

"I've been going back through everything, and—Cas, I talked to D.J. about this. He had no connection to Teplova, or her friends, or anyone else from Halberd. That phone number should never have been there."

"And you're claiming someone planted it to . . . to what, to help us? That's kind of far-fetched."

"No, it isn't. Not with people who make it their mission to, to watch, and nudge things along in the direction they want."

Fucking. Psychics.

"Rio thought they were involved all the way since this started," Simon said. "And I—I know it seems a stretch at first blush, but I agree. Because think about it. What's Pithica's stated goal?"

"Well, they try to smooth out all global injustice by manipulating everyone into world peace—"

And I cut myself off, because I heard what I'd just said.

Manipulation. They cured the world of ills by manipulating people, as many people as they wanted or needed to get their end results.

"This is how they operate," Simon said softly. "This is *exactly* how they operate. Coincidences and tiny changes, indirect steps from far away. Anyone who suspects a bigger web, that person will just end up being told they're paranoid. If Fifer was a threat—or, more likely, Teplova was who they viewed as the original threat, going off independent that way—Cas, they got Fifer to take care of one problem, and by embedding a person with a six-degrees connection to you, they then set you up to take *her* down. A few weeks later . . . problem solved."

Every organ in my body clenched, my skin tightening. They'd played me like a puppet—they'd endangered all of Arthur's family—"Why not just fucking do it themselves?" I burst out. "They're fucking telepaths. Wouldn't it be easier for them just to walk in and tell Fifer to off herself?"

"Cas," Simon said. "This *is* doing it themselves."

"They used me," I said hollowly.

"What you call telepaths—we aren't the only type of people they have," he agreed. "They could predict how you'd respond."

My fingernails were digging rivulets in the heels of my hands.

"Cas," Simon said. "I don't think you could have done anything different."

"We had a *deal*," I hissed.

"Not to attack each other. Now that they know about you . . . they're good at using the tools they know about."

Tools. Fuck.

Simon blew out a breath. "And, Cas, I'm—looking at what Teplova did here—I'm not certain they were wrong."

"*What?*"

"Wrong to manipulate you without asking you, yes. But this type of technology—what Teplova was doing with it, and the potential for misuse—"

"She wasn't misusing it at all," I said. "Not according to the real Willow Grace. She was just making a spectacularly good living. Nobody was *misusing* anything until Fifer came along, and you as much as admitted that Pithica put her there—"

"But if not Fifer, it might have been someone else," Simon argued. "And they—it's possible they were able to *know* that would happen eventually, really know it. I'm not defending them, and maybe they shouldn't have started that avalanche in this case, but I'm just saying—someone needed to stop Fifer. Heck, there are probably other of Teplova's clients who need to be stopped now. And Teplova might not have been the only one who adapted what she knew."

I forced myself to breathe and listen to what he was saying. "You mean there might be other, um, offshoots of Halberd and Pithica. Independents, like me, who might be using their powers to take over, or—or spreading them somehow, the way Teplova did. Creating more."

Creating more people with bizarre, otherworldly powers, like Fifer had wielded. Some would only use it for personal gain. Others . . .

Fifer had been about to build a world full of monsters, before we'd stopped her.

I squeezed my eyes shut for a moment. For the last few months, I'd become mired on the endless treadmill of trying not to go insane. Letting Simon into my head, maintaining some sort of equilibrium, trying to stay afloat in the face of the nightmares and voices. Somewhere in the middle of it all, I'd stopped looking ahead to accomplishing anything but those things.

I'd even gotten an office. A freakin' *office*.

Now Pithica was messing with our lives again, and we'd just seen evidence that a thousand other outfits could be springing up with similar tech, spawning more modified people who would multiply and mutate what they could do until they gained whatever power or advantage they desired. The city I'd failed was still suffering, and I'd betrayed a hell of a lot of people the past few years. I already had more to make up for than I could repay.

With some bitterness, I recalled my conversation with Checker about redemption. But I wasn't looking for redemption. I'd spoken truly when I'd told him I didn't believe it was possible. I might try to be better, but even if I succeeded in some small ways, there would be no balancing of scales. No making up for who or what I'd been.

No making me into a different person, even.

But I'd slowly started to want my life to be about more than what someone like D.J. was after. I couldn't do math anymore, but maybe I could do something.

God help me, I wanted *meaning*.

The last time I'd tried to be a hero, it had gone spectacularly badly. That just meant I needed another approach.

"Simon," I said.

His face turned toward me, surprised. I winced. I hardly ever talked to him without sarcasm.

"Go ahead," he said.

"I think we should start a research project." I held my breath, not asking the question.

He saw it anyway, as I'd known he would. "Yes," he said softly. Thoughtfully. "For this, I'm in. The world isn't equipped to handle these sorts of threats. Pithica was right about one thing. For this . . . people need us."

"Rio can't be involved," I said.

He nodded. "Because he's the one who made the deal with Daniela."

"No," I said. "Because I don't think he wants me on the front lines, and I'm going to be."

And if Pithica was the one who was pushing me into this . . .

Well, they were going to regret it, because I was going to figure out how to come after them again too.

.·.˙·.˙·.˙·.

I KEPT tabs on Arthur via nosy questions to Checker and Pilar, but I purposely delayed visiting him until they said he was on the mend. I didn't want to risk an argument spiraling him into further injury, and I was definitely planning to argue with him. Loudly. And at length.

About what, I wasn't quite sure, because after everything that had happened, I wasn't even sure he'd been wrong. But I wanted him to be.

When Arthur opened the door, however, he dropped his crutch and grabbed me in a bone-crushing hug.

I was pretty proud of my reaction time being fast enough for me *not* to reopen half his wounds trying to escape the embrace. I didn't really hug him back, but I sort of patted him on the back a bit until he was done.

"I'm never going to be able to thank you enough," he said, when he let go. His face was wet. "You got her back. You kept her safe."

Safe was probably a relative term, but I didn't contradict him. "You should thank Pilar," I said instead.

"Did already." He retrieved his crutch and limped back into his apartment. "Come in, Russell, please."

I did. Sat on one of his kitchen chairs. "I'm still pissed at you."

He'd gone over to the fridge, probably intending to offer me food or drink, but he stopped with a hand on the door handle, leaning against it. "It's all happy mediums, isn't it?" He wasn't looking at me. "I didn't know where to draw the line. I'm sorry."

"No," I said.

"I am, Russell. Believe it. Please."

"I didn't mean you aren't sorry," I said. "I meant I don't want happy mediums. That doesn't work for me." Recklessness overtook me, the type of giddy half fear that usually prefaced me doing something like jumping off a building. "I'm either your friend or I'm not. Isn't that how this works?"

He still wasn't looking at me.

"I don't mean you need to tell me everything in your life," I said. "But the things that . . . that make you happy, or are part of . . . the things that are important. I want to know." And I'd keep trying to be a better listener. I would.

"Yeah," Arthur said, after a minute. "Yeah. Okay. I'm in."

I let out a quiet breath. I hadn't wanted to acknowledge how much I needed to hear him say that. As if for weeks we'd been balanced on some invisible inflection point, and with those four words, he'd finally slipped us past.

"On that note," I said, trying to sound normal, "your ex-husband does these, um, Sunday dinner things. You know what I'm talking about?"

Arthur shrank a bit, his shoulders sloping in. Apparently giving up on the food, he limped back to the table and joined me, sinking into one of the other chairs and staring at the floor. "I did 'em. He kept going with it."

"Okay, well, Tabitha invited me for tomorrow," I said.

He swallowed.

"I told her I would only come if her dad said okay," I said.

"And, uh." Arthur's voice was very soft. "Did he?"

"I don't know," I said. "I'm asking him now."

Arthur took a shuddering breath, and then his head jerked in a very small nod.

"I also pointed out it would be super awkward to have me and Checker and Pilar all there without you," I said.

"Russell, don't . . ."

"Whatever sort of weird self-flagellation thing you've got going, you don't need to," I said.

"It's not that. It's—I don't want to make things awkward for anyone."

By *anyone* he meant Diego and Elisa.

"But why do you always have to be the person who gets shafted?" I said. "Why can't they grit their teeth and smile for two hours so you can come to one goddamn Sunday dinner?"

He raised his head to look at me. His cheeks were wet again. "Because . . . because I'm happier, doing this for them."

I punched him lightly in the shoulder. "Christ. You're such a fucking martyr."

"Yeah." He touched my arm. "Go. Have a good time. We'll do another dinner sometime, us and Tabitha and Juwon and the twins, and Checker and Pilar. Yeah?"

"Yeah," I said.

I left him there, sitting melancholy at his kitchen table, and called Checker as soon as I was out of the apartment.

The next day we came back at 4:00 p.m. precisely. Armed and ready.

"What is this?" Arthur said, when he pulled open the door to Checker's rapid knocking.

"We thought we'd bring Sunday dinner to you," Roy said, pushing past us to troop in with an armload of groceries.

"Yeah, and because we're young college men and therefore have the stunning culinary ineptitude of bachelors, you're doing the cooking," added Matti, following with more bags. "Don't say we never did nothing for you, Pop."

"I promise not to grow up like them!" Juwon piped up, only to be tackled by his brothers on the floor of Arthur's apartment. Tabitha ran to grab a pillow from the couch to start hitting them all with.

Checker, Pilar, and I hung by the door.

"You . . ." Arthur's eyes searched our faces. "You all did this? But what about . . ."

Checker gave him a half smile. "Elisa and Diego aren't monsters, you know. It's one Sunday. Of course they said it was fine."

Arthur glanced back and forth between us and his family, and his whole body seemed to relax in a way I'd never seen in him before.

"Well," he said. "Come on in, then. Guess I'm cooking dinner."

acknowledgments

ACKNOWLEDGMENTS ARE both easy and hard to write—easy, because I feel so much gratitude to the other people who have put such care and sweat into supporting these books, and hard, because I don't know how to find words of adequate appreciation.

Once again, my editor, Diana Gill, and her sharp editing eye have improved this book drastically from first draft to last. I am terrifically indebted for how she always manages to push my work up another level! She is joined at Tor by a team of incredible, hardworking talents, including her assistant, Kristin Temple; my cover artist, Jamie Stafford-Hill; my publicist, Lauren Levite; and countless others on the editing, production, and publicity teams who always go above and beyond in making my books as polished and successful as humanly possible. It's a joy to work with them and I am impressed and humbled by their skill.

My first readers for this book turned some feedback around for me on an embarrassingly short timeline, and I am once again so grateful to Maddox Hahn, Kevan O'Meara, Jesse Sutanto, and Layla Lawlor, who have been with me since the beginning and once more were so generous with their time for this book. Additional thanks on this one go to Tilly Latimer, who gave me support on the first few chapters early on in the process.

Finally, there are two people I continue to feel intense gratitude to not only for these books but throughout every aspect of this often-difficult career. More thanks than I can say go to my agent, Russell Galen, who championed this series, is a tireless advisor, and opens doors for me at every opportunity. And to my sister, who has been my first and original cheerleader, partner, and first reader in all things writing—I hope you know exactly how much you've mattered in helping create the writer I am today.

To list everyone else in my life who supports me in either my personal life or my writing would take the length of another novel. I am so lucky in not only my family, but in my friendships that have the strength of family, and in my web of personal and professional communities beyond that. I can only hope I can pay some of that gratitude forward, and that you know who you all are when I say: thank you so much.